WHAT OTHERS ARE SAYING ABOUT CAYMAN GOLD...

Hi suspense! Sustained! Intelligently done. Exciting concept. Told professionally. Highly recommended reading!

Al Haney
Author of *"Operation Primrose."*

"Cayman Gold" by John Hankins, is a fabulous book and the kind you can't put down once started. Realistic, a great story, descriptive, this book has it all. Can't wait to see "Cayman Gold" in movie form.

Thomas J. Hosted
Retired International Bus. Exec.

As a U-boat hunter during the days of World War II, I have been interested in all U-boat stories, both fictional and factual, and so I find this book to be exceptionally intriguing for portraying in such a realistic manner, a situation which could actually have occurred years ago. It's a great story with a surprising finish...

Neville Baker
Former RAF Bombadier

CAYMAN GOLD

GOLD

By John Hankins

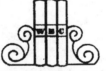

Writers Book Club
of
America

Houston, Texas

Dedication

To my wife, Nedra,

the source of my

many inspirations

John Walter Hankins

ACKNOWLEDGEMENTS

y grateful appreciation to the many people who made this book possible, in particular Mr. Tom Adam, a long time resident of Grand Cayman for sharing his knowledge of U-Boat activities in the Caribbean during WWII, and to many other unnamed individuals who shared what they knew as I made local inquiries.

My thanks also to Chief Inspector (now Superintendent) Philip Ebanks of the Caymanian police establishment who provided additional information concerning legal and other matters in the British West Indies.

From a technical and historical perspective, I am indebted to the staff of the Chicago Museum of Science and Industry for providing photos and other data relevant to the German submarine *U-505*. This type IXC submarine, which had been captured off the coast of Africa in 1944, has has been on display in Chicago since 1954 following its release by the U. S. Navy. *U-505* served as the model for this novel.

In trying to be as accurate as possible—yet still with an author's license to fictionalize material—I must also express my appreciation to Mr. Harry Cooper of the Sharkhunters Organization in Hernando, Florida, for providing insight and information into actual U-Boat Operations. Many of its members are former U-Boat officers and enlisted men.

As to the characters themselves, except for Martin Bormann, all others are fictionalized. Considering what I know of Bormann, I'm convinced he survived the war. Should that be the case, I hope this novel will serve as a vehicle for keeping the memory of his dreadful deeds before the public so they will never be repeated. What he and others did helped rob their nation of its young men and women. In the *U-Bootwaffe* alone, for example, out of some 39,000 members more than 32,000 died.

As for the American couple in my book—the Northam's—their names are real. I used them in honor of my newly-wedded Australian friends, Phillip and Janelle Northam, who allowed use of their names. Perhaps one day they too will have a little girl named "Tanya!"

FOREWORD

As a U-boat hunter during the days of World War II, I have been interested in all U-boat stories, both factual and fictional, and so I find this book to be exceptionally intriguing for portraying in such a realistic manner, a situation which could actually have occured years ago.

At the end of World War II there was a great deal of art treasures leaving the *Third Reich*. Other than U234 which was refitted in Stettin, Germany, and found to contain approximately Six Million dollars (1945 prices) worth of mercury hidden in its keel, no other U-boat--to my knowledge--was ever found with treasure within its hull. This does not mean however, that U-boats did not carry SS personnel and their illicit treasure, in their exodus, to South America and other safe havens. What we do know is this: At wars end, members of the German submarine force deliberately scuttled a large number of their U-boats. Conceivably, it is not unreasonable to assume a few of these could have been diverted for other purposes.

From former dedicated U-boat crew members who risked their lives every time they went out on patrol, I learned recently that before the end of the war was obvious, rarely if ever did SS and Gestapo personnel visit their boats, since life aboard these cramped vessels was much too dangerous for them. But, when the war began to turn against Nazi Germany, such individuals suddenly appeared on the scene, bringing with them what they regarded as "Spoils of War" --to enable them to start a new life in another country.

The story herein touches on concentration camps, the last days of the *Third Reich*, the effects of the air bombardment on Germany, the perils of undersea warfare and the utter ruthlessness of Himmler's elite SS corps--the worst of all Nazis. It's a great story with a surprising finish, and I am certain those who read this book will enjoy the twist and turns of *"Cayman Gold."*

Neville Baker
Former RAF member

INTRODUCTION

This story, though fictional, has its foundation in truth, fact, and history . . . .

For example, near the end of World War II when it became obvious to members of the Nazi hierarchy that the Third Reich was aout to fall, a number of them began making plans for their future by hiding illegally-acquired bullion and other treasures for conversion to their own use at some later date.

We know that a great deal of this illicit treasure was taken from Nazi death camp inmates before it was deposited in Nazi Germany's infamous Reichbank, where the dreaded SS maintained large accounts. Some of the gold bullion stored within its crumbling walls had been melted from gold teeth and turned into ingots while other stocks came from the treasuries of captive nations.

As the war intensified and Allied aerial bombing of Berlin increased, the treasury of the Reichbank was hastily moved to other parts of Germany. Portions of it went to Bavaria to be hidden in salt mines and other supposedly secure locations. What remained was supposed to have been distributed to other banks and organizations within the Reich, but history shows that a number of diversions took place!

When the Allies began occupying Germany and Austria, some of the hidden caches were uncovered and confiscated, but far more remains undiscovered. It's conceivable some of the missing loot could have been taken by Allied personnel, and this theory is not discounted in view of known arrests and convictions of Allied personnel. A recent Texas case is such an example, wherein an American Officer removed priceless church items, and almost fifty years later, his heirs discovered their value. According to newspaper accounts the items were redeemed for payment alleged to amount to a million dollars, even though they had been stolen originally!

In any regard, exactly how much more was hidden by the Nazis is difficult to say, but with the passage of time, stolen or missing items appear in various markets throughout the world. These include the sudden and unexpected appearanace of negotiable instruments and priceless objects d'art* While large quantities of gold bullion have been recovered, much more still seems to be missing, including huge sums of American and other foreign currencies known to have been deposited in the Reichbank.

* Like those recently found in the old Soviet Union.

Certainly, much of this missing treasure was secreted away by ex-Nazis—men and perhaps even women who assumed new identities and nationalities. A few of the more noted criminals like Adolf Eichmann have been caught, tried, and punished, but other equally infamous ones are yet to be found. Their means of departure from Nazi Germany sometimes bordered on the ridiculous, with the U.S. and its former allies, stupidly or intentionally—whatever the case, allowing former war criminals to escape from under their very noses. In some cases—irrespective of their past—many ex-Nazis (scientists more often than not) were deliberately taken into an Allied country and made honorable citizens in order to assist in that country's national agenda.

As far as possible avenues of escape for other Nazis war criminals, the use of German U-boats has strongly been suspected, for most certainly, many of them were still prowling the seas at war's end. The seamen who manned those deadly vessels of war are treated differently from the Nazis in this novel since most of them were guilty of nothing more than truly serving their country during a time of war. What their leaders did is another thing and must be dealt with separately.

The premise of using submarines as escape vehicles has many precedents—witness the evacuation of German personnel and other key officials from French seaports toward the end of the war and the remarkable escape of U-boat crews to South American countries like Paraguay and Argentina, where several surrendered.

Rumor ran far and fast back then, with at least one U-boat commander being accused of helping Hitler, Eva Braun Hitler, and other Nazi criminals to escape. The rumors were justified since many of the long-range U-boats like the type XIV and IXC40, were used to ferry raw materials to and from Japan. In fact, at the end of the war, one such trip included the transport of several dissembled jet fighter airplanes and heavy water, the latter universally known as a product essential for atomic bomb research and production.

Fortunately, the long-range U-boat never reached Japan. When informed their country had surrendered, its Captain reversed his vessels course and headed for the east coast of the United States where the sub and its contents were surrendered to U.S. Navy authorities. And there—according to reports from various sources—its highly secret contents were off-loaded and disposed in a manner known to but a few.

This now leaves us with the whereabouts of other Nazi war criminals who have never been caught. Where are they? What are they doing now? Could some of them be involved in the "neo-Nazi" movement which is flaring up again around the world?

Prologue

Bon Voyage

Wall Street, New York City—1990's

ostalgia had no place for consideration today; his mind had been made up. It was now or never! Phillip Northam, fortyish, tall and good-looking, had been a stockbroker and partner in the wallstreet brokerage firm of Nelson, Cardwell and Stevens for a number of years, and had finally decided to call it quits. For good reason too: Not only was his health in jeopardy, but so was his ten year marriage to one of New York City's most famous fashion models.

For the present his thoughts were on saying good-bye to his many friends and associates. They had given him a farewell retirement party, making it difficult for him to leave.

While all this was going on, Phillip looked around his office, to see if the movers had overlooked anything. As he suspected, they had. On the floor behind his luxurious executive desk was a shblow box full of medals he had earned for galantry in action and war wounds; all awarded for service in Vietnam years earlier.

1

Upon return to the U.S. back then he went to college where he majored in business administration. Upon graduation he went for a series of on-campus interviews where he was quickly identified by representatives of the brokerage firm he was now leaving, as being a candidate who seemed to possess the qualifications the firm had been seeking. They were right! Within a short period of time after employment Phillip shot to the top; first to a minor partner status, then to a full partner. He enjoyed the benefits of his labor, but there was a down side—stress at work and social disharmony at home!

It came to a head one day, after a routine visit to his doctor, but Phillip didn't have time to think about it now, since everyone was milling around him to wish him well. One person in particular, was Harry Witherspoon, a senior partner in the firm, who just happened to be the person who hired him straight out of college. They were old friends now, and both senior partners.

"You sure you won't change your mind?" asked Harry, testing the resolve of his friend.

Phillip shook his head.

"We're going to miss you," Harry added, while putting a reassuring arm around his friend's strong shoulders.

"Your friendship means a lot to me, Harry, and I'll miss you, too," replied Phillip, "but like I've said many times before, this is something I must do. In fact, with no offense intended, or reflection on this firm, which has been particularly good to me, "it's something I should have done long before now."

"Well, just the same," interjected Harry rather compassionately, "should you decide to come back to the rat-race, remember there will always be a place for you."

At that moment he grasped Phillip's hand firmly with his left hand, then quickly, so it wouldn't be noticed, wiped a small tear from his cheek.

Phillip would miss Harry and the others, including his dignified and efficient secretary, Margo, who had worked for him many years. Margo proved many times that she was worth every penny the company paid her. Now she too was in tears, especially when Phillip reached for his briefcase. Sight of her almost broke Phillip's heart. They embraced briefly, then it was time to leave. While everyone watched, he walked out of the massive office into the hallway leading to a bank of elevators.

There was more to this departure than Phillip's friends and associates knew. Weeks earlier his cardiologist had bluntly asked, "Have you made any plans for your funeral?"

2

Phillip thought the man was joking and responded somewhat casually with a "What?"

"Phil," Doctor Raymond said somberly, "I'm not kidding. What I've got to say is important, and from what I can see right now. . . from all these reports and tests, including my own personal examination, "you're a prime candidate for a coronary, a debilitating stroke, or both."

"Me?" replied Phillip incredulously, "I thought I was in good shape. How could that be?"

"Most of it is due to stress and poor dietary habits," replied the doctor. "In the kind of work you do, high tension and all that stuff, something's got to give, and stress is one way the body responds when it's overworked. Like an auto engine, it can only endure so much."

"So what do you recommend?" asked Phillip with great concern.

"Quit what you're doing and take a long vacation. Let it all out and just enjoy yourself. If you don't, then you can expect the worse . . . sooner or later. Perhaps sooner, if you don't do something about it."

Dr. Raymond's words stunned him at the time; he hadn't expected that kind of report! It was hard for Phillip to accept at first because he felt well, with only a minor ache or two . . . nothing else. Oh, he felt a little tired now and then, but that went with the territory. Never-the-less he considered his doctor's advice, especially upon realizing a vacation might be the solution to another problem as well: the mending of a marriage which was about to fail.

For some time now, Phillip and his wife, Janelle, had not been getting along. As a beautiful, highly acclaimed international fashion model, she was required to be away from home a lot, which, like Phillip's occupation, left little time for family life. In their ten-year marriage, Phillip and Janelle rarely ever spent a weekend together.

Given the circumstances of their careers, both parties realized that had it not been for the fact they had a daughter, Tanya, their marriage might have folded earlier. The fact it hadn't, had something to do with love for their daughter and a semblance of love which still remained for each other; the latter hurt more by absence from each other than anything else. And so, a solution to salvage what remained was imperative: Phillip would heed Dr. Raymond's advice .

Talking to Janelle that night was easier than Phillip expected. To his delight and surprise, Janelle was willing to put her career on hold for the sake of their marriage and the happiness of their daughter, and he, in turn, would retire from the firm. Why not? After all, he had been there long enough and had an excellent retirement plan to guarantee a secure retirement!

With this came plans for an extended vacation to the Caribbean, aboard their new forty foot, ocean-going yacht—a marvelously equipped vessel which they previously had little or no time to enjoy since its purchase. When told of their plan, Tanya was absolutely ecstatic. She wanted nothing better than to be with her parents instead of being shuffled by one or the other to private days schools while her parents worked. It had been a way of life for her, and she was glad to see it end.

Many options for travel were considered, but the one which held its own, was a cruise to the Caribbean, where pirates of old once roamed and buried their treasures. Phillip especially, liked that part, and made it quite clear he would do some treasure hunting upon arrival at their destination.

For Janelle, her thoughts were on the beauty of the islands themselves, with rest and relaxation on pristine beaches being uppermost in mind, as opposed to a working vacation which Phillip seemed to envision. Regardless, both felt they could do a little of each and still be content, and so they decided on the Cayman Islands in the British West Indies, three small islands situated between Cuba and the southern tip of Mexico off the Yucatan peninsula.

And so, as Phillip raced down the hallways of the firm, never looking back for fear of regrets, his mind focused not only on his reasons for leaving, but something even more pleasant: A leisurely cruise with his family aboard their fabulous yacht the *Lucky Streak,* to islands covered with fragrant flowers and exotic birds, to crystal clear blue lagoons surrounded on all sides by gently swaying palm trees.

"Oh, daddy," Phillip remembered Tanya saying just then, "it's going to be fun, we get to play *Swiss Family Robinson . . . .*"

With that his gait picked up and he whistled his way back to the parking garage below, where he promptly entered his Mercedes XL convertible and drove off. Excitement was in his blood and he could hardly wait to leave the mad, mad, streets of New York City. Nothing—in his mind at the moment—could ever cause him to think about returning. Nothing!

What he didn't know at the time was that his family's eventual presence in the Caribbean, at a particular time and place, would set off a chain of events no one would ever forget...

PART ONE

CAYMAN GOLD

Ruins of Hitler's Reich Chancellory

Chapter 1

The Führerbunker

Berlin—1945

he city was in shambles and still smoldering from an Allied bombing raid when a camouflaged half-track raced through the debris-littered streets. Flanked by motorcycles, it was heading for the Führerbunker, Hitler's concrete-reinforced bomb shelter buried deep in the earth next to the crumbling Reich Chancellery building.

As the occupants of the half-track traveled through the thick smoke that blotted out the morning sun like a dark blanket, they could not help noticing the catatonic shuffle of nearby refugees as they rummaged through the cordite-smelling ruins and streets in search of food and shelter. Most seemed impervious to their surroundings and the carnage around them.

In the minds of these people, like those of their military and civilian counterparts passing in and out of the guarded doorway leading to the underground labyrinth of the Führer's bunker, there was a silence—an absence of conversation. It was as if everyone had unilaterally agreed to suppress words in exchange for deep inner thoughts.

Clearly, the war was nearly over, yet almost everyone refused to believe the signs of defeat that were all around them. The deceit was almost complete in that those fallen victim to its lies had long learned to live with their situation. Many would even ignore sounds of incoming rockets and artillery shells fired upon the city by approaching Red Army units, that is, until a missile seemed headed in their direction. At that moment, all would be jolted back to reality again. Ears would perk up until the danger had assuredly passed. After that the citizens would return to their previous activities as if the enemy outside their city was about to suffer an enormous defeat and the Third Reich would be resurrected from its ruins.

The camouflaged half-track rumbled to a halt outside the Reich Chancellery and three men—two of them uniformed—raced up the chancellery steps. The sentry and duty officer guarding the entrance quickly snapped to attention, gave the Nazi salute, and cried out, "Heil Hitler."

One of the visitors, a tall, gaunt, black-haired SS officer with a boyish look, became agitated when the duty officer insisted upon examining his identity papers.

"Just following orders, Herr General," the captain replied respectfully while trying not to succumb to his superior's intimidating manner.

"Well, be quick about it then, and notify the Führer we've arrived," the General demanded.

"*Jawohl*, Herr General," the duty officer replied as he moved to a nearby alcove and reached for a wall-mounted field phone. He wound the crank several times while contemptuously eyeing the black-leather-coated man anxiously pacing the floor before him.

"*Jah?*" a voice answered.

"They're here. . . ."

"*Gut*, send them down. I'll inform the Führer."

Without delay, the captain returned all identity papers, saluted, then waved the visitors on with a comment all wanted to hear, "You may pass, gentlemen. The Führer is waiting."

The young sentry who had been watching the high-ranking officials from a position near his duty officer whispered a question as the visitors walked away.

"Sir, the general seemed upset. Do you think the Russians have crossed the Oder?"*

"Not from what I've heard," the officer replied, showing more tolerance and friendliness than was common between officers and enlisted men in the Germany army. In the last days, with the war going

* *River east of Berlin, on German-Polish border.*

8

against them, a closer understanding and camaraderie had superseded what had traditionally been a caste system.

"Rumor has it. . . ."

"Trash," the officer interrupted. "You can't believe everything you hear these days. If our generals don't know what's going on, how can anyone else?"

Both men turned to watch the general and his associates as they strode rapidly through the large building, heading for the stairwell leading down to the Führerbunker. Fragments of the general's conversation echoed back at them. What was heard took the form of a criticism: the futility of attempting security in a building containing more holes than a wheel of Swiss cheese. Laughter, then moments later, the general's voice, with those of his companions who appreciated the analogy, faded with the metal-on-marble sounds coming from the steel heels of the general's shiny black boots.

Waiting at the entrance to Hitler's anteroom was Martin Bormann, Nazi Party secretary, who extended an anxious hand to each man.

"Ah, General von Kleitenberg, Admiral Neumeister, and my dear friend, Doktor Funk," nodded the balding, slightly obese man who had long been a close associate and confidant of Adolf Hitler. "I thank you for coming. It was good of you to come so quickly under such interesting and exciting circumstances—for us especially."

With that, he led the three men into a cramped anteroom, where other officials waited impatiently, hoping to see Hitler. Upon seeing that he was not present, the new arrivals turned to their host, Bormann. He seemed unconcerned and more at ease than anyone in the room, despite the gravity of the situation. Minutes-old intelligence reports stated the Russians had begun crossing the Oder River, the last major obstacle between them and Berlin itself.

As his comrades, including himself, shed their outer garments to adjust to the warmer temperatures within the stuffy room, General von Kleitenberg leaned forward and whispered into Bormann's ear, "Any word yet?"

"It's like I said before, General," Bormann replied in a subdued voice. "He has a lot on his mind these days. But don't worry; he'll come along, especially on a matter as critical as this."

"But," the general complained as his comrades moved in closer to air their concerns, too, "we're running out of time."

Bormann smiled, irritating the general with his seemingly calm

9

demeanor. It was only a facade, and they all knew it. "As I said, one cannot push matters of this sort . . . beyond a certain point, that is. But, if I were to render an opinion, I would say he is coming around. In fact, at one point, I did hear him say something positive."

"Like what?" pressed the general.

"That your plan was a masterpiece of planning . . . similar in many ways to what he would have done had he been asked. That wasn't the case at first, however. In fact, when he first read it, he called it treasonous . . . until I told him you were an extremely loyal officer, who had the best interests of the Reich at heart, and that he needed to keep an open mind on the subject because it had merit."

"Well, that is encouraging," the general responded with a sigh of relief as his eyes studied the worried faces of his companions, who had had their reservations about endorsing his plan in the first place.

Doktor Funk, minister of economics and head of Nazi Germany's largest bank, the Reichbank, was affected more than anyone. For weeks he had been pressing the Führer, to do something about protecting his bank's reserves, but no answer had come. Then along came von Kleitenberg and his plan; it seemed to provide what was needed.

Doktor Funk's dilemma was critical indeed since the Reichbank had been devastated by Allied bombers and its contents were literally spilling into the streets from its many holes. Thus, much was at stake. He knew that if Hitler did not act soon to protect the assets of the Fatherland, they would soon fall into the hands of whoever took the city first. After that, to carry on any war effort without funds would be impossible.

Admiral Neumeister, a short, round-faced stocky man who came with Doktor Funk and the general, shared similar concerns. As a decorated former U-boat commander now serving under the commander-in-Chief, Grossadmiral Doenitz, he knew only too well the dangers of the sea, in particular, those faced by submariners in a warfare against an enemy now employing sophisticated weaponry and new detection devices. His role in implementing the von Kleitenberg plan was to act as liaison between the *Kreigsmarine* (the Germany Navy), SS, and certain other branches of government. In fact, though his actions and those of others had not yet been approved by the Führer, in a coordinated effort they had gone ahead anyway, confident Hitler would eventually see the wisdom of their actions. It was a nervy and risky thing to do, but Martin Bormann, a co-partner in the plan's development, had assured them he could get his superior's ear if they would remain calm while he "planted seeds."

This then was the day they had all waited for, and it couldn't have come any sooner since Allied victories were decreasing their options. The fact the Allies had captured all German submarine pens along the coast of France and were even now making unprecedented daytime aerial raids against those still in operation in Norway and the Baltic made them all the more concerned. It was today or never!

"Martin," the admiral piped in after a long break, "like von Kleitenberg said moments earlier, time is of the essence. If we don't act soon, we'll never be able to get any of our U-boats out of the Baltic and into the North Sea. Even now, of those still operating, we're lucky if any of them can make it back safely."

"I'm fully aware of that!" replied Bormann. "What else can I tell you? You know the man. He doesn't always go along with facts but more upon intuition, though he has assured me he understands everything."

"Then why hasn't he acted before now?" barked the general in a raised voice while quickly looking over one shoulder to be certain no one overheard his criticism. No one was listening; the others in the room were too engrossed in their own problems.

What irritated General von Kleitenberg about the others in the bunker was their slovenly appearance. They didn't seem to care how they looked any more or whether they shaved at all, something that went against the general's military training. It was clear the others, a mix of high-ranking military officers and civilian officials, were demoralized. Gone was their collective zeal about German invincibility and Nazi superiority, including the high regard and arrogant air by which they once had carried themselves. Defeat was in the air, leaving most of those present to hover themselves before the door of their all-knowing savior, Adolf Hitler, who could heal their wounds while offering sustenance for their emaciated spirits. And so they waited in hopes of being granted an audience.

Acknowledging von Kleitenberg's question, Bormann replied by pointing to a doorway everyone was watching. It led to Hitler and Eva Braun's living quarters. "Be patient. You have priority."

Seconds later, the noisy room turned strangely quiet. Though no sound preceded his entry, somehow everyone knew Hitler was about to enter. First came his adjutant, then the man himself. General von Kleitenberg, like those near him, stiffened, then rendered a salute. It was casually waved away by Adolph Hitler as he entered the room and moved toward the newly arrived guests. Near a large, over-stuffed chair and coffee table, he motioned for the general and his group to sit while simultaneously motioning to his adjutant to clear the room.

11

Within minutes, all were gone, leaving the Führer and the new arrivals alone. Hitler was the first to speak. He looked straight into General von Kleitenberg's eyes.

"I like your proposal, Kleitenberg," Hitler said. "Though I don't go along with its defeatist premise, your plan takes into consideration some rather interesting alternatives."

"*Danke*, you honor me, mein Führer", General von Kleitenberg responded happily as he rose from his seat and clicked his heels in acknowledgment. He wanted to say more but didn't dare. Like those gathered around him, he knew the end of the Thousand Year Reich was at hand and could not help but believe Hitler knew it, too, though he wouldn't admit it. At this point, the general reasoned, it would be better to wait and see what would come next.

"Tell me, Kleitenberg," invited Hitler as he motioned for him to sit again, "about your motivation and thoughts for the future."

"With pleasure, mein Führer," von Kleitenberg replied eagerly as he searched his mind for words to influence his leader. "If the Third Reich is to be perpetuated into the future, it is essential that we . . . that is . . . those of us who believe in the principles and redeeming values of National Socialism—to which you have devoted most of your life—do everything within our power to see that its successor, the Fourth Reich, completes the goals you have established."

"By using assets from the ruins of the Reichbank?" interjected Hitler, clearly testing his subordinates sincerity.

The general was equal to the test and responded immediately, "A necessity, Führer. As you know from your experiences, no worthy project can survive long without funds."

"From the Reichbank's point of view, Führer," interrupted Doktor Funk, "there is no objection to the SS removing their deposits, provided that's all they take."

"Sir!" responded von Kleitenberg, seconds before Hitler intervened to permit the Reichbankführer to finish what he had to say.

"No offense intended, Herr General," replied the nervous banker, who glanced often in Hitler's direction for moral support. "It's just that we have had some unfortunate situations arise in the past, most of which involved Reichführer Himmler himself and certain unexplained irregularities, that is . . . ."

"I can appreciate your concern, Herr Doktor, but I cannot be held accountable for what my former superior did. My first loyalty is to only one person—the Führer himself!" objected von Kleitenberg. "What the Reichführer did has nothing to do with me or the men under my command. And as I said earlier, our activities in your bank will be confined to our own accounts. Of this you can be assured!"

"For all our sakes, I hope so, Herr General," replied Doktor Funk. "Between your needs and those of the war effort, my bank faces quite a challenge. For instance, in addition to protecting what has been entrusted to our care, we must make certain everyone gets paid, from our valiant soldiers to workers and suppliers."

The Reichbankführer's concerns were well founded. Besides being custodian for Nazi Germany's lawful assets, his bank was also the repository of confiscated Italian bullion recently taken from Italy after Italy capitulated. It included hundreds of tons of other gold reserves; some $400 million in American bank notes and negotiable instruments, plus stockpiles of miscellaneous national currencies and priceless *objets d'art*, most of which had been stolen or confiscated from conquered nations and private collections.

"Führer, if that's all they will take, I will be satisfied," replied the bank director as he looked in Hitler's direction for a response. "That is, except for one more thing."

"And what is that?" asked Hitler.

"The assignment of adequate numbers of personnel, motor transports, and railway cars to help us move since we have much too much to move in such a short time. And, Führer, from what we've been told, you are the only person in the whole of the Reich who can authorize such an order."

"That is correct, and for good reason," replied Hitler. "If I didn't control everything, cowards would flee the city and the war would be lost!"

The war is lost, you damn fool! Get on with it! Why wait? thought Bormann as he watched his chief hedging over something he knew he had to do. It disgusted him, but still tact had to prevail, even as late as it was.

"You are right, of course, Führer," interjected Bormann to placate his chief while attempting to redirect his chief's thoughts, "but a decision must be made in this instance, or we risk losing everything belonging to the Reich."

The very thought that such a thing could happen angered Hitler. "Never!" he cried. "No true German would ever permit such a thing! He would rather die than let an enemy suck his blood!"

Bormann pressed on. "True, Führer, and that's why we need to act. But even now, there are other things to consider which need your approval."

"Like what?" inquired Hitler, silently fretting. His twitching fingers showed his apprehension.

"May I answer that, Führer?" interrupted von Kleitenberg. Hitler motioned for him to go on. "What Martin is referring to concerns the U-boats we have selected for our mission. Like the treasury which needs help to move, my men and I will need your authorization to tap whatever manpower and material resources we can to help us conduct our salvage operations in the Baltic. Without it, it's doubtful the U-boats can be refitted and ready for sea. And it all must be done at night."

"Why nighttime?" asked Hitler, ignoring more important questions he could have asked.

"To keep the enemy from knowing what we're up to," replied the general. "As far as the Allies know, these boats have been destroyed and are at the bottom of the Baltic and no longer any use to us. That's what we want them to think anyway. But we must move quickly."

"Mein Führer," interjected Admiral Neumeister, hoping to reinforce his colleagues' position. "I have to agree with the general. If we don't act soon, it will be impossible for those of us in the *Kreigsmarine* who would be responsible for much of the work to modify the two type IXC U-boats we have chosen."

"I'm always being given deadlines!" complained Hitler. "If I gave in to everyone who claimed he had an emergency, we wouldn't have anything left with which to fight the war."

"I cannot speak for anyone outside of this group, Führer, but I can assure you here and now that what we are asking for is nothing more than what we actually need—though I will grant you it is quite considerable in view of the project's magnitude and importance. But remember, sir, what we are doing is not for us but for you and the Reich."

"How much time do we have left in your estimation?" asked Hitler.

"According to our critical path schedule which we've worked out, Führer, two or three weeks at the most. After that, we've lost the momentum and anything can happen!"

Hitler shrugged; he didn't like what he heard. "We could have reverses on the front by that time, and there would be no need for a contingency plan," he argued, hoping others would agree with him.

Everyone in the room panicked. They could see Hitler was still grasping for one last hope, but in their minds it simply was not realistic. Something had to be done!

"Until that happens, mein Führer, we must not abandon von Kleitenberg's plan because far too much is at stake," interjected Admiral Neumeister nervously. "Even at that, though it is quite thorough, things could still go wrong with it."

"What do you mean by that?" snapped Hitler, abandoning his earlier position about a turn in the battle. This was a good sign to the others since his response revealed he wasn't too confident about another successful front. It was obvious that any threat to the program they were now contemplating had priority in his thinking even though he was trying to underplay his interest.

"There's always the possibility our divers could have made a mistake about the salvagability of the two U-boats we've decided to use though we don't think so after studying numerous underwater photographs of the damages inflicted upon them. Should the worst be the case—heaven forbid—we would have to find suitable replacements, and more time would have been lost. Fortunately for us, we still have time since the Allies do not have complete mastery over our inland seas as of yet, but they are rapidly closing the gap. When that happens, any attempt to get our U-boats safely through the Kattegat Sea would be impossible."

"Anything else?" asked Hitler, glumly. His concern was apparent, but again he tried to mask it.

"*Jawohl, mein Führer,*" the admiral replied. "There's still the matter of deep-water hydrostatic tests which each vessel must complete before it can be declared seaworthy. Otherwise we risk losing everything we have worked for."

"After that, Führer, assuming of course, all goes well," added the general in his quiet but dignified style, "the last thing we would need would be assistance from the *Kreigsmarine* and *Luftwaffe*, respectively, in particular, minesweepers to clear our path through Allied-mined waters and fighter aircraft to protect us from enemy patrol planes until we have reached the North Sea."

"If you're hoping for support from Goering's air force, forget it General!" scoffed Admiral Neumeister. "Like I said before, there's little or nothing left of it. On the other hand, when it comes to the navy's part, you can be assured we will do our best to see you get what you need, provided, of course, this meets with the Führer's approval."

"Führer, as you can see," said Bormann, anxious to speed up the process, "time is against us. Our boats will have formidable tasks as it is, just trying to leave the Baltic. Allied aircraft are everywhere now, waiting to pounce on our boats like preying pigeon hawks. Should any of them be unlucky enough to get caught on the surface recharging their batteries or submerged in shallow waters where they can be readily seen, their chance of escape is nil. In any case, without ground and air protection and sufficient time to make adequate preparations,

15

the project could be doomed from the start."

"I've heard enough!" shouted Hitler, cutting him off. "You don't have to repeat what I already know! Time is essential, that I know, but I need to be assured you have solved the problem involving weight, not some gibberish about how dangerous it's all going to be! War is dangerous—that's a fact, but so is victory over failure! So unless you have something else, don't bother me with trifles."

"That's why they're here today, Führer," Bormann broke in quickly while acknowledging the men around him. "We are the recipient of great news—it arrived only hours ago while you were resting. . . ."

Hitler's eyes lit up. "Well, get on with it."

"Word has been received from our research plant at Peenemünde that they've developed a new light weight alloy, the likes of which has never been seen or used before."

"And . . . ?" asked Hitler impatiently.

"Our scientists are ecstatic about it. They say this alloy could revolutionize our rocket and jet aircraft industry because of its durability, strength, ease of production, and low manufacturing cost. Of equal importance, from what they tell me, is the fact it could be used as a new light-weight outer skin on our rockets."

"What has this to do with what we're talking about?" asked Hitler.

"Don't you see, Führer?" interjected General von Kleitenberg. "It's the answer to the weight and balance problem we were anticipating, and it couldn't have come at a more propitious time since we had reached a decision that a number of important items would have to be left behind . . . until we could retrieve them at some later date. But now, all that's changed! With this new alloy, Peenemuende has given us an out!"

Hitler was skeptical. "I've been told similar things about our research on heavy water and the making of a new and more powerful type of bomb by the splitting of atoms and the like," he said, "but to date, nothing has materialized. So what makes you think the Peenemünde story is any different?"

"Because I was the one who approached them with the problem in the first place, and they did what I asked them to," replied Admiral Neumeister. "The men involved are close personal friends of mine and loyal Party members."

Hitler pondered the admiral's words before replying. Something in the man's tone urged him to reconsider. "If both reports—those on the device to harness the heavy-water project and the new alloy—are true, I would have to agree we are on the threshold of something great and glorious. On the other hand, if they turn out to be nothing more than grandiose figments of a lunatic's imagination, which has often been the case, then we're no further ahead than we've been and we will have to consider other alternatives."

"Mein Führer, I know the scientists personally, and they're not the type to exaggerate or misrepresent," the admiral replied. "Even now while we are sitting here talking, they are producing duplicates of the prototype for our use."

"How do you know they will work satisfactorily?" asked Hitler.

"Because the prototypes have already been field-tested. The most critical was the hydrostatic test, and it came out marvelously."

Hitler's countenance changed just then. Instead of one reflecting delight and pleasure, it went from enthusiasm to sarcasm, like he was still trying to prove something, only to change again after he had aired his thoughts.

"If you're right, it's about time they came up with something workable!" replied the Führer. "Don't forget; we've spent millions upon millions of reichsmarks on their many projects, most of which went up in smoke!" He paused and a schizophrenic-looking grin covered his face.

Everyone froze.

"You know," Hitler continued after a few interesting thoughts, "if your researchers are right, this discovery could revolutionize our entire armaments industry—and revive the Reich. Even space, which we have not yet conquered, would be no barrier to our future work."

"I agree, but only if we can get away in time," reminded the general with great care.

Hitler stopped speculating and turned his attention to other matters. "What about your U-boat crews? Have they been properly trained?"

"While we are here conversing, Führer," replied the admiral, "the men we have selected are undergoing intensive training in general and specific subjects. They are the best of the best."

"From where did they come?" asked Hitler as if ignoring or disbelieving what he had been told.

"Most are volunteers from the SS and the *Hitler Jugen (Youth)* while others are volunteers and conscripts taken from the regular establishment."

Upon seeing the frown on the Führer's face, which he had anticipated, the admiral hastened to clarify his last remark. "Of the last two groups, Führer, necessity caused us to revert to their use. We were short on skilled crewmen and had to take what we could, but with

17

considerable caution."

Hitler stared at the man for a moment, his mind analyzing everything. "What about the Grossadmiral—Doenitz? Does he suspect what you've been doing?"

"*Nein,* mein Führer. All he's been told—as suggested by General von Kleitenberg here—is that the *OKW,* the General Staff, under your orders had assigned me to a special 'top secret' project and that it had something to do with the testing of new marine-type weapons. Also, that he would be provided specifics at the proper time."

"I see," said Hitler. "And what was his reaction when told his top aide would be working for someone else?"

"He didn't like it at first but consented nevertheless, because—as he explained to me—he had enough things on his mind without being concerned about special projects being conducted by the General Staff."

"That's him, all right," agreed Hitler with a mischievous smile. "A task-oriented man. That's why I like him." His thoughts and eyes turned to General von Kleitenberg just then and the ruse he had used to keep the project secret.

"Clever, I must admit," said Hitler, "pulling the visor over Doenitz's eyes. I knew you were presumptuous and innovative, Kleitenberg, but I see you have an anticipatory nature as well, which adds a new dimension to your character. I like all these things in a man, particularly if he is loyal and can be trusted."

"Thank you, Führer. You're much too kind," replied the general, startled by the accolades.

"Surprising as it may seem, my dear General, I agree with every thing you've done so far even though you were presumptuous in my behalf. After all, there is no substitute for good planning, providing the people you select are trustworthy. That's where extreme caution must always be applied because one rarely knows who his enemies are until their loyalty and integrity are tested under fire."

"Your point is well taken, Führer," replied the general. Before he could say anything else, Hitler interrupted him.

"Wolf's Lair shall always be with me," Hitler said, showing remorse. "I shall never forget that day nor the traitors in my midst and the bomb that shattered my arm and nearly took my life. It could happen to you, too, believe me. So the less anyone knows about this project, the greater your chance for success. Do I make myself clear?"

"*Jawohl,* Führer," everyone replied.

Hitler addressed the general again to see what kind of response he would get. "Suppose during the course of your duties you find traitors and mutineers in your midst. What would you do?"

"There is only one thing to do, Führer," replied the man boldly. "Eliminate them immediately!" His words sent cold shivers running down the spine of the man next to him, Doktor Funk, whose blood pressure rose instantly, to the point he nearly fainted. "You know as I do, Führer, there is no room in our organization for cowards, deserters, or traitors!"

Hitler smiled. "Excellent! I hoped you would respond in that manner, Kleitenberg. In time of war, harsh punitive measures must often be used to ensure victory over one's enemies, irrespective of their rank or position—even to the exclusion of ethics and so-called moral standards."

"From the tone of your questions, Führer, may we presume you intend to approve the plan?" asked Admiral Neumeister, believing he had properly sensed Hitler's thoughts.

"In principle, yes," answered Hitler, "but the use of conscripts bothers me and goes against my better judgment. Couldn't others have been found?"

"If we had had the time, yes," admitted Admiral Neumeister, "but regrettably, most of the ones we would have chosen are either dead or incapacitated because of war wounds. And besides, we would be courting disaster if we pitted inexperienced U-boat commanders against an enemy armed with the latest in tactical weapons. Before I would do such a thing, mein Führer, I would tender my resignation here and now." His boldness surprised everyone.

"That won't be necessary, my good Admiral," said Hitler with a reassuring smile. "I was only testing your resolve."

Hitler's concern was not unreasonable as everyone noted. His caution and delay in giving his approval had other causes, something which they had not been aware of previously. One of the causes which they learned to their horror and dismay was his awareness of petty grumbling and dissension within certain military units—the *U-Bootwaffe* (submarine service) especially. Open criticism of his leadership and management of the war was rampant, much of it bordering on treason.

"We've heard similar reports, too, unfortunate and isolated as they are," admitted Admiral Neumeister in an attempt to minimize the severity of the problem, "but that will not happen with the men we've chosen. Disrespect or insubordination against you, our Führer, and those chosen to represent you is a court-martial offense punishable by death before a firing squad."

"Just the same," argued Hitler, ignoring the tough words which were intended to reassure him, "you must never relax your vigil. Traitors are everywhere. Take General Steiner, for instance, a man I would have trusted with my life until he disobeyed my orders to open another front. As a consequence, what do we have, I ask you? Disaster! What he did now affects the whole of Germany; can you believe that? Another traitor in our midst!"

"That's why the bulk of our staff consists of SS men," interrupted von Kleitenberg. "While I cannot speak for others, I know I can trust my men to see that Herr Bormann, myself, and other loyal Party members chosen for this trip get to our final destination in one piece." He remembered something just then. "And—oh yes—Führer, if you haven't already guessed, my hand-picked men will eventually replace the conscripts you're concerned about."

Again Dockor Funk's heart skipped more beats. *I wish he wouldn't be so explicit*, he thought. Unlike the general, who was the epitome of daring, he was just the opposite. To him, wisdom was more valuable than valor, so he decided to hold his tongue as much as possible. In the past, it had gotten him in trouble and he wanted to limit his exposure to danger.

"I admire your spunk, Kleitenberg," said Hitler, impressed all the more with the gutsiness of the man. "You are a true knight, and I shall never forget you."

What he meant by that, no one knew for sure, but they were pleased, nevertheless, though the others—besides von Kleitenberg— hoped he would toss a few meager accolades their way, too. He did not, nor did he finish his probing.

"There's just one more thing I'd like to go over, " said Hitler, still addressing the general.

"I am at your service, Führer," snapped von Kleitenberg.

"I would like to review your plan of implementation one more time."

"Of course, mein Führer," von Kleitenberg replied eagerly as he moved to a spot next to his chief. While everyone looked on, he removed a massive document from his valise and laid it before him. The cover was most impressive; it bore the raised embossed seal of the Third Reich, below which, again embossed in raised silver letters, was the title: PROJEKT U4R.

This is it! thought Bormann. *If Kleitenberg plays his cards right, we can be out of this damn place in a week or so. That is, unless Adolf gets carried away again. . . .*

In a matter of seconds, the general found the section the Führer was interested in. With great care, he explained each part, occasionally stopping when interrogated. Now and then a question had reference to another section, and he would quickly turn to it, explaining its relevance or meaning.

Naturally, Hitler didn't always grasp what was being explained. When that happened, he asked for clarification and the general willingly obliged. Though the pace was slow, the general, much to his surprise, found Hitler to be quite astute at grasping technical and other matters. This pleased the general and his companions because they could see by his response that Hitler was truly impressed with the depth, scope, and quality of the plan. At one point, while tabbing through the document, von Kleitenberg stopped at a section containing a folded nautical chart.

"Here, mein Führer," he said proudly as he unfolded it, "is a sample of the proposed course our U-boat commanders will follow, provided nothing happens to change their plans. As you can see, it is fraught with perils."

"Quite true," agreed Hitler, leaning back in his comfortable chair to rest his body, mind, and eyes momentarily. It was another ten minutes before he moved again, making some of those watching his limp body think he had either dozed off from exhaustion or had died before their very eyes.

While he was out of touch, those in his presence could not help wonder how long he—if still alive, that is, and given the strain he was under—could hope to survive? Clearly, his body showed the ravages of wear and worry. His skin was tallow and drawn and his eyes, when opened, were dull, almost dead, and no longer filled with the fiery spark which once leaped out hypnotically at his subordinates to challenge them at every turn. While those around him debated silently whether to touch him to ascertain his true state of health, remarkably, his exhausted body sprang to life again, like Lazarus being raised from the dead. Then, to everyone's amazement, he wasted no time revealing what had been going through his mind.

"Destiny has spoken. What must be done must be done! You have my approval, but under no circumstances—outside of this group and those who have a need to know—is anyone to learn of this project!"

"Oh, thank you, mein Führer. You shall never regret your decision," said von Kleitenberg, echoing the feelings and thoughts of his colleagues.

An air of excitement struck everyone in the room. The long wait was over! Hitler had approved the plan, and now all that was needed was for everyone to leave, to be on their way, since they had many things to do before dawn the following day. Hitler knew that when he looked into the eyes of those near him.

"Is there anything else you require?" he asked soberly.

"Your signature, mein Führer, that's all," answered the general as he pointed to the document on the table before him At the same time he withdrew a fountain pen from his breast pocket and placed it in Hitler's outstretched hand.

"You have done the right thing," said Doktor Funk, hoping to reassure his chief. Up to that point, everything would have been all right had he not added what seemed to him an innocuous statement, "After all, the war is lost."

The room exploded!

"Traitor! Defeatists!" shouted Hitler in an angry fit.

Oh, God! thought the general, like those near him who feared the worst. *That stupid ass! How could he say such a stupid thing at a time like this? His stupidity could jeopardize everything!*

"Traitor! Defeatist!" bellowed Hitler over and over again, causing the little banker to suffer an extreme case of anxiety.

Although what Doktor Funk said was true enough, it was a bitter pill for Hitler to swallow. He didn't need to be told how bad things were. He knew! Despite the chaos around him, Hitler hoped the thin thread which was still holding his empire together could be turned into one made of unbreakable steel. That was not likely, however, because the Third Reich had exhausted most of its defensive resources and was already sounding its death knell. In fact, its extinction was within hearing distance of Red Army cannons a few miles away. In a last bid to demonstrate his will over others, though he couldn't admit that was what he had in mind, Hitler decided to admonish the petrified banker as an abject lesson in leadership—in front of the others.

"Herr Doktor, if you value your position as a loyal Party member, never let me hear you express anything . . . anything at all that implies defeat or surrender to the enemy! Do I make myself clear?"

While everyone watched fearfully, feeling he was about to change his mind, he surprised them by switching topics as if nothing had happened to offend him, only this time, he fantasized his thoughts, something he did when deeply disturbed. Those watching during critical times like this could only wait until the phase passed.

"After all," continued Hitler, right after he had almost sent the nervous banker to an early grave, "we still have Linz to think about. If I should fall, who—tell me—in the whole of the Reich, would have the capacity and foresight to rebuild my beautiful city on the Danube? Don't forget; it was the only city in the whole of the Reich that succored me during my struggle for power. Because of its citizens, I was able to become the leader of the greatest nation on the face of the earth—our glorious Fatherland!"

Doktor Funk shuddered as he listened to his Führer rave about the past and his future ambitions for the Reich. He took the tongue lashing, then had to listen—along with the others—to his leader's dream of returning someday to his native Austria, where he planned to build a new Linz, a new city to replace the historic one now in ruins from repeated Allied bombings. Unlike Vienna, which had rejected Hitler when he was a struggling young artist, the old Linz near the place he had been raised had shown kindness to him, and he never forgot it.

When the Führer ended his mixed tirade, Doktor Funk apologized. "I . . . I am most sorry, mein Führer. No harm was intended, I assure you. As always, you . . . you are right, of course. Germany will never surrender and our soldiers will prevail—to the death if necessary."

As was typical of Hitler in these last days, once he had vented his anger, his countenance would change as if nothing had ever happened. It was a manic-depressive type behavior, one routinely observed by those near him. As to his mood swings, those closest to him felt his spontaneous and irrational outburst was due, for the most part, to the medicine his personal physician, Doktor Morell, had been pouring down his unsuspecting gullet for years. Everyone who knew the *doctor* considered him incompetent, a quack who somehow managed to ingratiate himself in the Führer's eyes. Though many tried to convince Hitler to sack the fellow and consult other physicians, he could never be swayed, so business went on as usual and Hitler's health continued to deteriorate, much like the war effort which was dependent upon his decisions.

Minutes later, much to everyone's surprise, Hitler was his old self again. Without a word and to the relief of everyone, he pressed von Kleitenberg's pen to the paper. Scribbly as it was, they were able to read and witness his scrawl: *A. Hitler.*

A sigh of relief swept through the room. The long waiting was over!

"I salute you, mein Führer. You have done a noble thing," said General von Kleitenberg as he scooped up the documents and stuffed them quickly into his valise. After repocketing the pen Hitler had borrowed, he went to an erect position, clicked his heels, then rendered a snappy salute. The others did the same.

With formalities over and matters concluded, Hitler gave the group permission to leave. The process of departure was difficult for him because he knew this most likely would be the last time he would see any of them. With difficulty he rose from his chair, shook their hands in a final farewell, then with Bormann at his side as usual, he hobbled like a tired old man back to his suite. At the door, he turned to watch the others leave before addressing Bormann.

"When will you be joining them?" he asked.

"As soon as von Kleitenberg sends word from Kiel that the U-boats are ready, if that meets your approval?"

With visible sadness in his eyes, an emotion rarely shown by Hitler, he signaled his approval with a nod of his head before turning to reenter his quarters. In some ways, Bormann pitied the man, but he had more on his mind than worrying about a dictator who had seen his day and lost it! Uppermost in his mind was survival, the need to save his own skin. His family had already been sent away, according to prearranged plans, and his wife told only as much as he felt she needed to know. Project U-4R was definitely not in that category!

When it came to fears, Bormann had his share. At any time before departure, when everyone else was out of reach, Hitler could change his mind, dooming those left behind in Berlin—him especially—to an unknown fate. That, more than anything else, Bormann wanted to avoid. With the enemy closing in from all sides, he didn't want his future to be determined by a supposed gesture of mercy and compassion on the part of the enemy, as opposed to the opportunity to enjoy a safe haven in a friendly country in another part of the world.

Before Bormann could close the door to Hitler's room, the Führer pushed it open again to remind him of something. "Oh, by the way, Martin, be sure to make sufficient copies of my testament for Doenitz and the others. I want everyone to know I have chosen him as my only true successor . . . not that fat pig Goering or that miserable whimp of a traitor, Himmler! And it must be delivered on time to the grossadmiral, no matter what the risk."

"I have, Führer, but I won't be able to send them out until you've put your signature to each document. As for Doenitz himself, I will deliver his personally. You can be certain of that."

"*Gut*," said Hitler. "I'll let you know when that is after I've had a chance to discuss a few things with Eva." He turned and hobbled away just then, leaving Bormann to contemplate his own future.

On the streets above, now cleared of debris for the passage of military and other essential traffic, the three men left as they came. Von Kleitenberg saw to it they were returned to their respective offices as quickly as possible before returning to his own office to finalize plans with members of his select staff. They worked late into the night perfecting them, then retired to await the signal to execute the first phase of *PROJEKT U4R.*

Obergruppenführer SS Ernst von Kleitenburg

Chapter 2

Aktion Rhinegold

Inside the Reichbank, Berlin

eneral von Kleitenberg was a most unusual man. Had his dossier been shown to anyone, that person would have seen how quickly he had risen within the ranks of the SS. The fact he did so, and within a relatively short time, was proof of his extraordinary skills and talents.

His success was due to many things, the most predominant being his ability to keep his own counsel, especially when it came to airing personal views about one's superiors, the Führer in particular. Beyond a doubt, the general knew Hitler was a sick man, a man who could no longer lead, much less accept the fact his empire was finished. If anything could save it from the ashes of defeat, it would have to be divine intervention, but given certain circumstances of which he and most of the SS were aware, that was not likely.

Irrespective of what he saw happening around him, von Kleitenberg was still a staunch believer in National Socialism. After all, he had grown up with it and, like so many others, had profited from that association. The gold bullion, much of it melted down from the teeth of death camp inmates, bore testament to his beliefs and participation in the willful extermination of human beings he had been taught to abhor.

One of his trusted assistants who worked with him deep into the night, was none other than Sturmbannführer Otto Reiter, a major in the SS, who had been ordered to Berlin by the general. With other members of their select group they perfected last minute details designed to put PROJEKT U4R into effect the next day, in fact, right after the air raid sirens sounded the "All Clear."

If anything could be said about Reiter, it was this: He was an intensely loyal and dedicated Nazi, one who never hesitated to carry out his orders, no matter how cruel, inhumane, or immoral. Naturally, such attributes made his services invaluable to the SS hierarchy and were the main reason for his original assignment to Treblinka, where he earned quite a reputation. In time, he came to the attention of an aspiring young colonel of the SS, namely Ernst von Kleitenberg, who was involved in the administration of the various camps. When reversals in the war effort affected the death camps, causing many to be abandoned, Reiter was the first to be recalled by his former chief--now a general--to assist him on a special project. Again, he was well suited for the job since it demanded ruthlessness and complete subservience to the will of his master.

Among some of the items reviewed in great detail that night was a contingency plan for removal of all gold bullion and other valuables belonging to other SS units known to be having difficulty reaching Berlin. The fact that von Kleitenberg's group would consider this did not bother them a bit. It was "dog eat dog" and whoever got there first got the spoils.

The second part of von Kleitenberg's plan was put into action that night. With the aid of trusted assistants and a small contingent of loyal troops, dozens of heavy-duty lorries and additional reserves of petrol were confiscated. After that, they waited for the early morning air raid by American B-17s. When it was over, his troops--and their confiscated vehicles--converged on the crumbling Reichbank. The bank president and his staff were already hard at work, releasing deposits to legitimate customers. It was bedlam at best, with debris scattered everywhere, hindering the orderly distribution of assets.

During the transition, a situation arose wherein an SS unit in the process of regrouping arrived to claim its deposits. Its commander, an Obergruppenführer (colonel), immediately demanded his unit's share from an account listed under the code name: *Aktion Reingold*.

Part of what the officer required involved the release of $100 million worth of gold bullion. When the bank official refused because the officer's papers were incomplete, the colonel angrily drew his pistol from its holster and pressed its barrel hard against the frightened man's temple.

General von Kleitenberg stepped in. He had foreseen such an occurrence long in advance and was prepared to deal with it. Before the startled colonel's eyes, he pushed an official-looking document bearing Adolph Hitler's signature in his office.

"All of it?" gasped the shocked man. He wanted to challenge the order's authenticity and the authority of the general standing before him but didn't dare since the general's troops far outnumbered the scraggly group he had brought with him.

"That's what it says, doesn't it, Colonel?" von Kleitenberg replied in a demeaning manner. In amusement, he watched with a subdued smirk on his face as the frustrated and bewildered man holstered his pistol, snapped to attention, saluted, then made a hasty about face before marching off with his men. Von Kleitenberg turned to the bank official, giving him something else to worry about. "He can't have it, but that doesn't apply to us, now does it?" he said authoritatively. Without hesitation, the intimidated man quickly wiped his brow and led the general's men to the cellar vaults without uttering a word in protest.

Later, loaded vehicles representing the different groups raced away; some were assigned to Doktor Funk's Reichbank staff while others represented General von Kleitenberg's special task force. Their destinations were as varied as the vehicles in which they rode.

Along with this exodus of Nazi treasure went an assortment of officials and support staff. The less astute of the group, those who failed to keep onlookers from drawing undesirable conclusions about what was transpiring before them, were barraged by these very people with curses and threats of violence for allegedly "running away" from the battle zone--Berlin--and leaving them to face disaster at the hands of the Russians. At that point, armed troops intervened with threats they would shoot anyone who dared interfere with the work at hand.

General von Kleitenberg's group, on the other hand, went very much unnoticed. Everything they did appeared to have "front line" marked upon it, a preconceived deception. They carried out the minutest of details with precision and in surprisingly good time. Thus, within hours after their portion of the treasury had been loaded aboard their waiting trucks, treasure, special cargo, and supervising officials vanished from Berlin, leaving no clue as to their route of travel. Even Martin Bormann, their prime contact, was left in the dark.

Then, after weeks of hearing nothing, a call from Kiel, a major seaport on the Baltic, reached the Führerbunker, asking for Martin Bormann. Eagerly, he raced for the phone.

"Bormann here," he answered.

"Martin," said the general. "Tell the Führer phase one has been completed and we're now embarking on phase two, though with some difficulties. They are minor at best and should be resolved in a matter of days, *verstehen sie?*"

As fast as Bormann responded with a positive "*jah,*" the general was gone. He was like that, never one to waste words when duty required him elsewhere. It was clear the program was behind schedule, since phase one should have been completed a week earlier. Shortcomings were anticipated, however, since transportation routes and communication lines were prime targets of the Allies.

With von Kleitenberg's report still in his mind, Bormann ran to Hitler's door, knocked, then entered after receiving permission. Like the Führer after the message was delivered, he, too, wondered what was happening in Kiel. Separately, each hoped von Kleitenberg would finish the next phase on schedule. The grand admiral still had a role to play though he hadn't been apprised of it yet!

Chapter 3

No Margin for Error

Kiel Harbor, The Baltic

ompared to American bombing raids over Berlin, those over the Baltic seaport of Kiel went unopposed by what remained of Nazi Germany's Luftwaffe. What the bombers left in their wake was chaos, the kind which threatened the very success of PROJEKT U4R.

The fact that Kiel and its major naval harbor facility—the Tirpitz dock in particular, was crumbling before his very eyes concerned von Kleitenberg greatly. In fact, this increasing destruction—much of it due to the lack of antiaircraft batteries to fend off attacking bombers— were seriously jeopardizing his staff's ability to meet the deadlines they had established for themselves.

To make matters more intense, the latest intelligence reports revealed British, American, and French forces had broken through German defense lines and were closing in on Munich, Hamburg, and other German cities.

In von Kleitenberg's assessment, it would only be a matter of time before the British would overrun Hamburg and move on to Kiel and other German naval seaports, cutting off all escape routes from Germany, so matters had to be expedited.

The minor problems to which he referred days earlier when communicating with Martin Bormann were not minor as he had said. In truth, they were major but he didn't dare admit things had gone awry for fear the Führer might cancel the project. The constant aerial bombardment had not only delayed delivery of the Peenemünde materials to which Hitler had referred weeks earlier, but had also delayed delivery of the specially modified U-boats which were expected to carry personnel and classified cargo to their new destinations.

As far as von Kleitenberg's special SS replacement crews were concerned, their training had proceeded as planned, though it too was often interrupted by unexpected and sudden aerial attacks. Crews without U-boats, however, were of no value to anyone, a fact which bothered von Kleitenberg.

The two vessels chosen for the mission would have been ready a week earlier had Allied bombing not destroyed Kiel's drydock and salvage facilities, so an alternative became necessary. They were sent to the south—to Luebeck—where newly improved snorkels and radar detection devices were located and final repairs could be accomplished. But even there, work was interrupted by air raids, sending repair specialists scurrying for shelter. When they returned, often they could not continue where they left off until power lines were restored.

If there was anything General von Kleitenberg couldn't stand, it was a delay of any sort. The role the Treblinka death camp played in his career had much to do with it. He knew that the failure of its commander to remove all traces of the camp's existence—which was now in the hands of the Russians—would eventually be linked to him. Also, once certain SS documents were found, he would be tried as a war criminal if captured, a situation he had to avoid at all costs!

Concern lined von Kleitenberg's face as he turned to his adjutant and barked instructions, "Get me Sturmbannführer Reiter at Peenemünde. And after that, get Admiral Neumeister—at Luebeck!"

"*Jawohl,* Herr General!" responded his adjutant as he picked up the phone on his desk and depressed the button on the receiver until an operator answered.

"*Bitte,* high priority. I need a line to the Peenemünde research lab."

A terse conversation ensued. The adjutant looked at his boss in frustration. The general stared back.

"No lines, sir. The operator says they're all tied up."

"Give me that!" von Kleitenberg demanded as he snatched the phone from the man's hand.

"Operator! This is General von Kleitenberg on a top security project for the Führer. What do you mean there's no line?"

The voice on the other end broke under his threats and could be heard apologizing while at the same time attempting to explain to the irritated officer that other priority calls were in progress and could not be interrupted. She gave a name.

"To hell with General Braunstein!" von Kleitenberg yelled when he heard one of the callers was a mere *Wehrmacht* general of lesser rank and stature. "My calls take priority over all priority calls—his included!"

Conceding to intimidation, the operator cleared the line, leaving General Braunstein with dead lines. After great difficulty, she managed to route von Kleitenberg's call through other switchboards to the Peenemünde plant operator, who then connected him to the proper person.

"Reiter! Von Kleitenberg here," the general yelled as soon as he recognized the voice on the other end. "*Vas ist los?*"

"Another raid, General. Killed some of our troops and disabled much of the factory."

"I don't need excuses," von Kleitenberg exploded. "I need those crates! Are they ready for shipment?"

"They'll be leaving by rail this evening, Herr General. That is . . . if we can keep the lines open."

"And what of the work detail that did the packing?"

"As ordered, General. Upon completion of their duties, they were dispatched according to plan."

"Excellent!" von Kleitenberg said, breathing more easily. He persisted slightly after that, showing his consistency for verification. In cryptic form he asked: "Once again, Otto, did I understand you to say the packing detail reached their *final* destination?"

"*Jawohl*, Herr General!" Sturmbannführer Reiter replied instantly. "Our security force returned a little over an hour ago, reporting all contents delivered on time, without difficulty."

"Fine work, Reiter," said von Kleitenberg. "You are to be commended for your efficiency."

"*Danke*, Herr General," the officer on the line responded, seconds before von Kleitenberg broke in again.

"There's nothing to keep you there now, so you'd better be on your way as quickly as possible. You know what to do."

"*Jawohl*, Herr General, but—"

"Yes, Otto."

"I thought you'd like to know, sir, Doktor von Braun and many of the scientists assigned to his project have abandoned the site."

"Oh—"

"Couldn't blame them," Reiter added. "The Russians have broken through and are heading this way . . . closing in fast."

"If they're smart, they'll commit suicide," General von Kleitenberg remarked, referring to the scientists. "If the Russians get them, they'll pick their brains first, then pickle what's left for future Pavlovian studies."

A horsey laugh was heard on the other end. Otto could shift moods and attitudes as quickly as his general. He was an accommodating soul, blindly loyal and gullible to a fault. And he knew exactly what his general meant.

As the general returned the phone to its carrier, he could hear Otto clicking his heels; he liked demonstrative obedience.

"Ready for Admiral Neumeister?" the adjutant asked while eyeing his commander. A brief moment of silence followed before the general nodded his approval. When that occurred, the eager young adjutant quickly picked up the phone and went through the same ritual he had gone through earlier.

While waiting for the operator to get back on the line, he watched as his superior walked slowly toward a steel-shuttered window in the reinforced concrete bunker they had been using as a temporary headquarters. It had been opened a few hours earlier, right after the bombers left. The general was looking out at what remained of the famous Tirpitz dock. Hulks of ships, many of them sunk, were everywhere, like the charred and crumbled remains of buildings which could be seen on the shore opposite the dock. What had once been a beautiful seaport town was in ruins. The devastation had an impact on the general as he stared out the window, causing his thoughts to wander, but his mind was never far from reality. When the operator answered, he turned quickly and waited for his adjutant to signal when the call had gotten through.

"Your call, sir."

"Well, Neumeister?" von Kleitenberg asked gruffly. "What excuse this time?"

"Another five hours—or so, General," a frustrated voice on the other end replied.

"That's what you said five days ago!" von Kleitenberg bellowed. "We're running out of time!"

"Both of our boats were hit last night," Admiral Neumeister

responded while trying to make himself understood over lines which crackled constantly.

"*Vas? Dummkophs*! How could you permit such a thing to happen?" the General yelled. "Don't you know how important this mission is?"

"It couldn't be helped, General," Neumeister explained. "A stray bomb found our camouflaged repair station, damaging both boats. But we were lucky; the damage was slight. We brought in extra help and generators, and repairs are nearly complete although an additional two- hour delay will be required."

"Delay! What for?"

"Diving test—to ensure their hulls can withstand extremes in hydropressure," Neumeister answered quickly. "Without it, we'd never be certain the boats would have any chance of running the blockade or surviving depth charges in case of emergency crash dives. If they pass, you can have the boats within hours."

"All right, all right, Admiral," von Kleitenberg snapped, accepting the answer. "Only be quick about it—if you can!"

The general showed his perplexity to those watching him, but he didn't voice his feelings to the admiral, sensing it would only complicate things. What bothered him more than anything was the Admiral's failure to protect the U-boats adequately. Instead of being separated, they had been dry-docked side by side, a critical error in judgment. Had the boats been destroyed or seriously damaged, with time running out, little or no time would have been available to secure replacements, thereby jeopardizing the mission to which they had been committed.

After considering the matter for a moment, the general decided on an easier tact. *After all*, he thought to himself, *medals are more plentiful than bullets these days.*

"I'm sorry, Neumeister," he apologized, "I had no idea you'd been through so much. And . . . to show you my appreciation, when I call the Führer, I'm going to recommend you for a decoration."

"That's very kind of you, but I don't deserve. . . ," the startled admiral stammered.

"If it hadn't been for you," the general interrupted, though he didn't really mean what he was saying, "we wouldn't have salvaged the two boats. And . . . besides, you deserve recognition for working under extremely heroic conditions."

"Thank you, General. That is very kind of you," Neumeister replied before cupping his hand over the mouthpiece to confer with an officer who had just entered. After taking the man's report, a broad smile swept his face. Without hesitation, he uncupped the receiver and spoke into the phone, "A last minute report, General, from my chief engineer."

"Go on," demanded the general.

Breathing a sigh of relief, the admiral replied, k"It's good news! Both boats have been repaired and are ready for their test crews. In fact, they are boarding them at this very moment. . . ."

"*Wunderbar*! Call me when they're ready to leave," von Kleitenberg said happily as he returned the phone to its carrier.

Those in the room with the general watched as he sat on the edge of the desk near the phone, elated over developments. After a few moments of contemplation, he said loudly, "It's done! Within days, Germany's future will be guaranteed!"

No one in the room was quite certain what he meant, but they felt he was referring to some kind of super weapon that was being installed on the U-boats which had been sent to Luebeck. If that were not the case, some asked themselves, why then was it necessary for the general and his specially trained SS crewmen to come to Kiel?

The crews gathered in the headquarters bunkers in the early evening, minutes after the raid over Kiel. Through the cracks in the steel-shuttered doors and windows, they culd see a fiery glow illuminating the city. It was like that coming from Hamburg further away, except Hamburg's was brighter because the target was bigger.

The adjutant called the group to attention as the general entered from a small side room which had served both as an office and temporary residence. Eager faces watched him enter.

"Be seated," he said as he moved toward the front of the crowded room and took a seat behind a small wooden desk. His adjutant, a highly skilled political officer, remained standing. He was prepared to admonish anyone who did not behave according to protocol.

Chairs clattered as men dressed in neat grey-green uniforms, the kind worn by submariners, scrambled for available seats. They were not regular navy men, but former SS troops chosen for the assignment. And true to form, under the watchful gaze of their adjutant, they quickly and quietly sat down in anticipation of orders.

"*Kameraden*," the young adjutant said as he raised his voice to be heard above the noise caused by bombs exploding in the distance. "It is my duty to inform you, as volunteers for this special mission, that the day we have been waiting for has come."

A great cheer arose in the small room. An eagerness which reflected a loyalty unknown by any other German military unit was seen on the faces of these newly trained crews of submariners.

"*Sieg heil! Sieg heil!*" they all shouted together. Their weeks of intense work under strenuous conditions found expression in their pleasure over the announcement.

The general and his adjutant permitted the outburst because they knew the men needed a break from the harsh training they had undergone. After minutes of jubilation, the signal was finally given for them to take their seats again and listen.

When order was restored, General von Kleitenberg stood up and walked in front of the desk and took a seat on one edge. In his hand, he carried a silver and gold-plated baton, which captured the eyes and minds of the zealous young men, all anxious to hear what their distinguished-looking leader had to say. The general couldn't have chosen his words better.

"Gladiators!" he said in a commanding voice to the glee and spontaneous applause of all present. "Like the brave men who stood before mighty Caesar in the glorious days of Rome, you too can claim preeminence! You are the Fatherland's finest, Germany's hope for the future!"

A volley of cheers followed, but some of the older SS men who had been chosen to lead the ranks of the new recruits did not respond quite so enthusiastically. Most were veterans of Stalingrad and remembered their own response when they were younger and idealistic. Still, they were loyal to Hitler and would willingly die for him before submitting to anything that would discredit his name. So the men who would make up this new task force, both young and old, shared a common vision, the type that defied the intellect of logical men.

"You are truly what I say you are," von Kleitenberg shouted to exhort his men, "men of valor." He waited for them to calm down again before continuing, "I can tell you here and now that within days—even hours—you will be doing great and glorious things for the Fatherland, and your work will help change the world!"

His words drew more applause and cheers, something he willingly accepted. In their minds, he knew they believed what he was saying even though they had not been told exactly what it was they were to do or where it was they were going. It didn't matter, however, because they had been taught to accept all orders of their superiors. Again he reached into their eager souls with words of glory and praise.

"Unlike the words of gladiators who stood before Caesar to die in hand-to-hand combat," said von Kleitenberg through use of an innovative analogy, "I say to you, fine and valiant warriors of the

Third Reich, today we live, and in three days—WE DIVE!"

The room exploded with joy. The moment everyone had waited for was near. As a consequence, an important promise would be kept. Within hours, all would partake in one great celebration before their final mission would begin. They had been isolated from other military men for weeks, suffering deprivation of every sort while undergoing intense training under the watchful eyes and supervision of the submariners they were replacing, navy crewmen who intensely disliked SS men.

As the rejoicing swept through the room, General von Kleitenberg prepared to leave. He waved his baton in the direction of his adjutant, who yelled loudly, *"ACHTUNG!"*

Silence swept through the room. Every man jumped to his feet and snapped to attention until the general and the adjutant departed. Then, pandemonium broke loose as they raced out of the building, heading for an underground bunker which had been colorfully decorated for their use.

Chapter 4

Farewell Banquet

Navy Barracks, Kiel

The navy band was playing patriotic tunes when the men poured through the bunker's many entrances. Anxious to meet their needs were dozens of mess stewards, carrying mugs of beer and trays of steaming sausages. Immediately, tongues wagged and eager hands reached for everything in sight. The program had been planned in advance by their general. He knew his men needed this time to relax and that this event could very well be their last, so it had to be good! But an important ingredient was missing, leading to a loudly voiced complaint.

"*Frauleins*! Girls! Where are the girls?" several high-spirited young men cried out, eager to find a few so they could dance and frolic.

"Sorry. Reasons of security," came a reply from one of the senior overseers, yelling over the din of laughing and complaining men.

Some of the more adventurous in the group didn't stop badgering their superiors. They pressed on jokingly, "Security? Over girls?

What for? They haven't got anything we haven't seen before."

Raucous laughter followed as the beer and schnapps began to have an effect, tempering the men in their demands for more than a one-gender party.

"Haven't you heard the American slogan, 'Loose lips sink U-boats'?" one crewman said to another who was still complaining. It was a paraphrase, but it had its effect.

"*Jah, Frauleins* talk too much," his companion admitted before taking another drink from a waiter. "Shotzies can be a detriment to one's health. Take my brother's experience for example. Got gonorrhea three times. . . ."

The missing gender was only missing in form, however. Every now and then, in jest, a drunken SS sailor would come charging through the room with a mop draped over his head, mimicking the missing women. Immediately, other crewmen would pretend to accost or woe them with various means and words of enticement. After that, they would go back to singing, with the *Horst Wessel* song predominating.

What they didn't know was that, in the bunker next door, General von Kleitenberg was carefully planning their last days in Germany. After the party was over and the men had sufficient hours in which to recuperate, he planned to have them ferried by armored motor launch to the two U-boats. The boats had arrived under cover of darkness hours earlier and were being kept anchored offshore for safety reasons.

The experienced captains who had been selected to command each vessel were to follow soon after to meet their respective crews and to prepare their vessels for specific tasks prior to final departure. In numerical sequence, each captain would be given sealed orders outlining duties for each day. After accomplishment, they would then receive their next set of instructions until it was time to rendezvous again and head out to sea.

Hours later, when the sound of revelry diminished and voices of drunken crewmen returning to their barracks singing *Lily Marlene* drifted off, General von Kleitenberg decided to call it a day, too. No person was without need of sleep, and he succumbed to its call, knowing he would be wakened by his orderly at the proper time. The last thing he noticed as he dropped into his bed was a view of the predawn sky over Kiel. It had a bright red-orange glow to it like a flame on a wick casting an eerie shadow on a wall, one that would not be extinguished until all the fuel upon which it fed had been consumed.

The flame reminded von Kleitenberg of a Berlin under siege and of Martin Bormann who, like the smouldering wick in the midst of that holocaust, was waiting anxiously for word from him that the final phase of PROJEKT U4R had been completed.

Upon receipt of this information, Bormann would immediately notify the Führer who, in turn, would sign the original order appointing Grossadmiral Karl Doenitz as the new head of the German government. It was to be hand-carried by Bormann to Doenitz at his new headquarters in Flensburg-Murwik, a naval seaport on the Baltic, not too far away. After that, Bormann would be free to join von Kleitenberg in Kiel.

Before he dropped into a deep slumber, von Kleitenberg's thoughts were still on Bormann—the fat, balding, pompous Party secretary of the Third Reich, who somehow had always managed to keep his own neck out of trouble to the detriment of others. Secretly, von Kleitenberg despised the man and hoped the Russians would capture that wick and extinguish it before it could reach him.

Führerbunker, Berlin

Bormann was quick to tell the Führer about von Kleitenberg's progress. The general had called at noon, informing him the U-boats had arrived and their new crews were on board undergoing last-minute indoctrination. Also, he reported that the long-awaited crates had arrived safely from Peenemünde and were ready for loading. Aside from that, only one item remained: the arrival of Bormann and his entourage. Departure was to take place within twenty-four hours.

Hitler, like Bormann, was ecstatic when he heard the news because everything around him was bad. The stopped-up toilet didn't help matters though he was the only one who didn't complain. More important matters were on his mind than a stench to which he had become accustomed.

"See, Martin," Hitler chided as he did a painful jig over the news. "There are still men loyal to the Reich, men and women who will fight to the very end to ensure victory over odds thought impossible."

"I agree, Führer," Bormann answered happily, his eyes aglow. That wasn't the way he felt the previous day when he wrote to his wife in Bavaria. She and their children had departed weeks earlier, at his insistence, to get out of harm's way and wait until they heard from him, sometime in the future. In his letter Bormann complained.

Liebling:

    Our project was approved by the Führer several weeks ago, but to date, only the barest of information has been received from our trusted comrade, GvK. Quite frankly, I fear something terrible has happened, and he is keeping the truth from us.
    On the other hand, if he hasn't been captured or killed by the enemy and is well and functioning, then that would inure to his benefit.
    However, we could all be wrong because we have been having difficulty maintaining radio and telephone communications to other cities. In these difficult times, paranoia sweeps quickly through the Fuherbunker, and the talk of spies and betrayals are constant topics. How unfortunate!
    If our mutual friend has done what we haven't anticipated, then the old saying 'Out of sight, out of mind' could very well apply. But we most certainly hope and pray that is not the case. He is in an enviable position, however, being able to do as he pleases with no higher authority to question his orders.
    Time is running out, and we have so precious little of it left to complete our mission. So we can only hope he will be true to his word.
    As for other things, I am happy you and the children are safe and no longer need to endure the stinking toilet. It's hard to imagine we have only one toilet to serve us—and an entire regiment of SS guards, who act more like pigs than soldiers! You'd think they'd have enough sense to carry some water with them to help flush the toilets! And, as for the Führer's architect, Albert Speer, he should have been shot for such a stupid oversight.
    Will contact you when the time is right. Give the children a kiss for me.

Love,
Martin

Chapter 5

An Unusual Cargo!

Kiel Harbor

Like schools of silvery fish swimming beneath the surface of the sea, the shiny torpedoes reflected the bright rays of the morning sun which were breaking through the mist of the fog-shrouded bay. Their glitter blinded those winching their long bodies over from the barge which brought them to the aft and forward loading hatches of the sleek, black U-boat moored nearby.

For those experienced in such matters, there seemed to be no appreciable difference in the torpedoes shipped from Peenemünde, other than they seemed more pliable than those normally issued from nearby naval ordnance depots. In fact, they tended to bend in the middle if not lifted according to instructions.

When questioned by the captain of the U-boat taking on this particular cargo—all twenty-four of them, the SS officer in charge, Sturmbannführer Reiter, grunted a simple answer, "Nothing to worry about."

"But they seem so fragile," Kapitänleutnant Wolfgang Schmidt complained as he watched the rough way in which the SS crewmen manhandled them before applying a layer of grease to each torpedo for a slippery ride down the loading tubes into the belly of the vessel. Once inside, other crews guided them into their temporary resting places—some into empty firing tubes and others into storage places below and above deck plates in the crew's quarters and aft motor room. This left little or no bunking space for crew members, causing some to wonder where they were expected to sleep.

"They're completely safe and more effective despite their outward appearances, Kapitänleutnant," replied Reiter somewhat irritably. "Their flexibility, along with newly developed warheads, constitutes an entirely new approach to submarine warfare," he lied to deflect the man's questions.

From Reiter's demeanor and response, it was quite clear to the young but seasoned U-boat commander that the older man's referral to his rank was intended to keep him in his place and to drive home the fact that, though their ranks were comparable, the younger naval officer's position was inferior to that of an SS officer—a major—who had been given authority second only to that of General von Kleitenberg himself.

Ill at ease, but still concerned over his forthcoming duties, the young U-boat commander dared to press further, "I don't mean to be argumentative, Herr Sturmbannführer, but have they been tested?"

"Why?" asked Reiter, not wanting to answer. More pressing matters were on his mind.

"Because the enemy is waiting out there," the officer said as he pointed to the north. "We don't need any more duds . . . like some of our earlier acoustical types which had been forced upon us without adequate testing."

The major looked toward the U-boat commander somewhat contemptuously before answering, "Doubting Thomas, eh? Well, for your information, my dear Kapitän, they've all been tested in our marine laboratory tanks, and have performed beyond our loftiest expectations, so as you can see, nothing can possibly go wrong."

"In marine tanks! Without sea trials?" the captain protested. "But—"

"There's no need for alarm," replied Reiter without turning his gaze from the scene below the U-boat's bridge, where crewmen were busily loading the torpedoes. "We have the word of our Peenemünde scientists that they will perform without such tests, and as expected . . . under combat conditions especially."

With that kind of reply, the captain dared say no more. The success

Kapitänleutnant Schmidt & Sturmbannführer
Otto Reiter on bridge of U-4R1

of German buzz bombs and V-2 rockets was now a legend, so he withheld further questioning lest he be charged with insubordination and treason, something he couldn't risk.

At that point, he looked down to the barge which had come out to their mooring site. A second batch of torpedoes was now being unloaded from their crates. For some unknown reason, though they appeared similar to the first group, they were quite different in that they seemed to be quite light, a fact which was quickly discovered by several crew members who almost tumbled over the side after applying the same amount of pressure they had used on the previous load. In this instance, Captain Schmidt had to speak out.

"Why the difference in weight?" the U-boat commander asked.

"You are very observant, Kapitänleutnant," Reiter answered quickly. "Just another version . . . with a different type warhead and propellant system."

"Oh?"

"As to its function, Kapitän, nothing has changed . . . other than the way in which they are to be fired. You will be given appropriate instructions in due time. Do you understand?"

"What else can I say?" replied the U-boat commander. "You're the one calling the shots though what we're doing is not standard procedure—without trial runs for effectiveness and safety's sake that is . . . ."

When Reiter refused to reply, the captain gave up. His thoughts went to other matters, in particular, the proper loading of his already overloaded and understaffed vessel. Though he was not told, he could readily surmise that the loading of additional supplies on the heels of a crew reduction meant only one thing: a prolonged journey. However, what pertained to his vessel, so he had been warned, did not necessarily apply to the other U-boat.

That's when his mind shifted to the sister U-boat. Hours earlier he had seen her slice through the foggy but gentle morning waters of Kiel Harbor, heading hastily for a mooring spot next to the devastated Tirpitz dock. While Reiter was looking the other way, busily shouting instructions to crew members on the foredeck below, the captain turned to look in the other boat's direction.

Instinctively Captain Schmidt reached for his binoculars and pressed them to his eyes, then adjusted the focus in time to witness the approach of a heavily guarded caravan of canvas-covered lorries. They were just pulling up to the loading platform opposite the other U-boat's gangway.

As the tarps on the rear of each vehicle were pulled apart, a number

of officials jumped out, then quickly raced down the inclined gangway and into the bowels of the sub. Support personnel followed, most
carrying suitcases and wooden cases. From their stance, it was clear
whatever it was they were carrying was quite heavy. In fact, many
needed assistance.

Upon seeing this, the young U-boat commander could not help
wondering what was going on, especially since his vessel had been
overloaded with torpedoes and miscellaneous supplies—minus sufficient crew—while the other seemed loaded to its bulkheads with
excess personnel and baggage. It was a strange sight—something he
couldn't explain.

"Don't you have something better to do, Kapitänleutnant?" Reiter
demanded as he tapped the startled officer on his shoulder.

"Just curious," the captain replied. "They seem to be doing
something different over there."

"Kapitän!" Reiter said brusquely. "What you see is none of your
business. And what you have seen—or observed—is not to be
discussed with anyone. And that's an order!"

"Jawohl, Sturmbannführer," the captain replied coldly, perplexed
by the secrecy surrounding the other U-boats cargo.

"Your binoculars, *bitte*," demanded Reiters with an outstretched
hand. "You won't need those for now. Anyway, you'll be informed
when its time to go.

Angered by the man's action and statement, the captain reached
over his back and grasped the strap holding his binoculars. He pulled
it over his head then handed it to the impatient SS officer who
promptly put the glasses to his own eyes to look in the same direction.
Through the haze near the pier, part of which was due to a low-hanging
fog, both men could see—with and without glasses—that whatever
had been going on was over. Water was now churning at the stern of
the U-boat, creating a visible trail of froth, and men were scurrying
across its decks casting off lines and pushing off the gangway that had
reached down from the dock.

On the pier, other activities were now taking place: The trucks
which delivered the officials minutes earlier were trying to escape
aerial bombs raining down on them. Unlike the U-boat which barely
managed t0 clear the ship channel by racing into a fog-shrouded bank
of clouds a few hundred meters away, the lorries were less fortunate.
All but one were blown to pieces.

Upon seeing a group of fighter and light bombers heading his way,
dropping their payloads, Captain Schmidt yelled hasty instructions,
"Clear the decks! Prepare to get underway."

The wave of panic which struck just then was routine for him, but not to new members of the crew. Most froze in their tracks when the order came. Even the brave Reiter, who was thought to be fearless, responded obediently when ordered below.

Fortunate for all on board, the last torpedo had been loaded and the barge—along with the tug which brought it—had been ordered away from the hidden cove where all the work had been done. The timing of these events for Captain Schmidt's U-boat could not have taken place any too soon because the barge and tug which had left minutes earlier, trailing a long white tail in their wake, had become a perfect target for enemy pilots seeking something to sink.

First came the strafing, then the bombs, all striking destructive blows. Within minutes both the barge and the tug burst into flames and began sinking. To those watching the disaster from the bridge and deck of the U-boat, it seemed fate had intervened. Unplanned as it was, the order to have the tug boat and barge leave saved the lives of those on the U-boats!

The raid was over, but not the carnage; it was widespread. Kiel, like its surrounding community and harbor facilities, was engulfed by more flames, with smoke more intense than before. For those on board the U-boat this proved to be a blessing, since a black haze had drifted away from the city, shielding it like it had done its sister earlier. This was confirmed by a brief radio communique on a pre-assigned frequency, the latter of which ended with instructions from the general himself: "Rendezvous."

Chapter 6

Today We Dive!

The Kattegat

ll hands, make ready!" each commander shouted, now joyous over being able to move from their hazardous locations.

When the boats were clear of debris and in deeper water, the captains issued orders from the bridges of their respective conning towers. Sometimes it was, "All ahead full, and steady as you go," or "Right, 10 degrees rudder," and so on until the desired surface direction had been achieved. Watches fully clothed in oilskins shared the responsibility, peering through binoculars tightly pressed to their eyes. They searched for mines which could sink them.

"If only we could have used the Nord-Ostsee Kanal," the young U-boat commander said while sharing the bridge with an intense Reiter, "it could have cut days off our trip... to the North Sea."

"Stop dreaming, Schmidt," Reiter replied, this time ignoring formalities. "It would have been too dangerous. And besides, it's impassable right now. A freighter was sunk halfway down, blocking passage."

The young captain wiped his face of the salt spray which had just swept over the speeding vessel. Properly garbed in foul weather gear, he could weather the storm but not his counterpart, Reiter.

The SS officer was soon to regret not taking the U-boat commander's earlier advice to prepare himself for inclement weather and stay below because now, in addition getting his uniform soaked throughout, he had gotten seasick. As a consquence, he was forced to abandon his post and go below for a rest and change in clothing. Following his departure, the radio operator cried out over the speaking tub leading to the bridge.

"Kapitän! A contact on our search antenna! Bearing 290 degrees. Approaching fast . . . ."

"ALARM!" the captain yelled quickly to the helmsman in the tower below after a quick view of the sky. The helmsman, in turn, pressed a button next to him which caused Klaxons to sound throughout the boat. The warning horns were followed by the captain's desperate voice as he yelled to the crew who quickly scrambled, "Clear the decks! Clear the decks!"

Moments later, after assuring himself the last crewman had slipped down the hatchway before him and certain his boat was in deep water and reasonably clear of the known "Rose Garden"—an anti-submarine mine field planted by the enemy, through which it had carefully worked its way—the captain dropped down too, pulling the hatch cover shut after him.

"Crash dive! Flood! Get this damn thing down—quick!" he cried.

What took seconds seemed more like hours as crewmen worked feverishly at their assigned post—some twisting valves, others checking gauges while calling out their readings, and others performing tasks necessary to ensure the U-boat's safe and quick descent into what was known as the "unforgiving" sea.

After that, the bombs fell, the boat rocked, its metal pressure hull creaked, and green submariners cried out when fuses exploded and light bulbs popped like artillery shells within the sub. The barrage was followed by bursting pipes and seals, many of which had only recently been repaired.

In the pandemonium which followed, Sturmbannführer Reiter forgot he was seasick. Though frightened out of his wits and confused by the bustle of activity taking place within the submerging vessel, he managed to keep himself together. Pride took over his demeanor, but only when certain he was everything was secure again.

Like other neophytes on board, but without specific duties to perform, he found it expedient to remain out of the crew's way especially that of the young captain whom he had treated so abominably earlier. And now, more than at any other time, he realized the captain was the only person who had the ability to deliver him and the crew from the dilemma which faced them.

"Damage report!" cried the captain. Within seconds and minutes, crewmen scurried in and out of hatchways leading to the control room to report what they found. Apart from blown fuses and minor pressure breaks, all was within reasonable limits of safety. The most important report concerned the condition of the pressure hull—it was undamaged.

Following this, the boat rocked again, but not as badly as before. Everyone breathed more easily this time after the captain speculated, "Single aircraft, probably . . . with a limited payload."

"You think so?" asked Reiter, who was standing nearby, almost too frightened to speak.

"One can never tell," the captain answered coolly. "In these narrow straits we're like ducks in a small pond, with little or no room in which to navigate. And they know it. . . ."

"Oh!" Reiter replied. "But we must get through!" he added more emphatically.

The captain ignored him, after noting several instruments showing the vessel's descent; it was too rapid. "Okay, Chief, level off. We're getting too close to the bottom."

"Aye, Kapitän!" responded the chief engineer, who yelled orders to others. "Trim tanks!"

Within moments the boat leveled off, creaking as it did, then the ride beneath the sea became calmer. It was then that the captain reduced speed, explaining to Reiter and those near him he didn't want to press his luck, just in case he had strayed too far off course and had reentered the mine field.

After several hours everyone got edgy, the captain included. Traveling blind under the water and in narrow straits was tantamount to courting disaster. Occasionally the captain would glance at his watch, then do what he usually did when under attack: sit back and listen without uttering a sound. Even Reiter dared not intervene, especially when the captain would take off his white cap, a symbol of his authority, and draw near the sound operator to put on a headset to listen for external sounds.

There was none, but from deep within the sea, he could not make a determination as to any danger coming from the sky overhead. The expression on his face was always under scrutiny by the crew, so he made a special effort to mask his feelings.

51

"Bring her up to periscope depth!" he finally ordered.

"Aye, Kapitän," answered the chief engineer, who quickly barked instructions again. A flurry of activity followed as crewmen quickly and methodically turned valves, causing compressed air to push water out of the boat's ballast tanks, leaving only enough to keep the boat at its desired depth.

Minutes later, after the vessel reached the proper depth, the captain raised the sky periscope to scan the horizon and sky overhead. A relaxed smile soon covered his face. He barked new orders.

"Blow tanks! Surface!"

The cheers were fast in coming, especially from the new submariners who knew little or nothing about the sea beyond what they had been taught. They were grateful to have survived their first attack and hoped their reprieve wouldn't be short- lived. They were in luck this time: nothing was in sight. Their safety was enhanced by the darkening overcast sky, one that prevented the moon from revealing their phosphorescent wake, although they were still subject to detection by enemy radar-equipped surface and aerial vessels, irrespective of the time of day.

In spite of the dangers, those on board looked forward to their rendezvous point and hoped the other U-boat, which had preceded them, would arrive safely. It was waiting for them when they got to a remote island in the Kattegat Sea off the east coast of Denmark. Greatly agitated, and standing on its bridge in clear sight of everyone, stood an impatient SS general.

After lines were cast and both vessels were winched in so a catwalk could be extended between the two, the general boarded and promptly demanded an explanation for their late arrival. While doing so, he pointed to his watch, thumping it over and over again.

"Well?"

"Enemy attack, Herr General," Reiter apologized while stiffening to attention. His answer did not phase his commander.

"An SS officer is as good as his word—remember that, Reiter," von Kleitenberg said even though fully aware of events beyond their control.

"*Jawohl*, Herr General," Reiter replied somewhat unhappily.

"*Gut*. Then let's get on with the mission. After all, that's what we're here for," the general added as he motioned for an orderly who was waiting for him on the other U-boat to transfer his belongings. In turn, Reiter called to a crewman standing near the conning tower to go below and fetch his gear, too, for transfer to the other vessel.

"Confused, Kapitän?" the general asked as the young captain

looked on, puzzled by events.

"A bit, sir."

"You need not be. It's all part of a plan," von Kleitenberg said. "You will have more details within the hour . . . along with your counterpart over there, Kapitän Braunau."

The young officer looked in the other boat's direction, then winced, showing he not only knew the man by sight but was aware of the man's reputation as an over-zealous U-boat commander who thought nothing about machine-gunning helpless seamen adrift in lifeboats.

"Now, if you will accompany me," ordered the general, ignoring the young commander's angry stare at the other captain as they climbed the conning tower to observe the transfer. Moments later, both descended into the conning tower below, then into the control room further down. "I will occupy your space, naturally," the general said as the captain followed, clearly showing he expected no resistance.

"Of course, Herr general," the captain replied although chagrined at having to do so. He had given it up earlier after Reiter boarded, so one more dominating intruder didn't affect him one bit. In any case, he didn't have time to worry since he would be doing other things shortly—preparing his boat for its final breakout into the Skaggarek Sea, where danger lurked. The next port for refueling purposes was Kristiansan, a Norwegian seaport still under control by German forces.

After that, from what little he could glean, both boats would then head for the North Sea before taking separate routes to a new rendezvous point in the middle of the Atlantic. Then, and only then, would their true mission be revealed. Despite this, the captain harbored a misgiving; it was something he could not explain. While everything seemed to indicate a secret mission designed to test new weapons, another purpose appeared more appropriate. It was something regular non SS crewmen felt also but dared not express, not at this time at least, though murmurs began to reach his ears.

"You may return to your post and proceed with your duties, Kapitän," von Kleitenberg said, "but remember what I said. Keep your men on the alert for mines and signs of the enemy."

With one quick swing, the general rolled himself into the captain's bunk, boots and all.

"As you say, Herr General," the captain replied while rendering a weak hand salute. "We'll remain surfaced all the way to gain speed and time—unless spotted by enemy radar. That's the only choice we

53

have, General."

"I know you'll do the best you can, Kapitän," von Kleitenberg sighed, moments before he put his cap over his eyes to catch a few short winks, leaving the captain with nothing to do but return to his duties on the bridge.

"Make clear! Cast off! Ahead one-third—both!" he called out minutes later. After that, his U-boat pulled away from the other, then proceeded at a slow pace until clear of known obstructions. Later, he ordered higher speeds while the navigator provided course directions and corrections to the helmsman for their next leg of the journey, one of many which were yet to come.

Refueling at Kristiansand was done quickly, though fuel reserves were in limited. When von Kleitenberg's all-black U-boats arrived, their conning towers blatantly emblazoned with the dreaded SS *Totenkopf* (skull and crossbones) emblem on its sides, personnel and requested supplies and services were immediately placed at their disposal.

The appearance of this special flotilla made many wonder as to the importance of their mission. They didn't have long to think about it, however, because they were gone as fast as they arrived, escorted back to sea by a number of armored "E" boats.*

Again fate took another twist. As each boat dived, the air raid sirens at Kristiansand wailed, warning everyone to run for cover. Within minutes, bombs were falling everywhere. Many were intended for the U-boats, which had been spotted by radar-equipped aircraft, but the attack came too late; both boats had dived and could no longer be seen from the air. This left the attacking aircraft with no other choice except to radio Allied surface vessels to be on the lookout for two German submarines.

"Is it like this all the time, Kapitän?" General von Kleitenberg asked sometime later, shortly after his command U-boat entered the North Sea and was confronted by a sub chaser. The enemy vessel wasted no time dropping lethal depth charges, one of which exploded violently outside the sub's pressure hull. Its concussion waves caused the sub to yawl violently, with loss of control being evident for a few anxious moments until the captain got the vessel under control again.

"Always, Herr General," replied the captain after a long wait as he looked up toward the ceiling as though he could see what was going on above. "We've never been given reason to expect anything less although, in the minds of many, our work is heroic and glorious." A smirk covered his face. "The truth of the matter is that it's filthy and dangerous, and our most common thoughts these days is 'Dive or Die!'"

The general was about to respond, but a distant explosion canceled his thoughts. Again the captain was at work.

"Rig for silent running! Quiet!" ordered the captain at the top of his lungs.

A tomb-like silence followed. All heads turned upward like the captain's earlier. They were now listening for the tell-tale high-pitched whine of zigzagging sub killers and the ping of their Asdic's (electronic submarine surveillance equipment) as they searched the depths of the sea for U-boats.

"More ballast," ordered the captain. A hiss followed as more air was released and water allowed to enter. Simultaneously, the vessel sank further . . . and further . . . until the propeller sounds of the pursuing vessel faded away to everyone's relief. The worst for now was over, but more was yet to come. It was something everyone expected, and they took the time they had to collapse from whatever ailed them—frustration, fatigue, and general exhaustion.

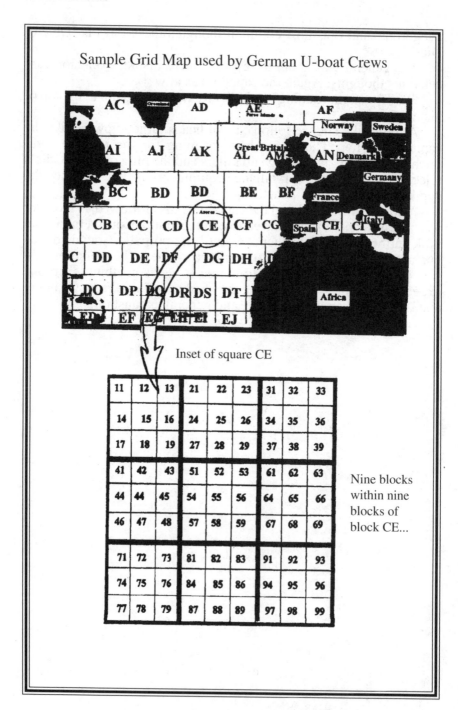

Sample Grid Map used by German U-boat Crews

Inset of square CE

Nine blocks within nine blocks of block CE...

Chapter 7

Grid CD-55

North Atlantic

T he circuitous passage through the North Sea between Great Britain and the Shetland Islands, then an equally complicated course a few miles south of the Faeroe Islands and into the North Atlantic, presented Captain Schmidt's partially seasoned crew with more dangers than they had expected.

In fact, repeated sightings of enemy ships plagued every nautical mile, causing him to order full dives and prolonged submersion beyond anything he had anticipated. He knew the enemy would chase him like a wounded seal, but he hadn't expected to use as much fuel nor had he anticipated prolonged use of battery power.

The original plan was to use the snorkel, but as luck would have it, the seas were not willing partners; they were unusually rough and high, limiting use of the tall, manually retractable air-breathing tube. Every time the sub rose on a wave, then dropped into a trough, tons of water would cascade down, causing its air intake valve to close. Problems immediately followed.

In one instance, the U-boat's diesels sucked out the sub's internal air supply to feed its air-burning engines. What followed next was loud screaming as crewmen writhed in pain from near-bursting eardrums. Their eyeballs were affected, too, feeling like someone was trying to pull them out of their sockets.

Choking black smoke added to the dilemma when engine room personnel dived out of their compartment into adjoining ones to escape fumes which could not be expelled through the diesel's exhaust system. Though the U-boat was only a short distance beneath the surface, outside water pressure was too strong to permit discharge of exhaust gases through the vessel's hull.

At this point, the situation became so critical, Captain Schmidt had no choice except to consider making an emergency ascent, at the risk of being blown out of the water by a destroyer which had been tracking it for hours. His only other choice was to remain below and use what precious few minutes he had to find a means to unjam the snorkel valve. Rapid movements of the boat up and down through use of the hydroplanes were attempted, but this, like all other attempts, proved fruitless. Excruciating minutes later, he gave up.

"Cut diesels! Switch to electric motors! Blow tanks! Surface!"

His words could not have come sooner. Men were in agony and sprawled everywhere, awaiting relief. Their situation was similar to that of a bottle of vacuum-sealed preserves. Unless someone could find a way to unscrew the top, all would soon perish.

Instantly, seamen scrambled, shutting and opening valves and switches. Air valves were opened, hissing loudly as compressed air rushed into the sub's ballast tanks to push out tons of water which had been allowed in earlier to keep the vessel at a certain depth. Bubbles soon emerged, surrounding the rising vessel.

Every eye that could watch the depth gauge did so. At the same time, and instinctively, every ear that could still hear listened for the telltale pings of the enemy's Asdic; it had been hitting the side of the boat for hours, warning them they had been detected. Luckily for all on board at this crucial moment, all was quiet. The pinging sounds had faded away.

"Battle stations!" Captain Schmidt cried out just as the depth gauge showed the U-boat had broken the surface. He wasn't taking chances the enemy might be waiting out of his boat's hydrophone listening range.

Within minutes, he and all the others scrambled through the forward, aft, and bridge hatches, coughing violently. As soon as they could, gun crews staggered to their deck guns preparing for action although most could hardly see through their smoke-blurred eyes.

Fearfully, everyone searched the horizon for sight of enemy ships. To their surprise, the sea was clear, allowing Captain Schmidt to order the diesel engines restarted, the internal air supply replaced by air pumps, and the batteries recharged. Then, a new course was established after the navigator got his bearings. "Steer one nine zero. Ahead one-half—both!"

Instantly, the helmsman who had just returned to his post in the conning tower complied with his instructions. The ship's telegraph registered the new speed, one that was automatically transmitted to a similar device in the motor room.

The next few days at sea were without incident. The snorkel performed well because the chief engineer had learned how to handle it better. On the third day, however, things changed for the worst. Upon reaching the periphery of grid *AL* on their patrol assignment chart, a position several hundred miles due east off the coast of Scotlan, danger threatened again. On the horizon out of nowhere came a gray tiger-striped destroyer. Within minutes, it was over the spot where Schmidt's boat, the *U-4R1* had just dived. It lobbed deadly depth charges after its escaping prey, causing the sea to roar and percolate like geysers.

To escape the lethal canisters, Captain Schmid, with General von Kleitenberg watching anxiously at his side, ordered his chief engineer to take the sub deeper, and deeper and to prepare for silent running. His evasive tactics eventually proved successful, but the sub and its crew were still in danger; their prolonged stay beneath the sea had seriously depleted the boat's battery power and air reserves. Fortunately, fate was on their side again. After hours of bombardment, the destroyer departed unexpectedly, allowing *U-4R1* to resurface, to purge the foul air from her interior, and to recharge her batteries partially.

A revised course was then set, leading to the predesignated meeting place between *U-4R1*, on Kleitenberg's command sub, and its sister, *U-4R2*, the U-boat on which Martin Bormann and other high ranking-officials had been placed. This rout, like the previous one, was not without complications. Within minutes of surfacing to recharge batteries, a massive convoy steamed into sight. It was ringed with escort vessels. On this occasion, as in others, Captain Schmidt's first impulse was to rise to the occasion and to sink every ship he could. "A-l-a-a-a-r-r-m! Take her down! Periscope depth!"

Klaxons sounded and lights flashed throughout the boat as the captain dropped down into the conning tower from the bridge to take a seat at the attack periscope. The seat and scope were one, being completely integrated. Whirs followed next as his feet depressed pedals at the base of the chair. In turn, the entire unit rotated in the direction pressed.

In rapid succession, Captain Schmidt called out coordinates, depth, distance, and other data, information which was rapidly entered into the boat's computer by the first watch officer.

"Prepare forward and aft tubes for firing!" An order like that meant only one thing—multiple targets. The crew scrambled again.

As a tension spread throughout the boat in anticipation of the attack and the retaliation everyone knew would follow, something unexpected happened. General von Kleitenberg burst through the hatch, bellowing angrily.

"Kapitän! What in God's name are you doing?" he demanded as he hastily reached out and grabbed Schmidt's shoulder.

"Preparing to sink the enemy, Herr General," said Schmidt as he continued to provide last-minute corrections to his first officer who was feeding the information into the bulkhead-mounted computer. He was unaware of the general's anger.

"You will stop this attack—immediately!" von Kleitenberg ordered as he pulled the shocked officer away from the eyepiece on the scope.

"Wha—?" Schmidt replied, stunned by the interference. "It's the enemy! They're out there! Ready to be sunk!"

"I give the orders around here, Kapitän" exclaimed von Kleitenberg as he clung tightly to the man's jacket.

"But—?"

"You will do as you've been ordered, Kapitän. We've got more important things to do than to jeopardize our mission for the temporary joy of sinking a few enemy ships."

"Belay those orders, Number One," Schmidt ordered reluctantly, addressing his first officer.

"Aye, Kapitän," the man replied as he uncradled the microphone and spoke into the ship's public address system to cancel previous instructions. A slight moan was heard from below, drawing a frown from von Kleitenberg as he looked down to see who could have been so insolent. Crewmen ducked out of sight.

"Kapitän. Enemy propellers. Closing fast." shouted the radio operator into his speaking tube.

Instantly, Captain Schmidt peered into his scope, then made quick rotating observations. The general's words were still hotly in his mind. Heading in their direction and closing in was one of the convoy's escort vessels, a corvette. Its screws aggressively churned the water through which it traveled.

"Damn!" Captain Schmidt cursed when he saw the fully armed vessel steaming toward him. "They must have spotted the scope. Left it up too long. . . ."

The contact couldn't have come at a worse time. *U-4R1* was just entering block *CD* near the latitude and longitude which had been designated as a rendezvous point between his boat and *U-4R2*, Captain Braunau's boat.

Like Schmidt and the wireless operator who cursed first, General von Kleitenberg added his own curses, knowing he was partly responsible for their detection. His concern was based upon what he had learned about submariners. He now had a better appreciation for the men who had dared to travel beneath the sea in "iron coffins." The glory they enjoyed, as seen by others, was temporary from what he could observe. In fact, it was terminal for most of the men chosen to fight the enemy from this weapon of war—the U-boat. While high sinking scores had been achieved at the start of the war, America's entry had changed everything; U-boats were being sunk as fast as they were being built and sent to sea.

"A-l-a-a-r-r-m!"

Again the fateful cry went out. Expecting the worst, Captain Schmidt ordered his vessel's hydroplanes into their most extreme diving position for an emergency descent. What followed next, however, surprised everyone: For hours upon hours, the warship merely circled overhead, dropping nothing.

Below, questions arose. Some crew members ventured reasons. Some thought those on the surface vessel were trying to scare them into surrendering, so they could capture the sub and acquire some of its secrets such as the Enigma, the sub's decoding machine, and its highly secret torpedo computer, the latest of its type. The crew was never able to determine the motive of those on the vessel overhead because it steamed away. This puzzled everyone on the U-boat because they knew they had been pinpointed and the ship had the ability to destroy them at will.

Hours later, the sub resurfaced to charge its near-dead batteries and to take new bearings leading to the rendezvous point it had abandoned earlier. It was in the middle of grid *CD*, one of a series of rectangular blocks superimposed over a large map showing the United States, Europe, and the seas and oceans which linked them. Each box was further divided into nine equal parts, and another nine

John Hankins

within that to assist everyone in determining precise locations.

The concept had been cleverly conceived by the German Naval Command. Grid *CD,* where von Kleitenberg's command sub, the *U-4R1,* had surfaced, was located in the middle of the Atlantic at a point halfway between the U.S. and Spain. And it was here that Captain Schmidt, von Kleitenberg, and their crew were to remain surfaced if necessary until the arrival of Captain Braunau's U-boat and a surprise package to which the general often alluded. What that was, the general would not reveal other than to say, "You'll not be disappointed."

Chapter 8

The Milk Cow

Mid-Atlantic

irst came Braunau's boat—the *U-4R2*. It rose out of the depths of the sea a few hundred meters away from its sister ship, *U-4R1*, but right behind it, to Captain Schmidt's complete surprise, appeared another lumbering giant—a milch cow— an ocean-going fuel resupply and repair submarine.

It was, as the general had promised, a surprise, but the joy of seeing it was short because of the danger both vessels posed to *U-4R1*'s course; both were dead ahead.

"Hard aport!" Captain Schmidt yelled at the top of his lungs to the helmsman in the tower below. The helmsman responded in time to avert a serious collision.

"All stop! Emergency astern full—both! All stop! Ahead one-third," and so on went Schmidt's rapid barrage of orders before making his final adjustment and approach to both vessels. He didn't need a life-threatening surprise, and he, like the general standing near him, cursed the near miss.

His thoughts went to the cow, its hull ravaged from wear and unpainted. She was a welcome sight, but no one, not even Captain Schmidt, ever dreamed of seeing one again. From his own knowledge—and those of his associates—every refueling and resupply sub in the *Kreigsmarine* inventory had been sunk or taken out of service some time ago because of their vulnerability to attack. They were slow, difficult to maneuver, and subject to easy detection. Even though they were needed, previous efforts on the part of naval personnel to replace them with better models had been abandoned for more critical war needs.

As the young commander studied the resupply sub rolling in the sea off his port bow, bobbing up and down like a cork in a large bathtub of water called the Atlantic Ocean, it became clear to him why General von Kleitenberg had repeatedly ignored his warnings about the possibility of fuel shortages being brought about by unexpected deviance from their original course. Everything had been preplanned. The type XIV resupply U-boat had it all—fuel, food, torpedoes, replacement parts and service, leaving little to be desired, except knowledge as to the final destination of *U-4R1* and *U-4R2*. The general had said the information would come in time, piece by piece. This had been the pattern from the beginning, and there was no reason to expect anything different now.

Fortunately, the sea had turned to glass, a rare occurrence in the Atlantic. This allowed both U-boats to maneuver into positions opposite the refueling tanker. Lines were tossed, followed by the hauling in of a heavy rubber hose like an umbilical cord of a fetus connected to its mother, which was to supply diesel fuel instead of nutrients to her metallic ocean-diving children. After the subs coupled with the tanker, supplies and fresh food—along with scuttlebutt—were regurgitated from the milch vow.

Its crewmen—exhausted, grubby, and unshaven like those on the U-boat after weeks at sea—brought the gossip. What they had to say was distressing to their counterparts exhausted submariners who had endured one harrowing experience after another for weeks and days on end. What they didn't need was more bad news, especially from home!

It started with a whispered comment about the death of Hitler and the appointment of Grossadmiral Karl Doenitz as Germany's new head of state. Confusion followed as more details were passed from sailor to sailor.

On the one hand, some understood the war to be over while others understood it was to continue and yet others said they overheard some of their officers discussing coded signals and radio messages calling for the surrender of all German armed forces to the nearest Allied forces.

"Propaganda! Lies!" barked General von Kleitenberg from the bridge of the milch cow, the lumbering sea giant which he had boarded earlier to quell the rumors and bickering which were in progress. He was not alone. Sturmbannführer Reiter, Martin Bormann, and several other high ranking-officers had joined him on the bridge, all bent on stabilizing the situation while reasserting their authority.

"*Kameraden*," von Kleitenberg yelled into a megaphone from the sub's bridge in hope of getting everyone's willing attention. When little or no response was forthcoming, he motioned to several of his armed guards to take key positions among the crew. Upon signal, they fired their weapons into the air.

"*ACHTUNG!*" yelled a bo'sun's mate after piping the men to attention. All but one crewman froze in their tracks. The sailor, a young petty officer who appeared disturbed, yelled up to the bridge, "General, the war's over. We want to go home to our families."

"It is not!" von Kleitenberg replied in anger.

"That's not true, sir!" the man countered, challenging his startled superior by his unheard-of audacity. "I was present when the signal from Grossadmiral Doenitz was received!"

"Who is that man?" General von Kleitenberg demanded, as he looked to the fore deck below, while nudging Reiter to go below.

"My chief wireless operator, sir," the captain of the milch cow admitted apprehensively. As he watched what was taking place on the deck below, several SS men, with Reiter leading the way, encircled the startled operator.

"You seditious, undisciplined, and traitorous sea worm," von Kleitenberg shouted from his intimidating position on the bridge. "It's vermin like you who have brought grief to our country, but we in the SS know how to deal with traitorous dogs!"

"Me? A traitor?" the man protested, shocked by von Kleitenberg's charge. "I was only. . . ."

He stopped as several men grabbed him and pushed him closer to the base of the conning tower, just below the general. Like everyone, he looked nervously upward.

Von Kleitenberg's face was flushed red. The veins in his neck and temple pulsated heavily as the anger within him grew. Everyone waited for his next move. It came when he stiffened and pointed a long accusing finger downward in the petty officer's direction. The shape of von Kleitenberg's gloved hand resembled a pistol, and the thumb on the same hand, its hammer. When he snapped the latter, a loud bark sounded below.

Bang!

Before the shocked eyes of the assembled crew, the radioman slumped to the deck, bleeding profusely from the head. Those standing near were shocked by what they witnessed; a small piece of skull, a wad of flesh, and spurt of blood went swishing into the sea like the bullet that caused it all.

Crewmen moaned softly as the body hit the deck, but none dared intervene for fear of a similar fate. The message was clear: the war was still on, even if only in the minds of their leaders who said it was. The rest of the general's instructions followed after a tarp was hastily thrown over the man. Before leaving to board his own vessel, he left the glum crew with a message about the dead man.

"He has been tried and found wanting, but you may rest assured his military record will remain untouched . . . to spare his family knowledge of his traitorous acts."

"Dismissed! Return to your duty stations!" piped the bo'sun, minutes after the body of the seaman was slipped into the sea. It was calm, receiving its charge more respectfully than those who sent it there. Then, upon a signal given by von Kleitenberg, the U-boats, with their engines throbbing, prepared for departure. Seconds later, their captains shouted orders, "Cast off! All ahead slow! Clear decks!"

"Kapitän Braunau," said Major Reiter from the bridge of *U-4R2*, minutes after the milch cow was a few hundred meters away from them, preparing to dive.

"Sir?"

"Tubes ready?"

"Yes."

"What are you waiting for? You have your orders."

"It doesn't seem right," Braunau replied. "The war's over. What is there to be gained?"

"You must be anxious to face an Allied tribunal for war crimes against torpedoed merchant seamen?" Reiter replied harshly.

"But these are German sailors, not the enemy . . . ," Braunau argued.

"Do I have to use this on you?" said Reiter as he angrily withdrew his chrome-plated P38 automatic pistol from its holster and pushed it against Braunau's temple.

"That won't be necessary," Braunau replied hotly and boldly while pushing the weapon aside. He sneered defiantly in Reiter's face before adding, "What I did, I did for the glory of the Fatherland! Just like what you did at Treblinka, or have you forgotten your good works there?"

"Swine!" Reiter replied, shocked that he knew.

"If I can't forget mine, why should you?"

Reiter reholstered his weapon. "Touche'," he hissed with an evil smirk. "At least we understand one another," he added before turning away to look at the departing resupply U-boat.

At that moment, the captain peered through a pair of high-powered, range-mounted binoculars, then shouted instructions to the helmsman in the tower below. He waited for confirmation. It came moments later, "All tubes ready Kapitän."

"Flood tubes!"

"Tubes flooded!" came a confirming reply seconds later.

"Los! Fire!" Braunau shouted.

The U-boat reeled when a salvo of torpedoes sped toward their unsuspecting target. Upon entry into the water, the small propeller on each torpedo began to turn and, after gaining the required revolutions, armed their electronic sensing warheads.

The resultant explosion was violent, more devastating than was thought possible. No one had taken into consideration the torpedoes, fuel, and other explosives the refueling U-boat still carried, and the collective devastation which would send shock waves racing back. The explosion had ripped the cow from bow to stern, leaving no survivors. As the supply boat settled into the sea, heading for its final resting place, a look of satisfaction crossed Reiter's face; it was a carbon copy of the one on General von Kleitenberg's some distance away as he watched the same thing. The sinking could have gone by without some hard feelings between Reiter and Braunau had the SS major not smiled when he asked the next question.

"Dead men tell no tale, *jah*?"

Captain Braunau's face turned white. What Reiter said reeked with insensitivity, and he didn't like it, orders or no orders! Though he had been a Nazi Party member from the beginning, he was still a sailor.

"One day you will go too far, Reiter," he warned as he looked hard into the SS officer's face. "It's only by circumstance we're in the same boat, so don't press your luck!"

"Is that a threat?" Reiter challenged as if he wanted a confrontation.

"Call it what you want," Braunau answered defiantly as if he didn't care anymore. "But remember this, *kamerad*. Without me this boat goes nowhere." He slapped the bridge rail hard just then, causing the bridge crew to look his way.

The message struck home. Reiter was startled by the response, something he hadn't faced before. Whatever he was thinking at that moment was interrupted when Braunau suddenly yelled into the conning tower beneath their feet.

"Clear the decks!" He turned to Reiter just then and challenged him. "And that means you, unless you want to swim . . . to wherever it is we're going."

Reluctantly Reiter obeyed and quickly entered the hatch.

A few hundred meters away, von Kleitenberg watched the *U-4R2* slowly submerge. His thoughts paralleled those of his trusted assistant, Reiter. Both knew the success of their mission required secrecy, and any breach—no matter how small—could spell disaster. Thus, the death of the officers and crewmen of the supply boat was justified in their minds.

Captain Schmidt of *U-4R1*, unlike his counterpart on *U-4R2* who knew beforehand the milch cow and its crew were to be destroyed, had no idea he and some of his men would witness the deliberate destruction of a German U-boat by their own people. When h and the others cried out in disbelief over what they had just witnessed, von Kleitenberg ordered them to remain silent.

"But why, General?" Captain Schmidt dared to ask as he looked out into the sea where the resupply vessel had gone down. An oil slick was rising, bringing with it pieces of charred debris.

"Military expediency," replied the general irritably. He was unaccustomed to being questioned by subordinates. Yes, he too—like Reiter with Braunau earlier—realized he could not do without an experienced U-boat commander.

"Does the end justify the means? At the cost of innocent German lives?" asked Schmidt, determined to get an acceptable answer.

Angrily, von Kleitenberg turned his tall body away from the rail of the bridge where he been observing the emerging debris to face the short U-boat commander who had questioned his authority.

"If I thought for one moment, Kapitän, that you were disloyal and were unworthy of command, I would have you shot right now!"

"Disloyal! Me? Never!"

"Tell me, Kapitän," asked von Kleitenberg, suddenly changing the subject, "what do you think we're doing out here in the middle of the Atlantic?"

"On a mission to save the Fatherland . . . and to bring victory to the Reich!" Schmidt responded.

"Victory? Over what?" laughed von Kleitenberg. "Haven't you heard—the war's over? We lost!"

"Over? You mean . . . the radio operator on the supply boat spoke the truth?" Schmidt asked, overwhelmed by the general's statement.

"For others, but not for us!" said the general, taking note of the stunned faces before him—that of the first watch office, commonly referred to by the captain as "Number One," and the captain himself. The remaining duty personnel were SS crewmen. He didn't worry about them; their loyalty was to the general.

"I . . . we don't follow you, sir," said Captain Schmidt. Still fresh in his mind were the radio operator's death and the unjustifiable destruction of the supply sub. It all seemed senseless.

"You seem to have forgotten something, Kapitän. We still have a mission to complete," the general answered.

"Mission? How can there be a mission with the war over?" Schmidt asked. He looked at his assistant. The man, he could see, shared his thoughts.

"It makes no difference. All this was taken into account when the Führer entrusted me with this plan," von Kleitenberg responded enthusiastically as if he expected the two U-boat officers to share his zeal.

Captain Schmidt didn't know what to say just then. His thoughts were muddled; they were still on the U-boat that had just been destroyed, and on the men who went down with her, German sailors who would never see their homeland or families again.

"But why did the men on the cow need to die?" Schmidt asked after getting up more nerve.

"You're a fool, Kapitän, a man without vision," von Kleitenberg chided, adding, "The war was lost long ago, but the Reich will live forever. And you and I, and all the men on these two boats, will be its progenitors."

Schmidt and his first watch officer couldn't help but smirk. It drew an angry look from the general, who hastened to explain, "For the past year, while your shipmates were dying needlessly at sea, there were those of us in the German High Command who knew the war was lost. And because we believed in the ideals of National Socialism, we received the Führer's permission to look to the future. This is that day! A day of glory! One that will someday resurrect the victory which has been stolen from us by our enemies."

"But how, Herr General, and with what?"

"Hah!" von Kleitenberg scoffed, again clearly indignant over the question. "You are not very alert, my dear Kapitän."

Von Kleitenberg turned just then to survey the sea for signs of aircraft or surface vessels, then the sky overhead where a lone sea gull remained suspended on a light breeze. After a brief pause, he turned back to face the waiting officers.

"Tell me, Kapitän. When you took command of this vessel in Kiel, did it ever occur to you to check the *Kreigsmarine Registry of Ships* . . . to see if this U-boat is listed? Or, better yet, haven't you noticed or wondered why the commissioning and dedication plates are missing?"

"No, sir," Captain Schmidt replied to the first question with his first watch officer agreeing. As to the second, they were suddenly aware of something they knew about, but never questioned. Their last-minute assignment and the work they had accomplished to prepare for sea duty had kept them from asking questions.

"Why is that so important, Herr General?" Number One asked. Often he remained quiet, but circumstances dictated otherwise now. Too much had happened.

"Because you would have found nothing!" von Kleitenberg replied slyly. "No records at all. . . ."

"I—we don't understand, General," Captain Schmidt interjected. Von Kleitenberg laughed.

"See what I mean? You're too simple in your thinking. SS men are taught to think ahead . . . to anticipate the unexpected so they can outwit the enemy."

"And—?" asked Schmidt, still uncertain what the general was getting at.

"To beat the enemy, you must think like them. Had we used U-boats known to the Allies as still being afloat, instead of salvaged ones, every Allied vessel in the Atlantic would be looking for us right now."

"What!" Schmidt exclaimed, caught by surprise. "This boat—and Braunau's—they're salvaged vessels?"

"Of course, Kapitän," von Kleitenberg answered, pleased with their shocked response. He laughed again before continuing. "That's why we had to take the most regrettable and extreme action against a vessel of our own flag. We cannot surrender nor can we fail to go on with our plan for the future."

"We are still combatants then," the captain interjected. He, like his assistant, was distressed by what they were learning.

"All part of the plan," von Kleitenberg acknowledged proudly as he looked into the bright sky overhead. "Whether you know it or not, Kapitän Schmidt, you, your men and mine are most fortunate in having been chosen as the nucleus for the rebuilding of a new Reich—the Fourth Reich!"

"And how will we accomplish this?" Schmidt asked skeptically. "I'm surprised at you, Kapitän. For a seasoned war veteran, a man of outstanding accomplishments against the enemy, you seem to have no understanding of military strategy and political necessity. Surely, you must know by now that the SS does not undertake any venture without first weighing the consequences? Why else would we train SS men to serve as crewmen on two of the Fatherland's finest U-boats?"

"But we were only told we had been selected for a special mission—to test new weapons!" Schmidt protested. "Not the rebuilding of the Reich."

"I know what I said, but that was only a ruse to disguise our true mission. Risk and sacrifices were required, and we had to take them. The milch cow was one of the sacrifices."

"I could never have done a thing like that!" Schmidt answered.

"That's precisely why I'm a general, and you're what you are," von Kleitenberg shot back impatiently. "I'm disappointed with you, Kapitän! I thought you'd have more imagination and zeal."

"But how do we know you're not running away?" Schmidt interjected suddenly, hoping to catch the general off guard.

"Insolence!" von Kleitenberg shouted, countering the unexpected statement from an inferior officer. "Don't ever challenge my loyalty again! No true Nazi, no true Aryan—one who believes in the principles expounded by our great and glorious Führer—could ever desert the party which has changed the face of the earth. Remember that! Heil Hitler!"

As he said that, von Kleitenberg raised his right hand in a Nazi salute. Schmidt and his first officer stiffened and returned it reluctantly. Uneasiness coursed through their bodies. It was made more intense when they looked through the conning tower hatch to the deck below. The eyes of SS men in the tower below were upon them, crewmen loyal and ready to serve the general. All he needed to do was to give the order and they would follow his command, even to the giving of their own lives.

Captain Schmidt's eyes searched the sea again, just as they had done earlier, to study debris still coming to the surface. A few bodies surfaced just then. He drew the general's attention to their corpses.

"It's regrettable," said von Kleitenberg after looking in the same direction. "We had no choice. It was them or us. War requires sacrifices . . . the lives of one's co-workers at times."

"Us?" asked Captain Schmidt, seeking further clarification.

"You still don't understand, do you, Kapitän?" von Kleitenberg said contemptuously. "Had we allowed them to surrender as they planned, the Allies would have learned of our existence and every warship in the Atlantic would be looking for us right now. We couldn't permit that. . . ."

At that point, Schmidt knew questioning the general further would serve no useful purpose. He and the few loyal crewmen upon whom he could depend were outnumbered and outgunned. They were at the mercy of the general and his mission and had no choice except to obey.

"In that case, Herr General, since we are still at war, may I suggest we leave the immediate area as quickly as possible since we are in danger of being detected and destroyed?"

"You're quite right, Kapitän," agreed von Kleitenberg as he reached into the breast pocket of his coat and removed a large envelope. He handed it to the man. "Your orders," he continued while adding a note of caution to everyone within hearing distance. "From this moment on, gentlemen, and on penalty of death, none of you is to divulge what you have just heard or seen. Further, you are advised not to deviate from these orders without my explicit consent. Is that understood?"

"*Jahwohl*, Herr General," Captain Schmidt answered.

"Good. Then you may open your orders, Kapitän," von Kleitenberg said before stepping down into the hatch leading to the control room below. "I'll be in my wardroom resting, should you need me."

"Bastard! Swine! Murderer!" Captain Schmidt cursed softly when the man was out of sight.

"Careful, sir," Number One warned. "The bulkheads have ears."

"How could they have done such a thing? They were German sailors!" Schmidt moaned.

Upon seeing one of the SS crewmen looking up from the conning tower, Number One took the initiative.

"Prepare to dive!" he yelled into the speaking tube next to him. Immediately, excess personnel in the tower descended into the bowels of the vessel, heading for their duty stations.

"Thank you," the captain replied, understanding why he did what he did.

"Don't forget your orders," Number One added.

"What? Oh, yes," Captain Schmidt replied as he opened the brown envelope. He scanned the order then turned it over to his assistant to read.

"The Caribbean! By way of Cuba? That takes us right through enemy territory!" Number One exclaimed.

"Clever, aren't they?" Captain Schmidt snorted.

"It's suicidal," Number One complained. "Why would they choose such a route?"

"Who knows?" the captain replied dejectedly. "Perhaps it has something to do with those damn torpedoes, the ones they've been making such a fuss about."

"You know," Number One replied in a whisper. "I've been thinking the same thing. For the past few weeks or so."

"Why?" asked Schmidt.

"It might be coincidence, but I don't think so," replied Number One.

"Explain yourself," pressed the captain.

"Coincidence, maybe," the man replied, "but a couple of weeks ago . . . the chief approached me, complaining about not being able to perform routine torpedo checks and overhauls. When asked why, he said the new SS torpedomen responsible for them said it wasn't necessary any more."

"They give any reason?" asked Schmidt.

"Nothing other than they didn't require maintenance of any sort."

"That is strange," the captain said. "I've never heard of a maintenance-free torpedo, have you?"

While Number One pondered the question, the discussion triggered something in the captain's mind. It dealt with an encounter with an Allied convoy, weeks earlier. When preparing to fire a volley of torpedoes at the enemy, von Kleitenberg had abruptly and angrily canceled his orders. No reason was given for his actions other than the excuse he shouldn't jeopardize their mission for the questionable glory of sinking a few enemy ships. Besides, he had been told, it was a waste of good torpedoes.

That was a strange thing to say and to do, he remembered thinking at the time. *But now, in view of what is happening, perhaps it wasn't so strange after all, that is, unless the torpedoes aren't what they're purported to be."*

"Time to go, Kapitän," Number One said as he looked down the hatch at the waiting helmsman. Everyone below was expecting a follow-through of the dive order.

"After you, Number One."

The first officer immediately slipped down the ladder into the conning tower, followed by the captain.

"Take her down!"

Horns sounded and lights flashed as the captain clanked the hatch down after him, then twirled the compression wheel until he couldn't tighten it any more. Pressure built up around the hull.

"Take a heading of two zero zero degrees, and hold her steady at snorkel level, Chief," the captain yelled as he dropped feet first to the steel deck of the control room. "Course correction will follow."

"Aye, Kapitän," the chief answered, bare seconds before barking orders to men already prepared to open and close valves, including those manning the diving planes.

"Hold her level, dammit, Chief," the captain yelled suddenly, right after the boat dived too deep, causing the snorkel to close and suck out precious air.

"Sorry, Kapitän," the chief apologized. In haste he called out a series of orders to others. Moments later the boat began to rise. "Angle on bow . . . ."

After the boat was balanced, rumors spread throughout the compartments about the loud explosion outside. Most of the talk came from the regular crewmen. They were worried and wanted an explanation. After making inquiries of their SS counterparts, they noticed a new coolness from the SS men, which worried them. To quell destructive rumors, they sent a spokesman to the captain.

"Kapitän, may I speak with you, sir?" the petty officer chosen for the job asked after making certain he couldn't be overheard.

"Yes, what is it, Karl?" Captain Schmidt answered. He lowered his voice upon noticing the man wanted to speak in private.

"It's about the resupply boat, sir."

"What about it?" Schmidt asked cautiously.

"Someone said it was sunk by *U-4R2*."

Shocked that word had leaked out, Schmidt pulled the man aside and whispered, "Who told you that?"

"One of our own men overheard one of the SS crewmen bragging about it," the petty officer replied. He looked around the control room, then motioned in the direction of a hydroplanesman who was manning his post on the opposite side. The captain looked around to see who it was.

"That the one?" Schmidt whispered to be certain.

"Yes, sir. He's the one all right," the sailor answered cautiously.

Captain Schmidt recognized the man as being present on the bridge when the supply boat was sunk.

"Is it true, Kapitän?" the worried man asked, interrupting his commander's concerned thoughts.

Captain Schmidt thought quickly before answering. "Yes, it's gone, Karl," he admitted, "but not in the way you might have heard it. You know these SS men; they tend to brag a lot, just to look good." He smiled just then, hoping the man believed the story until he could do something to defuse the problem. The answer was quick in coming.

As the greasy young machinist mate looked on, the captain stood up and walked to the center of the compartment and reached for a bulkhead-mounted microphone. While doing so, he motioned to the machinist mate to stand fast. Silence traveled through the boat when his words rang out.

"This is the Kapitän. I'm sorry for the delay in making this report, but more pressing matters kept me from telling you about the explosion you heard a while ago. Yes, it's true; our resupply boat is no more! Regrettably, she struck a mine, taking all hands with her. We grieve for our fallen comrades, and pray for their souls. *Enden*."

A few murmurs followed as the shock of the loss traveled throughout the boat. Then, as was true in the life of submariners, work continued with little or nothing being said about the tragedy though there was a sudden and noticeable change in attitudes, especially between SS personnel and nonSS crewmen.

Though the captain had adequately explained the unexpected sinking of the supply U-boat, he had not discussed the sudden and unprecedented execution of milch cow's wireless operator to the non-SS crewmen. In their eyes, he was entitled to a court-martial, but he didn't get it. Consequently, their suspicion grew and their seafaring minds began to wander. In fact, as the days passed, it was becoming increasing clear to them that the men who served in the SS belonged to a military service branch with a value system foreign to their own. As such, concern for human life and suffering meant little or nothing to them when it came to obeying the orders of their superiors. Blind obedience predominated!

Under such conditions, tensions grew and petty officers were put on the alert to quell any would-be confrontations. The desire to remain alive and fears of reprisal kept interpersonal relations from exploding. Despite their political and philosophical views, the men knew they had to work together since the skills of one were dependent upon the skills of the other.

John Hankins

Chapter 9

Alternatives!

The Caribbean

t had been three days since receipt of his last instructions. When no word was passed from the general, Captain Schmidt decided it was time to speak to his superior about his concerns. Uppermost in his mind was the upcoming passage through Cuban waters; it would be the last and most dangerous part of their journey.

"May I come in?" asked Captain Schmidt after he pushed the green security curtain aside so he could look in.

Von Kleitenberg was sitting at his small desk, writing something. Next to him, its cover and title clearly visible, was a book entitled *Military Strategy and Political Doctrine for Newly Commissioned Officers.* Upon reading the title, Captain Schmidt frowned.

"Something on your mind, Kapitän?" von Kleitenberg said as he pushed his writing pad aside. The pounding of the boat's diesels almost drowned out his words.

"I believe we need to talk, sir," replied Captain Schmidt.

"Take a seat," replied von Kleitenberg as he motioned for the commander to sit on his bunk. There was no place else to sit since the stateroom was filled with files and the general's personal effects.

"General, I don't mean to question your orders," said the U-boat commander as he pulled out a crumpled document from beneath his fowl weather gear, "but after thinking long and hard about our sealed orders, I just had to tell you that, if we continue as we are, we will be inviting disaster of the worst sort."

"It's all part of the risk we must take," replied the general.

"But Guantanamo, off the southern coast of Cuba, is where the American's have their largest concentration of warships! To attempt a crossing of that area is about as dangerous as trying to break into the Mediterranean by way of the Gibraltar blockade! Few if any of our U-boats ever made it!"

"You seem to forget something, Schmidt," replied the general. "The war is over, and they won't be looking for us."

"But, sir—"

"Kapitän, need I remind you that we are still on a 'top secret' mission, one specifically approved by the Führer himself . . . before he died?"

"I understand all that, General," Schmidt defended himself, "and I'm sorry our leader had to give his life in such an ignoble way, but..."

"But nothing, Schmidt!" interrupted the general. "Every detail was established long before you and your men were selected by a committee comprised of top intelligence officers . . . before being submitted to the Führer for approval. In fact, I was there when he reviewed the records of eligible U-boat commanders and when he personally selected your name from the list."

"You met with the Führer himself?" Schmidt exclaimed, suddenly and temporarily feeling proud about his selection and at such a high level. He had no idea so much had gone into the planning.

"Of course," replied von Kleitenberg while turning to his desk again to retrieve the book lying on it. Captain Schmidt noticed the name of its author: SS GruppenFührer (Lieutenant General) Ernst Wilhelm von Kleitenberg.

"Your book, sir?" he asked.

"Yes. I wrote it for aspiring young officers like yourself. Have you read it?"

"No, sir," replied Schmidt with some reluctance as if he would be chastised for not having done so.

"I'm not surprised. Only a few copies have been printed and circulated to date. Shortage of paper and reverses at the front prevented adequate distribution, but it's quite good if I might say so myself. Its focus is upon leadership and the importance of National Socialism as a political and social tool for world unification."

"Oh, I see," Captain Schmidt replied, feigning interest.

"I hope you do," von Kleitenberg said doubtfully.

"You see, more is involved than meets the eye . . . like this U-boat you're commanding and what I asked about it earlier."

"Oh?"

"If any ideological thought is to have a profound impact on the world, strategic planning is a must. Our Führer knew this, but unfortunately he died before he could see his hopes and dreams turned into reality. He did, however, leave a legacy for you, me, and other to pick up where his leadership left off."

Captain Schmidt listened attentively as the general spoke on, not totally convinced, but he needed to learn as much as he could about what had transpired prior to his being called to Kiel to take command of his boat. Up to now, he had never been told. It helped explain some of the things which happened at sea several days earlier after the milch cow arrived on the scene bringing news which shocked everyone. Also, he hoped to learn the reason for radio silence prior to that time.

"Tell me, Kapitän," von Kleitenberg asked, returning to a statement he had made earlier. "Didn't you think it odd, when you assumed command of this boat, that it was devoid of identification plaques?"

"No, sir. Like I said before, I was much too busy to notice," came Schmidt's answer.

The general gave a perceptible snicker. "You see, that's the difference between you and your men compared to men of the SS. My men would have noticed immediately; they're trained to be alert and pay attention to detail."

Captain Schmidt bit his lip, angry over not being able to respond vehemently to the general's subtle but demeaning manner.

"That's what I mean when I talk about preparedness . . . and pre-planning," continued the general as he opened his book and thumbed through it until reaching a specific section. "You might be interested in this chapter." He handed the opened book to the captain. "It's on the importance of pre-planning."

"I'm aware of such matters, sir," Schmidt snapped, offended by the implication. "There isn't a mission on which I have gone when pre-planning wasn't an important part. It would be foolish to do otherwise."

"You don't need to defend yourself, Kapitän," von Kleitenberg interrupted. "I was merely making a point about the need to pay attention to the smallest of details. And this mission is no different."

"Oh—?" replied Schmidt, more calmly this time.

"Her, let me show you," said von Kleitenberg, surprising Schmidt by his openness. He reached over to the desk for his leather briefcase. He opened it and pulled out a selection of large black and white photographs. "Ever see any of these U-boats before?"

Captain Schmidt studied the photos for a while before handing them back to the general. "Yes. I know them. They were sunk some time ago, with all hands."

"You're certain about that?" asked the general.

"Yes, sir. It's a matter of record, and besides, I knew their captains quite well," replied Schmidt.

"I think you'd better look at these, too, and their *U* numbers in particular," said the general. Without a hint of what was going through his mind, he passed the second set to the young officer. The response he hoped for was not long in coming.

"I. . . I can't believe it! These can't be the same boat?" he stammered, incredulous over what he was seeing.

"Took them right from under the eyes of the enemy," replied the general, "in the middle of the night. And the best part yet is that you're now the Kapitän of the one formerly commanded by Korvettekapitän Hermann Schultz."

"Schultz! He was one of my best friends," gasped Schmidt upon hearing the name.

"Oh! I'm sorry. I didn't know that. Otherwise I would have used more tact in advising you," replied the general with a startling display of compassion.

"It's like being in a coffin, now that I know," said Schmidt as he looked around the recently repaneled stateroom as if sensing the spirits of lost souls looking down on him. "Did you find their bodies?"

"Yes. What was left of them. But they were all given a proper burial, I assure you. It was performed in secrecy, however, because we had to protect the purpose of the salvage."

Schmidt's faraway look did not escape the general's notice. "You're not superstitious, are you, Kapitän?" he asked.

"No, sir, but it's just don't feel comfortable about being on a resurrected sub, especially one once commanded by one of my closest friends."

"Well, you'll get over it, Kapitän,'" said von Kleitenberg, "even more so when you have had a chance to test all the latest in technology we've incorporated into the salvaged version."

Sensing the man still had something on his mind, the general pressed on. "Anything else?"

Schmidt thought for a while, then decided he had better say what was on his mind. "Yes. There is something else."

"Go on," urged the general.

"It's about the milch cow, General. Destroying the U-boat I can understand, but not its crew."

"A duty I did not cherish, Kapitän, but it had to be done," von Kleitenberg replied in a strained voice. He had hoped to win the young officer over to his side by providing him with some insight into things which preceded his arrival at Kiel, but he was failing. So he applied the only tact he knew. "The answer to your question comes under the heading of 'The Art of Decision Making,' with a subtitle we in the SS refer to as the exigencies of the service. In other words, duty to one's country before all else, even if it means ordering the demise of others for the good of the whole."

"I'm afraid I could never do such a thing, General," interjected Schmidt.

"That's why you're only a Kapitän in the *U-bootwaffe,* and I'm a general in the SS," countered von Kleitenberg. "Had you been trained by the SS, however, you would be thinking differently."

"For you and others perhaps, General, but not for me. I wouldn't have the stomach to order the destruction of my fellow officers and crewman. I'm not the SS type."

The general's face took on a stern look, then shifted gears almost as fast, giving way to a subtle smile. He had to admire the young officer; he had guts! There was logic in what he had to say, but he had to agree, Schmidt was not SS material.

"What I still don't understand, General, is why, if the milch cow crew knew about our Führer's death and the grossadmiral's orders to surrender, they even bothered to continue on their resupply mission to us?"

"Simple," replied von Kleitenberg, surprisingly open. "The truth is that they didn't, that is, until the radioman broke his pledge. But up to that time we were relying on you."

"Me! For what?" asked Schmidt, unsure what the general meant.

"Yes, you," answered von Kleitenberg slyly. "It involved a little subterfuge, and it worked."

"What do you mean?" asked Schmidt, all the more confused.

"Come now, Schmidt, surely you're not naive or dense. It was your reputation as a U-boat commander, rivaling that of Guenther Prien* and some of the others, that drew our attention to you. What you have done is legend amongst submariners, and we decided to

* *Captain of U-47 which sank the famous British battleship, Royal Oak.*

capitalize on it in order to get non SS U-boatmen to volunteer for this secret mission. Clever, don't you think?"

"I had no idea," admitted Schmidt, "that all this had preceded my assumption of duty as Kapitän of this boat, any more than why a most hated U-boat Kapitän—Braunau—had been selected either."

"If you knew the magnitude of this project, my dear Kapitän—which I am not at liberty to disclose as of yet—and its importance to our future Reich, I am certain your attitude would be much different. Including your attitude toward Braunau and the unfortunate sinking of our resupply boat."

"I'm not so sure it would, on both issues," replied Captain Schmidt honestly. "As for Braunau, don't you know he's the most despised U-boat commander in the *U-bootwaffe?*"

"True, but a great U-boat commander, yes?" interjected the general to test Schmidt's ability to separate military expediency from moral values.

"I can't argue with his being a great submariner, but that doesn't change my contempt for the man."

"What he did was in the line of duty, and no different from what I had to do when ordering the Milch Cow's destruction!" replied von Kleitenberg. "Am I a criminal for doing what I had to do?"

"I'm sorry, General, but I can't answer that," replied Schmidt nervously, knowing he wanted to say yes, but that he couldn't if he valued his life and command. So he provided another answer. "You're the senior officer in charge, sir, and I'm not qualified to judge whether it was proper or not."

"I admire your tactfulness, Kapitän," said the general. "You answered correctly. Yes, 'yours is not to reason why: yours is but to do or die,' as Tennyson so aptly put it." His penetrating eyes never left Captain Schmidt's; they were intent on establishing dominion over the junior officer.

Captain Schmidt avoided his eyes as much as possible. By using his intellect, he had gotten through another challenge to his integrity. After all, he was still a military man following orders, and in every respect, true to his training which demanded a strong sense of duty to his superiors and the Fatherland. Despite this, however, a conflict arose within the him. It pitted his moral, spiritual, and ethical values against his military teachings. For a moment, he thought he had overcome the differences until he remembered something else, *My God! The war is over!*

"Well?" asked the general when no reply came.

"I understand," Schmidt lied to fill the gap. *You bastard*, he thought to himself, *all you're trying to do is to justify your own misdeeds! Say what you will, but it's not going to change anything!*

.   "I'm pleased you do, Kapitän, because I would be greatly disappointed if my recommendation to the Führer turned out to be poor judgment on my part," said von Kleitenberg with a sinister note.

"You need not concern yourself about my loyalty and competence," Schmidt replied quickly. "I will do what I'm ordered to do."

"Good, because we're on a mission of the great importance, Kapitän Schmidt," reminded von Kleitenberg as the captain's thoughts wandered again.

Schmidt hastily convinced himself he had to say what was on his mind even though wisdom, which had brought him through so many encounters thus far, dictated otherwise. "Does our cargo of torpedoes have anything to do with the mission, sir?"

Von Kleitenberg's eyes narrowed just then, and he jumped to his feet shouting, "Torpedoes! What do you know about the torpedoes?"

"Not a thing, sir!" Schmidt answered nervously. He hadn't expected such a reaction.

"Good! Let's keep it that way! You have only one purpose in this mission, and that's to get us quickly and safely to our final destination. Is that clear?"

"*Jawohl,* Herr General!" Schmidt wanted to know more but didn't dare ask, for the moment anyway. While his words were stifled, his thoughts ran wildly, with the subject of an unusual assortment of torpedoes being uppermost in his mind.

"You will follow the course specified in your orders until *U-4R2* rejoins us," continued the general.

Schmidt bit his lip. "Anything else, sir?"

"Yes. In a matter of hours, we will be monitoring radio stations on our shortwave radio in anticipation of messages from our agents in South and Central America and Mexico."

"May I ask why, sir?" Captain Schmidt asked, daring to press his luck again.

"For a final destination report," replied the general. "Our agents—and we have many of them in many countries—are trying to determine which one of our safe havens we should attempt first. Out there," he said as if pointing to a specific place, "we have as many enemies as we have friends, and where we go depends upon a number of things. Access to one of our unique sanctuaries is one of them, and the hiding of our two U-boats for future use is the other."

"I understand," Captain Schmidt replied, though many other questions remained to be answered about his superior's statement. For the moment anyway, he had learned something else: how complex the project was. He decided to ask another question, thinking it was okay, "Is Argentina under consideration?"

"It is, but the political situation is unstable now because the Argentinians have aligned themselves with the United States," came the general's frank reply. "As a consequence of this, we're not certain whether we should disembark there or go on to other places where— though quite remote—strangers are soon forgotten, either by memory or bribe." A mischievous smile crossed his face, showing he was full of surprises.

The pounding of the sub's diesels began to quiet down just then as did the speed of the vessel. A voice called down from the bridge, "Kapitän to bridge. Unidentified object off port bow."

Schmidt jumped up and made a clanging dash for the steel ladder leading to the bridge. The general was right at his heels. "It's got to be *U-4R2*," he said as he climbed up to the bridge. "They're due about now."

"Action stations!" cried Schmidt. as a preparatory order just in case the object ahead proved to be unfriendly.

"It's a U-boat, Kapitän," shouted the radioman from below. "Bearing two seven zero. Propeller sounds confirmed."

"Maintain stations!" Captain Schmidt cried out as he burst through the tower hatch and peered through a pair of binoculars handed him by a crewman.

"Why battle stations?" asked Number One. "It's one of ours."

"Maybe so, but we're in dangerous waters. Until we know for certain who's out there, it's better to practice caution."

"Well said," interjected von Kleitenberg from behind, making the captain mad enough to vomit, especially when he added, "Much like a chapter in one of my books on the subject of 'Preparedness: the Essence of a Good Leader.'"

"Shithead!" replied the captain under his breath. Lucky for him von Kleitenberg was looking from the back rather than from the front, and the roar of the wind was coming from the rear rather than from the opposite direction. Had the general heard the words which had been drowned out by the wind, Captain Schmidt might not have lived to utter other commands.

"All clear, Kapitän," came the radioman's voice from below. "Air and sea clear except for the U-boat!"

A flashing light, using the international Morse code emanated from the approaching vessel just then. The first officer read out the letters and everyone shouted joyously as he called them out, "*U-4R2*."

"It's Braunau!" exclaimed von Kleitenberg with an anxious sigh of relief. "For a moment, I was afraid he had run into trouble."

"Ahead two-thirds, both," ordered Captain Schmidt to pull his vessel in closer. At the same time, he issued orders to men on watch to be on the lookout for enemy ships and planes.

In the meantime, Number One was busy directing other crewmen. "Prepare to take on passengers!" he yelled to those assembled on deck.

As the work proceeded, the U-boat's telegraph reflected other orders through mechanical changes which reached to compartments below. The last change came with the command, "All stop," issued by the captain.

The sea was calm that evening, a situation not uncommon in the Caribbean. Even so, men looked out over the horizon nervously. They were fearful of being discovered, yet as their captains had cautioned earlier, there was little to fear once they had erected artificial super-structures made of canvas hung from cables stretched from bow to stern. This improvisation gave each vessel the appearance of a small ocean-going freighter. Nevertheless, the men fretted while maintaining a sharp vigil.

In the bowels of *U-4R2*, a number of officers crowded around the navigator's plotting table in the control room while others gathered around the sound room, listening intently to radio broadcasts from different countries. A good many took notes.

One of the officers standing next to the radio operator was a fluent linguist. As the situation warranted, he would tell those near him what was being said. Sometimes it met with outbursts of joy, and at other times, with anger and frustration when the news was bad, like the latest from Brazil. A German U-boat, *U-530*, had surrendered there, and the boat and crew were turned over to U. S. military authorities. During lulls, those gathered around the radio room would mingle with others until the time came to listen to another frequency. The most significant message was yet to come, minutes before the station was to go off the air.

Chapter 10

Turning Point

Radio Vera Cruz, Mexico

"Éste El Radio Mexico! Viva Mexico!" boomed the radio announcer's voice moments after he gave his last commercial and played Mexico's national anthem to end his long broadcast day.

With that behind them the special group of officers assembled aboard U-4R2 turned to a junior S.S. officer responsible for interpretation of the hidden message. When he finished, everyone turned to the general who was waiting patiently with Bormann in the center of the control room to listen to what he had to say.

Crowded and stuffy as the room was, an air of formality permeated it. Reiter was responsible for making the setting appear officious. Above the navigator's plotting table, he had managed to find a place to hang a picture of Adolph Hitler and a small flag bearing the symbol of Nazi Germany, the swastika.

"Well, gentlemen?" said von Kleitenberg as he watched those near him mumbling over their choices. "You've heard tthe report. We have very few options. It's Venezuela or Mexico. The others are definitely out! Too many obstacles and too risky while..."

"I agree," Bormann said as he looked down at the map spsread out over the navigators table. He studied it closely while running a rubber-tipped pencil along Mexico's long coastline. "I hope they know what they're doing," he said, referring to the message which came from the Mexican radio. He assumed that was where they would go if the rest of the group agreed with him.

"I'm for Maracaibo," said another officer, quivering as he spoke, preferring Venezuela.

"Field Marshal," von Kleitenberg replied as he looked at the gaunt and sickly man with disgust and impatience, "we've been over that before. It's much too dangerous now, and we must go where we find open doors, irrespective of the number of people we must bribe!"

"Oh—oh, yes," the tired man replied. "I forgot."

"Mexico's our best choice," said Bormann, "since we still have a number of strong allies there—former German nationals, men and women who are still loyal to the Reich. With a little time on our side, there's no reason to believe we can't all be assimilated into Mexican society until the time is ripe to start over."

"I agree. This particular site is the best one for the time being, as opposed to the others, since it is quite remote from large cities—outside of a few fishing villages here and there," said a thin, bespectacled civilian engineer, a loyal Party member and former director of a construction team of the infamous Todt organization, which had built most of the submarine pens along the French coast.

"Can we hide our U-boats there?" asked the field marshal.

"If it's good for ducks, it's good for U-boats," the engineer stated with authority. "I believe you will be pleasantly surprised when you get there, and while our facility in Mexico is somewhat different from those we left behind in France, you can have my word it will be more than adequate to meet your needs."

"What about the locals? Won't they be suspicious?" asked another member of the group.

"Just a few fishermen and duck hunters, who rarely venture beyond their villages, the kind who are easily bribed."

"Where will we enter the lagoon?" asked von Kleitenberg.

"Through one of two places, with the best one being here," the man replied as he pointed to the main inlet, which was opposite a small village named Ciudad del Carmen. "It's a sleepy old fishing village dominated by squadrons of mosquitoes. Anything else about the place I cannot say. I'll leave that up to the agent who has been posted there for some time."

"I'm not so sure I'll like the place," said the field marshal after hearing about the hoards of insects, poisonous snakes, and dangerous reptiles residing in the area.

"I can assure you, Field Marshal," comforted Bormann, "it's not all that bad. As Herr Gruber says, the facilities are modern even though they were not built to the standards of the others."

"If the name Laguna de Terminos means what I think it does," said another member of the group, "I'm not so sure I like going there either. We could get trapped if it leads to a dead end."

Bormann was quick to respond by reminding him and the others of the song they had heard over Radio Mexico some hours ago, South of the Border, Down Mexico Way, and about the meaning of the advertisement promoting an ideal place for duck hunting—the code word they all had been waiting for.

Their Mexican hideout was located in the lagoon behind a long island which ran north and south along the east coast of the Mexican mainland in the Bay of Campeche. Because the island blended with the shoreline, the northern and southern inlets were hidden from the sea. Ciudad del Carmen dominated the northernmost part of the island, and the only way of reaching it—outside of a ferry boat and small fishing boats—was a small, infrequently used airport.

"Did it have to be so cryptic?" an officer asked, referring to the complexity of the radio message. Bormann replied, "We wouldn't want someone to take the man up on his offer, now would we?"

Everyone laughed.

Bormann went on to explain the ridiculous advertisement. The announcer, a clownish person appreciated by Mexican audiences for his outlandish jokes and sense of absurd humor, without his own knowledge, had been used as an innocent intermediary to reveal their final destination. The so-called hunting grounds were not for persons with no stomach for jungle living, as the announcer warned, because it could only be reached by sea. That was the final clue they had all been waiting for! Also, to add more humor, he said that those who had prepaid their way would get their money refunded if they returned alive to complain about their mosquito-ridden accommodations in the swamp. Another clue!

Von Kleitenberg supplemented Bormann's explanation by telling the others that Mexican listeners would only conceive the man's ravings as one of his many jokes and would not take him seriously. After all, what better way could there be to contact U-boats—without the enemy knowing—than through some ridiculous radio program!

When it came to the most important part of the announcer's message, everyone was confused. It had dealt with an inducement to go fishing in the lagoon, using a seasoned guide who would meet them. He would be riding a pink dolphin.

"What does that mean?" everyone asked at once.

"I'm not sure, but like everything else, I'm certain the answer will be waiting for us when we get there," replied Bormann.

"There's another part we shouldn't overlook," reminded the interpreter, "which confirms everything."

"Like what?" questioned Bormann.

"The song about the cockroach, remember?" came his prompt reply. He was referring to La Cucaracha, a lively song about a three-legged cockroach. The announcer played it immediately after the announcement, then— to the surprise of everyone—cut in the middle with the words, "Then there were only two."

"It was the final clue, the part that put all our plans together," interjected von Kleitenberg to seize the initiative. "No one except our trusted agents knew of our plans to reduce the number of U-boats to two. So, as you can see, all is in readiness, and our people are prepared to receive us. Once we're agreed upon our final destination, all that will be required of us is to send a return message by short wave."

"And how do you propose to do that, General, without giving our position and existence away?" asked the field marshal, thinking he had outwitted a general of the SS, which was a rival to the Wehrmacht, the legitimate army of the Fatherland. Von Kleitenberg was equal to the challenge.

"Simple, my dear Field Marshal. Once we've reached an accord, we will contact our agents on a preselected frequency to let them know what we've decided. They in turn will confirm receipt of the message surreptitiously in case unfriendly ears are listening in."

"Shall we take a vote, meine herren?" interrupted Bormann, anxious to see if everyone would be in agreement. He looked around the dimly lit control room for objections.

"Yes, we must decide," agreed an officer standing near the hydroplane control panel. Others joined him.

"Good, then let's get on with the vote by scribbling your choice on these sheets of paper," said Bormann as he handed a sheet to eager hands. "Before we begin, let me remind you that a majority wins, and no quibbling will be tolerated."

Minutes later, Sturmbannführer Reiter retrieved the sheets, then tallied them. Under watchful eyes, he counted each ballot, then released the results.

"Thirteen votes for Mexico—two for Venezuela!"

A sigh of relief traveled through the tired group, overshadowing the moans of the two who disagreed.

"Gut! Then it's off to Mexico!" Bormann announced happily. He turned to von Kleitenberg. "Well, General, you were right. Our agents have done their work well, and as always, you've been vindicated by your planning."

"Danke," von Kleitenberg answered respectfully as he quickly looked around to acknowledge the thanks of others.

"I thank you, meine herren, for your kind support. I must warn you, however, that we still have a long way to go. In fact, our sea route to safety is still full of obstacles, with detection and destruction by Allied forces being the most serious."

"With snorkels, that shouldn't be a problem, Ernst," Bormann interjected. His use of the familiar name was unusual, surprising von Kleitenberg.

"That depends, Martin," von Kleitenberg replied, taking the same liberty.

"On what?"

"Weather conditions, location of Allied vessels and aircraft, depth of water for diving purposes, time of day, plus proper coordination and communication between vessels. And the possibility we might have to separate and go in different directions should enemy warships be encountered."

"Anything else?" asked Bormann, reflecting concern again.

"Only this," came the reply. "The passage between Cuba, Haiti, and Jamaica is going to be difficult and dangerous, but it's the shortest and fastest way for us to go."

A few moans came through just then but were quickly suppressed when Bormann pressed on.

"You have an interesting way of stimulating our imagination, General," he replied jokingly though he was quite serious, too. "I hope you can do the same thing when it comes to ways and means of avoiding annihilation." He studied the general's face, knowing he would get some kind of reply.

"Yes, I can. In fact, if you will recall, we are privileged to have two of the Reich's finest U-boat captains to guide us. They've brought us through countless battles already without so much as a loss of life (other than what had to be done to the cow), and they are familiar with the gulf through which we will travel."

Those around him knew what he meant, and nodded their heads in agreement.

"Speaking about U-boat commanders, General," said one of fifteen men in the compartment. "I'm reminded of something most important: the final disposition of nonSS crewme and their commanders of whom you just spoke. Have you made a decision in regard to this vital matter?"

The man could speak freely and didn't need to look around to see if only loyal SS men were present since everyone except the fifteen had been excluded from participation in the highly secret meeting. The others had been ordered to remain on deck and away from hatches while the conference was in progress. SS guards were posted to ensure privacy.

"Not yet," replied von Kleitenberg guardedly. "Of one I am certain, but—as to the other—my captain, it's still questionable."

"We'll speak of that later," Bormann interrupted. "We've more important matters to consider at this time. We mustn't forget our first priority is to reach a safe haven, so whatever their loyalty, we still need them! Anyway, whatever happens later is up to our committee to decide."

He like von Kleitenberg turned to eye all those present in the event questions still needed to be answered. Upon seeing none, Bormann took the next step by announcing adjournment, followed by a raspy "To our glorious Führer. Heil Hitler!"

"Heil Hitler!" the others enthusiastically replied before noisily collecting their papers for departure to their assigned places.

"Oh, by the way, Martin," said von Kleitenberg as he prepared to leave U-4R2 to return to his own vessel.

"Yes?"

"There's something I need to warn you about." His face showed he was quite serious. "It concerns the torpedoes."

"What about them?"

"Your captain needs to be thoroughly indoctrinated as to which ones he is to use should he have to fight."

"Why? Did something go wrong with yours?"

"As much as I hate to admit it," replied von Kleitenberg, "we did have some trouble several days ago after my captain ran across enemy ships on their way to Europe. He was about to shoot when I stopped him."

"Good grief! All could have been lost!" exclaimed Bormann.

"I know, but it was corrected though I had a hard time keeping the truth of the torpedoes from the captain. He's much too inquisitive for his own good."

"You think he knows? Can he be trusted?"

"I'm not sure, but I know he knows there's something special about them . . . because of their markings."

"I'm surprised at you, Martin. You, of all people, allowing a thing like that to happen! I thought you never made mistakes!" chided Bormann. He was delighted to find the general was vulnerable like everyone else.

"We all make mistakes," admitted von Kleitenberg, "no matter how infallible we might think we are." His frank admission surprised Bormann, and he took it to heart since the same thing could happen to him if his captain attempted to fight off an enemy attack.

"Anything else?"

"Yes, one thing more. In case we get separated or fall under attack, do not, under any circumstances, allow any of your torpedoes to fall into enemy hands. If you have to dispose of any of them, remember where you left them so we might retrieve them later."

"Good advice," admitted Bormann as he grabbed von Kleitenberg's outstretched hand in a farewell intended to last until they greeted each other off the coast of Mexico.

Major Reiter saluted, then shook hands with the general. After that, he followed von Kleitenber through the hatch to see him safely off. Minutes later, the General and a member of his guard pushed off in a rubber dingy, heading back to U-4R1 where Captain Schmidt and his gun crews were anxiously waiting.

"Heave to," the first officer yelled into the megaphone to the deck crew below as the dingy approached. The sea was calm except for a few gently rolling waves.

Quickly crewmen tossed lines and pulled in the small craft, holding it fast until its occupants could disembark. Moments later, the coxswain scaled the ladder, too, then assisted the deck hands in dragging the dingy aboard for storage. More orders rang out when that was done.

"Clear decks! Ahead one third—both!" cried the first officer with the approval of Captain Schmidt after he had received a nod from von Kleitenberg, who had just joined him on the bridge.

"Your orders, sir?" Schmidt asked, anxious to move on. For a few moments, von Kleitenberg said nothing. His eyes were trained on the departing U-4R1. The water at its stern was churning white and its engines were throbbing rhythmically. Through the silk-screen, moon-illuminated sky, he could see the silhouette of the snorkel-equipped vessel outlined against the darkening horizon as it slowly slipped into the depths of the sea like a huge whale anxious to evade pursuers.

"Sir—," said Schmidt again after his first attempt to elicit the

General's attention failed. What followed was unexpected.

"Do you speak Spanish, Kapitän?" von Kleitenberg asked as if he hadn't heard the man.

"No, sir," replied Schmidt.

"Good, then you and I will learn together," replied the general.

"I—"

"Take her down, Kapitän," von Kleitenberg ordered, sounding more like a U-boat commander. "Hold her at snorkel level, then see me in my cabin after it's done. We'll talk then."

"As you wish, sir. Same heading?"

"Yes, until further notice."

"Aye, aye, Kapitän-General," Schmidt replied while rendering a snappy salute in a jesting manner.

"I like men with mirth and imagination," said von Kleitenberg while inching his way down through the bridge hatch, heading for his stateroom even further down.

"Thank you, sir," answered the captain as he followed him down while issuing new orders to those around him.

"You heard the general," he called out. "Prepare to dive! Flood!"

The U-boat was engulfed in a cacophony of sounds after that as escaping air roared through the vents, water entered from below, and the hull began to feel the pressure of the outside water against its plates. It creaked like a tin can being crushed by a heavy boot, but there was a difference; this can was made to withstand extremes of pressure. It needed to be that way since men were living within, men who were now busily asking each other, "Where do you think we're going?"

"Wir fahren gagen Mexico!" von Kleitenberg said after Captain Schmidt entered his stateroom.

"I suspected as much, sir," replied Captain Schmidt, showing no surprise.

"Why Mexico?" inquired the general, curiously. "We could have gone elsewhere. There were other alternatives?"

"A U-boat Kapitän, like SS officers, must consider alternatives too, sir," replied Schmidt. The general caught the inference.

"Ha! You're more perceptive than I thought, Kapitän," replied von Kleitenberg with a smile on his face. "I like that. I like your candor. Please go on; I'm interested in your reasoning."

"It's not all that spectacular, sir," the captain responded. "Since you made it quite clear we were not to scuttle the boats, it was only logical to conclude that time, distance, fuel, supplies, and a mysterious cargo required a port, where a submarine wouldn't be discovered."

"And?" challenged the general. "That is true of most of South and Central America."

"Perhaps," the captain replied, "but if I were concerned about the nature of our cargo—and the type of passengers entrusted to my care, then . . . ."

"Enough!" von Kleitenberg demanded, ending the conversation. "You are wiser than I thought. Excellent points, however, and I do commend you on your excellent observations, Kapitän."

"You asked, sir," Captain Schmidt quickly replied, "and I was only trying to comply."

"I know, Kapitän, and you are right, of course." He looked to the distant bulkhead before speaking again to see if their conversation was being heard. No one was listening; it would have been impossible anyway since the loudly pounding noise of the diesels drowned out almost everything.

"Yes, Kapitän, we have made a decision," admitted von Kleitenberg. "If we're lucky to break into the Gulf of Mexico undetected, the balance of our journey should be easy . . . in my estimation."

He pulled out a map just then, and pointed to a series of lines he had drawn. "You are to follow this course, Kapitän."

"Not through there!" protested Schmidt. "It's full of enemy warships. I know; I've been through this passage before!"

"But they're not expecting us this time, and the water is over a mile deep, which would make it difficult for surface and air vessels to detect us."

"I know, but that's what scares me," countered Schmidt. "If we should be depth-charged and the ship disabled, it might never rise again, and we would be crushed like an egg—with no survivors!"

"So?" replied the general, seemingly impervious to the captain's concern. "Either way, we're lost—unless you think surrender is the best alternative?"

"I wasn't implying—"

"We still have a mission to complete," interrupted the general, "and the Führer has provided well for us."

Captain Schmidt said nothing. It was foolish he knew to argue with a man like von Kleitenberg who was a fanatic for detail, and an idealist. One thing did cross his mind just then, the general's statement containing the Führer. He wasn't sure what it was that Hitler had provided. Unless. . . .

"I haven't forgotten, sir."

"Good, then let's alter our course as I've directed. We still have a way to go before making our next contact."

"Contact?"

"By our agents, of course. As I told you before, preplanning is crucial to the success of any mission, ours especially."

"I see," replied Schmidt, feeling somewhat relieved over what he had just learned. Previously, each leg of the voyage had been revealed piece by piece. Now, however, he was getting the culmination of all preplanning.

"As a matter of caution, Kapitän, I would suggest you have your navigator familiarize himself with the lagoon and the channel leading into this area here."

Captain Schmidt leaned forward and studied the spot, then pushed his cap back on the top of his head, awed by what he saw.

"We can't afford mistakes, Kapitän," von Kleitenberg emphasized as he positioned himself in the center of his bunk, laid down, then pulled his cap over his eyes to catch a quick catnap. He left the captain with a final word, "I have every confidence in your abilities as a naval officer, Kapitän, so please go on with your duties as stated."

"Thank you, and as you say," replied Schmidt as he turned away, pulling the green curtain closed after him. Minutes later, the general was fast asleep.

In the control room, the captain assembled some of his officers, then issued new orders after conferring with his navigator. "Come right, for a heading of two nine zero degrees," he ordered. "Careful now . . . maintain depth. Ahead two thirds, both. All right now, steady."

As orders were passed, voices duplicated them, confirming execution. After a while, things returned to normal for the different shifts, with different ones taking turns occupying bunks vacated by those going on duty. The IX-C, like other U-boats of other types and classes, were never built with bunks for every crew member. Space was too critical for that, so bunk-sharing was the way of life with one man's sweat warmly bathing the next occupant.

On the other hand, the officers and petty officers were much luckier. Rank had its privileges, but not much more than one would have expected, that is, until the general boarded. After that, the officers doubled up, with the captain receiving priority over everyone.

"Take over, Number One," Captain Schmidt said as he passed his first assistant in the narrow passageway. "Call me if anything is spotted, no matter how insignificant."

"Aye, Kapitän," he responded, happy to assume some of the burdens. He passed the general's compartment on the way to the control room; the green curtain was still drawn. A guard stood by, watching intently.

John Hankins

Chapter 11

War Is War!

The Windward Channel

assage through the Bahaman chain of islands had been much smoother than everyone had expected. Of course, traveling at night with a bright moon to light the way helped considerably. The trip was made even easier because of the artificial superstructures which had been erected. Passing ships took the disguised vessels as another tramp steamer traveling between islands. Their chief engineers saw to the realism by deliberately causing their diesel engines to expel smoke up through the false smokestacks. With a flare for authenticity, each added red and green lights to the port and starboard sides of their respective boats.

By light of early morning, the scene had changed. Aircraft were noted in the distance, making everyone edgy. Luckily, none flew their way. Signal lights between the two U-boats followed shortly after the first aircraft was sighted, and after several hectic back and forth flashing minutes, both U-boat commanders agreed they would continue traveling on the surface at top speed for as long as they could. In the meantime, while keeping a safe distance from one another, they would also dismantle their false superstructures so emergency diving would not be hindered.

Like the navigator on each sub who urged caution, every crewman knew how critical it was for each U-boat to enter the Windward Channel between Cuba and Haiti in the evening. It was a heavily trafficked sea lane, and as much distance as possible needed to be maintained between the two boats. They had not forgotten the previous night's activity, wherein each vessel literally had to feel its way among shoals, reefs, and shallow-water passages between the various islands that made up the Bahaman chain. In fact, these outcroppings acted like a protective wall as though they had been intentionally erected to keep intruders from entering the Caribbean from the Atlantic!

Aboard Captain Braunau's U-Boat

"A-l-a-a-r-r-m!"

Bormann's command sub trembled with activity when its captain ordered all engines stopped and a switch to electric motors for an impending dive. He wasn't concerned about *U-4R1*. It had dropped back hours earlier to repair a bearing and was expected to catch up later. He was concerned about the large black ship on the horizon which seemed to come out of nowhere. He watched it through his powerful binoculars and called out coordinates as it continued its approach.

"What's happening?" asked Martin Bormann as he climbed through the bridge hatch, breathless, unshaven, and disheveled. He looked terrible; seasickness had plagued him most of the way, but it was only in the last few days he managed to develop "sea legs"—at least that was what the submariners jokingly called his stance.

"A coastal steamer, from what I can see," replied Braunau, never taking his eyes off the subject.

"Have they seen us?" asked Bormann, all in one breath.

"I don't know. Unfortunately, we're close enough for them to see us," replied the concerned captain.

"Damn the luck! What are we going to do?"

His answer came through a series of orders given by the captain to his crew. "Action stations! Prepare tubes one, three, and five for surface firing, and no others." He repeated himself to make sure his order was properly understood.

"Aye, Kapitän," came an instant response from below, reconfirming what he had already ordered.

"Are you sure we should do this?" asked Bormann, not certain what was correct. "It's possible they haven't seen us."

"Perhaps, but we can't take a chance," replied Braunau with a grim look on his face.

As both men watched the approaching vessel grow in size, the first officer took over, calling out range, depth, and heading. Captain Braunau listened as the statistics were repeated below, only to call out additional instructions after seeing a flurry of activity on the approaching vessel.

"Open bow caps! Flood! Gun crews on deck!" Within seconds, crewmen poured through the forward and bridge hatches, some to man the twin 20mm and 37mm AA cannons on the platforms aft of those on the bridge and others to operate the specially mounted 88mm cannon on the forward deck.

As the captain and others watched the other vessel, they could see its crew scrambling. It was clear they had spotted the U-boat but were not certain what to do. A few tried waving as if to advise the war was over while others ran to safety amidship like they knew the men on the U-boats hadn't heard Germany had surrendered.

Whatever the real situation, for Captain Braunau it didn't matter. He ordered his crew to fire on the defenseless vessel. The second the first tracer streaked across the waves heading for its target, the captain of the merchant vessel altered his ship's course. As more shells followed him, he zigzagged, hoping to avoid the deadly shells which had found their objective and were now penetrating the hull of his boat.

"Kapitän!" a voice from below sounded through the speaking tube. "They're sending an SOS."

"Oh! Shit!" Braunau cursed, his voice quivering with rage. "That's what I hoped to avoid!" In rapid succession, he shouted new orders to his crew and ordered his helmsman to turn to starboard to permit all guns to concentrate their fire on the vessel. "Get that damn antenna! Shoot it down! They're signaling!"

Concentrated cannon fire swept the departing ship with increased intensity just then, as gunnersmates zeroed in on the mast to which the antenna had been strung. Minutes later, a shell found its mark. The splintered mast fell to the decks below, dragging the antenna wire with it.

The next order was harder to take, but every man obeyed his

commander. "Sink her! No survivors!" Captain Braunau shouted.

While the deck crews raked the unfortunate vessel with cannon fire, the first officer made torpedo range corrections in preparation for firing. As quick as that was done, Captain Braunau shouted orders to those in the conning tower, "Tubes one, three, and five—*Los!*"

The sub jerked back like the recoil of a rifle as each torpedo left its tube, heading in the direction of the retreating vessel.

"They're getting away!" Bormann shouted, upset over seeing the merchant vessel suddenly outdistancing them. Its captain had ordered full speed ahead by demanding more boiler pressure. Billowing smoke filled the sky as his engine room personnel complied by shoveling more coal.

"They're slightly faster than us," Braunau yelled back, admitting the gain, "but they're fools to think they can outrun or outmaneuver our T5s, our acoustical torpedoes."

He said that with certainty, and he was right. Within minutes after they were fired, the fleeing ship received the first of the steel fishes. Bulkheads ruptured and creaked when the vessel's boilers exploded, flinging large metal plates into the sky as rivets exploded out of their holes.

As submariners watched, a gaping hole in the side of the vessel appeared, allowing the ocean to enter in a foaming surge. At that juncture, the ship began to list, then settle. Seconds later, it was sped to its watery grave when two more torpedoes buried their explosive heads—one in the bow and the other near the stern. So extensive and complete was the damage that the ship's crew were unable to lower their lifeboats.

The death throes of the vessel and its crew was not something anyone could watch with joy, submariners especially, but they had their orders and had no choice but to comply. All listened as bulkheads creaked and the vessel slowly settled, giving off steam and smoke.

"A survivor—over there!" pointed one crewman as others looked in the direction shown. A man was swimming toward them. He cried for help. Soon others in the same predicament cried out.

"Shoot him!" shouted Braunau. Shots rang out as gunners aimed and pressed triggers, silencing those in the water. To be certain no witnesses remained, the sub quickly circled the spot were the ship went down. They had a hard time seeing because it was getting dark.

"Kapitän! Radar contact! Bearing 010 degrees," shouted one of the sound room personnel.

"Clear decks!"

Again alarms sounded and men dived through hatches after

hastily securing deck weapons. The last hatch to be banged shut was the captain's.

"Dive! Dive! Dammit! Let's get the hell out of here!" Braunau screamed at the top of his lungs. Bormann had long preceded him, nearly breaking his leg in the process. He had lost his grip on the metal ladder.

"Take her down to 70 meters," the chief engineer shouted. "Hydroplanes down . . . ."

"Prepare for depth charges!" the captain yelled out. Another lesson in survival had begun for the exhausted crew. It wasn't new. In fact, for the past two months, all had experienced the rigors of diving and resurfacing, either to elude Allied patrols or to surface for replenishing air supplies and recharging batteries. In the process, too, all had learned what it meant to stay submerged for days on end. Their faces, bodies, and clothes were covered with grime and sweat. In short, they stunk badly, just like the interior of the U-boat.

Aboard Captain Schmidt's U-Boat

"The damn fool!" cried Captain Schmidt from the bridge of *U-4R1* as he surveyed the horizon in front of his vessel. He had arrived just in time to see Bormann's command sub diving near the debris left by the merchant vessel it had sunk. He didn't have time to dwell on the subject; an anguished warning came from below.

"Radar contact!"

"Where?" cried Schmidt as he and his men searched the skies while awaiting the bearing.

"280 degrees, Kapitän—and closing. Range, 6000 meters approximately."

The spot in the sky was like a shining star. It had captured the dying rays of the setting sun as it headed in the U-boat's direction. The second officer was the first to see it.

"There, Kapitän. At two o'clock," a member of the watch called out.

All eyes on the bridge followed his outstretched arm. It was a plane all right, but because of its distance, no one could ascertain its type, that is, military or civilian. Whatever the case, it posed a problem for all on board; they had been discovered.

What to do next depended upon what those in the plane would do. If military and armed, it could attack. If civilian, it might just circle out of range and report its findings by radio to the nearest Allied base.

Captain Schmidt was faced with a dilemma, and a decision was required: to order his crew to man the deck guns in preparation for an attack or to order everyone below for a crash dive. The plane's distance prompted his decision, risky as it might have been, since he knew it wasn't to his advantage to wage a surface battle with an airplane that could call for backup while delaying the U-boat's departure.

"Clear decks!"

Everyone on deck wasted no time diving through open hatches, heading for their duty stations.

"Dive! Take her down fast, Chief!"

"Flood! All hands forward!" yelled the chief.

Instantly crewmen raced from the aft and mid sections of the U-boat to the forward torpedo room and dropped.

"Hydroplanes down full!"

The weight of the men in the forward compartment, along with the extreme diving condition, caused the bow to dip at a sharp angle, and men to cling to whatever they could to keep from destabilizing the boat's descent.

"Level off at 90 meters, Chief," cried Captain Schmidt. "Prepare for depth charges!" He, like the general and the others, waited for what they knew would come next and was surprised when it didn't. The silence couldn't be explained.

"What's going on, Kapitän? Are they decoying us?" von Kleitenberg asked after a long silence.

"The worst, General!"

"A destroyer?" asked von Kleitenberg.

"No! It's that *dummkoph* Braunau! How could he do a stupid thing like that?"

"What's he done?" demanded von Kleitenberg, confused by the captain's angry words. Schmidt lost no time explaining.

"He sank an unarmed merchant vessel!" Schmidt replied angrily as he strained to hear external noises, the kind all submariners dread.

"What! When?" asked the general all at once. His face had taken on a pallor, then flushed to red when the impact of the incident struck him. His explicit instructions to every U-boat commander was to avoid confrontation unless attacked.

Captain Schmidt didn't answer right away; he was busy listening for external sounds, in particular, those made by planes dropping bombs or depth charges. The general recognized his stance and did not press him further. When nothing was heard, Schmidt turned to the soundman.

With earphones plastered to his ears like protective earmuffs, the operator turned the handle of his hydrophone listening device, his face contorted as he strained to hear.

"Well?" asked Captain Schmidt impatiently.

"Nothing, Kapitän," the operator finally replied.

Captain Schmidt turned away to face his superior, who had been standing by. "You should have seen it . . . the carnage. Dead bodies and debris everywhere."

"Is there any chance of the wreckage being spotted? Soon?" von Kleitenberg asked as if oblivious to what had happened.

"Yes, sir . . . but not before morning, I believe," Captain Schmidt replied.

"What makes you so certain, Kapitän? The time of its discovery is crucial to our mission."

"Because it's too dark outside to conduct a search from the air. But when it comes to U-boats, that's another story. As long as we're on the surface, we're subject to detection."

"Then we're safe for the moment," von Kleitenberg replied, breathing more easily now.

"I'm sorry, but that's not true, sir. Actually, we're more in danger now than in previous encounters with the enemy."

"Why do you say that?" asked von Kleitenberg, taken aback by his commander's statement.

"Because the ship gave its coordinates before it went down."

"That does changes things, doesn't it?" said von Kleitenberg, clearly perturbed by the news. He paced the control room, stopping later to ask another question, "Do you think our presence has been reported?"

"I'm afraid so."

"What about the ship? Are you certain it sent a distress signal?" the general pressed on in hopes of finding a flaw in the U-boat commander's evaluation.

Their conversation was interrupted when the chief radio operator burst through the hatchway. Captain Schmidt pulled him near while addressing his superior.

"Ask him, General. He's the one who heard the signal."

"Is that true, radioman?" asked von Kleitenberg. "Did the merchant vessel report anything besides the SOS? Like being attacked by a U-boat?"

"Yes, sir, it did, and it was *U-4R2* which sank it. I heard its screws—and the fish—the torpedoes she sent out, including the sound of the other ship's propellers too . . . before it went down."

"Idiots!" von Kleitenberg bellowed, angrily lifting his symbol of authority—the baton he always carried—high into the air, then bringing it down heavily into the palm of his gloved hand, where it made a loud whacking sound, enough to frighten anyone.

"Sir—" Captain Schmidt tried to speak but was cut off.

"I told Bormann to instruct his captain not to use the real . . . I mean . . .use his torpedoes except in case of a dire emergency!" His slip of tongue did not go unnoticed by the captain, who kept what he heard to himself.

"It's Braunau's fault . . . the carnage," inserted Schmidt, clearly showing his disgust. "What are you going to do about him, General?"

"That's a matter that doesn't concern you, Kapitän," von Kleitenberg replied. "I'll deal with it in due time."

As *U-4R1* glided silently under the water, her electric motors humming, Captain Schmidt looked around. The faces of his men were as taut as his own. They had come a long way, had escaped every obstacle, and now all were faced with the possibility of discovery and death, yet they were not the ones responsible for the sinking.

Captain Schmidt knew, like his crew, that their U-boat—not Braunau's—could end up being the one tracked by enemy search vessels. It was logical since *U-4R2* had already fled the area and his surfaced boat was the only one in the area at the time the plane made its appearance. Unfortunately, distinguishing one U-boat from the other was virtually impossible. To avoid detection, only one choice remained: head for the Gulf of Mexico waters as quickly as possible.

An hour was to pass before *U-4R1* was to surface again, but only after a thorough search for surface noises was made by the sound operator.

"All right, Chief, take her up to periscope depth," Captain Schmidt ordered. The chief complied, and the boat rose slowly, guided upward by a well experienced engineer.

Peering through the night periscope, Captain Schmidt surveyed the area. He turned round and round, then called out again, "Surface!"

Within minutes, *U-4R1* rose gently out of the sea into a pitch black night, a white wake churning at her stern. Then, like a cat vomiting an undigested meal, she emptied her guts to allow the navigator and watch crews time to climb onto her bridge before allowing the others to come topside.

The eyes of each watch member searched their respective 90 degrees of the compass, for a grand total of 360 degrees, or four sectors ranging from 0 to 90, and 90 to 180, and so forth. It was a tried and proven method, one long employed by submariners to help search out the seas for enemy vessels.

While the watch members surveyed everything in sight, the navigator conducted his duties by studying the sky and looking for breaks in the overcast sky from which he could take bearings. In time, he found what he wanted, taking notes in the process. When finished, he slipped below deck to consult charts and to determine *U-4Rl's* current location and speed and to plot its future course from what he had learned. Before he could complete his calculation, however, nature called and he dashed for the nearest head.

As he was passing the hydrophone operator's station opposite General von Kleitenberg's stateroom, he had to stop. The operator was in a panic.

"JEE-SUS!" the radioman shouted. "Oh, God! It can't be! Yes, it is!"

As the navigator watched, knowing what he would hear next, the operator yelled into his speaking tube to the captain on the bridge above.

"High speed screws, Kapitän! My guess is it's a destroyer. Now we're in for it!"

Sailors knees buckled and their hearts throbbed heavily upon receipt of the news. They had been through enough, but duty called. In distress himself, the navigator knew what he had to do before the order came. The thunder bucket* had to wait. He raced back to his station, wetting his pants as he did. No one noticed because getting wet and stinky was routine on board a U-boat. Besides, they were impervious to smells—irrespective of the source!

"A-l-a-a-r-r-m! Clear the decks!" came the captain's cry.

With that, Klaxons sounded and lights flashed as men dropped into the belly of their stinky home for another round with destiny. There wasn't enough time to recharge the U-boat's batteries nor to purge the interior of foul smells, much less fill nearly exhausted compressed air tanks, but despite the shortcomings, the U-boat sank into the sea, reaching for a depth never attained before.

Air hissed out of vents as water filled ballast tanks, almost generating as much noise as the speeding ship which passed overhead, minutes before its sonar started pinging against *U-4R1's* steel hull.

"This is it!" Captain Schmidt cried angrily as his eyes followed the arrow in the sub's depth gauge. Occasionally his eyes searched upward as if trying to visualize depth charges tumbling down at him and his boat.

B-L-A-A-A-M!

More followed, and more. . . .

107

It was a nightmare for the crew of *U-4R1*. More than twenty four hours had passed since they lost contact with the avenging destroyer. It had tracked the sub like a hound dog on the trail of a wiry coon.

The whole affair had been an episode of wit with the advantage clearly being on the side of the pursuer. Other vessels had joined in the chase to make the situation on board the U-boat all the more untenable. Nerves were stretched to the limit as crew members panted for want of air.

Captain Schmidt had kept the boat down for as long as he could, but the accumulation of carbon dioxide plus depletion of air reserves left him no choice except to raise the boat before they would have nothing left with which to blow the ballast tanks.

"Blow tanks! Periscope level!" came his order. Everyone listened apprehensively as the hissing traveled through air lines. The pressure was down, and the boat seemed to take its time rising. Someone tapped the depth gauge and the needle moved. It had gotten stuck, but slowly rotated upward. Cheers followed.

"Periscope level, sir," the chief called when the needle reach the mark he had been waiting for. "Trim tanks. Hold her steady. Ahead one-third."

In the tower, Captain Schmidt manned the periscope to study the sea and sky above. To his relief, the sea was clear and calm, but the sky overhead was overcast, allowing only the barest of light from the moon to penetrate and illuminate the area. Satisfied with what he saw, he snapped up the bars on his scope. "All clear, Number One. Down scope."

Moments later, crewmen burst through hatches like fire ants escaping an ant hill that had been saturated with gasoline, then set on fire by an irate farmer. All were gasping heavily and wasted no time breathing in the pure, cool air. It was invigorating, but all too short. With the exception of watch personnel, most were sent below to help repair damage caused by the depth charging. A bent shaft was their worst worry; it occurred when the diesel engine to which it had been connected was shaken loose from its mounts during the bombardment.

On the bridge, Captain Schmidt had other things on his mind as he shouted into the speaking tube leading to the engine room. "Chief!" he yelled. "I need damage reports."

"Aye, Kapitän," a muffled barrel-sounding reply came from below.

"Do you know where we are?" von Kleitenberg asked as he pushed his tall body between the commander and his first officer.

Captain Schmidt did not answer right away. He and his first officer had their eyes glued to their binoculars, studying a pair of small islands off their starboard bow. They were far away and barely visible. Upon noticing this, the general looked, too. Except for a few scattered lights, everything else was clothed in darkness. On the port side, it was different. A bright glare could be seen in the distance, illuminating low scattered clouds of the night sky.

"Well, Kapitän, where we are?" von Kleitenberg asked again.

"I'm not certain, General," Captain Schmidt replied. "Maybe our navigator can give us an answer." He called below decks, "Number Three to the bridge!"

"Permission to come up?" asked the navigator as he worked his way up the steel ladder to the bridge hatch.

"Permission granted," came the captain's quick reply.

"You called, Kapitän?" the navigator asked as he worked his way through the hatch, then took a place near the captain.

"Got any idea where we are?"

The navigator looked up at the sky before withdrawing his sextant from its case. "I doubt it, Kapitän. I need a clear patch of sky to take a reading of the constellations."

"See what you can do," urged Schmidt.

Number Three, like everyone else on the bridge, took another look, but shook his head in frustration. "We're going to have to wait a while, I'm afraid."

"Can you venture a guess—a wild one?" asked the captain, hoping for something positive.

"We're somewhere off the Cuban coast, I'd say . . . or near some of its offshore islands. I can't be certain, of course, since we made too many evasive turns and dives to keep track, and there's no telling how far we've been pushed off course by the currents."

"I know all that," said Captain Schmidt unhappily. "I just wanted an educated guess, though I pretty well knew what you would say."

"If only some of the clouds would clear away," sighed the navigator, thinking wishfully. "In minutes I could have the answer . . . ."

Like the others watching the same sky, he knew it wasn't likely though there was always a chance a strong front might pass through, pushing enough of the clouds away to give him the kind of clear sky he needed.

"Damn!" cried the captain with concern transfixed across his young face. "I just know we're in dangerous waters. And if I'm right, this area is loaded with Allied warships and seaplanes, some based at

Jamaica and Guantanamo and the U.S. bases off the coast of Florida."

Von Kleitenberg, his face grotesquely illuminated by the red light coming through the tower hatch, decided to add a few thoughts of his own to hide his own fears.

"Let's not panic, Kapitän," he said as he looked at the man whose face was barely visible in the night sky. "We need to do things by priorities—in the first instance, to analyze our present status."

"That's already in process," interrupted Schmidt, almost disrespectfully, but clearly abruptly. "My chief engineer is already working on it. We should have a report shortly."

"That's all very well and good, Kapitän, but we must also consider our strengths and weaknesses if we are to make appropriate decisions."

"Excuse me, General," interrupted the captain who had little time for lectures. "I think I'd better go below; the engineer must have run into difficulties." At that point, he lowered himself into the bridge hatch, then through the one in the conning tower's floor to the control room below in time to meet his engineer who was dragging his tired body through the aft hatch.

"How's the port shaft?"

"Not good, sir. It's bent beyond repair. Without a repair ship, we can do nothing. As for the bearings, they can be repaired, but what good is that if the shaft can't be fixed?"

"We can still move, can't we?" asked the general, who had walked up and overheard the conversation.

"*Jawohl*, Herr General, but with only one screw to propel us to wherever it is we're going," the chief replied. "We can use the bent shaft in case of an emergency, but I wouldn't recommend it because it would help the enemy pinpoint our position."

A gloom covered the faces of everyone, the general's included. Von Kleitenberg's thoughts turned to the captain. "Any solutions? Recommendations?"

"Any idea where we can find a spare milch cow?" replied Schmidt to the shock of everyone around him. "We're crippled! Like a newborn babe without its mother on whom it can suckle and the only thing we can do is crawl!"

Von Kleitenberg's face reddened; the implication was clear. He resented Schmidt more than anything now but held his composure.

"I asked for suggestions, not criticism, Kapitän!" von Kleitenberg warned. "And while I'm at it, may I remind you, Kapitänleutnant Schmidt, that I am still in command and respect is required at all times? Is that understood?"

Captain Schmidt gulped, then nodded his head in acknowledgment after noticing one of the general's bodyguards pushing forward, ready to act if directed. To everyone's relief, the general motioned the guard off.

"If we have other problems, I need to know them now, Kapitän Schmidt!" von Kleitenberg demanded. "And whether yoy believe it or not, I know from experience that, if one searches deep and long enough, he's bound to find a solution."

"Truthfully, General, our situation is critical. Aside from the damaged shaft, we have many other problems. For example, all of our listening devices—underwater and bridge-mounted—have been damaged beyond repair, and there's no place to get replacement parts."

The news was bad indeed, striking deeply into von Kleitenberg's mind and heart. His thoughts wandered to the supply boat he had ordered sunk. Though it carried the parts they needed, its destruction—in his way of thinking—was justified. The same reasoning applied to the destruction of its crew. It was militarily expedient to blind permanently blind a hundred pairs of eyes and bridle half as many tongues—more or less—than to risk destruction of the entire project. Of course, he could have waited until the mission was almost complete before ordering the milch cow's destruction, but then again, they could have been separated somewhere along the way, the mission still would have been jeopardized. So he did what he had to: ordered their demise, for the good of the service and the welfare of the Fatherland!

As everyone near the general waited for new orders, his next statement to the U-boat commander shocked those who knew differently; it was a clear challenge to the captain.

"*Kreig ist kreig!* War is war! No one could have predicted the presence of the mine, Kapitän. I hope you're not implying I had anything to do with milch cow's unfortunate end?"

Recognizing it for what it was, Schmidt avoided the trap. Had he done otherwise, he could have been summarily court-martialed for questioning his superior's veracity and authority under wartime conditions, that is, if he was lucky enough to be afforded that courtesy. It wasn't likely, however, if the execution of the radioman on the milch cow was any example of how the general planned to conduct future breaches of discipline.

Before answering the man whom he knew expected a reply, since in some ways they were made of the same stubborn cloth, the captain searched his mind for appropriate alternatives. He knew that in some respects he had the upper hand over the general since he was the only

111

one qualified to see the U-boat through its various trials. By the same token, he also knew he had to play each hand carefully because he still had others to think about, in particular, the safety of his crew—those who did not belong to the SS elite.

"You are right, Herr General," he answered after a brief silence.

"About what?" von Kleitenberg asked to make sure they were in agreement.

"About the need for preplanning. Obviously, the enemy did just that, by dropping antisubmarine mines in our path in the middle of the Atlantic. And now we have no spare parts or means to repair our boat . . . other than what we brought with us."

"To err is human," replied the general with a confident smile on his face, "but in this case, I don't think that applies. Most likely it was a stray mine, one that just happened to float our way, unfortunate as it was for us."

While most of those listening to the exchange did not understand the nature of the game being played, there were some who did. Of this group, those who were close to the captain feared for his life while those aligned with the general wondered when he would exert his authority and get rid of the dissident factor within their midst. On the other hand, all groups knew that the time was wrong for such action since the captain, for the time being anyway, was indispensable.

"What are the odds against such a happening?" Schmidt asked the general, subtly testing his luck about the presence of such a mine. "One in a million?"

"KAPITÄN!" interrupted the general, tiring of the game. His face was beet red now. "Forget it! The milch cow is gone and there's nothing we can do about it! If you don't understand what I mean, there's a chapter in the book I told you about which covers in depth difficulties like the one we're now in and how to avoid recriminations and panic. I suggest—when you have the time—you read it from cover to cover. After that, you'll know what I've been talking about all this time."

To make certain his words impacted everyone, von Kleitenberg looked around the crowded control room, his eyes challenging the eyes that met his until they turned away or looked down to the steel decks, a sign of their continued subservience.

"Anything else, Captain?" pressed the general one more time, clearly ascertaining his authority.

"Nothing more than what I've already said, Herr General, though we're still able to get underway."

"Good, then head for those islands off our starboard bow. I've decided upon a plan which should help ease our situation."

"As you say, General," replied the captain as he turned to his first officer and engineer who were waiting anxiously for some form of direction. "You heard the general; adjust our course accordingly. And you, Chief, continue with your repair work on the bearings in case we might need to use the shaft for an emergency dive."

"Aye, aye," both men responded before running off to their various stations. Within seconds, a series of orders traveled through the boat, repeated by those affected by them. Again a flurry of activity followed with valves and wheels being opened and turned and motors engaged. After that, the boat pushed forward slowly.

"Anything else, sir?" asked Number One just to be certain nothing had been overlooked.

Captain Schmidt considered the matter, then answered. "Yes, keep a lookout for a break in the sky, so we can determine our present location. And when we're within a mile or so of the closest island, advise me immediately."

"Aye, Kapitän," Number One replied before returning to his duties where he happily left the captain and general.

"Kapitän," said the general after things had settled down to a routine, "I would like to talk to you privately if you don't mind. Please join me in my stateroom as soon as you can; there are a number of things we need to discuss."

He pushed his way through the large hatch leading out of the control room down to his quarters below. Captain Schmidt followed minutes later, after making certain everything was operating as well as could be expected.

"All right, let's go to work," ordered the chief engineer as he rounded up some exhausted men in another part of the sub, where he directed their attention to its idle shaft. The repairmen weren't as fortunate as other crewmen positioned near the general's stateroom, who listened with ears perked in that direction, hoping to hear what was being said between the two adversaries. Most of their efforts were doused by the sound of pounding diesels and the playing of a record *Lilly Marlene,* on orders of the general. It was his favorite.

"Fat slob!" complained a hydroplanesman to his companion after learning the singer was Reichmarshall Goering's wife. "I hope his ass rots in hell!"

"Quiet! Talk like that isn't good for your health," the chief interrupted after overhearing what the man said. He had just returned to the control room after overseeing work being done by others in the motor machine room at the stern of the boat. Curious like the others, he cast a glance at the thin green curtain to the general's stateroom.

The outlines of the captain and general were projected against the curtain like puppets against a blank screen. A heated debate was taking place within, and it was clear the general was doing most of the talking. The mostly one-sided discussion continued for another ten minutes before the captain emerged, shaken but relieved. Minutes later, he assembled his officers and issued new orders, including special ones for his favorite chief to institute.

"Prepare to dive. Snorkel depth!" cried the chief in rapid succession. "Bow planes down. . . ."

Minutes later, the vessel, with its snorkel protruding above the surface of water, cut a white path through the calm sea. In its path, a trail of exhaust fumes poured into the air. Concurrently, the vessel's course toward the distant islands was being monitored by the first watch officer who was as anxious as anyone to get there. When within two miles of the first island, he notified the captain and was promptly ordered to take a circular course around the island. All during this time, both von Kleitenberg and the captain took turn sitting at the periscope, studying the island before them. It seemed devoid of human habitation.

"Looks clear to me," said von Kleitenberg, now as much at ease with the periscope as he was with his silver-handled baton.

"I agree," said Schmidt after he took a final look. "What now?"

"Get in as close as you can get to that reef, then I'll tell you the rest," replied von Kleitenberg.

After verifying the spot, Captain Schmidt issued new orders to his helmsman. "Take a heading of 5 degrees starboard to 78 degrees true."

An hour later, after taking depth soundings which they could not totally trust, the U-boat, with its one operating diesel turned off, withdrew its snorkel and maneuvered with great care in waters which were unfamiliar to everyone on board. From that moment forward, the sub was bathed in sweet silence until it stopped.

In the atmosphere which now prevailed within the vessel, both men—von Kleitenberg and the U-boat's captain, shrouded by a soft red light which illuminated the interior of the conning tower— continued to take turns monitoring their approach to the unknown island through the night periscope. As they did, other eyes, most of them from below, looked up through the hatchway, hoping to hear what was being said.

"See anything?" pressed von Kleitenberg as he watched Schmidt swivel electrically in many directions.

"Not a soul," replied the captain softly. "A good night for ghosts, if you believe in them . . . ."

Von Kleitenberg took over just then. Like the captain, he twirled round and round, then stopped. "It's clear all right."

"What now?" asked Schmidt.

"Prepare all tubes for firing until all torpedoes have been jettisoned."

"Firing? All? And at what?" asked Schmidt all at once. He was dumbfounded by the order. He hadn't expected it.

"Over the reef and into the lagoon directly in front of us," came the general's immediate reply. "Think you can do it?"

"I can try, Herr General, but I don't know how much clearance we have since we don't know where we are."

"It doesn't matter," said von Kleitenberg, "so long as the torpedoes end up somewhere in the immediate vicinity."

"All right. If you say so, General. You know, though, we'll have to surface later to get the torpedoes stored under the deck plates?" said Captain Schmidt as he reached for the bulkhead-mounted microphone to the ship's public address system to comply.

"Understood," replied von Kleitenberg. "Proceed."

"Prepare all tubes!" announced the captain. From below came an instant response.

"Bow tubes ready."

"Aft tubes ready."

"Set depth for surface run," the captain ordered. "Range 2000 meters, heading 85degrees. . . ."

"What's out there? Enemy ships?" the first officer asked as he poked his head through the hatchway from the operations room below.

"Nothing," the captain replied while keeping his eyes pressed to the periscope eyepiece.

"Then why are we loading our tubes, Kapitän?" Number One asked, feeling he had a right to know, just in case.

"We need to get rid of some weight so we can leave this area safely," answered the general without revealing what else was on his mind.

"Oh!" came Number One's short reply. He returned to his post below, prepared to execute additional instructions when they came.

"Open fore and aft torpedo tubes. And flood!" Schmid t ordered.

The message was repeated below.

"Fore tubes ready."

"Aft tubes ready."

"*LOS!*" Captain Schmidt yelled. The boat instantly trembled and rose, a condition which was expected. As others waited, Schmidt watched as tiny white streaks stirred the plankton in their path as they passed through the sea. Minutes later, they passed over the foamy reef and disappeared from sight.

"Reload!" Schmidt shouted again, instantly putting crewmen back to work in the fore and aft sections. Sweat poured down their bodies as they pushed their bunks aside to lower ceiling-mounted torpedoes into their tubes.

Again the order came. "*LOS!*"

Again the torpedoes traveled toward the coordinates given by the captain. The numbers were slightly different from before, but only to compensate for the boat's movement, not the torpedoes' destination.

The men in the torpedo rooms were puzzled when they didn't hear any explosions. What they did note, however, more than anything else, was the disturbing readjustment of the boat's depth. As each volley of torpedoes was expelled, the U-boat got lighter, causing it to rise. At one point, it actually resurfaced, causing the chief to go into a near panic. Within minutes, however, he overcame the problem with a rapid flooding of ballast tanks.

When the last of the internal torpedoes went speeding to their destination, new orders were issued through the sub's telegraph to machinists in the motor room. In rapid succession, they turned valves, opening some, closing others.

"Surface! Prepare to load deck torpedoes!" shouted the chief.

"Here we go again!" a weary man grumbled as he joined others in the control room to scale the ladder leading up through the bridge hatch. They were not alone; others required to assist congregated around the aft, galley, and forward hatches also, waiting orders to go up.

"QUIET!" yelled petty officers, seconds before a loud roar engulfed the boat, causing it to rise again. Not a whisper was heard when the first hatch was opened, nor did anyone dare move until ordered.

"Zero!" the chief yelled.

"Equalize pressure," Captain Schmidt ordered seconds later. A hissing sound followed, then his hatch flew open.

"I go first this time, Kapitän," von Kleitenberg ordered as he pushed the captain out of the way and climbed out quickly. "Rank has its privileges, you know."

"And its liabilities too," Captain Schmidt interjected quietly as he followed the limber officer to the bridge.

A loud but dull thud echoed through the boat just then, causing everyone to hold their positions and look around for the answer.

"What the hell was that?" asked the general.

"Damned if I know! It came from outside the hull. Driftwood, perhaps," speculated Captain Schmidt.

Just then, a high-pitched voice—a terrified one—cried from the sea, startling everyone. Every ear turned, startled and puzzled by the strange sound hitting their ears.

"AAAeeeeeee!"

U-4R1 in an unexpected and tragic evening
encounter with a Caymanian fisherman and his
grandson off Little Cayman

Chapter 12

The Fisherman

Little Cayman, July 1945

onathan Bowman had no thoughts the afternoon he set sail from George Town, Grand Cayman Island, that his fishing trip with his young grandson, a scraggly little boy of mixed ancestry, would be anything more than ordinary.

For years, and long before the war had started, he had always fished at his favorite fishing cove off the tiny island of Little Cayman. It was quiet there, and few if anyone ever fished there.

Now a man in his seventies, Jonathan Bowman could trace his roots to African slaves who had been transported to the Cayman Islands. They had been freed many years later, after bitter debate by the British Parliament that slavery was not only inhumane, immoral, and against God, but was also bad for one's health.

Like his ancestors before him, Jonathan preferred the old ways. He believed in witches—both good and evil—and monsters which rose out of the sea. They were a part of him, and he respected their position when it came to honoring a god for this and a god for that. With equal zeal, he passed these beliefs on to his children, though

119

most would not believe what they had been taught; they had become civilized!

But the same did not apply to his grandson, Joseph. Little Joseph was a quiet boy who adored his grandfather—most probably because the old man didn't go around boozing all day like his father, who thought work was for slaves. No wonder! With that kind of attitude, he never got to work much. No one, not even children of former slaves, would offer him a job, that is, except for a rare unwary tourist, who had the misfortune to seek his guide service. Regrettably, he managed to fleece most of them before they knew they had been taken. What was regrettable is that he never got reported because the tourist was either too busy to bother or too ashamed to report the misdeed. It's too bad, too, because had they done so, his drinking money would have dried up and the islanders would have been better off with him behind bars.

Of course, Little Joseph couldn't understand all this. He was just six years old when his father's reputation swept the island. Unlike his father, who despised work—fishing especially, the little tyke took to it like fish to an aquarium. His grandfather was responsible for this passion, after recognizing at any early age how fascinated the boy was with the sea. Often, the grandfather would take him fishing in what had once been a lifeboat on a passenger vessel. Its owners had given it to him after he risked his life to help passengers off their ship when it went aground.

Until this day and evening, a day which was to change everything, Grandpa Bowman had never before taken his small grandson away from Grand Cayman Island to a sister island in the chain some sixty miles away. Months earlier, Little Joseph's parents refused to let him go, but now all that had changed—Little Joseph had been orphaned and deserted at the same time! His father had died after a bad bout of cirrhosis, following a heavy drinking spree with friends at Pedro's Castle, an old fort turned restaurant, high above one of the island's rocky shorelines.

When referring to his father's affliction, local church-going people called it "mango fever," a fictional, rare disease presumably contracted through the ingestion of contaminated mangoes. In reality, the cover-up was a humanitarian attempt on the part of the local folk to disguise the true nature of the man's death for the sake of his son, Little Joseph.

There was some truth to the story, however, and it had to do with the color Yellow. One got "yellowed" either from drinking too much alcohol (jaundiced) or from eating too many mangoes. To those who knew better, however, if one contracted the latter, it was only the result of a juice stain—nothing else!

Others held a different opinion as to how the matter should be handled, with local mango growers and importers being more vocal. They preferred to be more open and honest about Little Joseph's father's demise, "Good riddance!"

The boy's mother, on the other hand, deserved equal attention. Upon news of her husband's colorful end, she packed her bags and simply disappeared. No one knew for certain where she had gone although a rumor or two came from friends who said she had run off with a tourist to Miami.

With no one to object, both grandfather and grandson were free to sail at will, that is, until school authorities started to track the boy down, insisting he be sent to school for a "proper" education. Jonathan Bowman didn't mind that so much, so long as he could keep his grandson and go fishing with him on weekends. The authorities agreed.

So this Saturday, two months after the war ended, they sailed for Little Cayman, a sister island many miles away. Their plans were simple: to fish until the boat in which they came was filled to capacity and to do some treasure hunting if time permitted. The old man's favorite fishing spot was outside a long, partly submerged circular reef which enclosed a beautiful sandy beach on the island itself. Within this enclosure was a much smaller island, which also offered a small beach, but it was less desirable than the first.

There was something magical about that island besides its offering a place for rest and solitude. It had a way of soothing one's nerves while providing refuge for a weary soul. At other times, the opposite could be true, especially around hurricane season. Then, a contrast would take place, dramatic as day is bright and night is dark. The surf would roar like a ravenous lion and crash upon the reef with a fury that drove the tropical birds that normally chirped happily far away until the passing of the season. That's why Grandpa Bowman chose the spot. It was a place where no one could disturb the bond which existed between him, as a caring, loving grandfather, and his little grandson.

He hoped for a respite, but fate dictated otherwise as a long, black shape moved ominously into his favorite outer-reef fishing grounds, disturbing what had been a gentle rolling sea. The sudden and unexpected swells coming from the submerged creature caused his small boat to rise and fall, frightening his grandson. An answer to the superstitious man's dilemma was needed to calm the lad.

"Might be the sea god," he said reverently to his grandson. "Like the god of the sky and land, you've got to give him something or he

121

might get mad."

As his grandson watched with fearful eyes, Jonathan reached down to the floor of the boat to find a piece of bait. He squinted while doing so. The glare of the lantern was hard on his cataract-covered eyes; its rays distorted his sight, but he went on.

"Understand?" he asked his intense and curious grandson.

"Yes, Grandpa," little Joe answered in a soft voice, its volume weakened by fear.

"What do you understand?" his grandfather asked.

"That we're supposed to give something back," the boy replied hesitantly.

"Yes—and never forget that," the old man charged proudly, just as bright moonbeams flashed downward through a break in the partially overcast sky. They illuminated his white teeth, which sparkled like new ivory, and something else too, which puzzled him and his grandson.

They couldn't explain it, but a number of white objects, cylindrical in shape, each leaving white trails behind it, streaked toward the reef near which they were fishing, then passed over them and disappeared from sight.

Fish, the old man thought before going back to what he had been telling his grandson. "As I said before," he continued, "one must always give the sea god something in exchange for what we take."

"All the time?" little Joe asked while trying to stifle a yawn. The long trip over had exhausted him.

The old man smiled, then reached into his pocket and pulled out a small leather bag. He opened it, then pulled something out. Their tinkle caught the young boy's attention.

"What's that, Grandfather?" he asked, leaning forward to see what the old man had hiding in his fist.

"You really want to know?" his grandfather teased.

"Yes, yes," the boy replied enthusiastically, now fully awake.

"It's treasure!" said the old man with a happy laugh as he opened his hand to reveal several gold and silver coins.

"What's treasure?" asked little Joe innocently. His question didn't surprise the grandfather because he knew his grandson was too young to fully understand its meaning.

"It's money, like we use in Grand Cayman, except it's old. It was left by pirates who lived here a long time ago. I found 'em ... dug 'em up," he added while returning most of them to the tiny bag in which they had been stored. He pulled a draw string to secure it, then gently tied it around the boy's neck. "Here, you hold them for a while. It'll bring you favor with the sea god," he added to the boy's delight.

"Oh!" exclaimed little Joe, totally thrilled. A question crossed his inquisitive mind. "Grandpa, why isn't it like the money we use in George Town?"

"Because it came from the sea—from the god of the deep—who allowed me to find it," replied the grandfather, moments before his countenance changed from contentment to worry.

For some unknown reason, the sea beneath the boat started churning and then came large swells, all of which made the tiny boat dip and sway. It wasn't like the first disturbance they had experienced minutes earlier, right after he and his grandson noticed a series of silvery objects, trailing white streaks, crossing over a nearby reef, then into a lagoon located on the other side.

At first glance, the old fisherman concluded they were dolphins because of the manner and ease over which the reef was traversed. It wasn't a bad thought because this was a dolphin playround, and the creatures were everywhere.

As Jonathan Bowman searched the depths for the cause of the new and unusual disturbance, his grandson's eyes followed his, but nothing could be seen. That's when another thought struck the old man.

"I think I know what's wrong," he said finally, after giving the matter some thought. "It's the sea god. He's angry because we haven't given him anything yet."

"Then do it quickly, Grandpa," the frightened little boy pleaded, as he clung to the gunwale to keep from falling out. "I'm scared."

"Hah, hah," the old man laughed. He had only been joking, but in reality he did fear the sea and the god who supposedly controlled it. The turbulent sea and bubbles now rising from it worried him. "All right," he replied quickly to appease his grandson and the sea god at the same time. "We'll give him something right now so he won't be angry anymore."

As the boy looked, the old man tossed into the sea the coins he had withdrawn earlier. They plunked into the water some distance away.

"Ahh—now he'll be happy," the old man said before his grandson could speak. "Pretty soon he'll quiet down, and then we'll catch all we need." The certainty in his voice made the young boy relax though that wasn't true for the old man; he was petrified because the sea about him was doing something he had never seen before.

Less than a minute later, it erupted like a new volcano, spewing water everywhere. After that came a violent and unexplainable jar and a back-wrenching thud which tossed the boat from side to side, nearly spilling its occupants.

123

As quickly as they could, both occupants looked in the direction of the problem, in time to see a giant monster rising out of the sea. It had a hideous bony face, denude of eyes. It had arms too, long bone-like ones, bleached white, which crossed the eyeless bony skull on both sides to form an *X*.

"Pirates!" screamed the old man as he jerked his grandson from his place in the boat and pushed him under a canvas tarp near the bow. He didn't have time to explain what the threat really was, though he thought he recognized the shape and symbol which frightened them. "Stay here, and don't move until I tell you," he said with a firmness never before used on the boy.

The old fisherman, his eyes wide with fright and his curly hair nearly standing on end, looked up then to the cause of their troubles. Before him, a large metal vessel with tons of water cascading off its black deck rose higher and higher out of the sea, dwarfing the tiny boat.

"AAAeeeeee!" cried the frightened old man as the grotesque structure rose higher. His heart pounded to the point of bursting when suddenly before him, black-garbed men scrambled over the monster's back, shouting words he could not understand. Then, to add to the confusion, a ray of bright light reached downward like a finger in the dark, illuminating and blinding him. Its brightness kept him from seeing the men in the conning who were shocked and dismayed upon discovering his presence.

"Good God! A man! What in the devil is he doing here?" bellowed von Kleitenberg as he looked down with extreme frustration to the frightened figure of a gnarled old man cowering in a small boat near *U-4R1*'s barnacled hide.

"*Sheiser!*" snapped Captain Schmidt as he perceived the same thing. "As if we haven't had enough surprises for one day."

"Gun crews to the bridge," the general ordered without bothering to ask the captain. A flurry of activity followed as SS crewmen emerged like ants from ant hills.

"Please, General . . . I beg you," Schmidt pleaded as he studied his superior's intent face. "Can't we make an exception?"

From his position in the boat, the old man could only watch; the shock of events had robbed him of his senses. It was made worse by his superstitious mind and thoughts of pirates who once forced men off the plank at sword point. He tried rising to his feet to plead for mercy, but his words were drowned when a barrage of orders brought more men to the sub's back.

"Pirates!" the old man cried out, just as fiery sparks burst from the barrels of superstructure-mounted cannons. Von Kleitenberg's orders had been carried out though under protest by Captain Schmidt.

"We're still at war, Kapitän, or have you forgotten so quickly?" reminded von Kleitenberg.

"But he's just an old man. What could he possibly tell the authorities? That he saw a German U-boat? We would be long gone by then."

"It's not that easy, Kapitän," von Kleitenberg shot back dispassionately. He looked down into the sea again. The old man had dropped to the bottom of his boat which was riddled with holes. Von Kleitenberg motioned to one of the gunners. "Sink it!"

Captain Schmidt and his aide looked away, powerless to do anything as a burst of gunfire racked the splintered boat. Its noise drowned a small voice coming from under an innocent-looking tarp within the boat. Though barely discernible, several persons reported hearing something like a child crying.

"Night birds," offered a member of the bridge watch. "They put out a shrill cry."

"What was he doing here?" Number One asked after gaining courage to look back.

"A fisherman is my guess," replied Captain Schmidt. "Didn't you see his nets and tackle?"

"That reminds me, Kapitän," von Kleitenberg interrupted as the U-boat pushed away from the sinking fishing boat. "We have some fishing of our own to do."

His message was quite clear: They had surfaced to withdraw their spare torpedoes from their sealed containers beneath the deck plates and it had to be done quickly. As it turned out, the process took longer than expected since hand-operated winches and cumbersome tackles and pulleys had to be used to pull the torpedoes from beneath the deck plates before sending them sliding down their respective fore and aft chutes to the interior of the boat, where they were systematically fired toward the shore.

The entire procedure took a little over three hours and with each shot, the sub rose higher and higher, and with each meter of rise came a corresponding increase in list from one side to the other. Weight loss was responsible and directly attributable to the torpedoes which had been launched.

"Clear the decks!" shouted Captain Schmidt as soon as the last torpedo sped through the dark waters toward its final destination. A short time later, he dropped into the conning tower, bringing the hatch cover down after him, then quickly twirled its wheel to make the lid watertight before dropping to the floor.

The boat's electric motor started humming, propelled forward by the one usable propeller. A gentle swishing followed as it gained speed. Captain Schmidt hesitated as he listened to the whir, then followed through with orders everyone had been waiting to hear.

"Take her down!"

Those near him repeated the order, causing a flurry of more activity. Soon the boat began its descent.

As soon as activities quieted down, von Kleitenberg walked over to Schmidt and tapped him on the shoulder. "We have lost enough time already, Kapitän. Let's get out of this area as quickly as we can."

Schmidt wiped his face before answering. The old fisherman was on his mind. He knew that sooner or later someone would report the old man missing, and a search would begin. It might even be sooner if the man lived on the island they had just left, though he didn't think it was inhabited. *Whatever happens*, he thought, *there had better not be a U-boat in the area of the wreckage!*

Kapitän, pressed the general. "Did you hear what I said?"

"What do you think I'm doing, General?" reponded Schmidt irritably. "We've had enough of Braunau's folly for one day, don't you think?"

"Just being cautious, Herr Kapitän. Experience has shown it never hurts to ask the question," the general explained. "In fact, there is an interesting chapter in my book about such matters, if you're interested," he added as he turned away, heading for his wardroom.

Schmidt's eyes followed him. They were full of contempt and loathing for the man.

Von Kleitenberg was hardly out of sight and hearing when Schmidt spat on the deck then cursed. "Damn him! Who does he think he is? God?"

Number One walked up at that time. "Careful, sir, the bulkheads have ears, you know."

"Good! I hope their eardrums burst!" Schmidt replied carelessly before trudging off to the officers' wardroom, where he hoped to catch a few winks.

"Any orders, sir?"

"Yes, take this damn boat out of here."

"What heading?"

"Due north and clear of these islands until we can determine our location. After that, steer for the tip of south Mexico and let me know when we're no more than 50 miles offshore." He crouched low to enter the next compartment.

"Whew!" Number One responded. He started to issue orders but stopped short when the captain poked his head through the hatchway.

"Oh, by the way, Number One, if you need additional instructions while we're enroute, ask your new Kapitän, the general. He seems to know everything."

Number One said nothing; he didn't dare.

The general heard the remark through his curtain but decided to ignore it; his thoughts were elsewhere. While others were bent on their various tasks, he turned to his own by pondering the map before him. *Bormann, you slob,* he thought to himself while thumping his rubber-tipped pencil on the desk, *you'd better be there when I get there!*

Minutes later, he decided to lay down and read. The book he chose was his own. He thumbed through until reaching his favorite chapter, "Management of Subordinates: The Art of Discipline." *Where have I gone wrong?* he asked himself. *By now, Schmidt should have been subdued!*

The hum of the electric motor soon lulled those off duty into a deep sleep. All were physically and emotionally drained from the night's work. Nothing disturbed them, not even the cook who had worked hard to prepare a hot meal. In disappointment, he walked back to the galley, mumbling misgivings to himself.

"Coffee?" the cook asked as the chief engineer just happened to pass by. He had been working on the burnt bearing and the dislodged motor for hours and looked terrible.

"You know how to get at my heart, Kuchie," the chief responded wearily.

"Did you get it fixed?" the cook asked, hoping he did. He was anxious for conversation and company and wanted the man to stop and visit a while.

"The mountings and bearings, yes, but the shaft's beyond us."

"Oh! Sorry. You tell the Kapitän yet?"

"Told him earlier, before he sacked out. He's asleep right now and needs all the rest he can get. Might be required to get up at any time, you know. . . ."

"I understand," the cook replied before switching subjects. "What's Mexico like, Chief?"

"Don't know. Never been there myself. Why?"

"Because that's where we're headed!"

"Schultz! You been fermenting apricots again?"

"How can you say such a thing!" responded the cook.

"I know you, my friend," the chief replied with a mischievous

smile. "Remember the crock of apricots I found in the thunder box .
. . the one we converted to storage?"

"But that was a long time ago," protested the cook. "Anyway, it's
true about us going to Mexico. Go ask the captain; he'll tell you."

"All right, I will. After he wakes up," the chief replied as he
dumped copious amounts of sugar into his cup. "Need the energy, you
know," he said while the cook looked on in astonishment. He walked
away, heading aft toward the control room.

"Nobody wants to talk," the cook mumbled to himself as he
reached into the oven to pull out a pan. He cut a slice of some sweet-
smelling pastry, then gingerly nibbled at it to keep from getting burnt.
A voice called out just then, waking those in the petty officers'
quarters next door.

"Hey, everybody! I smell strudel."

The pantry became a beehive of activity as the word spread, giving
the cook his *muchj*—sought after—attention. It was short-lived,
however, when the men returned to their quarters sleepier than before.

Chapter 13

Radar Contact

Cayman Trench, 1945

 is Majesty's Ship, the HMS *Winston*, a sleek new destroyer only three months old, was the pride of the British navy when she put to sea for service in the Caribbean. Besides sporting a fresh black-gray striped coat of paint which covered her steel sides, she was one of the best-equipped vessels of her type in the British inventory of ships. Displayed proudly for all to see was an impressive array of weapons and sophisticated gear, including a huge radar antenna—the latest of its kind, which crowned the top of her bridge, very much like the crown that had been placed on King George's head at the time of his coronation.

Complementing the vessel's sophistication were her crew, the majority of whom were seasoned navy veterans who had been pitted against German naval forces time and time again, mostly while assigned to other ships. Collectively, they brought to his majesty's service some five hundred years of experience.

With the war over, many of those on board looked forward to

leaving the Caribbean to return to their homes—some to England and others to Scotland, Ireland, Canada, India, and other nations of the Commonwealth. Naturally, some of the men would soon be discharged and others would take leave and continue in active service until retirement.

The radio operator on board the *Winston* was one of the latter, a career serviceman from England. Like the others aboard ship, he was anxious to go home on leave. His expectations were dashed, however, when an urgent radiogram from the commandant of the U.S. fleet at Guantanamo came in, addressed to his captain. It was explicit:

> "Brazilian merchant ship, sunk in the
> Caribbean approximately 2100 GMT,
> yesterday. X. No survivors! All
> massacred. X. Original distress call
> giving coordinates garbled. X. Air
> reconnaissance of debris in area confirms
> presence of one U-boat—possibly more.
> X. Believe U-boat responsible for
> sinking. X. Sonar contact made yester-
> day by our destroyers who depth charged
> area. X. Cannot confirm a kill. X.
> Advise search in your immediate area. X.
> U-boat believed damaged. U.S. vessels
> combing area from Guantanamo southward,
> beginning with longitude . . . ."

When reading the document, the captain of the *Winston* was incredulous, calling the leader of the attack on a civilian vessel in peacetime "either a lunatic warped by the maniacal ravings of a madman or some misguided U-boat commander who wants to carry on the war all by himself."

It was simple enough to give credit to the uninformed, but it was not that easy to erase from the minds of everyone the tragedy which wiped out so many lives.

"All hands lost, what a pity!" Captain Smith moaned as he looked out over the ocean through the thick pane-glass window on his bridge. The radiogram was in his hand.

"Yes, sir," replied chief radio operator Peter Smythe of the Royal Navy as he studied the serious look on his skipper's face. It was strange working for a man who had a name similar to his own, yet spelled and pronounced differently. The difference was national!

Captain Smith was Canadian; Peter hailed from England.

"Is there anything else, sir?"

"Yes," the captain replied after thinking a bit. "Send a reply to the commandant of the U.S. fleet, Guantanamo. Tell him we are conducting a search in the areas specified in his signal. And we will keep him advised of any developments."

"Is that all, sir?"

"Just that you and your boys keep a good ear, that's all."

"That we will, sir. Thank you, sir," Smythe answered sharply as he stood erect, lifted one foot, stamped, then did an about-face and walked out.

"My, you boys do know how to impress a newcomer," the captain said, addressing his first officer who had been waiting nearby.

"Tradition, sir," the officer answered proudly. "The British navy has had a long time to develop it."

"I know. That's why most Canadians have flat feet, you know," the captain replied as he walked slowly away while trying to hide a subdued smile.

A strange look covered the first officer's face; he wasn't sure whether his captain was joking or serious or whether he should laugh or maintain a stiff upper lip as was his custom in such matters.

While he pondered his thoughts, Captain Smith walked over to the helmsman. "What's your heading, sailor?"

"One six zero degrees south, sir," the man responded.

"Good, steady as you go, sailor."

"Aye, captain. Steady as you go," the young seaman repeated as he stole a glance at his captain who was now walking onto the open bridge wing on the port side to survey the horizon and to air his thoughts. They were many.

Captain Smith, a thoughtful, tall, and robust-looking man, weighing slightly over 200 pounds and a former athlete in his own country, was concerned about the recent sinking. With the war over by some two months, it seemed incredible that a German U-boat could still be out in the wide watery expanse before him, searching for unarmed merchantmen.

It must have been an accident, he thought. *Yes, that's it. There's a lot of old tubs floating out here, most overdue for Davey Jone's locker—the deep six.* On the other han, knowing what he knew about German atrocities, he let his thoughts tack another way, *Of course, the sinking could have been deliberate!*

"Captain," a voice called from behind.

"Yes, what is it?" Captain Smith replied as he turned to face his

131

executive officer.

"We have an Asdic contact, sir. Sound says it could be a sub, but he's not sure. Radar is searching, too."

"Where away?"

"About twenty miles, sir, bearing due south, 180 degrees."

"Close the distance, mister," Captain Smith ordered with great calm. "Give her all she's got and don't spare any fuel."

"Aye, aye, Captain," the seasoned officer replied enthusiastically. "Shall we sound General Quarters?"

"Most certainly, mister. From all appearances, we're still at war. And, oh yes, be sure to warn all stations to be on alert for the possibility of other U-boats."

"Very good, sir," his assistant replied as he walked briskly back to his duty station on the bridge.

He gave orders to others when he entered, causing a rash of alarms and bells to resound throughout the vessel. Within seconds, while alarms bells continued to clang, officers and seamen alike raced to their duty stations. Soon heavy guns were moving up and down in anticipation of action.

Throughout it all, loud speakers blared, providing last-minute instructions to everyone. Cooks, apart from those designated to perform additional duties, could be seen darting in and out of hatches or up and down gangways, carrying food and beverages to different stations.

"What's your screen saying?" asked Captain Smith from his station on the bridge. He had a direct line to the command room where all the sophisticated radar and other electronic listening gear was located.

"Ten miles and closing, sir," the chief radio operator replied.

"Still think it's a U-boat?"

"Almost certain, sir, but I can't explain why it's moving so slowly?"

"Maybe it's been wounded?" the captain replied.

"Hadn't thought about that, sir. It could explain why—" The man stopped suddenly, then listened more closely before speaking again. "Captain, we're picking it up better now . . . on our sonar. I can hear its screws—I mean, screw. Only one." He faltered for a moment while trying to figure out why that was. "There's a racket on board . . . like they're experiencing some kind of trouble."

"Where away?" the captain asked anxiously, hoping to pinpoint its exact location.

"Dead ahead, sir!" the radar man suddenly interjected in a high-pitched voice. "You should be able to see her now. She's surfacing, and I'm getting a large blip on my screen."

"Unidentified object dead ahead!" a lookout on the bridge shouted just then, verifying the find.

Captain Smith and his first officer raced out and onto the deck adjoining the bridge, then looked through their binoculars in the direction pointed. A small black speck could be seen emerging in the relatively calm sea. All was not right with her, as indicated by billowing smoke which poured out of her hatches, obscuring much of her.

"It's on fire!" another lookout yelled.

"All ahead full!" Captain Smith ordered. His message was quickly relayed through the ship's telegraph to the engine room.

As more steam was supplied, the destroyer cut through the calm sea like a sharp knife.

"It's a U-boat!" shouted another lookout. Some of the smoke which had hidden her identity cleared and it was now easy to make out her profile, in particular, her conning tower and snorkel.

"Battle stations! Prepare for action!"

On Board *U-4R1*

Before the trouble started, Captain Schmidt had been sound asleep. Then someone shook him violently, and cried, "Kapitän! Get up! Emergency!"

He could barely think straight when awakened from a deep slumber, but the danger was immediately apparent. Besides a smoke-filled vessel, he had to contend with burning eyes and eardrums on the verge of bursting.

Confused as he was, he managed somehow to feel his way into the choking control room Mass panic and confusion best describes what he saw. He found Number One.

"What happened?" he demanded though he felt certain he knew the answer.

"Our snorkel failed!" Number One shouted to be heard over the din.

"Who told you to use the snorkel?" demanded Schmidt. "It was damaged during the last attack—don't you remember?"

"I know, but—"

"But what?"

"I was only following the general's orders," replied the frightened man.

"What's the general got to do with it?" Schmidt yelled angrily.

"Don't you remember, sir? You told me I was to do whatever the general ordered—until we reached Mexico . . . and that's what I did."

"Damn!" Schmidt cried as a severe cough cut off his words. He put a handkerchief to his face to filter the air going through his mouth, like the others. While it helped a little, it did not relieve the searing pressure in his ears. The situation was desperate, and something had to be done.

"Karl! Anything upstairs?" yelled the captain to his radioman, who was barely able to maintain his station at the hydrophone.

"Can't tell, Kapitän. Can't get anything to work."

"Then we're going to have to take a chance and go up, enemy or no enemy. Surface! Blow tanks!" yelled Schmidt, unable to bear the screams of his stricken men any longer.

"Surface!" the chief cried out, repeating his words. "Blow all tanks! Up hydroplanes!" His eyes watered from the blinding smoke as he pushed his face next to the boat's depth gauge to make sure its needle was moving. When it hit its mark, he yelled as best he could, "Zero, Kapitän—the boat is surfaced!"

Captain Schmidt headed the evacuation by nearly being blown out of the conning tower. The release of internal air to stabilize conditions had been excessive, causing pressure to build within the hull rather than to match it to the outside atmosphere.

"Everyone on deck," he called from the bridge. He didn't need to give the order because it was impossible for anyone to stay below. Upon emerging, a number of crewmen fainted while others fell to the decks gasping and convulsing violently. Only a handful appeared fit for duty, and those marginally.

The sight was appalling. More than anything, Captain Schmidt hoped to avoid another mishap with the snorkel, so he blamed himself for not giving specific instructions to avoid using it even though it was von Kleitenberg himself who had given the original order. What the general did not know was that Number One had little or no measurable experience in such matters, and by taking it upon himself to lead, he too had jeopardized the entire mission. Though Number One was unquestionably loyal and willing to obey all orders issued him, he was not command material, the reason for his never having gotten a U-boat of his own.

"Post your watches, Number One, and secure that damn snorkel before anything else happens!" Captain Schmidt ordered after noticing an absence of lookouts on the bridge. He wasn't aware Number

One had collapsed to the deck, gasping for air like the others, until he heard a hacking reply coming from the deck near the periscope housing. He gave the man a hand.

"Aye, Kapitän," Number One coughed as he reached up, grasped the extended hand, then grabbed hold of a steel railing to steady himself before descending to the foredeck to muster sufficient help. Minutes later, while a number of submariners were working on the damaged snorkel trying to lower it back into its berth beneath the foredeck, a lookout spotted something on the horizon.

"A-L-A-R-M! DESTROYER! DIRECTLY AFT!" a panicky lookout cried at the top of his lungs.

Heads instinctively turned.

"That's all we need!" Number One cursed, seconds before a shell screamed overhead, exploding near its bow.

"Hoist the black flag!" ordered Captain Schmidt.

At that moment, von Kleitenberg ran up. "What are you doing?" he demanded angrily.

"Surrendering. That's what!" cried the young captain.

"That's what you will not do!" ordered von Kleitenberg.

"But we haven't a chance against them," argued Schmidt, trying to be heard above the noise which permeated every part of the vessel.

"All guns on the enemy!" ordered von Kleitenberg as he pushed the captain aside to face his men directly.

"Are you mad?" demanded Captain Schmidt as he grabbed the man by his arm and turned him back to face him. "Can't you see there's no way out! It's too late! We'll all be killed if you continue!"

It seemed like a thousand eyes were on the pair. The sympathetic ones—including a few of the SS—were in agreement with the captain while the majority of the others were prepared to die or fight to the end.

"Belay those orders," demanded Captain Schmidt to countermand the general, "and raise the flag!"

"Kapitän, I order you to desist," demanded von Kleitenberg as another missile—another warning shot—crashed near the bow, causing the vessel to toss more violently this time.

"You might be loyal to a dead cause, but not me or my men!" replied Schmidt, seconds before a volley of bullets penetrated his body. As he dropped to the floor, a shocked look crossed his face as if he could not believe what was happening. He tried to say something but could not.

"Well? What are you waiting for?" demanded von Kleitenberg as he looked at the crew members who had seen it all.

The aft 80mm gunners and those on the promenade deck manning the twin 20mm's managed to get off a few rounds, but accuracy was impossible due to the tossing seas and smoke which hindered their efforts, making the general realize his boat was no match for the destroyer which was rapidly closing in. One last choice existed.

"Clear decks!" von Kleitenberg yelled loudly, resigned to whatever was to happen next. "And you, Number One, take command! You're the Kapitän now."

When the man failed to move fast enough, as a direct consequence of his shock over seeing his captain murdered before his eyes, von Kleitenberg pressed the pistol to his head. "Did you hear me?" von Kleitenberg demanded.

"Aye, General," gulped Number One, immediately regaining his sense and composure. In a flash, he walked over the lifeless body of his former superior and yelled, "Clear decks! Dive! Dive! Bow planes down full!"

It was a dangerous thing for him to do since the U-boat's fantail would lift high out of the water, making itself a perfect target for good marksmen, but he didn't know that since he hadn't had much experience.

As the U-boat's bow dug into the deep, dark sea in a steep angle of attack, exposing its tail much like a whale about to dive, a violent explosion struck it, causing it to twist and turn uncontrollably. The concussion and violent movements tossed crewmen everywhere, incurring grievous injuries to most.

In a desperate attempt to regain control, Number One, from his new post in the conning tower, yelled a question to the chief engineer in the control room below, "Chief! Why isn't she going down quicker?"

"She's too light, sir," the chief called back in a loud and panicky voice. "We took off the torpedoes and she's too light. It takes longer to flood now."

Oh, God! thought Number One. *I forgot about that! What do I do now?* In his haste to obey the general, he had forgotten a basic but critical rule: to be mindful of the effect of weight on a floating object. It was a critical error in judgment on his part, one which he knew Captain Schmidt would never have made, and that was why Schmidt was a captain and he wasn't. *What would Kapitän Schmidt do*, he asked himself, *if he were here?*

"Do something, Number One!" demanded von Kleitenberg in a sudden display of panic. "Surely you know how to get us out of this, don't you?"

Number One looked up for a split second into the the face of a man who never before showed he was capable of emotion. The skin was paler than he had ever seen before and it wasn't because of the low wattage lamps which illuminated the tiny tower. Von Kleitenberg, the pillar of strength, was literally frightened to death and was hurriedly taking off his clothes as if ready for a swim. Number One didn't have time to ask him why. Instead, he did what he had to, after remembering something Captain Schmidt had once told him: *If you ever have to go down quickly, give her everything you've got, no matter what the price. Remember, there's always the chance the enemy might make a mistake.*

"Engage the damaged shaft!" he ordered.

"It'll burn the bearings and give us away," the chief protested.

"To hell with the bearings," countered Number One. "We've got to compensate by adding power. And everyone forward—now!"

A grinding metallic sound swept through the boat and surrounding water seconds later, almost as fast as the speed of light, and with it, nerve-wracking vibrations convinced almost everyone on board the sub was about to blow apart.

At that moment, the shelling stopped, giving them a moment of relief, but only for a moment. What those on *U-4R1* did not know was that the destroyer commander had decided upon a different strategy. With great skill, he guided his vessel over the spot where the U-boat had disappeared, then ordered an array of lethal depth charges—"squids" as they were called—fired upon the fleeing sub.

Unlike anything ever used before, it was a forward firing mortar-type weapon which could hurl a 350-pound explosive package hundreds of yards away. It was a late comer to the war, but late or not, it was a devastating device when used properly. In fact, when fired within a reasonable distance of a fleeing U-boat, it never failed.

B-L-A-A-M! B-L-A-A-M!

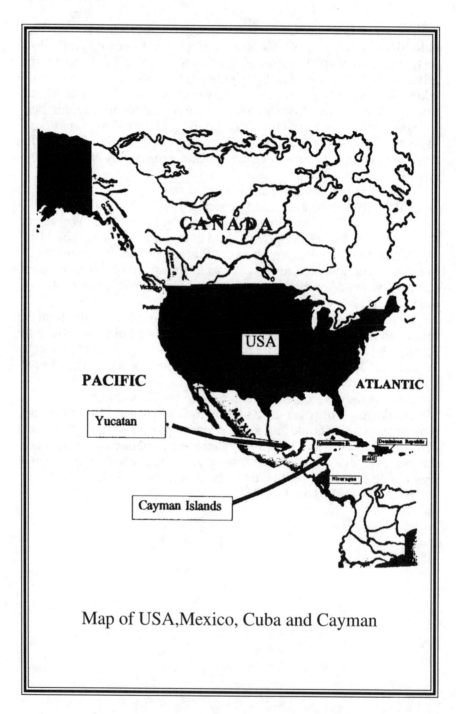

Map of USA,Mexico, Cuba and Cayman

Chapter 14

Driftwood

HMS *Winston*, Greater Caribbean Sea

aptain Smith felt the pain of the sinking vessel as it expelled its final breath in the form of huge bubbles which rose from the depths of the sea. He rejoiced in the victory that brought the sea monster to its decline but cried in his spirit for the souls of the men entombed in its steel body, men who were accompanying it to an unreachable grave thousands of feet below. Its grave marker was a huge oil slick which blanketed the water over the spot where it had begun its twirling and descending motion to the ocean floor which awaited its arrival.

Cheers went up as sailors on the HMS *Winston* watched what they knew was a final farewell to an enemy vessel, but a somberness followed when the truth of the U-boat crew's extinction drew a parallel to the fortunate existence of those who were left alive—the men on the British destroyer compared to the men on the U-boat, those who had the misfortune of being annihilated by the technical superiority of an adversary whom they had once sought to destroy.

Because the surprise catch came a half hour before sunset and because the surface of the ocean was littered with large chunks of oil-covered debris, a search for survivors was difficult. As a consequence, a survivor could easily be overlooked. In spite of it all, the search went on, cautiously of course since no one knew for certain whether other U-boats were lurking in the sea below, waiting for the opportune time to get even.

"A man!" shouted a lookout as he pointed excitedly at an oily lump which was barely visible in the darkening sea. Other voices cried out too after spotting the same thing.

"Where to?" asked the captain from his place on the bridge. A seaman pointed. He looked in that direction, then made a quick check with personnel in the control room as to subsurface sounds.

"None, Captain," a technician reported. "It's clear!"

Captain Smith looked back to the sea, observing the sight first, then ordered lights to illuminate the area. About two hundred feet off the starboard bow, a man totally covered with oil and surrounded by debris came into view. He appeared dead. Buoying him up was an oil-covered emergency-ascent breathing apparatus.

"Bring her about," yelled the captain in an effort to maneuver his vessel as close to the man as possible. Minutes later, after reassuring himself he had accomplished what he intended, he issued another order, "Longboat away!"

A coxswain several decks below complied with the order, minutes after an officer and several seamen entered the motorized lifeboat which hung from its davit by greased cables. Upon a signal from the armed officer, he struck a locking device, then pushed a lever, and the longboat descended with a metallic whir to the sea below.

Several cautious minutes later, seamen manning both ends of the longboat cautiously and simultaneously coordinated the release of the boat's security hooks. It wasn't an easy thing to do, however, since release had to be effectuated when the sea had risen evenly; otherwise a dangerous spill would have occurred. But the men doing the work were more than well qualified for the task and managed to get the boat into the water without incident. It motored away after that, guided by strong searchlight beams which helped lead them to the floating man. They reached him minutes later.

"He's still alive, and breathing, sir!" cried the first sailor to touch him.

"Haul him in, I'll signal the captain," ordered the sublieutenant who had directed the recovery.

While sailors worked feverishly to pull the greasy, waterlogged man into their boat, their lieutenant aimed his signal gun at the slowly circling destroyer. He sent a series of dots and dashes, telling them what he had found.

"All stop! Maintain General Quarters," cried the captain after checking with the operations control room for any change in subsurface conditions. He was a cautious man.

Simultaneously, the ship's telegraph clanged as instructions were mechanically relayed to the engine room. Reversal of engines followed, then a full stop.

"Lend a hand here," a deck officer ordered men near him as he wrestled with the recovery of the longboat bumping against the ship's hull not far below. As soon as both hooks were reattached, he signaled the okay for the boat to be winched in.

The unconscious man was an ordinary sailor from the looks of his clothes. A physician came to supervise his removal to the ship's infirmary. Within minutes, the German was whisked away in a metal litter basket and carried—with great difficulty—through a series of narrow hatches and passageways.

"Mr. Peabody," called the captain from the darkened bridge above, addressing the ship's doctor.

"Sir!" answered the doctor who knew the skipper's voice though he could hardly see him for all the shipboard lights.

"Please advise me of his condition as soon as you can."

"Aye, sir," the doctor called back up before entering a hatchway to join his assistants. He could hear the German seaman moaning as his beaten body was transported through a narrow hatchway marked "Infirmary."

"It's a miracle he made it at all, sir," said the executive officer, Mr. Hawkins, as he reviewed the sinking with his captain after he returned to the bridge. "I wonder how he got out?"

"It's possible he was one of the men on deck," guessed the captain.

"Might have been blown off before it dived," Mr. Hawkins added.

"We'll know in time," said the captain before issuing new orders. "Secure from General Quarters, Mr. Hawkins, and take her home. And by the way, do keep a sharp lookout for other U-boats. Guantanamo seems to think there might be more."

"Aye, Captain," replied the first officer before translating his orders to others. "Ahead one -third, and steady as you go, for a heading of 180—home."

While the helmsman adjusted his course, another member pushed the ship's telegraph handle back and forth to signal those in the engine room below what to do.

U-R42 meets the Pink Dolphin in Campeche Bay
off the tiny village of Ciudad del Carmen

Instantly, a trail of smoke poured out of the vessel's stack as its diesel engines responded to the throttle. Then, slowly at first, it began to move. A wide 180-degree turn followed, then more instructions from the bridge to increase speed, which dissipated the rolling back and forth it had been experiencing at a full stop. It had caused some of the newcomers to sea to head for the rails.

As it sliced through the water like a sharpened knife through a medium rare sirloin, HMS *Winston* was once again in charge of the ocean rather than the other way around, and those who had been sick began to feel better.

When everything appeared in order, Captain Smith left the bridge; a visit to the infirmary was in order since too much time had elapsed since his instructions to the ship's physician to keep him informed. He wondered why. Had the man died, or was the doctor still patching him up? He hoped the latter was the case since there had already been enough deaths for one day.

After hastily skipping steps to get to the lower decks, he approached the infirmary and walked in after bending his head. He was a tall man and had to duct again as he passed first through a small office, then into a larger room, the sick bay. Beyond that was the treatment room, a tiny surgery area called the amphitheater, wherein emergency procedures could be performed if necessary.

The doctor and his assistants were in the sick bay, tending to their patient. While the corpsmen were bandaging various wounds, the doctor was checking his blood pressure and other vital signs. It wasn't a good sight. The man appeared to be on death's doorstep; his face and much of his body were covered with bandages. He was extremely pale and his breathing was shallow, a fact which bothered the doctor.

"Well, doctor, will he make it?" asked the captain after waiting for a while. Concern and compassion covered his face.

"It's hard to say. His blood pressure's dropping. A ruptured spleen is my belief," he said unhappily while directing one of his corpsmen to set up several IVs for the administration of glucose solutions and plasm supplements for blood loss.

"What are his chances?" asked the captain.

"He'll die if we don't operate," replied the weary doctor with a face of gloom as he directed his captain's attention to his tiny operating room. "It's not much, but it's all we got."

"Then go to it," urged the captain. "There's a life to lose or one to preserve."

"That's the problem, Captain," the doctor said quite candidly. "I haven't had any recent surgical experience, and I don't think I'm

143

equipped to do it. You see, my specialty is psychiatry, not general surgery."

The room turned silent. Had it been anyone else besides this captain, curses against the admiralty for permitting such an assignment to take place might have occurred, but it did not. Captain Smith was a calm, theoretical, and practical man, one who respected not only his own limitations, but those of others. The practical part of him spoke this time.

"You're still a doctor, Doctor!" he said with strong emphasis on the man's profession. "All of us have to take risks—just like this man here when he agreed to go to sea," he said while pointing to the dying man. "And since you have some surgical experience, irrespective of whether it's your specialty or not, you've got to use what you know. Is there any other choice?"

"None, Captain," the doctor replied, agreeing. "You're right, and I . . . we will do what we can, sir."

As the doctor was about to turn back to his patient, a question crossed Captain Smith's mind. "Any idea who he is or what his duties were on the U-boat?"

"From what we've been able to learn, based mostly on what he was wearing, one would be inclined to say he was a cook though he doesn't look much like one," replied the doctor.

"What makes you doubt it?" asked the captain.

"Well, for one thing, he's too thin. Most of the cooks I've ever seen were fat from being exposed to an abundance of food, but this one is thin, and outside his injuries, he is in rather good shape for a man his age."

"Looks are deceiving," countered the captain. "He could have lost weight if the sub had been at sea for any length of time. As to age, I don't know anything about U-boat service requirements."

"On the other hand," interjected the doctor, "we do have other things which seem to support our theory about his being a cook. He was wearing these." The doctor turned to retrieve a wet, oily, white jacket, the kind commonly worn by mess personnel, along with a set of metal dog tags and a wallet containing identity papers displaying a likeness of the man.

"Seems conclusive enough," said the captain as he glanced at the oily material, then briefly thumbed through the wet papers, "but one never knows." He dropped the wallet and tags back on the chair.

"What should we do with all this stuff?" asked the doctor.

"Hold on to them until we get through this crisis," the captain answered. "If he makes it, we'll have enough time to interrogate him.

There's a lot of questions needing answers about him and the boat he was on."

"I understand," replied the doctor as the captain turned to leave.

"And by the way, Doctor," the captain added with a confident smile before exiting. "Good luck. I'm confident you and your competent assistants will do your best."

There was a silence in the sick bay as everyone looked at each other, saying nothing. The doctor broke the silence. "Any of you guys ever scrubbed before?" he asked.

The answer was "No." All were recent graduates of the Royal Navy school for medical assistants and had never been to sea before, let alone had any significant training and experience in a hospital setting.

"Then we'll all learn together," said the doctor stoically as he ordered them to prepare their patient for surgery.

The captain heard the exchange, shrugged his shoulders, then muttered something to himself as he scaled the ladder to go topside, "Poor devil. I hope he makes it."

Chapter 15

Hide and Seek

Campeche Bay, Mexico—Early Morning

ight had fallen as *U-4R2* inched its way off a darkened coast. On the bridge, watch personnel kept a close lookout. The closer in the vessel got, the lighter and more shallow the water became, causing everyone on board to worry since the sub was traveling through unfamiliar waters and its depth guage was inoperable.

Where are they? fretted Captain Braunau as he scanned the shoreline for sign of an approaching vessel. Martin Bormann and Sturmbannführer Reiter were beside him, straining their eyes, too.

"Be patient, Kapitän," advised Bormann in a soft voice. "Our agents know what they're doing. A delay perhaps, but they should be along shortly."

On the dimly lit bridge, Captain Braunau could see that his superior wasn't too confident about what he was saying; his taut face showed it.

Again the men resumed their watch, saying little or nothing as they looked in the direction of a series of lights they had been told was the tiny fishing village of Ciudad del Carmen, their waiting place. Behind it, from what they had been told, was an expansive lagoon which could only be accessed through one of two ways: through inlets located at the northwestern end of the long slender island on which it was located or through a much smaller inlet at its southeastern tip. Only the northern one opposite the fishing village could be used because only it could accommodate a vessel as large as a German U-boa with its deep draft, provided an experienced pilot or escort vessel could lead them through.

Bormann broke the silence this time. Thoughts of the missing U-boat, and von Kleitenberg, were on his mind.

"Do you think they've been discovered?" he asked.

"Out there, everything's possible," replied Braunau with a hint of disdain while motioning with his head in the direction of the sea through which they had recently passed.

"Perhaps he's decided to go elsewhere, leaving us to fend for ourselves?"

"Not my general!" Reiter interrupted.

"I was merely speculating," Bormann replied defensively.

"Sir! General von Kleitenberg is a man of honor! He'd never do such a thing! And besides, he's taken the sacred oath," countered Reiter.

"Oh, yes, the oath," Bormann smirked, remembering its importance to Himmler, especially. "I'm sorry. I almost forgot how you men of the SS can always be counted upon to obey orders . . . even to the death!"

"That is correct, Herr Secretary," Reiter said proudly. Out of habit, he stiffened, then clicked his heels together, showing he hadn't lost any of his zeal for anything SS.

Captain Braunau, who listened to the exchange, said nothing. The expression on his face said it all; it was one of contempt—for both men now.

The conversation stopped when Bormann realized he was treading on sacred ground and getting in deeper than he wanted to. He needed to be more discreet when talking about the general, but like the others, he needed to know where the man was. That very thought caused him to look at his watch.

"Damn!" he said loudly so everyone would hear. "It's been over fourteen hours since our last contact with the General. That's too long! Something must have happened."

"He could have run into enemy warships and had to play a mouse being chased by a cat," suggested Braunau. "Otherwise he should have been here by now."

"God! I hope not!" exclaimed Bormann. "If he should fall in enemy hands, everything would be lost! Including everything on his boat!"

To defuse his concerns, Braunau interrupted, "Don't forget, *U-4R1* had bearing problems. That alone could cause a serious delay in their progress."

"Even at that, he should have been here by now," argued Bormann, still unconvinced.

"Depends," reasoned Braunau patiently, "if he had more bearing trouble or had to deviate from his regular course due to the presence of enemy warships."

It was a plausible answer, one that helped allay Bormann's worst fears.

"You could be right," Bormann agreed as Braunau's attention was drawn to a shadowy object slowing approaching them. Its red and green running lights could be seen bobbing up and down in the heaving sea.

"*Was ist das?*" asked Reiter, noticing the same thing. "Do you think—?"

"Where? Show me," Bormann asked excitedly as he searched the dark night.

"There," said Captain Braunau as he pointed to an object in the distance; a foaming white trail marked its path. A light flashed, emitting a series of dots and dashes.

"Someone is signaling," said Reiter.

Braunau called out the letters, "D-U-C-K-S. Ducks."

"It's them!" Bormann shouted happily. "They're here at last!"

Braunau flashed a return signal, using the letters P-I-N-K, then waited. In turn, the approaching vessel flashed another series of letters, D-O-L-P-H-I-N, confirming for everyone that their long-awaited escort had arrived.

Bormann was ecstatic beyond words and could hardly stay out of the way of crewmen who popped out of the bridge hatch to join others on the foredeck below, where they would assist in the tie-up.

With minutes, everyone on deck could not only hear the putting sound of the small fishing boat's engine, but could also see its superstructure and rigging. Fish nets and cables covered its booms, showing it was a shrimper. What better way to hide a clandestine activity than through a simple fishing boat that looked like it was going out to sea to catch some of the world's finest jumbo shrimp!

As the shrimper grew closer, everyone could see a man standing on its bow, shouting instructions in Spanish to the vessel's captain, then in German to converse with the U-boat's deck crew about special needs.

"Standby to receive lines," the second watch officer called from the bridge to the deck crews below. Much activity followed, which brought the vessels together. As it happened, something else besides the man on the bow of the shrimper drew everyone's attention. It was the vessel's outlandish color—pink! Of equal importance was its name, painted in large blue letter, Dolphin!

Now, the mystery was solved, making everyone originally involved with the use of the code name rejoice. There really was a Pink Dolphin, and there was a man riding on it at the bow, just like the Radio Mexico announcer had said!

Soon both vessels were tethered securely with a long gangway extended between them. The man on the bow, a European-looking fellow, was the first to climb aboard. After a quick exchange of words, a petty officer escorted him to the bridge, where introductions were made hastily.

The man, a Herr Mueller, who seemed a little nervous and agitated, wasted no time getting to the business at hand.

"Where's the other U-boat?" he asked, looking around.

"We don't know," replied Captain Braunau as he motioned in the direction of the open sea again. "We haven't heard from him, have you?"

Herr Mueller winced, clearly perturbed. Like Bormann earlier, he looked at his watch. "We can only stay a half hour at most; otherwise we risk detection. And besides, it will take some time to get your boat to its new berth."

"What if *U-4R1* should come after we've gone?" asked Braunau.

"He'll just have to wait offshore," replied the man, "until we can arrange another meeting."

"But—?"

"That's all we can do, Kapitän. We'll come out again tomorrow night, I assure you. And besides, if he still has a working transmitter, we'll be able to monitor him."

"After greasing more palms, eh?" chided Bormann as he nudged the man jokingly.

"*Moneda*, they call it here," the man replied. "It's a way of life here, and everyone has a price, irrespective of position, government officials especially. And it works quite well, believe me!"

Onboard HMS *Winston*

"Captain, can you come up?" asked the bridge officer on duty after reluctantly awakening his chief.

Captain Smith had gotten into his sack hours earlier after a gruesome night of searching the surrounding sea for other U-boats. While he slept, per his instructions, a message was sent to the commandant, U.S. Naval Forces, Guantanamo, advising him of their successful search and destroy mission of a German U-boat and of the sailor they had rescued.

"What is it?" Captain Smith asked groggily as he wiped the sleepiness from his eyes and cleared his throat to speak into the telephone.

"We're not certain, Captain, but it looks like pieces of driftwood, with someone—a child, sir—clinging to it."

"Are you certain?"

"It may sound stupid, sir, but that's exactly what it looks like."

"I'll be right up! Carry on," Captain Smith replied as he returned the phone to its receiver. Hhe pushed his weary body out of his bunk and reached for his pants. Minutes later, he was back on deck, peering through his binoculars at a small object rolling in the bright morning sea next to pieces of what had once been a lifeboat. The sea was gentle as the ship altered its course to maneuver closer to the bobbing object before coming to a full stop.

Again the order, "Lower longboat!" was given by the captain. It was the second time he had ordered a rescue mission in two days.

"You were right!" Captain Smith said, addressing the officer who had called him while slowly sipping a cup of freshly brewed coffee brought to him by an observant orderly.

Minutes later, another patient was admitted to the ship's infirmary, screaming at the top of his lungs about sea monsters who threw sparks at his grandfather, killing him, and hurting him in the process.

"He's delirious, Captain, and has a nasty wound in his thigh," the ship's doctor called up to the bridge from his infirmary after a preliminary examination.

Captain Smith pushed his phone aside for a moment until passage of a piercing scream emitted by the boy.

"Must have experienced something dreadful," he said into the phone when it passed. "But what puzzles me is how he got way out here?"

Before the doctor could reply, the chief boatswain's mate entered the bridge carrying a large piece of flotsam to show it to the skipper. It had numerous holes in it like it had been attacked by seaworms.

"Hold on, doc," the captain said as he interrogated the chief. "Where'd you get this?" he asked while the doctor waited.

"The boy was clinging to it, sir," replied the man.

"Looks like bullet holes!" said the captain before turning back to the phone, this time with something else on his mind.

"Tell me, Doctor. Could the wounds on the boy have been caused by gunfire—bullets?"

"I was just going to tell you about that," replied the doctor excitedly. "There's a tiny hole on one side of his leg and a gaping exit point on the other, like the kind a bullet would make."

"Meaning . . . ?" asked the captain.

"He's been shot! And there's extensive muscle damage which will in all probability leave him with a nasty scar and limp."

"Anything else?" asked the captain while motioning for the chief to leave the piece of goods and go on with his regular duties.

"His state of mind, at this time," replied the doctor. "As for his wound, I used the standard treatment—sulfur powder. Other than that, he's okay, and we'll manage."

"Thank you, Doctor. Carry on, and please do keep me informed."

"You can be certain of that, sir," the doctor replied while adding, "I'm glad I'm not in his shoes because he's badly traumatized."

"If his case has any connection with the U-boat we sank yesterday, then God help all the other innocent victims permanently maimed by the wickedness of evil men," said the captain.

"You sound like a philosopher rather than the captain of a warship, if I may say so, sir," the doctor interjected with a bit of mirth.

"Had leanings that way," replied the captain, "but my father won out. But enough of that for now. In the meantime, what is the status of Jerry?"

"He came through the surgery okay, sir, awake and hungry."

The captain smiled, "Guess you were right, bones. He must've been the cook."

The doctor laughed at his new name, before adding, "Just a hunch which proved correct, sir, though it has been confirmed by one of my orderlies who speaks a little German. He told me the first thing out of Heine's mouth—or Jerry as you put it—was a question about strudel."

"Strudel?"

"That's right, sir. It seems he had left a fresh batch in the oven just before the boat went down and is still upset about losing it."

"A one-stomach mind I'd say, wouldn't you?" joked the captain before become more serious. "In the meantime, until I can find time to talk to him, keep him well and comfortable. There's still a chance he's not what he says he is. Anyway, let me know if you learn anything else—about the sinking of that Brazilian ship in particular. And anything he might know about the boy."

"Strange you should mention that, Captain," replied the doctor, "because something rather interesting did happen a while ago though it might not mean anything."

"Let's hear it anyway," urged the captain.

"Well, in between short sleeping spells, we've noticed Heine looking at our new patient like he knows something about him, though I could be wrong because he keeps falling asleep and there's no way to pursue the matter, not now anyway. . . ."

"That might be significant, or just plain curiosity," Captain Smith replied thoughtfully. He remembered something just then. "By the way, did you see any strange tattoos on his body? Under his left arm especially?"

"Anything in particular, sir?"

"Like two SS lightning bolt-type letters, the kind used by SS troops."

"None that I know of, sir, and I mean that because we have wrapped his body from head to foot and would have noticed. It's the absence of a tattoo which makes him unique, if you ask me."

"Explain yourself," prodded the captain.

"Well, for a seafaring man, you'd think he'd have one or two. Maybe even a little one with the name of his best girl, but he is clean throughout."

"That's not unusual. I don't have any either, but I do agree with you; most sailors do succumb to local tattoo artists during port calls. Anyway, keep your eyes and ears open until we can get him to a place where he can be properly interrogated."

"Aye, Captain. Will do," replied the physician as a click on the line signaled an end to the conversation—and to his curiosity.

"Take her home, Mr. Hawkins," Captain Smith ordered after cradling the phone. His thoughts were troubled as he turned to leave the bridge for his comfortable cabin on the deck below. More than anything, he needed a few more hours of rest, but the mystery of the boy's mid-Caribbean appearance gnawed at him. He turned long enough to pose a question to his second officer, the navigator.

"Mr. Goodfellow!"

"Sir!" the young officer snapped.

"Would you be kind enough to study your charts and report back to me when you're finished about any relationship that might exist between the U-boat we encounterd and the one chased by the Americans off Guantanamo—including the spot where the young boy was found adrift."

"I've already done that, sir," the officer replied with a bright smile on his face, startling his chief. "I took the liberty—on my own, sir—to see if there was an connection."

"Oh? And what conclusion have you reached?"

"It could be one and the same boat, sir."

"On what basis?"

"Almost in a straight line, sir. But . . ." he faltered.

"Out with it, Mr. Goodfellow, I haven't all day."

"Calculated at known U-boat speeds, surfaced or submerged, our U-boat should have been much further away. By the same token, when considering reported sightings in connection with the plotting of a course from where the U.S. Navy lost contact, the finger still points toward the boat, sir."

"Why do you suppose that is?"

"I don't know, sir, unless it had been damaged earlier . . . slowing it down."

"Very perceptive, if I may say so, Mr. Goodfellow. Thank you, it makes sense. Perhaps we'll have the answer we're looking for if and when Jerry wakes up."

With that, Captain Smith turned and walked away, yawning heavily as he did. As he disappeared below, his heels clanged heavily until they were heard no more.

"I wouldn't want to be in Jerry's shoes," the second officer said, referring to the German prisoner they had below.

"Me either, if his boat was responsible. . . ."

Villa at Laguna de Terminos

Bormann was pleased with the accommodations. The entire operation had gone off without a hitch. Herr Mueller was thorough in everything he did. As a consequence of bribes, local officials were absent, and when the U-boat went through the inlet, no one was in sight.

"Are you satisfied, Herr Secretary?" Mueller asked.

"The Führer himself would have been pleased beyond words," Bormann responded.

"*Danke,* Herr Secretary, but it was nothing, really."

"To the contrary, Herr Mueller. Your work has preserved the Reich."

Bormann's words were well chosen for, indeed, what had occurred minutes earlier could not have been done by incompetents or fools; it was done by experts.

With the "pink dolphin" leading the way, the U-boat had been carefully guided safely through the northern inlet, then into the lagoon itself, and further on in to a large section of marshland. After carefully negotiating cleared areas, the boats encountered what looked like a tall growth of impassable weeds, which gave way suddenly to reveal a long, narrow waterway. The tall brush which appeared to be an extension of the shoreline was not that at all; it was an artificial gate camouflaged to look like the real thing.

Everyone on the U-boat's deck who had been required to assist in maneuvering could not help being amazed by what they were seeing and experiencing. The facade gate, when it closed behind them, fascinated everyone, but not quite as much as the next surprise.

At the base of what looked like an ancient Mayan ruin towering over them, a gigantic door swung open, revealing a huge internal structure. The shrimp boat did not enter. Instead, it made a narrow circle in a small turning basin, then went back in the direction from which it had come.

"*Wunderbar!*" Bormann exclaimed as did others around him, but with different words, as *U-4R1* slid gently into a waiting slip, big enough to house two or more U-boats!

"By German engineers, sir!" Herr Mueller proudly explained as he looked around the huge dome under which the U-boat had come to rest. After the gigantic door to the huge, partially prefabricated shelter banged shut like the artificial bush gate a few hundred meters away, a barrage of bright lights came on, illuminating the interior as if someone had let the sun in. This overwhelmed all the newcomers.

"I can't believe it!" Bormann gasped. He was joined by Braunau, who shook his head in utter disbelief.

"It's another Brest . . . St. Nazaire . . . La Pallice and La Rochelle," Braunau said in awe.

"No, not quite," Mueller interrupted with a smile. "This one isn't built to withstand bombs like the ones you've been accustomed to, Captain."

He was referring to the bombproof U-boat pens built on the French coast on the Bay of Biscay after Germany occupied France. The Allies were never able to bomb them out of existence.

"I'm dumbfounded," admitted Braunau as he continued to look

around. Mueller looked on, pleased by his response. "To build something like this with all the dredging and the like, without anyone's knowledge, had to take a lot of preplanning."

Mueller's face lit up again. His human hull was nearly bursting as he told the rest of the story. "Yes, it did! It was the brainchild of General von Kleitenberg."

"But—?" Braunau gasped, confused by it all. "I thought he didn't know anything about where we were going until a few days ago?"

"That's true, Kapitän. He didn't know," the man replied with delight, "but what you don't know is that this shelter is one of several. There are others. . . ."

"More? Like this? Why didn't anyone tell me?" Bormann demanded.

"I thought you knew, Herr Secretary," Mueller replied apologetically.

"I was never told anything like this existed," insisted Bormann as he looked around the huge pen.

"It was the general's idea to build it here, like the other ones . . . in out-of-the-way places—Brazil along the Amazon, to name one, and the Orinoco in Venezuela, to name another. If the political climate in the other countries had been better, you mostly likely would have gone on to South America."

In an effort to hide his ignorance, Bormann spoke up. "Just like Ernst," he said, "always planning ahead! Can't blame him, though, for being so secretive. Now I understand why he didn't want to scuttle the U-boats after our arrival. He had other plans, I see."

What he didn't say bothered him—in particular, just how long had von Kleitenberg been working on the project and with whom, because this was no last-minute plan as he had originally been duped into believing. Undoubtedly, it had to have started much earlier; that much was clear! And on the presumption he was correct in his thinking, Bormann wanted to know what else von Kleitenberg had in mind which he hadn't shared with anyone else—Hitler included. The answer was to wait since Mueller was anxious to get everyone settled.

"You haven't seen it all, sir," Mueller said proudly. "There is much more."

"Like what?" asked Reiter.

"We have a villa too, Sturmbannführer."

"Villa?" asked Bormann.

"Oh, yes. A large country residence on a few hundred thousand acres of virgin land, with no one but us to enjoy its benefits, except for a few *peones*—peasants, who never bother us and an isolated village or two."

"Can they be trusted?" Bormann asked instantly, worried over the possibility of betrayal and discovery.

"Nothing to fear," Mueller replied with an all-too-confident smile. "The peonies are simple people. All they know is that the estate is owned by rich absentee landlords who are foreigners and that they will visit from time to time."

"My!" Bormann like the others near him exclaimed, fully impressed.

"Now, as for your men," Mueller added suddenly to change the subject, "everything is in readiness. They will be sheltered in nearby bungalows, where they will undergo intense indoctrination and be issued new clothes and identity papers. If they do not speak fluent Spanish, tutors will be provided until they do."

"In the tradition of General von Kleitenberg, I see," said Reiter, totally impressed.

"Yes, he thought about everything," said Mueller before returning to the subject of the U-boat's crew. "When the time is right, if they have met all our requirements and have successfully completed their training, your men will eventually be relocated to other parts of the country, where they will live as ordinary citizens until called to duty for the resurrection of our glorious Reich!"

"It is so good to hear you speak that way," Bormann interjected warmly and deceitfully. There were some unanswered questions in his mind. He planned to play along until he could learn more—von Kleitenberg's plans, in particular. "The Führer would have been proud of what you've done."

"Thank you, Herr Secretary. You're much too kind. I was only doing my duty," Mueller added before picking up where he had left off. "Since the general has not yet arrived, then I shall proceed with my instructions in accordance with his wishes."

"And what is that?" inquired Bormann while the others listened.

"First of all, I must see to it that your men are properly cared for, but not before I've had a chance to speak privately with Sturmbannführer Reiter," he said as he gently grabbed the man's arm and pulled him aside. While doing so, he motioned for Reiter to look to the foredeck below, where the crew was assembling.

"What's this about?" asked Braunau, who looked down, too, disturbed by what he saw.

"This doesn't concern you, Kapitän," Mueller said as he took on an officious air. "For the record, your men are now under my jurisdiction. Your mission is over for the time being, and you must now prepare for your future work—the re-outfitting of *U-4R2* into a modern, highly sophisticated submersible—as close as you can get to the type XXI."

Braunau gasped. "I was never informed of this!"

"It doesn't matter," replied Mueller. "As a loyal Nazi Party member, you know you didn't need to be informed, or have you forgotten? Our mission here, Kapitän, even if it kills us, is to be done! So cheer up, my dear fellow, because you will have the opportunity to be part of a much bigger picture. Think of it!" Mueller added with great enthusiasm. "The latest in science and technology will be at your fingertips, and you will live to see the Reich rise again and her enemies pushed into the earth in disgrace."

Braunau whistled in disbelief. "That's a tall order," he said though he had to admit by what he saw that a great deal of planning had gone into the project already. But one thing bothered him. "Assuning you're right, where will all the money come from?"

Mueller laughed. "You brought some of it with you, my dear Kapitän, but the best is yet to come, and that's with the general."

Braunau was speechless. He had suspected as much but never saw any evidence to prove that the strange torpedoes they had loaded in Kiel were anything other than what they had been presented to be— new marine weapons! A thought raced through his mind, dominating every neuron. *Good God!* he thought. *Why didn't I think about it before? The answer was obvious; it was right under my nose all the time!*

A second thought struck him, superseding the first, about an incident on *U-4R1* in which Captain Schmidt had been vigorously admonished for trying to sink enemy ships with the new torpedoes. *How strange*, he had thought at the time, but now the mystery no longer eluded him; the torpedoes carried something other than explosives, and items of value—whatever they were—were concealed therein.

"Wait until the general arrives; then the rest will be obvious," continued Mueller.

"Herr Mueller!" interrupted Bormann. "You've said enough! Kapitän Braunau has not been made privy to all our secret. Not yet anyway!"

Mueller appeared embarrassed and apologized profusely before excusing himself to be with Reiter as he had planned. When out of hearing distance of Braunau, he posed a question, "Do you have the names of the eligible ones?"

"Right here," Reiter replied as he pulled a crumpled sheet from his coat pocket and handed it to the man.

"Does it include the questionables?"

"Of course. I've been through situations like this before," Reiter replied while pointing to the paper. "The ones circled in red are definite, and the ones marked in blue are the questionables."

"Good!" Mueller said as he pocketed the list. "You have a copy, don't you?"

A smile covered Reiter's face as he provided the answer. "Shame on you," he teased. "You should know by now that no true SS officer would ever think of doing a job haphazardly, no matter how trivial. And that applies to the making of adequate copies."

Their movements did not escape Braunau's eyes. He couldn't help wondering what they were up to but didn't dare push his luck. Bormann, on the other hand, was wondering what Braunau was thinking. It was clear from their looks, both men didn't know whom to trust any longer. Their thoughts stopped when Mueller rejoined them to address the U-boat commander.

"Kapitän," Mueller said. "I know your men are tired, so please be kind enough to dismiss them from their duties. Warm food and shelter has been prepared, and when they have filled their stomachs, they will be taken to their new quarters where they can bath and relax until called for their first assembly."

"That is very kind of you, Herr Mueller," Captain Braunau replied politely. He turned to his first officer. "Number One, assemble the crew."

"Aye, Kapitän," the first watch officer replied.

Within seconds, crewmen from within the sub left their posts to join their shipmates on the foredeck.

"*ACHTUNG!*" the chief bo'sun shouted after piping the scraggly, smelly group to attention with his shrill whistle. After they were properly aligned, he looked up to the bridge, saluted, then gave his report. "Ship's company ready, sir."

"What shall I tell them, Herr Mueller?" Braunau asked after returning the salute.

"That they are to accompany my security guards who will see to their well-being after they've been separated into manageable groups."

Braunau issued the order quickly since his men were exhausted and needed rest. What he didn't notice, because he was too exhausted, was the way in which his crew as being divided. Those of the SS went with one set of security guards while those of the regular navy, except for one or two, went with the others.

In the dining room hours later, where the refreshed SS crew

159

members—and the few mentioned earlier—had gathered, the absence of the balance of the crew became apparent. When questioned about this by Braunau who sat in the section reserved for officers and VIPs, a hush fell upon members of the local cadre sitting at his table.

Mueller explained it all. "Nothing to be concerned about, Kapitän. They've been taken to another camp . . . for reorientation and training in the philosophy of National Socialism. You will be able to see them later, I assure you."

When pressed again for an explanation of muffled gunfire-like sounds coming from nearby marshes sometime earlier or whatever it was that sounded like shots, Braunau received another plausible answer.

"Hunters—they're everywhere. You'll get used to them."

Braunau, like Bormann and the others who arrived on the U-boat—minus one group, went to bed after that, exhausted from their months at sea, including their final night's work. What lay ahead of him, he didn't know nor did he feel he could envision a good answer.

He dreamed heavily that night, mostly about enemy destroyers attacking his U-boat. Hours later, dripping with sweat, he woke with a start. Part of his dream haunted him. In it, he saw a U-boat in dire distress, twirling toward the bottom of the sea, its hull crushed like paper. Later, floating on the surface over its tomb, he saw the body of a submariner; the victim's face was contorted in horror. He looked more closely to see if he could recognize the face; it was his!

Top View

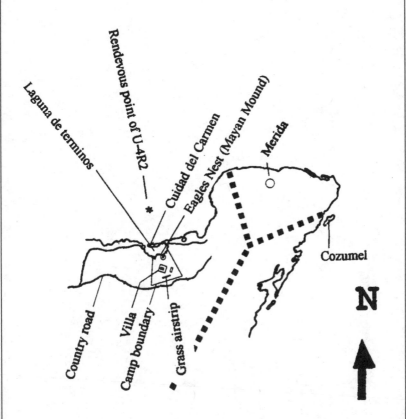

Laguna de terminos

Rendevous point of U-4R2

Cuidad del Carmen

Eagles Nest (Mayan Mound)

Merida

Cozumel

Country road

Villa

Camp boundary

Grass airstrip

N

Yucatan Peninsula, Southern Mexico

John Hankins

Chapter 16

Eagle's Nest

Laguna de Terminos, Mexico

t was not yet daylight when three men hurriedly entered the brightly lit bunker they had left the night before to take positions in a steel-caged elevator cab located in its midsection.

Following the press of a button, electric motors began to whir, causing steel cables to slap each other in rhythmical harmony as they traveled over pulleys which lifted the elevator. The trio was riding to dizzying heights above to a lookout station some four and a half stories above the bunker's belly, as Mueller called it.

The exterior of the bunker, which had been designed to imitate nearby prehistoric vegetation-covered Mayan ruins, could easily accommodate two type-IXC U-boats, plus other types in the third slip. In that slip, swaying gently in the calm water was a sleek, 40-foot cabin cruiser.

As the cab continued its upward climb, Mueller eagerly pointed to the belly below, noting some of its finer qualities, in particular, an

163

ultra-modern machine shop complete with spare parts. While Bormann looked down without ill effects, Reiter did not; he was showing significant signs of distress.

The higher the cab rose, the more his pallor intensified and the more tightly his hands clung to the safety rail near his side. Despite all efforts to have him look down to the technical wonders below, no amount of coaxing him could make him do so. He had, to the surprise of everyone, a morbid fear of heights.

"You're missing something exciting," said Bormann as he and Mueller continued to study the scene below, *U-4R2* safely tied to huge steel mooring posts—bollards—in its tranquil berth. And over her, like swarming bees to a new hive, were a number of workmen. Some were making repairs while others were stripping her interior of cargo, the torpedoes especially.

As the workmen carried out their duties, supervisors with colored arm bands, in the company of armed SS guards, kept an account of everything coming off the sub.

Unlike Reiter, his counterpart in the SS, Herr Mueller, the *Lagerführer* responsible for the entire bunker and villa complex, wasn't phased by anything; he was used to going up and down in a swaying bucket while others around him tended to get sick. If they were of equal rank, he delighted in their distress and often teased them. When he observed the pallor spreading across Reiter's face, almost matching his wife's white-colored facial cleansing cream, he couldn't resist exploiting his associate's condition.

"Come now, Reiter. Surely a little height can't scare a tough SS man like you?"

"I fear nothing," Reiter protested above the din in the dome despite the fact he was about to vomit if the elevator didn't stop soon.

Lucky for him, it reached the summit and Reiter burst out, right after an attendant opened the steel safety gate to allow the trio to exit. Once they were off, the attendant slammed the elevator door shut with a loud clang, then sent it on its way back to the ground floor.

"Our 'Eagle's Nest,'" announced Mueller proudly as he led the newcomers into a huge, softly lit room. "Not as luxurious as our Führer's mountain retreat in Bavaria, but it will do."

The room was large enough to accommodate twenty or more persons, was sparsely furnished, and from what the guests could see, was more than satisfactory for the purpose it was built—observation. This was evident because a series of rectangular plate-glass windows, about 3 by 10 feet, could be seen mounted in each panel making up the wall.

"Are you ready for the next surprise?" asked Mueller with a broad grin while at the same time activating an electrical switch near him.

Before either man could reply, the room was transformed into a discord of sounds and motion which left them aghast. Like the iris of the human eye—shutters over each panel slid open and tiny beams of light streaked in from the rising morning sun. The more Mueller allowed the shutters to open, the brighter the room got until it was bathed in as much light as was available at such an early hour.

Bormann and Reiter ran toward one of the panels, where they got their first glimpse of the lagoon and sea through which they had come the night before. What they saw got them thinking.

"Can we be observed?" asked Bormann before Reiter could ask the same thing.

"I knew you would ask," laughed Mueller. "Everyone does. There's nothing to fear, gentlemen; we're beyond detection."

"How have you managed this?" asked Bormann.

"It's quite simple, really," replied Mueller. "Let me show you," he said as he directed the two men to the opposite side—the land side of the room—to look out.

In the distance and not too far away, with their ghostly tops barely visible through the morning mist which lay heavily at their bases, stood the crumbling remains of several Mayan ruins. With each passing minute, as the sun rose above the eastern horizon, they became more prominent and perceptible, drawing indescribable awe from their beholders.

"See what I mean?" said Mueller. "They're everywhere. All we had to do was to modify them a bit, by burrowing into the one that best suited our needs and then taking the liberty to add certain embellishments—like camouflage to match the topography. We took great pains to duplicate it so as not to draw attention to ourselves . . . outside of the things we wanted the locals to know."

"Unbelievable!" exclaimed Bormann. "I have to admit I am absolutely overwhelmed! Such genius!"

"German ingenuity," Mueller boasted. "No detail has been missed as you can see. Security included!"

"You have done well," Reiter agreed with a nod of his head while looking around the room to mentally record everything as he had been taught.

When Bormann walked to another panel, Reiter and Mueller did the same thing. As they looked down upon the dense jungle, the sun was dissipating the mist which had obscured a better view earlier. Beyond the jungle was the marshes, and even further, the lagoon and

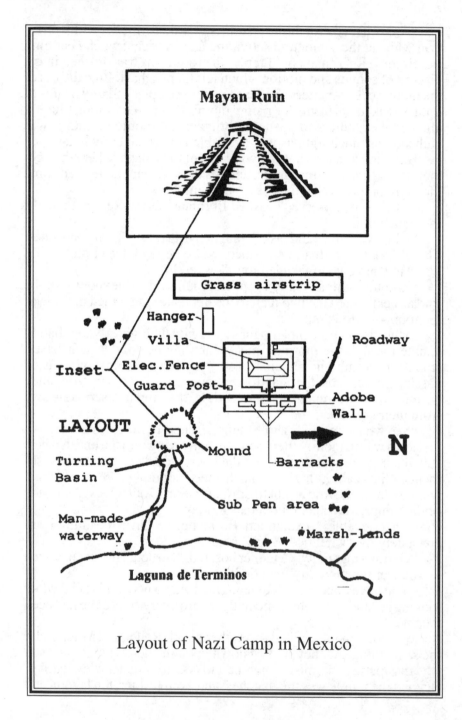

Layout of Nazi Camp in Mexico

sea, where all their thoughts suddenly rushed.

"It's beautiful, even though treacherous at times," said Bormann in a pseudo-philosophical manner as he watched with deep fascination the sun's rays bouncing off the sea's greenish-blue surface like millions of sparkling sapphires and diamonds.

"What?" asked Reiter, having missed the point.

"The surface of the water," said Bormann irritably. "It sparkles like precious jewels, too precious to behold."

Surface. The very mention of that word captured everyone's thoughts. Three pairs of eyes simultaneously looked to the horizon in hopes of seeing the approach of *U-4R2*. Search as they did, it was nowhere to be seen! Gloom followed.

"You're wasting your time," Mueller said after a long look. He was trying to be realistic—practical. "Let's face it," he added. "Even if they were out there somewhere, they wouldn't be able to show themselves until after dark."

"You're right, of course!" agreed Bormann.

"If they come, how will we know?" asked Reiter, answering the question himself. "By radio?"

"Yes. To an assigned frequency which the general himself selected," replied Mueller. "So far, however, we haven't heard a thing."

"So what do we do in the meantime?" asked Reiter, again anticipating the answer. "Wait?"

"That's all we can do," replied Bormann unhappily while still searching the sea. Except for a small fishing boat or two, nothing out there even looked like the hull of a German U-boat.

"Suppose they've been caught," Reiter asked suddenly, "which is not beyond the realm of possibility. What then?"

Bormann pondered his question deeply, wrinkling his almost bald forehead as he did. There was no escaping it—the question was valid.

"They're out there—somewhere!" he finally answered, with a qualification however, "maybe even at the bottom of the sea . . . as a consequence of an encounter with the enemy. Whatever their situation—whether good or bad—we must move on. Unless. . . ."

"Unless what, Herr Secretary?" pressed Reiter, not certain what his superior meant.

"There's been a deliberate change in plans, which does not include us. . . ."

Reiter's face dropped, his pallor replaced by a bright red.

"Surely, you can't be serious, Herr Secretary?" he questioned. "No one knows the general better than I, and I know him to a fault. He's a man of honor, who would never betray his country or trust!"

"You have judged me much too quickly, my dear Sturmbannfurher," reprimanded Bormann in an effort to minimize the unexpected confrontation. "It's not the general I'm referring to per se, but others around him, those who shared the same vessel. After all, as you know, there were some undesirable elements on his boat, and God only knows what they might have done in our absence."

The explanation penetrated Reiter's mind. Bormann, the Reich Secretary, his senior by rank and position, had a point and it had to be recognized for the truth it represented. Also, Bormann himself required respect, making it imperative he, Reiter, mend fences as quickly as possible.

"Forgive me, Herr Secretary, for jumping to conclusions. You must understand, sir, I was only trying to defend the honor of my general as I am sworn to protect yours," Reiter eloquently replied.

A good answer!

"Nothing to apologize for, Sturmbannführer," Bormann lied. "I would have done the same thing had I been in your position."

Truthfully, Bormann despised the man, mainly because Reiter was a shadow of himself, always waiting hand and foot on his boss, the general, in much the same way he had behaved toward Hitler. There was more than a subtle difference, however, for Bormann was high in the Party hierarchy and a close Hitler confidant to whom everyone gyrated if special favors were needed. That's how the general came to him.

Anyway, that was all behind him now, and more important matters needed to be resolved—in particular, if things changed for the worse, and they appeared to be, he would need an assistant, and Reiter appeared to have all the qualifications he needed, that is, providing *U-4R1* failed to materialize within the next few hours. His thoughts returned to Reiter and his expected reply. He had to win him over to his side if von Kleitenberg never returned.

Reiter's reply was one of relief for both men. "*Danke*, and thank you, Herr Reich secretary," said Reiter warmly. Concerns about the general's fate and his future status were uppermost in his mind. If he played his cards right, he would not lose prestige and position, and this included his ability to show a reasonable amount of concern for his former boss, but not with too much vigor so that there would be room in which to ingratiate himself to the man who might become his new boss. What he said next fit the bill, "I'm pleased to know you think as highly of him as I do."

"I do indeed, Reiter," agreed Bormann happily while also taking into account the *Lagerführer's* reaction. Fortunately, it was neutral, which delighted him to no end. At that point, he decided to address Reiter and Mueller together.

"Gentlemen," he said with great care, "as you both know, in times like now anyway, we must all be particularly careful as to whom we bring into our confidence . . . no matter how much we like them. Believe me, when it comes to personal ambitions, nothing is beyond the realm of man's cunning—deceit especially!"

By the look on his subordinates' faces and the uneasiness which they demonstrated, Bormann knew he had struck a nerve. It didn't matter which one or what kind, so long as there had been an effect. As far as the original project went, he had only a small part in its development as compared to that provided by the general, but now, with von Kleitenberg gone, with uncertainty surrounding his whereabouts, he saw an opportunity to take over, provided of course von Kleitenberg was lost forever. On the other hand, if the general did come back, nothing would be lost. In that case, he'd simply go on living off the assets of the Reich, but not like many of the others in his Party who had consistently dipped their fingers into the Reichbank's till for years while he played nursemaid to Hitler.

"As for *U-4R1*," he continued, "I don't quite know what to say. Not yet, anyway. There are too many variables."

"She should have been here long ago," Mueller admitted, "and that's what worries me."

"Why?" asked Bormann.

"Well, if she's gone to the bottom with all hands, our mission and purpose here could be jeopardized," he responded.

"Perhaps, but not necessarily so," Bormann countered in an effort to demonstrate his leadership abilities. "True, while we might be crippled for a while, all is not lost. Remember, we still have *U-4R2* and everything she carried, which should be more than adequate to support our initial program for years to come."

"Yes, but there's more than just money aboard *U-4R1*, not to mention its special cargo which is vital to our future," replied Reiter. "Without it, we might not have enough for what we have to do, and we could spend years trying to overcome our loss—if at all. That is . . . if we can presume the worst has happened."

Mueller broke in just then. "For the moment, I'm not presuming anything. But suppose, for a moment, *U-4R1* has ran afoul of something and will never reach us. In that case, what will be our next step or course of action?"

"There's only one that I can think of," replied Bormann.

"For instance?" Mueller asked. Like Reiter, he too was deeply

concerned over von Kleitenberg's failure to appear within hours after
U-4R2's arrival. Though he was willing to wait and do nothing in the
meantime, an inner voice within him, like Reiter's, prodded him to
protect his interest by siding with Bormann, just in case.

"To search the entire Caribbean—and elsewhere in the world if
required—until we find them, irrespective of cause. Whether their
absence is by mishap or design is unimportant compared to other
matters, in particular, their precious cargo. What they have is what we
need, and what we need is what we must retrieve. There's no avoiding
the issue!" said Bormann quite correctly as he summed up their
dilemma.

The room went silent. Bormann's words impacted Reiter and
Mueller; their options were few and they knew it! Like Bormann, they
too knew that the undertaking of such a search would not only require
vast sums of money and personnel, but could go on for years—
without any guarantee of success. So what options did they have? In
everyone's mind, none—unless, by pure chance, *U-4R1* suddenly
appeared off the horizon, returning plans to normal.

With Bormann's words still echoing in their ears, the thoughts of
everyone suddenly turned to the sea beyond Cuidad del Carmen. In a
somber mood, they studied everything in sight, often mistaking local
fishing boats for their missing U-boat. Laughs of joy would follow
only to evaporate when the object turned out to be something other
than what they hoped for.

During the lull in their conversation, the beauty of the local
scenery distracted Bormann. He watched in awe as the bright morning
sun rose slowly above the horizon, then into the sky overhead, casting
its golden beams on the white clouds floating overhead and onto
beautiful wildflowers in the jungle and marshes below. Before long,
its rays chased the morning darkness away, revealing a topography
which stretched for many uninhabited miles. This caused Bormann to
say something more concisely and resolutely.

"We must continue as planned as if our brilliant general were here
personally. Since he is not, however, then according to protocol and
plan, I shall assume command and issue orders along with his—and
our beloved Führer's wishes—before he died."

He said this without hint of reservation, in some ways surprising
Mueller and Reiter, though they each had anticipated his assumption
of command. Both posed questions.

"What about the men who came with us and the permanent cadres
who are already here? What do you expect of them?" asked Reiter.

For Bormann, somehow the answer was obvious and came

quickly. "Some of them must be trained as operatives—to search out *U-4R1* while others will undergo training as originally planned, to await the glorious day when their boots will once again march to the triumphal tune of *Deutschland Uber Alles* and they shall carry the standard of the new Fourth Reich high over their heads for the whole world to see and admire."

The inspiring words caught Reiter's fancy. They were patriotic, and he loved them! His body transformed itself from a slouched, bent-shoulder position to a stiff and erect posture. Simultaneously, he pulled in his fat chin, pushed out his sagging chest, sucked in his bulging belly, then eagerly rendered a regulation Nazi salute to the sound of clicking heels. He bellowed joyously, "To the Fourth Reich and our great and glorious Führer! Heil Hitler! May his memory live forever!"

Mueller was impressed by his compatriot's enthusiasm and promptly returned the salutation, but Bormann, on the other hand, was less demonstrative, a fact that did not go unnoticed by the others.

Immediately after that charged moment, something struck Reiter's mind. He was quick to confront Bormann, "Have you given any thought to the status of Kapitän Braunau?"

"I was about to ask you the same thing," interrupted Mueller. "He's been on my mind too . . . ever since I met him. Frankly, I don't trust him even though he's been a Party member from the beginning . . . ."

Both men looked at Bormann expectantly.

"Try him, and if he doesn't measure up, then do with him as you will, but not until I've been assured a competent substitute, one having similar if not better qualifications, can take his place."

That was a reasonable statement, making Reiter breathe more easily. He hadn't expected that out of Bormann. A reply was in order.

"That's all I wanted to know, Herr Secretary. I feel as Mueller here does though he doesn't know the captain like you and me."
He nudged Mueller for support.

"There's something wrong with him, and it keeps gnawing at me," said Bormann, knowing he knew something about the U-boat captain as well. "You do know, don't you, that he's a long-time Party member?"

"Party membership has nothing to do with it," Reiter replied bluntly. "It's his character that counts, and what he does even in his social life!"

"I need more than that," replied Bormann.

"Well, for one, he drinks too much and is a womanizer, which

171

makes him a security risk in my opinion. In addition, he doesn't know how to control his tongue or temper."

"I'm aware of some of these things," said Bormann almost sheepishly because he had broken a few of the cardinal rules himself. "Go on."

"Then there's his unpredictable moods, which swing back and forth like a pendulum on a clock—argumentative at times, pleasing at others," continued Reiter. "As a consequence, tension builds up between him, his fellow officers, and his crew, which makes him almost unbearable to work with. You saw some of this behavior on the trip, I'm sure, and that's why I believe we've got to get rid of him— before he can do some real harm."

"My thoughts exactly," said Bormann, agreeing.

Bormann turned around, once again redirecting his eyes to the open sea. Occasionally, he would glance down at the remarkably camouflaged man-made waterway leading away from the bunker's base to its secret entrance a quarter of a mile away. Within the boundaries of the straight waterway, movable artificial shrubbery had been expertly placed to break up its line and to prevent detection from the air.

As others waited for an answer, Bormann's mind searched for something profound to say.

"Think of it, my friends," he said with great vigor as if he were Adolph Hitler himself. "What an opportunity we have to remold the world. And while it sleeps, we will be mobilizing their youth, first with our own, who will be thoroughly trained before being sent into local communities, where we expect them to be assimilated—and even marry—until it is time for them to take up arms again. After that, to other groups of nordic or germanic origins who would like to join our cause."

"All because of *PROJEKT U4R,* a brilliant plan," Reiter reminded everyone. "Our Führer would have been so proud had he lived to see what Obergruppenführer von Kleitenberg had conceived of for the glory and honor of the Fatherland!"

He hummed a patriotic *Waffen* SS tune and unabashedly strutted around the room like he was marching in a parade again in sight of the Führer and hundreds of thousands of worshipers.

When he got to the other side of the room at a panel and side he hadn't looked through previously, he stopped. His eye, like the others which had followed him out of curiosity, swept across the vast jungles now fully visible and fell on something unusual. It was a villa—a huge, beautiful, multistoried structure of Spanish colonial design, complete with a red-tiled roof. All around it was a tall wall several feet thick with guard houses strategically located.

The magnificent villa dominated the center of a large clearing, one containing thousands upon thousands of hectares of land, where herds of beef cattle grazed. In addition to the villa, a number of other buildings could be seen in and about the area. Some served as housing for staff members and the others—as Mueller explained after he saw what the others were looking at—were barracks and training facilities. Beyond the clearing was an impenetrable jungle. A scattering of impassable swamps comprised the balance of the terrain. For access, a lone road linked the circle to a little traveled and poorly maintained highway miles away. The road was fully guarded, as the trio could see, by watchdogs and armed men on foot and in vehicles.

Sensing the thoughts of the new arrivals, Mueller was quick to remind them of his earlier discussion concerning the uniqueness of the place.

"It's as I told you," he said proudly. "We're completely isolated from the outside world. No one can get in or out without proper credentials." He smiled; there was no misunderstanding what he meant. "Now as for contact with the outside world, should the need arise, we can reach any village or city within minutes or hours."

"You don't say," said Bormann, wondering how that was possible.

Mueller laughed, happy to provide some answers. "Oh, yes, we've got everything under control," he said. "In addition to having a variable fleet of motor transports, we also have a number of small planes and boats to carry us to wherever we need to go."

While the others listened, he pointed to a long and narrow grass airstrip and some metal buildings not far from the villa; the strip was being mowed.

"The planes are hangered in those structures near the field . . . and the boats and cars are at other locations within the bunker and compound."

Bormann and Reiter beamed, overwhelmed by the complexity and magnitude of the project.

"Think of it," said Bormann in a more relaxed manner. "While the Allies are scouring the whole of Germany and Europe for us, here we are—thousands of kilometers away—safe and secure in a paradise of luxury and splendor. What more can we ask for?"

"Nothing, really," Reiter responded, "except the return of our U-boat. There's still the possibility all could be lost if the general fails to return."

"Reiter! You know better than that!" admonished Bormann as he walked up to the man and looked into his round face as if ready to spew fire into it. "What makes you think the mere loss of an SS general could bring failure to a project so brilliantly conceived? Even von Kleitenberg knew he was expendable!"

Reiter cringed, sorry for the slip, and didn't know quite how to respond. Bormann did it for him. To ease the man's pain, since honey draws more flies than something caustic, he decided upon a more subtle approach.

"I will admit the loss of the general would be most unfortunate, but by no means must we ever consider his loss—presumed as it is for the moment—to be anything more than a setback, so to speak. And as you know, neither you or I—or Mueller here for that matter—should ever expect to be treated any differently. In comparison to the mission's importance and the cargo we must find, our personal well-being means very little."

While Reiter seethed over what he considered to be the Party Secretary's lack of regard for his lost commander, he had to admit the man's point was well taken.

Sensing he was gaining the small-thinking man's confidence, Bormann tried another approach. More than anything now, he needed the man's full support and loyalty. Thus, in an uncharacteristic gesture, he placed both of his hand on the man's shoulders and squeezed them gently.

"Come now, my dear comrade," Bormann said warmly. "Surely you have not forgotten who you are and what you mean to the cause, have you?"

"*Nein*—no indeed, Herr Secretary," came Reiter's prompt and qualified reply. "I have always been a loyal soldier and expect to die like one!"

"*Gut!*" Bormann replied as he gripped the man's shoulder's more firmly. "In that case then, I'm sure you won't mind answering several questions?"

"Not at all, Herr secretary," came the reply.

"Very well then," continued Bormann, looking straight into the man's eyes. "As an SS officer, is it not true that you have taken an oath requiring you to uphold the Führer, his appointed officers, and the Fatherland, for always?"

"That is correct, sir! On my honor as an officer of the SS," Reiter barked proudly.

"And is it not true that, as a member of the SS, you are duty-bound to obey the orders of your superiors—willingly and unquestioningly—irrespective of any adverse circumstance to you personally?"

"*Jawohl.* It is, sir!" Reiter again replied, even more proudly this time.

The questioning had brought back memories. In his youth, he had been a zealous, unbending member of a *Hitler Jugen* brigade. Years later with equal enthusiasm, he enrolled in the SS academy, where he underwent stringent indoctrination and training. While not at the top of his class, he did gain a few honors; marksmanship was one of them. He graduated finally after barely passing some stiff qualifying examinations. Pomp and ceremony marked that day. *Oh, what days those were*, he thought.

"Excellent," said Bormann, interrupting his pleasant thoughts. "I see we understand each other. Any questions?"

"None, sir," Reiter replied. His superior's point had been well taken; there was no need for further clarification.

Bormann didn't stop there, though. He went further with Reiter.

"I must say, Herr Sturmbannführer Reiter, you have proven yourself most worthy today, and as an expression of my gratitude, I'm going to let you in on something quite confidential."

"Oh? Like what, sir?" Reiter asked.

"It concerns a replacement for General von Kleitenberg, should he fail to return." Reiter's heart thumped heavily, almost stopping from the shock. He listened attentively. "Should he not return to claim his rightful post at this station, the next senior SS officer in line will have to assume his post."

Bormann dropped his hands, leaving Reiter to contemplate his future. In the background, watching everything with envy, was Mueller, who said nothing.

Reiter's facial expression didn't take long to change from an expressionless, stern look to shock, then to one full of hope and great expectations. *It can only be me*, he thought to himself. *I'm the next senior SS officer in line. The other officers don't count.* With these thoughts in mind, for the first time in days, Reiter did not miss his general. After all, like Bormann had indicated, the man was expendable. Remembering Bormann just then, he responded as the man expected him.

"Herr Reich Secretary," he said quite boldly. "You were right to remind me of my duty as an SS officer. One must never forget his oath. Above all, duty comes first, not the petty wishes of insignificant men. I am at your service, sir!"

With an outstretched hand and a smiling face, Bormann warmly took Reiter's hand in his, then shook it firmly. In a similar move of solidarity, Mueller joined in, pledging his loyalty, too. He bowed politely and clicked his heels when Bormann offered him a hand.

With amenities over, the trio returned to the open window. Again they searched the surface of the sea, but nothing was there. If they could, they would have searched its depths as well, but that was not possible now, given the current state of deep sea research technology.

Occasionally they would take turns peering through a large tripod-mounted telescope. After adjusting for distance, they would make sweeping observations of the sea stretched out before them. It went on for hours until Bormann decided to call it quits. In anger, he vented his frustration.

"Dammit! Where are they? We need its cargo," he muttered to himself, without reference to the general and those under his command.

At the Villa—A Meeting of Minds

The afternoon sun was beginning to set, casting as it did long shadows over the jungle and lagoon near the villa. Inside Martin Bormann's new office, Reiter, Mueller, Captain Braunau and a selected few of the senior officers who had accompanied him aboard *U-4R2*, excluding others who had no interest in the project other than anonymity and escape from Allied war crimes tribunals, had gathered to study oceanographic charts. They were intent on determining *U-4R1*'s last course. To combat the heat, ceiling and floors fans were turned to high speeds, often scattering papers and critical nautical charts.

Captain Braunau, his white cap pushed slightly back over the top of his head like a typical U-boat commander, was in the middle of the foray. Every now and then, he would offer his thoughts or would be asked to explain certain nautical matters.

As the room darkened, lights were turned on, revealing the haggard look of all and the frustration which they felt. When it came time to break for dinner, a sweaty and breathless wireless operator who had been working in the radio transmission station room next door burst in.

"Sir!" cried the man excitedly, addressing Bormann. "News!"

"Is it about *U-4R1*?" many voices cried at once.

"We . . . we're not sure," the man stuttered, not knowing whom to address. A lot of brass was around. "It's from Radio Havana! They just released a story about a U-boat being sunk by a British destroyer somewhere in the Gulf of Mexico."

"Are you certain?" demanded Braunau.

"Could it be von Kleitenberg's?" a loud voice at the back of the room cried out, overshadowing Braunau's question.

"Are you sure it was a U-boat?" asked Bormann, trying to conceal the fact he hoped it was because he could lose his new status if it wasn't true.

"I only know what our interpreter told me, sir," said the apprehensive operator. "It's written here—all of it!"

Bormann snatched the paper out of the man's trembling hand, then scanned it quickly before summarizing its message and dismissing the radioman.

"According to Radio Havana," he said, "a large German submarine, one suspected of sinking a Brazilian merchant ship, was attacked and sunk late yesterday afternoon in the waters east of the Isle of Pines and north of the Cayman Islands and one survivor, a cook, who's not identified by name, was the only one to come out of it alive."

Braunau, like others near him, groaned. "To think," he said, "while we were here in the bunker, they were going to the bottom of the sea." He stopped talking when Martin Bormann signaled he wasn't through.

"The report goes on to say that the warship which sunk it, a British destroyer having the latest in antisubmarine devices, had been asked by the Americans to assist in a 'search and destroy mission' and had done that with no loss of life or damage to themselves."

"It wasn't the British who sank that ship! It was us!" complained Braunau remorsefully, moments before he reached for a bottle and took a sip to soothe his jangled nerves. "We are the ones who should have gone down—not them!"

"That's enough!" ordered Bormann. "You've sunk too many ships, Kapitän. You can't let it get to you. What's done had to be done. It was them or us, and you above all people should know that!"

"Yes, but look what has happened!" he replied sadly. "They got caught because of us!"

Braunau didn't make any friends with his remarks; the others didn't want to be reminded of the circumstances leading to the resultant tragedy. It was clear from the look on their faces, Bormann's and Reiter's especially, that he had incurred their wrath. In some ways he didn't care. His conscience had been freed unexpectedly, even though temporarily, by discovery and use of a remarkable and almost undetectable (odorless) alcoholic beverage—Mexican tequila.

When Braunau settled down, Bormann returned to the message he had taken from the radioman so they could discuss the balance of the news report and what remained to be done.

"The report says the captain of the British warship advised authorities he had spotted the U-boat about a hundred miles due north of the Cayman Islands, wherever that is, and when he first spotted it, it appeared to be in distress. Before engaging the vessel, a lot of smoke was seen coming out of it."

"The snorkel!" Braunau suddenly cried out, interrupting Bormann. "It couldn't have been anything else!"

"After closing the distance," continued Bormann, "several warning shots were fired over the U-boat's bow to surrender, but those on board chose to fight. Having no choice, the destroyer's captain had her sunk."

"Dogs!" cried an irate officer at the grim news.

"Bad luck, that's what it was!" suggested Mueller.

"Luck—hell!" Braunau cursed. "It was that damned snorkel! It's happened before! No U-boat crew could ever hope to survive if it malfunctioned at a critical time."

"Any other survivors besides the unidentified cook?" asked another member of the group.

"It doesn't say," replied Bormann after rescanning the document.

"Where did they say the boat went down?" asked Braunau suddenly while reaching for a set of charts.

"Somewhere between the Isle of Pines, which belongs to Cuba, and the Cayman Islands, the report said," another member answered.

As others looked on, Braunau ran his fingers across a chart of the Gulf of Mexico and pointed to the general area where the boat went down. He studied some figures.

"Damn! They've gone down in the Yucatan channel. It's too deep, more than five miles down," he cried. "At that depth, a U-boat would be crushed like a tin can struck by a sledgehammer."

His graphic description turned a few stomachs—the old field marshal's, especially. Others winced. Bormann, on the other hand, wasn't bothered by that kind of talk; he was too busy thinking about his next move. He needed to know the approximate location of the sunken U-boat before considering alternatives of action, so he joined Braunau to evaluate the situation.

Occasionally Bormann would ask Braunau and others a question or two. This went on for hours. Eventually he stopped what he was doing to bring the attention of the others to the radio report they had received and what it had revealed to him.

"Gentlemen, if you will recall, Radio Havana also stated the

U-boat might have been involved in another incident—the killing of a Caymanian fisherman and the wounding of his young grandson, who, incidentally, managed to survive."

"What are you getting at, sir?" asked Mueller.

"If that's true," said Bormann, "it could be a clue to the course von Kleitenberg was following, which means we need to know where the encounter took place. And even though it appears we may have lost the U-boat and its contents forever, there's still the possibility it might have been another U-boat. Or . . . if it was *U-4R2* that it didn't go down in deep water, leaving the possibility of recovery wide open."

It made sense to everyone but Braunau, who felt they were suffering from delusions of grandeur. He opted to listen and sip his cognac.

As the small group listened, Bormann offered a thought, "Put yourselves in von Kleitenberg's shoes. For example, if you were he, entrusted with a cargo of immeasurable value—under conditions of war—what would you have done to preserve that cargo knowing imminent destruction or capture lay ahead?"

"We don't know that for certain," said someone skeptically. "He might never have gotten to that point. . . ."

"True, but it's still an interesting thought, don't you think?" pressed Bormann, determined to get support.

"I'd dump the cargo or as much as I could in a safe place," suggested Mueller, the first to take the bait.

"Exactly," said Bormann. "No man as clever as general von Kleitenberg would ever risk a cargo of such value if he knew his vessel was in danger of being sunk or captured, so if that's a reasonable assumption to make, then it would seem appropriate to conclude—if he didn't get caught off-guard first—that he left his cargo elsewhere."

"A wonderful thought, but—" interjected a member of the group before being outranked by Reiter.

"Assuming you're right, Herr Bormann," asked Reiter, "where do we begin looking?"

"Somewhere in this circle," said Braunau as he opened his calipers and drew a circle which encompassed all of the Cayman Island group, part of Cuba, and some smaller islands off its coast. He took into consideration the U-boat's estimated daily range, in a submerged and surfaced mode, including its estimated speed under varying conditions known to them.

Moans swept the room when those who studied the chart realized how much area was involved.

"It could take us forever to find it!" Mueller groaned.

179

John Hankins

"Or a short time too," Bormann interjected. "The general was no man's fool. In my opinion, he dropped his cargo in some little-known but accessible place. But where?"

"It could be anywhere," another argued while moving and pointing to positions on the map. "Here . . . here . . . or even here."

Reiter agreed by attempting an example. "Knowing the general as I do, I'm convinced he wouldn't have left anything undone. His efficiency at Treblinka for example—I mean—Kiel," he corrected, "went without a flaw. So I know, given the right situation, he'd have disposed of his cargo as early as possible—in a place no one would guess . . . so it could be retrieved later."

A lot of heads nodded just then. Most present knew the general and his modus operandi. They knew Reiter was right and that the young and brilliant general had done what they thought.

"So where and when do we start?" a senior officer asked.

"Here," replied Bormann as he pointed to a group of islands paralleling what appeared to be the course *U-4R1* taken. The spot he identified lay off the Cuban coast. "It's a guess of course, but that's the best place to start. We've got to find that cargo, no matter how long it takes."

He reached for a half-filled bottle of cognac and poured small portions for those present. What he had said about Braunau's drinking earlier, no longer applied. It was time to celebrate. "I give you a toast," he said as he lifted his glass high for all to hear and see.

"To our success in finding *U-4R1*! Heil Hitler!"

PART TWO

FIFTY YEARS LATER

George Town Jail, Cayman Islands, BWI

Chapter 17

A Man Called Crazy Joe

Grand Cayman, B.W.J.—1990s

s birds chirped cheerfully outside the high-barred, open-air windows of George Town's only jailhouse and flitted back and forth excitedly outside one of its cells, their shadows were cast down like the cell's over the lone figure of a man laying prostrate in his own vomit on its cement floor. He was impervious to their presence.

Moments later, frightened by a loud clanking sound, the birds flew away, taking their shadows with them, while leaving the cell's behind. It was the jailor struggling with the lock to the cell's heavy steel-barred door. Seconds later, he opened it, then walked in and nudged the snoring man with a heavy boot. At the same time, he clenched his nose to keep from smelling the stench.

"All right, Joseph, time to get up," he said irritably.

Suffering from a hangover, Crazy Joe—as almost everyone called him—moaned and groaned as he rolled from side to side, spreading the sludge he made earlier.

183

"Come on. The magistrate's waiting," the guard said as he reached down to grab the filthy little man from off the floor where he had slept during the night, being careful in the process to keep from getting soiled.

"Ohhhh, where am I?" moaned Crazy Joe, a question he had often asked his jailor many times before.

"Where do you think?" replied the jailor as he looked upon the poor excuse for a human being before him. In some ways, he felt sorry for the scrawny fellow, but after years of trying father-like counseling, he had given up all hope for the man's rehabilitation. Crazy Joe was the town drunk and showed no inclination to change.

"Was it bad?" Crazy Joe asked, not certain what the charges would be this time or what he might have done the night before.

"You'll find out soon enough, after you've made your appearance," the jailor replied caustically. "Now let's get on with it," he added as he nudged the groggy, emaciated man down the line of jail cells to the washroom at the end of the building, where he was forced to shower and change into jail clothes.

The jailor didn't push Crazy Joe too quickly because he knew from previous experience that nights on the hard, cold, concrete floor agitated an old wound of his; he often complained about it, and this morning was no exception.

The lame leg served a useful purpose, and to those who shared his secrets, Crazy Joe made no bones about capitalizing off the injury he had gotten many years earlier while fishing with his grandfather. The incident—or accident—supposedly happened off a remote fishing spot on Little Cayman, a sister island. The story, gleaned from experts at the time, was true enough except when told by Crazy Joe; he often embellished it a bit to gain more sympathetic listeners. Thus, people would ply him with drinks to loosen his tongue. Unfortunately, that's when his future problems began. In his adolescence, he became addicted to alcohol, more as a way of drowning his memories and sorrows than for the love of drink. Most of his memories were connected to the tragic loss of his beloved grandfather, a man he idolized, and the balance concentrated on his permanent injuries.

Later in his life, as alcohol began to dominate more and more of his earthly existence like his father's before him, fantasies took the place of the truth. When he was partying, they would become more bizarre. Delirium tremens, hallucinations, and temper tantrums became more frequent. His escapade the previous night, from what he could glean from his jailor's words, was not quite like the others. In fact, it was worse from what he could discern.

184

The Court House

"All rise," the orderly called out as the magistrate responsible for public order walked into the packed courtroom and took a position behind his ornate bench. Everyone bowed at that moment.

"This honorable court is now in session. God save the queen," cried the orderly once again, and again those present bowed.

The judge was a tall, impressive, black-robed man whose hair was snow white. As he sat in his symbol of authority, a large, overstuffed leather chair behind the mahogany bench from which he judged cases, he gave everyone the impression that if he were not God Himself, he was darn close to it.

Exalting him all the more was the Cayman Islands coat of arms which was attached to the front panel of the huge mahogany bench. The inscription around its perimeter came from the Bible: "He hast founded it upon the seas."

Again, the bailiff called out, "You may be seated!"

A noisy shuffle of chairs followed as visitors and locals alike pressed in closer to watch and listen as the public prosecutor stood up, ready to present his cases.

"What's your first case, Mr. Prosecutor?" asked the white-haired magistrate as he pushed back into his comfortable seat while waiting for a reply. He seemed bored already though the day had only begun. It was 9 a.m.

The Crown versus Joseph V. Bowman, Your Honor," replied the man.

"Is he back again?" asked the judge in an irritable voice as he pressed forward in his seat to peer over the top of his bench at the cowering figure of a man who was trying to appear inconspicuous in the prisoner's docket. "Is he represented by counsel?"

"No, Your Honor. He's still destitute and places himself at the mercy of the court."

"What are the charges this time?" asked the judge, resigned to his task.

"There are three, Your Honor," the prosecutor replied.

"Go on," said the judge as he motioned with an outstretched arm.

"Charge one, drunk and disorderly in a public place. Charge two, possession of and discharge of a dangerous weapon in a public place, and charge three, defacement and destruction of private and Commonwealth property."

"My, my, Commonwealth property, too!" said the judge cynically

185

as he glanced in Crazy Joe's direction. "I must say he's certainly been busy this time."

He swiveled his chair to get a better view of the trembling little man who was now being supported by two police officers.

"Well, Joseph, how say you?" the judge asked. "Innocent or guilty?"

"Not guilty, Your Honor—by reason of temporary insanity," Crazy Joe replied.

"Aren't you getting tired of that plea?" the judge asked with a disgusted frown.

"Well—it's true, Your Honor," Crazy Joe insisted to the judge's chagrin.

"All right, you may proceed," said the judge, addressing the public prosecutor. "Let's hear the details."

"Well, sir, according to our report," began the man, "last night, at approximately 7:30 p.m., the defendant here, Joseph V. Bowman, entered Clancy's Bar on Seven Mile Beach, where he began drinking. By 11:35 p. m. approximately—according to witnesses—he became drunk and disorderly and was warned by the barkeeper that, if he didn't behave himself, he would have to leave."

"Go on," pressed the judge. "Let's get to the good part."

"Well, Your Honor, according to witnesses, he behaved himself for a while until he overheard someone bragging about a big fish he had caught off Little Cayman. It was from this point onward that the defendant—the prisoner here—became irrational and unmanageable. Without any provocation—according to witnesses again—he began screaming something about a devil fish or something crawling over the wall where a number of the bar's clients were playing a friendly game of darts."

"Sounds familiar," the judge interjected. "Anything else?"

"Yes, Your Honor. After that, he became unmanageable, and while in a frenzied state—again according to statements from witnesses on the scene—he informed everyone present he was going to kill that fish before it killed him."

While saying that, the prosecutor put his index finger to his temple, then moved it in a circular motion; the gesture did not go unnoticed by the defendant.

"I protest!" cried Crazy Joe. "I'm not crazy! What I said about the fish is true!"

"Quiet! Or I'll hold you in contempt of court!" ordered the judge as he banged the bench with his gavel. "You'll get your chance to speak in your own defense."

With the restraining arms of his guards pressing his shoulders, Crazy Joe sat down and kept his mouth shut.

"You may continue, Mr. Prosecutor," said the judge.

"Thank you, sir," replied the prosecutor. "The barkeeper and proprietor of Clancy's Bar, Mr. Clement Bodden, reported that he tolerated the defendant as long as he could but had to physically remove him when he kept disturbing his dart-throwing customers about a strange 'devil fish' he saw creeping up the wall next to them."

"Still seeing demons, eh?" the judge said directly to Crazy Joe as he peeked over the top of the tall bench in his direction.

Crazy Joe gulped uneasily before responding, "Yes, sir, just like the last time, I'm afraid."

The prosecutor continued when the judge nodded in his direction and asked: "Is there more?"

"Yes, sir. According to witnesses previously mentioned, after the proprietor expelled Mr. Bowman, it was only a matter of minutes before he returned—only this time he came armed with something resembling a large harpoon, to which—as we now know—he had attached an explosive device, complete with battery and wires."

"And?" pressed the judge, his interest suddenly growing.

"Once inside he wasted no time tossing his weapon at the offending wall, blowing it away. In fact, the explosion was so great, it knocked our revered monument to shipwrecked sailors in the park just opposite the wall completely off its pedestal."

"Good Lord!" exclaimed the judge. "Was anyone hurt?"

"That's the good part, Your Honor," replied the prosecutor. "By the grace of God, almost everyone had left by the time he returned."

The courtroom came alive with loud whispering and murmurs, preventing the prosecutor from adding a few things he still wished to cover. Irritated by the disorder, the judge pounded his desk vigorously.

"We'll have order in this courtroom," he ordered, looking sternly at the audience. "If there are any more outbursts, I'll hold those responsible in contempt of court."

BANG!

The courtroom resembled a mausoleum; not a sound was emitted except those coming from the front of the room, where the judge presided.

"Anything else, Mr. Prosecutor," he said, "now that the dignity of this court has been restored?"

"Yes, sir, the third and last charge: damage to Commonwealth property, which includes destruction of the wall in the bar, plus damages to the pedestal of the monument and its base after it was moved by the violent blast."

"Joseph Bowman!" the judge said, as he addressed the little drunk who had often been before him for minor offenses. "What in the world ever possessed you to do such a thing? You could have killed someone!"

"It's that thing, Your Honor. You know . . . the one that's been bothering me all these years."

"I've heard it all before, and I've tried to be patient and understanding with you, Joseph, but this time you've gone too far and there's a limit to what a magistrate can do. Instead of getting better, you keep getting worse. And . . . and that incident, the one to which you referred earlier—that happened more than forty years ago! For all I—we know, it might never have happened."

"But it's true, Your Worship!" cried the small, dark-complexioned man as he rubbed his hands nervously. "I'm not lying, Your Honor—Judge. I can still see it! Like it was yesterday . . . coming out of the sea. Skull, bones, and all. . . ."

"In a bar?" scoffed the judge with a disbelieving smile. "Not very likely. Besides, you could have killed someone. The creatures you saw came from your abuse of alcohol. That's what I think!"

"Some of them, maybe," he replied, "and I agree I've been drinking too much, but I know that I know there's a creature out there somewhere that wants to get me, but I'm going to get him first. After that, I'll stop drinking."

The judge shook his head, and turned to the prosecutor again. "Any estimate of damages?"

"Eight hundred Caymanian dollars for the wall, two hundred for resetting the monument and its pedestal in their proper place, fifty dollars for repair of the park fence, plus fifteen hundred dollars for interruption of business," the prosecutor replied as he approached the judge and place an assortment of papers on his bench.

The judge put his spectacles to his eyes to study the estimates, then shook his head before removing them again to peer down at the prisoner; he was only nearsighted.

"Joseph Bowman," he said as he looked with disgust at the man standing before him, wringing his hands anxiously, "as I said moments ago, you've gone too far this time. What you've done is not only disgraceful and destructive, but an embarrassment to us all. Consequently, you leave me no choice but to do what our laws require."

Another hush fell over the audience as they waited for the judge to render his verdict.

"Joseph V. Bowman, I find you guilty of all charges," the magistrate proclaimed loudly. "Have you anything to say in your own behalf before I pronounce your sentence?"

"Have mercy, Your Worship!" pleaded Crazy Joe. "I'll do anything—even quit drinking, but not Nort'wd!" he cried pitifully. He was referring to newly built Northward Prison, located at the other end of the island.

"I could send you there, all right," the judge replied, agreeing with Joe as to the options, "but that wouldn't solve your problems. I've heard all your promises before, and you've never kept any of them. Soooo," he continued, drawing out the word as he did, "this time we're going to try something different."

"Like what, Your Honor?" Crazy Joe asked.

"I'm going to divide your punishment into two parts," said the judge as he studied the estimates and charges before him. "In the first instance, I'm going to fine you the sum of two thousand dollars—Caymanian—for being drunk and disorderly in a public place and for the willful destruction of public property. The fine, naturally, will be used to compensate all injured parties for damages inflicted against them and to defray court costs."

The judge paused for a moment before continuing, "as for the second part of your sentence, you are hereby ordered confined to George Town Jail for a period of ninety days, during which time you will be visited by a competent doctor—at public expense, who will monitor your withdrawal from alcohol. And if anytime within this period you are deemed substantially recovered by the medical authorities, you will be released providing your fine has been paid. Otherwise, I will send you to jail for the damages you have inflicted."

"But—I'll never be able to pay the fine," protested Crazy Joe. "I'm broke."

"No pay, you stay," said the judge, showing he meant it, before adding, "though you might contact some of your waterfront drinking buddies for assistance."

While Crazy Joe was thinking, the public prosecutor spoke out.

"Your Honor, if it pleases the court," he said as he asked to approach the bench while at the same time trying to untie the cords of a small brown bag which he carried. "I believe we have more than enough here to satisfy the judgment."

Curious eyes followed him as he took a position before the judge and opened it up. The bag was familiar to many of the people in the courtroom; it belonged to Crazy Joe. He always carried it around his neck like it possessed some kind of magic power, only this time, someone else had it—the police. They had stored it for safekeeping after he was arrested.

"What is it?" asked the judge as he watched the man pull the bag open, then empty its contents on his bench. Loud tinkling sounds followed.

"NO! You can't take them! It's my bait! To catch my big fish!" cried Crazy Joe, his eyes bulging wildly from their sockets. A guard restrained him when he tried to leap out of the prisoner's docket to recover what belonged to him.

Spectators in the audience wondered what he meant. Some thought he had gone out of his mind while others familiar with his fish story took it all in stride; to them it was something quite ordinary.

"It's all I've got left," he cried.

"Are they what I think they are?" asked the judge as he studied a number of gold-looking coins.

"Yes, sir. All collector's items, and valuable," replied the prosecutor. "Doubloons, pieces of eight, solid gold crosses, and the like—enough to pay his fine, I believe."

"Any ideas as to value?" asked the judge.

"Five thousand at least, I would say . . . at today's market prices."

"Good! That should cover everything with some left over for him," said the judge as he grabbed his gavel and pounded his desk again. "Remove the prisoner."

"Don't take it, I beg you! It was given to me by my grandfather before he died!" Crazy Joe cried pitifully.

"It's true, Your Honor," interjected the court orderly who had been seated next to the judge. He had known Crazy Joe since childhood and knew how much he cherished the bag and its contents.

The judge shook his head just then, remembering something. A look of pity crossed his face. He looked back at the courtroom; all eyes were following his, registering similar degrees of discomfort.

"Very well," the judge added. "We will not confiscate these coins in view of mitigating circumstances now known to members of this court, but we will keep them in safekeeping until the fine has been paid and the period of confinement has been satisfied."

Down went the gavel again.

"Oh, thank you, Your Honor," Crazy Joe cried gratefully through copious tears while kissing one of his guard's hands to demonstrate his appreciation. Embarrassed, the guard snatched it away, then nudged him toward the door leading out of the court.

"Next case," the judge called as he annotated his journal before motioning to the bailiff to remove the coins and turn them over to the court clerk for proper disposition before the next defendant could come from the rear of the courtroom.

"The Crown, versus Silas Jonesbury, Junior," cried out the bailiff moments later, disrupting the judge's thoughts.

A young teenage boy, accompanied by his mother, nervously took the docket. The judge studied him sternly, then motioned for the prosecutor to present the case.

"What is the charge?" the judge asked.

"Speeding, Your Honor. Sixty-five in a forty-mile-per-hour zone."

"How do you plead?"

"Guilty, Your Worship—Honor!"

"How old are you, young man?"

"Sixteen, Your Worship."

"Do you have anything to say in your behalf . . . to justify your conduct, son?" asked the judge with a sober face.

"No-o-o-o, sir," the nervous boy replied.

"You have anything to say before I pronounce sentence?" the judge asked.

"He's never done anything like this before," the boy's mother interrupted in hopes the judge would show compassion.

"And he'll never do it again," the judge replied abruptly. "It's a serious thing he did, and he should have known better. We can't allow teenagers to violate traffic laws; someone could get killed! Guilty as charged," declared the judge.

Both the boy and his mother wept.

"I hereby fine you one hundred and fifty dollars, Caymanian, and order your driver's license suspended for a period of three years."

B-L-A-A-A-M! went the judge's gavel.

"Next!"

A loud voice from outside overpowered the distressed cries of the teenager who had just gotten his license and now had lost it. It was Crazy Joe, yelling at the top of his lungs for all to hear.

"Mark my words, I'm going to kill that thing someday!"

"Tch, tch, poor chap," the bailiff remarked to the judge after he returned. "After all of these years, one would think he'd have gotten over it . . . ."

Forty-Five days later

Following confirmation by Crazy Joe's doctor that he had responded to therapy, the judge ordered his release.

Exhibiting good health, with more weight to prove it since he had been eating regularly, Crazy Joe wasted no time heading for a small makeshift restaurant on the shoreline of Hog Sty Bay. Once there, he planned to drink to his quick recovery with his many friends, all of whom were anxious to hear his most recent exploits, including some he had with a nurse or two when he was required to undergo two days of tests at the local hospital.

To get him started, they had taken up a small collection since they knew he would be would and bought the cheapest booze they could find. He could repay them later—along with the money he collected to pay his fine—after he reestablished his guide business.

While they sat beneath a shade tree in the hot morning sun waiting for their friend to arrive, one of their number strummed a guitar while singing. He stopped and waved when he saw Crazy Joe approaching, a huge smile plastered across his dark brown face. Crazy Joe's eyes were bulging with excitement in anticipation of their reunion.

A sleek sailboat entered the bay just then, motoring its way through the crystal clear waters of the bay toward the dock near him. Its presence distracted Joe. He stopped and looked, admiring what he saw, hoping all the while he could own one like it someday. In his present state he knew he couldn't, so he settled for just meeting its owners. Offering his cheap guide services was the way to go.

"Hey, Joe!" one of his Caymanian friends called impatiently, guessing what was traveling through his conniving mind.

Joe turned for a moment and looked.

"Look what we got, Joe," his beach-bum friend called out while holding a brown bottle of whiskey high in the air.

Crazy Joe's mouth watered. His friends knew what he needed. With a big broad smile covering his face, he made a quick dash toward them and was soon reveling in his freedom through drink and idle conversation. Soon he had his friends to the point of hysteria about his presumed exploits while in the hospital. It didn't matter whether any of them were true or not but whether they were entertaining. They were that.

Intending it as a joke only, a friend slipped badly when he asked, "Hey, *mon*, you see any more devil fishes lately?"

If there was any laughter left in him at that moment, it departed quickly along with a happy smile which had flowed across his face seconds earlier. Clearly, Joe was disturbed. The others watched in silence, knowing the statement shouldn't have been made because it evoked an emotional pain within him which he could barely stand— the loss of his grandfather many years earlier. Tears rolled down his now saddened face into many streams, much like the many thoughts which ran through his tortured mind.

"Hey, *mon*, why'd you go and do that?" demanded one of Crazy Joe's friends while giving the man who asked the question a swift, hurtful punch to his right upper arm.

"I was only joking," the first man responded, painfully favoring the arm.

"Well, it ain't nothin' to joke about," the second man responded. "We're sorry, Joe," he said, apologizing for everyone.

Joe had clammed up. Silence fell on the group, the laughter had disappeared, and everyone waited for Crazy Joe to speak again. As they watched, he sipped.

"I know what you're thinking," Crazy Joe finally responded, using a cliche, "If I've said it once, I've said it a thousand times: it happened just like I said . . . a long time ago. And don't ask me what it was because I don't know. I was too young then, but I swear I saw the thing with my own eyes — these!" He pointed defiantly to his eyes with a long, bony finger.

"Yeh, we know," the more sympathetic drinking partner replied, speaking for the others. "What say we forget it for a while, okay? Have some more to drink, then we'll talk some more."

"No, I've already had too much to drink," Crazy Joe replied sadly, "and besides, I think I should've listened to my doctor. He said I shouldn't drink because it's bad for my liver and I'd soon be seeing bad things again if I continued drinking."

At that point, Crazy Joe's eyes wandered. He looked down into the clear, emerald-green bay in front of him, Hog Sty Bay. Despite its name, which implied "dirty" and "muddy" and only suited for pigs, it was all but that. Nearby, novice scuba divers in the company of their instructors were diving in the tranquil bay. Further on out and directly across from him was the pier where merchant and small passenger vessels docked to unload their cargoes. The only vessel in sight just then was the sleek yacht, its American flag waving in the gentle breeze at its stern.

"I think I'll take a walk," Crazy Joe said, as he lifted his body off the ground and proceeded unsteadily in the docked boat's direction. His drinking buddies looked on, sensing fully what he was planning to do, but said nothing. Employment was Crazy Joe's quest, and they knew better than to try and stop him. Only a word of caution escaped from his friend's lips.

"No more trouble with the law, brudder, you hear?" the man called after him.

Crazy Joe motioned back in disgust; his intentions were honorable. The only time he got in trouble was on payday. That's when he celebrated. But payday didn't always come, so he compensated , satisfying his need for celebration by brewing his own—fermented mangoes, potent as the concoction was.

"Hey, mister. You need a guide?"

Crazy Joe. A well-known character around George Town

George Town, Grand Cayman Island
British West Indies

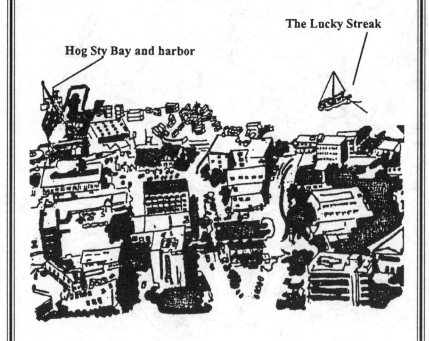

The Lucky Streak

Hog Sty Bay and harbor

Chapter 18

The New Yorkers

Hog Sty Bay, Grand Cayman Island

our papers are in order, Mr. Northam," the casually dressed customs inspector said as he handed the documents to the tall handsome man before him.

He smiled at the pretty young girl standing next to her father, then at the exceptionally attractive woman who had just joined them. He guessed it right; she was a fashion model, as the handsome man was quick to point out.

The customs inspector and an assistant had boarded the yacht a half hour earlier to check for correctness of papers and contraband. All had been found in order.

"You may tie up to your assigned mooring at any time, sir, after you've paid entry and mooring fees," the inspector said.

"Guide, sir?" called a voice from behind the man, greatly disturbing him. He looked around to see who it was, then cringed. "Crazy Joe, get off this dock. You know you're not supposed to be out here soliciting business."

A mischievous smile was on Crazy Joe's face as he stared at the newcomers while trying to give his best impression. "I'm just trying to beat the others, that's all," he said while waving to the little girl.

"You can do it from the shore," responded the customs agent as he grabbed the little man by the shoulder, twisted him around, then directed him in the way he should go. "Now get on with you," he said with a little push.

The agent turned to the address the Northams.

"These guides," he said. "Pests! All of them! Don't know when to take no for an answer."

A voice called over his shoulder from the man who had just been ordered off the pier.

"Oh, mister!" yelled Crazy Joe, getting Phillip Northam's attention. "When you need a guide, don't forget to call me. I'll be waiting over there," he said while pointing to the concrete landing area. "I'm the best guide around . . . and I'll show you everything."

"Don't mind him," the customs officer remarked.

"Is he as good as he says?" asked Janelle Northam.

"To be truthful, ma'am, yes, except when he's drinking," replied the man.

"Bye. I'll be waiting. I know the best fishing, scuba, and snorkeling places, including places to look for buried treasure," called Crazy Joe again before making a hasty retreat.

The last statement intrigued Phillip Northam!

"Does he really know where to look for buried treasure?" asked Phillip, the newly arrived skipper of the sleek new yacht, *Lucky Streak,* tied snugly to the protected pier.

"Knows most of them," the agent replied. "His grandfather helped him."

"Grandfather?"

"Yes, sir, an old fisherman who died at sea over forty years ago. He knew the best fishing grounds and a lot about places frequented by pirates. Used to do a lot of digging for buried treasure. I suspect he passed some of his knowledge on to his grandson."

The scrawny, dark-skinned Caymanian pricked Phillip's interest with each passing word. His purpose for choosing the Cayman Islands, unlike the motivation of his wife and daughter, had been stimulated by articles in travel magazines about Spanish galleons which had floundered in the rough seas and ended up on nearby reefs and about pirates who raided treasure ships returning to Spain, then buried what they had stolen on nearby islands. True, some of the articles were for publicity purposes, but he knew for certain some of what he had heard and read was true, for example, the finding of the *Atocha*, a treasure-ladened galley, off the southeastern coast of Florida by the famous treasure hunter, Mel Fisher, and the *Senora de la Concepcion*, by Burt Webber.

"You're here on a vacation, I hope?" asked the head customs agent who had caught the adventurous and faraway gleam in Phillip's eyes.

"Why do you ask?"

"Well, because if it's pirate gold you're after, you'll probably have a hard time finding any."

"Oh?"

"It's here all right," the customs official quickly reassured Phillip, "but a good deal of it has already been discovered. And if there's any more anywhere, the chances of it being found on this island are quite remote."

"But the brochures said pirate treasure is still to be found and we can keep what we find?"

"Under certain conditions, that is," replied the inspector without saying what those conditions were. "If I were you, I'd enjoy myself first, then try my hand at treasure hunting, but not here. You'd have better luck out on Cayman Brac and Little Cayman than on Grand Cayman. They're virtually untouched and pirates were known to frequent them. In fact, a bloody battle took place at Cayman Brac . . . ."

"How far?" asked Phillip, interrupting.

"Eighty to eighty-five miles by boat, and less than an hour, more or less, by small plane."

"Now that sounds interesting," replied Phillip with a gleam in his eye to his wife's chagrin.

"Phillip!" Janelle protested. "Not now. We just got here! And besides, you said you wanted to get away from the rat race for a while . . . to spend some time with your family."

"I know," admitted Phillip. "But just think of it," he added with excitement in his eyes, "we could find a bonanza!"

He turned to the customs officers.

"Is there a dive shop in town?" he asked.

"There are a number, sir. The closest is Shipwreck Charlie's, right down this street here, and beyond that is Soto's," replied the official as he pointed. "It's at the corner of Harbor Drive and Cardinal Avenue. Their prices are reasonable."

"Good," Phillip replied. "I'll need some diving equipment and supplies."

"Well, while you're doing that, I'm going shopping," Janelle said in a huff, agitated by her husband's unwillingness to undertake mundane things like shopping and sightseeing first.

A voice called out from the cement pier, causing everyone to look that way. It was Crazy Joe, advertising again.

"Don't forget me," he called.

"Why don't you go with him while I go to the dive shop?" suggested Phillip, still intent on preparing for a treasure hunt.

"No!" she responded sharply. "Where you go, we go!"

"Didn't mean to start a family quarrel," the customs officer broke in timidly while handing Phillip a booklet on rules and regulations for the operation of boats in Caymanian waters and a form on which he had entered a series of charges. "Your charges for mooring and entry fees. Cash or money orders only," he added.

Phillip looked.

"They're reasonable," he said as he reached into his rear pocket for his wallet. He removed several bills, collected his receipt, then bade the kind official and his assistant good day.

An hour earlier, from a position outside the bay by ship-to-shore radio using channel 16, they had contacted Cayman port authorities for docking instructions. After informing port authorities of the number of souls on board, port of registration of their vessel, and other pertinent data, they were directed straight to the dock to await arrival of customs personnel. With that behind them now, all that remained was to enjoy themselves.

As Phillip started the tiny auxiliary engine so he could carefully back up the yacht, Janelle, with the help of customs officials who released the mooring lines, did her part by hauling in the lines. Tanya, in the meantime, was cautioned to stay out of the way while her parents concentrated their efforts on getting their vessel safely to its newly assigned mooring buoy. A half hour later, they were safely moored and ready to ride to go ashore.

In a matter of minutes their dingy (zodiac brand) zipped away, made a sharp U-turn to the left of the docking pier, then headed straight for the concrete landing platform where Crazy Joe, interestingly enough, was still standing. As they disembarked, he greeted them with a broad smile, the kind reminiscent of early American billboards—before antidiscrimination efforts banned them—showing a bright-eyed, happy, young black boy who is getting ready to sink his sparkling white incisors into a slice of ice-cold watermelon.

"Guide?" he asked enthusiastically while offering a hand to Phillip as he maneuvered the dingy into position so everyone could get out.

"How much?" Phillip asked as he climbed out and looked around before reaching down to grab Tanya from her mother's arms.

"I come cheap, sir," Crazy Joe replied in a flash. "And I'm the best guide in the Cayman Islands."

"How much?" Phillip asked again.

"Fifty dollars a day, and that's a bargain!"

"What!" exclaimed Phillip while Janelle looked on and waited for him to lend her a hand.

"Forty—" countered Phillip, not certain whether he really needed a guide or not.

"Thirty-five—with expenses?" countered Crazy Joe.

"Too high!" replied Phillip, prepared to dicker. "Twenty-five and expenses, and that's my final offer."

"Ah, I can see you are accustomed to bargaining, sir," Crazy Joe responded with a happy laugh before being interrupted.

"Had to," acknowledged Phillip. "Vietnam taught me a lot of things."

"A shrewd bargainer indeed, sir," Crazy Joe responded with flattery, knowing it could get him everywhere—immediate employment especially—if he played his cards right.

"Well?" pressed Phillip, running out of patience.

"I accept!" Crazy Joe replied quickly, after sensing he might have pushed too hard and did not want to overplay his hand.

At that moment, Phillip Northam, a New York stock broker who had made it good, a man who had often been challenged by the best of Manhattan's hard-sell merchants and street vendors, wasn't certain whether he had been had or was about to be. In his haste to bargain, he had forgotten to define the meaning of "expenses."

"Phillip!" pleaded Janelle, who was still standing in the shaky boat trying to get out. "Have you forgotten me?"

At the same time, Crazy Joe took his job seriously. First he helped secure the dingy, then worked with his new boss by helping Janelle disembark. Secondly, he yelled at the top of his lungs to a taxi he saw passing by. It screeched to a stop, backed up, then parked near the seawall.

"Where to, boss?" he asked as he quickly opened the back door and politely allowed Janelle and Tanya to enter first. Then came Phillip, who sat next to them. With everyone properly seated, Crazy Joe took his place in the front seat next to the driver. He winked at the man. Phillip noticed the exchange but said nothing.

"Where to, boss?" asked the driver.

"Shipwreck Charlie's Dive Shop," replied Phillip.

John Hankins

"Great place and great prices," said Crazy Joe, making Phillip wonder whether there was a conspiracy of payoffs going on.

While he considered the possibilities of collusion, the driver shifted gears and sped away, first by making a life-threatening turn in front of a car that already had the right-of-way, then into a side street on the wrong side of the road—so he thought—until he remembered that Caymanians drive on the left side of the road like the British!

In three minutes, the taxi made a U-turn in a non-U-turn zone, stopping in front of a dive shop crammed full of diving gear and other water sports equipment, including locked displays of treasure and other artifacts which had been found in and around the Cayman Islands. The sight of them stirred Phillip's appetite for adventure.

He addressed the proprietor.

"Got any suggestions for out-of-the way treasure hunting?" he inquired testingly.

"I most certainly do, sir," replied the dive master and proprietor of the shop, delighted to be of assistance.

Phillip leaned in closer, speaking so he wouldn't be overheard. The dive master, with a subtle smile on his face, accommodated him by pressing in closer.

"I've been told by supposed experts," he said, actually referring to the customs official to whom he had spoken earlier, "that there's a special place not too far from here where I can search for treasure."

"On Little Cayman and Cayman Brac," said the dive master in a voice louder than Phillip wanted.

"Yes, yes—those are the places," replied Phillip.

"For what you want to do, sir," added the man, "few if any of the tourists ever visit those islands, which makes it good for you."

"Why is that?" asked Phillip.

"Because there's no easy way to get there except by small plane or boat. And they don't have the comforts found here."

"That's no problem for us," replied Phillip anxiously. "We came by private yacht, and we're free to travel at will—with no time constraints."

"For you, maybe," Janelle interjected while standing at his side, "but not for me. Remember I've got an important modeling job next month."

The dive master was impressed with what Phillip had told him, but was even more so after observing his wife. He had a hard time taking his eyes off the attractive woman and the pretty little girl whose hand she held. His mind shifted then; she was married and was a mother. Tough luck!

Unaware of his thoughts, Phillip asked, "How do we get there, and what kind of equipment would you recommend?"

"It would have been much easier had you asked what don't we have, sir," the man answered proudly, before adding, "Tell me what you need and I'll get it for you."

"Everything," replied Phillip as his wife looked on apprehensively and while his daughter fingered everything within reach of her curious hands.

The proprietor smiled.

"We have bargains incomparable, sir! From air tanks and regulators to snorkels, masks, fins, weights, shark repellant, swimsuits, beachballs, and portable compressors to refill your tanks, to name a few."

Two hours later, the waiting taxi, with its meter still running and its driver still smiling, chugged away completely full.

"Look what the nice man gave me," Tanya said happily as she held up for her parents to see the beautiful beach ball and a quart-size sand pail—with matching shovel—the proprietor had given to her.

"Honey, he could afford it after what your father did for him," replied her mother with a hint of sarcasm, taking into account all the equipment and supplies her husband had purchased from the shop, the bulk of which was crammed into their tiny taxi.

The remark escaped the little girl, but not Crazy Joe. He had watched his new boss chalk up charges on his American Express Gold Card without batting an eyelid. He liked that because that was the kind of gold to which Caymanians were accustomed—plastic! And besides, credit cards were more negotiable than treasure supposedly buried by pirates centuries earlier and certainly more reliable than tales of supposed caches fed to unsuspecting tourists by unscrupulous merchants in order to shore up the economy. Of course, no one would ever admit to that, but then again, what was wrong with it so long as all parties—locals and tourists alike—benefited? For the tourist, it meant enjoying the scenery and magnificent beaches while for the locals, it was a way to improve one's standard of living. Fair is fair!

Minutes later, the taxi pulled up to the seawall and parked, emptying itself of passengers and cargo before returning time and time again to the dive shop to retrieve diving gear, then back again to the seawall until there was nothing left to carry. Naturally, these trips pleased the driver and his silent partner, Crazy Joe, since each trip meant more money, and the more money they earned, the more they divided. It wasn't a bad deal for the driver because Crazy Joe was particularly good at drumming up business, especially during off-season times.

If the taxi bill was outrageous, Phillip Northam made no mention of it because he had gotten everything he wanted, and more! Now he was anxious to sail away to Little Cayman, but it couldn't be. Not this day anyway. Janelle had put her foot down right on top of his right foot and said, "No! Not until tomorrow."

So he had to pacify her or face verbal destruction in the shop they had just left, something he didn't want because he knew she was right. Treasure hunting could wait another day or so, but in the meantime, he had to tend to the needs of his family. Divorce was unpalatable.

While he fiddled with his newly purchased metal detector, Phillip couldn't help thinking about the trip to the neighboring island to see if it worked. While doing so, he thought about the lagoon on the map the dive shop owner had shown him earlier and the minor obstacles they would face upon arrival. The most prominent was a semi-circular reef surrounding the lagoon, one in which a small island—Owen's Island—could also be found.

Once in the lagoon, as the diver master had stated, it would be up to the Northams to select which pristine beach they would use—the one on the main main island or the one on Owen Island. They were both beautiful. That was music to Phillip's ears, so he had wasted no time buying promotional literature, which pleased the shop proprietor.

If he could, Phillip would have left right then. He could not only taste the place but could also visualize their yacht anchored safely outside the reef, rolling back and forth in its clear, aquamarine waters while he, his wife, and daughter basked in the sun on the island's remote, uninhabited beach. There was a person or two on the island, so he had been told, but he would be lucky to see any of them. And besides, if he did, they wouldn't bother anyone. Also, there was a grass airstrip there for emergencies, but it was rarely used. Most intriguing of all, however—again according to the dive master—was his unique opportunity to dig for buried treasure. Some had been found there in the past, and it was worth going over to see—according to the man— since most Caymanians had no way of getting there, tourists included.

"Have enough fun for one day?" asked Janelle as she watched her husband, accompanied by Crazy Joe and the driver, moving the beeping metal detector across the earthen part of the seawall. Most contacts turned out to be discarded soft-drink tops, plus a modern coin or two.

Phillip heard her, then sheepishly quit what he was doing and returned to the dock to continue loading the rubber boat while his wife and child remained behind to watch everything. A number of trips were required before he could finally take them back to the yacht, hungrier than starving bears after a hibernation.

Tanya was the first to complain.

"I'm hungry, Mamma," she cried.

Phillip looked to her, then to her mother as if saying, "How about finding your child something to eat?"

Sensing what was on his mind, Janelle cut him off, "We're eating out, remember? And I'm not cooking, not while we're in port!"

The message was clear!

Minutes later, and reasonably dressed, Phillip and his family reentered their rubber boat and headed for shore, where much to their surprise, they were met by their guide, Crazy Joe, who was still exhibiting his memorable toothy smile.

"A place for dinner?" he asked.

"Know one?" replied Phillip.

"The best in town," he replied, showing absolute boldness. "And reservations have been made."

"My!" exclaimed Janelle, pleased with his foresightedness and consideration.

"At your service, madame," he said, bowing graciously as his taxi driver friend screeched in next to the seawall to a full stop. Another driver had tried to move in, but gave up after a hot exchange of words, some too bad to repeat.

"You don't happen to own this taxi, do you?" Phillip asked after recognizing the driver.

"No, sir! That would be a conflict of interest," Crazy Joe countered in something mimicking indignation.

"All right, let's go. . . ," ordered Phillip, "to where it is you've planned."

"Your tie, sir," the maitre d' said politely as he handed Phillip one to match his outfit. He had selected one from a group hanging on a nearby wall.

"But—?"

"Sorry, sir," the man replied, anticipating Phillip's response. "It's house rules. Proper attire is required at all times, except at noontime."

"As you say," Phillip acquiesced while showing a slight tinge of embarrassment as others more formerly dressed passed by. Reluctantly he put the tie on, then took a seat next to his family to wait for a vacant table. Crazy Joe went outside to wait, but not before the maitre d' crossed one of his palms with a green note of "thanks."

"A lovely place," sighed Janelle, happy to be out again after weeks at sea cooking, scrubbing, assisting her husband with the sails, or relieving him at the wheel.

"I thought I came here to get away from all this," Phillip whispered softly into the air, referring to the hustle and bustle of New York City.

"It's so exciting. Breathe the fresh air," Janelle urged, ignoring his complaints. It was a tropical night, full of fragrant smells, and she enjoyed every moment of it.

As darkness set in, she listened to the waves pounding the rocks nearby and absorbed the fresh clean smell of the roaring sea. After a while, her thoughts and eyes shifted to the sky above and the innumerable stars twinkling there. When she had looked enough, her thoughts returned to the sea and its sweet smell. It elicited a response in her, but not like the aroma which twitched her, her husband's, and her little daughter's nostrils, evoking extreme pangs of hunger. The smell of chef-prepared gourmet seafood being served to a patron at a nearby table was more than any of them could stand.

"I'm hungry, Mamma," Tanya moaned while rubbing her stomach.

"You'll have to hold on a little longer, dear," her mother replied. "It won't be too much longer; we're waiting for a table."

She was right. Within minutes, the maitre d' returned, then escorted them to a table on the veranda near the open sea.

"Your order, madame?" asked their waitress after allowing them sufficient time to study the menu. Her voice was almost drowned out by the pounding surf and the beautiful music played by an accomplished pianist.

Phillip's thoughts were not on the menu, but on the islands beyond his sight. Nevertheless, after seeing his family satisfied, he selected what he wanted, then thought about other things for a while—New York in particular.

"Wall Street was never like this," he said, sighing heavily.

"I'm glad to hear that," replied Janelle, thinking he could never get his mind off his work. "One needs to relax now and then, you know?"

Phillip had to agree his wife was right. He did need to get away, relax, and forget business for a while, including the graffiti-splattered subway cars and walls he had to ride and pass each day and the hoodlums who rode along in search of easy pickings.

While somewhat colorful, the graffiti didn't bother him too much because their gutter-minded creators—or similarly minded individuals—updated them on a regular basis, providing variety for curious minds which followed each alteration. The muggings, on the other hand, were another matter. Most of the victims were weak or old men and women who couldn't defend themselves. Not so for Phillip. He had been a Green Beret and had learned the ways of the enemy so he could defend himself without difficulty. In fact, his face became so well known that his previous, would-be assailants always ran the other way when they saw him coming.

Another reason for getting away from the madness to which he was exposed had to do with his many multimillionaire clients; they ran him to a frazzle. So when the day finally came to get away and relax or face a possible coronary at age thirty-nine, he reluctantly agreed to comply with his doctor's suggestion, but only after his cardiologist—with his wife's full support—confronted him with a soul-searching question: "To whom do you wish to leave your estate?"

The message sunk home, and he and Janelle, his wife of ten years whose beauty and figure were often publicized in national and international magazines, had agreed to revitalize their sinking marriage by taking an extended trip to the Caribbean aboard their newly purchased yacht.

Phillip and Janelle were sailing enthusiasts. They often sailed the waters off the New England coast and the Great Lakes, but their excursions became less and less frequent as their work schedules conflicted, and even less frequent after Tanya came along. Then came a trip to the doctor for an annual physical. When he said, "Go," Phillip wanted to say "No!" but Janelle, who insisted on coming along and heard the verdict, intervened by reminding him he had another heir to think about besides herself—Tanya!

The look in Tanya's innocent blue eyes and the color of her hair—golden blond—did something to his thinking just then. She was as pretty as her mother, and as stubborn as himself, so when both mother and daughter ganged up on him to get want they wanted, he couldn't resist. Grand Cayman Island in the British West Indies was the place they had decided to go.

Phillip's thinking changed from the past to the present. He saw gold again, only this time it wasn't the gold in his daughter's hair. It was a different kind, and it was in a place not too far from where they were now—about seventy miles away, to be specific, and just waiting for him.

The taxi ride back to the dock was uneventful. It took less than five minutes to get there from the classy restaurant, and during this time, Phillip hummed happily. To this, his wife attributed the mai tai's he had been sipping all evening. The drinks had loosened him up so much that he would break into song quite often, with selections from *Carmen* being his choice.

"You have a good time, boss?" Crazy Joe smiled as he helped him out of the cab.

"Did I have a good time?" Phillip repeated. "You can say that again, ole boy, and I've got to hand it to you, George. . . ."

"Joe—it's Joe, boss," Crazy Joe corrected with great tolerance. He knew the exhilaration his boss was experiencing—and the consequences after the fact, too.

"Oh, yes, Joe," Phillip replied, happily correcting himself.

"He's had too much to drink, I'm afraid," Janelle apologized, showing she was somewhat disgusted. "And I'm not getting into the boat until he sobers up."

She looked to where the boat had been tied. One of Crazy Joe's buddies was sitting nearby, occasionally sipping from a bottle of beer.

"Who's that?"

"Your guard," Crazy Joe replied when he noticed her stare. "Had to hire him to keep crooks from stealing your outboard."

"Oh?" replied Janelle, not certain protection was required. "What's it going to cost this time?"

"A mere five dollars," he answered. "The taxi fare is separate, of course."

Janelle frowned, resigned to her situation. She looked back into the cab; Tanya was fast asleep. In fact, she had fallen asleep in the restaurant and had to be carried out by one of the waiters after her father had demonstrated his inability to maneuver safely between crowded tables. A few customers had been unseated as a consequence, requiring dining room staff to come to their rescue.

The taxi was waiting when they got outside, thanks to Crazy Joe. Upon seeing Phillip in his condition, Joe took over by helping everyone get in the waiting taxi before getting in himself. He did the same thing again after reaching the seawall at Hog Sty Bay.

"Ge—o-r-g-e," said Phillip, slurring the name.

"It's Joe, sir," Crazy Joe corrected again.

"Oh, y-e-sh-sh, Joe," Phillip giggled while trying to work his way down the short flight of stairs leading from the elevated waterfront to the small landing below. Joe helped him.

"What do you know about that little island out there?" He pointed to the sea over his shoulder.

"Little Cayman . . . or Cayman Brac?" Crazy Joe asked.

"Tha's it, Lil'l Cayman," Phillip slurred again.

"Why do you ask?"

"Ask him tomorrow, dear," Janelle interjected.

"No! I want to know right now 'cause thas where we're going tomorrow morning."

Crazy Joe's eyes grew large, and he began to quiver. His thoughts raced madly when pains of the past came to mind.

"Well?" pressed Phillip as he descended carefully. He hadn't lost his train of thought.

"I wouldn't go there if I were you, sir," Joe replied softly as he assisted him to the landing below. "Not to Little Cayman, anyway."

"Oh? Why not?"

"Because a big sea monster lives there and it kills people," replied Crazy Joe with a nervous twitch on his face. It didn't escape anyone's notice, including Phillip's as saturated as he was.

"A what?" asked Janelle from her position at the head of the stairs. She barely heard the comment.

"Surely you don't believe in sea monsters?" Phillip asked.

"It's not safe out there, ma'am," Crazy Joe called up to Janelle, temporarily ignoring Phillip. It was difficult serving two masters.

"Why?" asked Janelle.

"Sea monsters—that's why!"

"There are no such things," Janelle replied, almost laughing. "We've been sailing the seas for years and have never seen anything larger than a whale."

"It wasn't a whale, ma'am," Crazy Joe replied loudly. "I don't lie about things like that—ask my friend Moses here," he said as he directed her attention to the guard standing nearby. "Ain't that right, brother?" he added, addressing the man who had heard what he said.

"Well?" Asked Phillip and Janelle simultaneously.

The thin black man seemed embarrassed and hesitated answering until prodded by Crazy Joe.

"Go'n; tell'em. They ain't goin' to bite you."

"Well," he answered softly, "all I know is what he's been tellin' us for twenty or more years, but I do have to agree with him that something bad happened out there a long time ago and he's got proof of it."

Phillip's eyes turned back to Crazy Joe as did Janelle's.

"What proof?" they both asked.

Crazy Joe didn't need to be prodded. In a flash, he pulled up one of his pant's legs to show a large jagged scar over which ugly keloid tissue had grown. It accounted for the limp with which the man walked.

"How'd you get that?" Phillip whistled. He was closer to the man and could see it quite well. Where the wound had been sutured, stitch-like marks were still visible.

"The monster did this," said Crazy Joe.

"A shark perhaps," ventured Phillip, now sobering up.

"Sharks don't make these kind of marks" Crazy Joe countered. "I know sharks. I've been around'em all my life. It was the monster, I tell you. Bigger than your boat. And I saw it . . . them," he corrected, "with my own eyes."

"Them?" asked Janelle, puzzled by the word.

"It carried demons on its back who fired darts at me!"

"Oh, come on," Phillip laughed, thinking he was being put on. "You can't be serious?"

"I'm quite serious, sir, and one thing I don't do is lie abut my injury!" said Crazy Joe with a very sober face. To the surprise of everyone, he began to cry, making everyone ashamed of themselves.

"I'll get Tanya," Janelle remarked, unable to cope with the situation. She went back to the taxi, paid the fare, then helped her sleepy daughter down the short flight of stairs to the boat, where Phillip was waiting.

With his family safely aboard the Zodiac, Phillip started its outboard with a turn of a key and the pressing of its starter button before asking the men on shore to release the mooring lines. Moments later, he revved the engine, and away it went toward the center of the bay.

An anguished voice called from the darkness just then. It was Crazy Joe issuing a warning. "I wouldn't go if I were you, sir. Not until I get a chance to kill it. It killed my grandfather."

"Oh, dear," Janelle remarked as the tiny rubber boat pulled away from the landing. "I'm afraid he needs help."

"Did you see his leg?" asked Phillip.

"Not very well," Janelle admitted.

"Well—whatever it was, it had to be real."

"Not by a sea monster, surely," Janelle replied guardedly. She thought for a moment before asking a question. "You know, it could have come from some kind of accident, which he's turned into a comfortable way to make a living. . . . by playing on other people's sympathies."

"It's been done before," Phillip agreed, "but I'm not so sure that's true in this case. He's too sincere."

"Watch out!" Janelle yelled in a nick of time to keep Phillip from running into a small fishing vessel which had just crossed their path.

"Whew!" said Phillip after swerving in time. A collision late at night could have been disastrous—even fatal. Janelle's look told him many things; he had drunk too much to be driving a boat in the middle of the night. To clear his muddled mind, he dipped his hand in the sea and splashed cool water over his face. It helped.

Minutes later, the Zodiac pulled alongside their yacht and the Northams got onboard. For a while, the cabin lights remained on until everything and everyone had settled down for the night.

"Are they going to Little Cayman?" asked the taxi driver when he approached Crazy Joe and his friend Moses while giving him his cut of the fare.

"That's what they said, but they don't know what they're in for," Joe replied as he extended an eager hand to collect his commission.

"You know, outside of you, no one has ever seen a sea monster like the one you've been talking about all these years," the driver said. "Not even the folks who live there now."

"It doesn't matter if you saw it," replied Crazy Joe in defense. "What matters is the fact that I saw it! It's out there all right. Gone away for a while maybe, but it's going to come back someday, and that's when I'm going to get it. I can feel it in my bones," he said, "especially on the wound because it's been feeling kind've funny . . . . strange. So I know it's coming back."

Theiy turned their eyes to the sea, pondering it for a long time without speaking. Then when a police car stopped by, flashing its search light in their direction, they decided it was time to go.

First went the cab driver, then the part-time guard, Moses, who was supposed to be followed by Crazy Joe. The latter, after they were gone, decided he needed to air his thoughts a while longer. It took only a half hour before he was distracted. Not far away at a spot next to a closed diner on the opposite shore, he heard singing. He recognized some of the voices and decided to join his drinking buddies. He knew he would be welcome.

Soon their jovial and drunken voices reached to the bright and shining stars in the sky overhead, to the tune of a hastily composed ballad dedicated to one of their members. It was titled "*When Joe Kills Mo*," a takeoff on the novel *Moby Dick*. It worked perfectly, lifting Crazy Joe's troubled spirit. He fell asleep after that without so much as an apparition to mar his dreams.

Initially that wasn't true for Janelle; she had a nightmare within the hour. She dreamed a huge monster rose out of the sea and grabbed her. She woke with a start, turned on the light and realized she had had a bad dream, so she took a sleeping pill before going back to her bunk to wait for it to take effect. She rested peacefully after that just like Crazy Joe on the beach nearby.

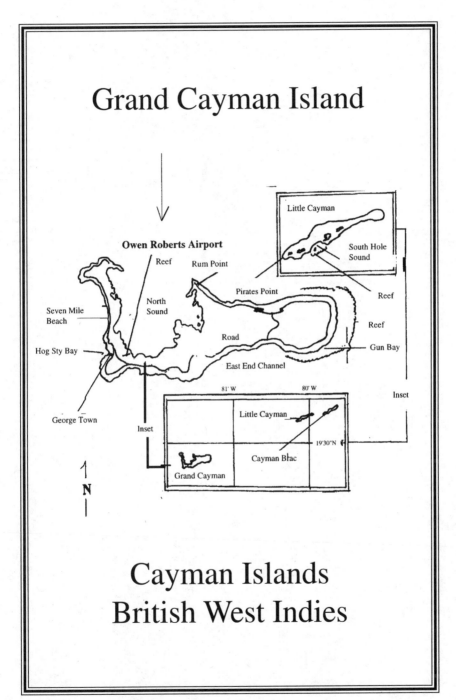

Grand Cayman Island

Little Cayman

Owen Roberts Airport

Reef Rum Point

South Hole
Sound

Pirates Point

Reef

Seven Mile
Beach

North
Sound

Reef

Road

Hog Sty Bay

Gun Bay

East End Channel

81' W 80' W

Inset

George Town

Little Cayman

Inset

19'30"N

Cayman Brac

Grand Cayman

N

Cayman Islands
British West Indies

213

Chapter 19

All That Glitters

Little Cayman, B.W.I.

s fast as the sun's rays penetrated the portholes, Phillip was up, bursting with energy. Excitement was in his eyes when he shook his sleeping wife in the bunk across the aisle from his. Tanya was asleep too in the next compartment.

"Go'way," Janelle moaned sleepily as Phillip nudged her.

"Come on; it's great outside. The sun is shining, the sea is calm, and the skies are bright blue—without a cloud in sight," Phillip said cheerfully, hoping she would respond.

"That's great. Enjoy it," she said groggily while flipping over from her back to her stomach.

Not to be discouraged, Phillip patted her on her soft, shapely rump. It appealed to him, so he dived into the sack with her, only to find himself painfully on the cabin floor.

"It's time to go," Phillip said angrily.

"You go," Janelle moaned again, seconds before he reached under the covers, grabbed her legs, then pulled her out to the floor alongside him. She screeched, then tried to resist his amorous advances, but couldn't; he was much too strong for her.

Minutes later, Janelle was preparing breakfast. Tanya had awakened after the loud crash in the cabin. It stopped the early morning play between her mother and father. For the Northams, breakfast was great; it couldn't have tasted better as they ate out on deck in the open air under an umbrella of blue sky.

"We're still going?" asked Janelle.

"Of course," Phillip replied. "Couldn't ask for a better day."

He pulled out an oceanographic map and began studying it closer. With a protractor and rule, he drew a line, then measured the distance from Grand Cayman Island—the big island in the chain—to Little Cayman. Then he studied other points on the map, the location of radio beacons in particular as a safety net if his satellite-tracking device failed.

"Not too bad," he murmured softly, drawing a pursed lip response from his wife.

"I'd rather stay here a few more days," Janelle said as Tanya happily dove over the side and dog-paddled near the boat. Janelle interrupted her train of thought just then to address her daughter as Phillip looked on without concern. "Be careful, dear. Don't go too far."

"Mamma, look at me," Tanya called from the clear green-blue water where the bottom could be seen. Tanya showed how well she could float on her back and back-paddle.

"Nice, dear," responded her mother before returning to her point of contention with her husband. "A day or two certainly won't hurt."

"We can do that when we get back," Phillip argued gently. He didn't want to make her mad, lest he be required to abandon his plans. "When we find the trea-s-u-r-e," he emphasized as he grabbed her affectionately, pulled her to his lap, then planted a captivating kiss squarely on her mouth. Janelle melted under such attention.

"Besides," Phillip continued after both released their grips for want of precious air, "it'll only be for a few days, and we can come back for a longer stay."

"Promise?" Janelle smiled.

"Yes, dear," he replied as he held three fingers up. "Boy Scout's honor."

Janelle laughed as she watched his boyish grin. Phillip had been a Boy Scout, and a good one. In fact, he still had all his awards and badges; they covered the wall of his study along with those earned in Vietnam, in a much harder and tragic way.

"All a-b-o-a-r-d!" Phillip called happily as he motioned for Tanya to return to the boat.

Tanya was happy to return. She had her mother's mannerisms, but her father's adventurism in her soul. She held up one arm and Phillip lifted her out of the water, wiped her down, then sent her to help her mother below decks as he prepared the yacht for its departure.

The whole episode took the better part of an hour. Janelle's reluctance to go had caused some delay, making Phillip worry about having sufficient wind to propel the sleek yacht to its destination before the end of the day. Assuming wind conditions were proper, the entire trip—according to his calculations—could be made in six hours or less, provided nothing happened like being becalmed. In that case they would drift for a while, and the voyage over would take longer then planned. He hoped that wouldn't happen since he wanted to reach Little Cayman by late afternoon. As things went, it looked like the best he could hope for would be early evening.

As Janelle stood by on the bow watching for his signal to release the line from their buoy, Phillip started the vessel's tiny diesel engine. It sputtered to life moments later.

"Okay, let her go!" he cried out.

As soon as Janelle released her line, Phillip engaged the vessel's propeller, and the boat began to move. Phillip carefully guided it to the harbor entrance, then into the open sea beyond. A half hour later, he stopped the tiny engine, and with Janelle's assistance, went through the routine of unfurling the yacht's sails, which quickly bloomed wide and white over the dark blue ocean like the wings of eagles.

What Phillip and his family did not see was the worried look on a little Caymanian's scraggly face. The man who watched them intently from the shore was Crazy Joe. He had come to like the New Yorkers and feared for their safety. He waved, but no one saw him.

Hours later, after the yacht circled around the coast of Grand Cayman Island heading on a tacking course for Little Cayman, the winds died suddenly, leaving the Northams stranded—adrift. All they could do at that point was wait and take occasional readings off the navigation satellite to determine their position, so when they did finally move with updated data, they would make appropriate course corrections.

"Think we ought to use the engine?" asked Janelle after a long wait.

Phillip frowned before answering. "Wouldn't be wise. We might need the fuel in case we get close to any reefs."

"Oh!"

"Wind should come up soon," replied Phillip as he turned the helm over to Janelle. "I'm going below to listen to the weather broadcast . . . to see what they're forecasting."

"Good, it's getting hot up here," Janelle replied while pulling her thin cloth shirt over her shoulders and making a minor adjustment of her sun visor cap to protect her eyes from the bright sun. At the same time, she looked at Tanya, noticing how red she was getting. She sent her below decks for a while.

Before Phillip emerged with his news, Janelle already knew what he had to say. The wind had strengthened, and the sails were already flapping in the breeze again, propelling the yacht.

A child's voice called from the bow.

"Land ho!" Tanya shouted. She had learned sea lingo from her parents and had been watching intently for the first sight of land.

She was right. A long, flat mass loomed before them. To be sure they were in the right place, Phillip took another satellite reading and traced the coordinates on his nautical chart.

"It's Little Cayman all right. Everything matches up, including the contours of the island."

"You sure it's not part of the Isle of Pines group next to Cuba?" asked Janelle. "We've been sailing long enough."

"Nope—they're further north," Phillip replied, "and besides, if we were near Cuba, we'd know it. It'd dominate the horizon in front of us."

They reached Little Cayman an hour later, and upon finding the channel to South Hole Sound, switched from sails to diesel in order to insure better maneuvering of the *Lucky Streak*. The seaward side of the channel on their right was bounded by an impassable semi-circular reef within which was a small, flat, vegetation covered island— Owen's Island—and a shallow, sandy, white-bottomed lagoon that gave the surrounding waters a clear, emerald-green color. It was hypnotic to watch, much like the white-gold beach on Owen's Island, which seemed more appealing to the Northams than the other on the much larger Little Cayman Island because of its isolation. So they decided to spend a few days there first.

Their arrival could have come at a better time because the sun was dropping rapidly in the west, leaving them little time to find an adequate mooring site before daylight disappeared.

"Okay, let her go! Drop anchor!" cried Phillip.

In response, Janelle struck a small lever, which caused the anchor to plummet quickly into the sea, stopping the vessel. It swung around moments later, facing in direction of the prevailing current.

"Ah, what a way to sail," Phillip said after he had secured the helm so it wouldn't swing back and forth and get fouled or damaged. "It's unbelievable what modern technology has done for sailing. Think of it, autopilots, electronic satellite tracking, emergency beacons. . . ."

"Stop dreaming and help us," Janelle called as she and Tanya secured the sails and wrapped them. "There are some things which must still be done by hand, you know."

Reluctantly, Phillip got up to lend a hand. His mind was really on the shore. His interest showed every time he glanced in the island's direction. It was barely visible now, but that didn't stop him from looking. An occasional light scattered here and there indicated people lived there. How many he didn't know, but from what he had been told, no more than twenty souls or so.

Soon he and his family were below decks, washing and preparing for dinner. Janelle and Tanya, with some help from Phillip—on request, had prepared a good meal. In addition to the battery lights which illuminated the interior, they used candles to celebrate their safe arrival and to underscore their hopes for a successful venture. The lights went out a few hours later, except for the ones on the fantail and on the mast above, which alerted other vessels of their presence.

That night, Phillip could hardly sleep. His mind was on buried treasure, just waiting to be found. On the other hand, Janelle slept quite well. Her thoughts were on the quaint shops and boutiques back in George Town. As for Tanya, hers were on the new sand pail and shovel she had been given and how she would use them once ashore.

Janelle's sleep was suddenly disturbed when Phillip shook her.

"Where's the valium?" he asked apologetically.

"Where it's always been," Janelle mumbled sleepily. "In the medicine cabinet, of course!"

"Oh! Thanks," Phillip replied, embarrassed he had woken her up because of a lapse of memory. In defense of his actions, he added, "Getting old, I guess."

"Now go to sleep, and don't wake me again," Janelle moaned groggily.

As the boat swayed, so did Phillip, but he found what he was looking for—where it was supposed to be. He popped a ten-milligram pill in his mouth, then went back to his bunk and waited for relief. In a short time, he was snoring heavily to his wife's extreme distress.

"Wait till he wakes up," she mumbled as she tossed and turned before deciding she too needed to visit the medicine cabinet.

She had dark circles under her eyes the following morning even though she had medicated herself to help her sleep. As a professional

The Northams Motoring to Little Cayman

model in great demand, a person often called upon by the biggest and best advertising firms to model the very latest fashions of their clients, her every success in the industry depended upon her looks and good health. Unfortunately, she and Phillip were in stressful occupations, which was not good for either of them, so their family physician had prescribed a mild tension-reducing medication to help them.

While urging caution in its use, he also—like Phillip's cardiologist—vigorously recommended they take a badly needed vacation away from the stresses of city living. His advice also contained an "or else" admonition.

The "or else" part was important to Janelle. The romance in her life was waning, almost falling apart, because of her—and her husband's tension-filled careers. As a consequence, they no longer enjoyed normal family relationships and that was adversely affecting their daughter's life. They tried a private school, thinking it would help, but it was no substitute for the presence of a loving mother and father, a fact which soon became obvvious. Thus when several doctors, and counselors, too, suggested a vacation to help heal things, even though Phillip was reluctant at first, their recommendations could not be ignored. Consequently, their future plans were sealed.

So far, for Janelle anyway, everything was working reasonably well, that is, except for Phillip's obsession with finding pirate treasure. It was beginning to get under her skin. What happened next was unexpected.

"Hey, what's the matter with your eyes?" her husband asked as he affectionately pushed in beside her while sincerely inquiring, "Didn't you get enough sleep last night? There's black circles under them."

"Out!" screamed Janelle as she pushed him toward the cabin door while trying to contain her tears.

Bewildered, Phillip flew out of the cabin seconds before she threw her bedside clock at him.

"Women!" he said to himself after taking a`seat next to the helm. "Boy! She sure is touchy this morning."

"That's because she didn't sleep most of the night, Daddy," Tanya interjected after overhearing his words.

"Why?" he asked innocently.

"Because you snored all night, that's why."

"Oh! Oh!" replied Phillip as he considered ways to make up.

Janelle came up on deck later, looking much better. She had fixed her self up, being sure to cover the dark rings beneath her eyes. She didn't say anything to Phillip, which turned out to be a good thing. In penitence, he was conciliatory to her needs and pampered her most of the morning even when it came to helping her cook and wash the dishes. And until he was certain she wouldn't bite his head off, he decided to delay working on his new diving gear.

When the time came, he went below to gather their diving equipment, beach umbrella, and a host of other items and gadgets, then took them topside for transfer to their faithful Zodiac. While he was busy doing that, Janelle and Tanya were in the cabin preparing a picnic basket to take with them. Janelle, by this time, was her normal self again, mostly because of Phillip's efforts to make amends.

"Beautiful place, isn't it?" said Phillip when his wife and daughter joined him on deck, fully prepared for sunbathing. Both were drenched from head to toe with suntan oil and wore identical Cayman-made straw hats to shield their eyes from the bright morning sun.

Janelle looked toward the island and took in a big breath of air. It was sweet and invigorating, carrying with it the fragrance of many flowers. "It is beautiful," agreed Janelle. "Like one of those picture post cards, the type one sees in stationery stores."

"I know what you mean," her husband agreed before directing her thoughts back to the beautiful coconut and mangrove-rimmed island before them. "What a place to get lost and what a place for pirates to hide their gold!"

"And a perfect place for us to get a tan," Janelle interjected, her thoughts on more practical matters. She looked around for Tanya, who was waiting by the small ladder for her father to help her into their Zodiac.

Phillip preceded his daughter, getting in first to make room for everyone. Besides beachballs, a large beach umbrella and a collaps-ible chair, he had his diving gear and metal detector to rearrange before his family could get into the overloaded rubber boat. Despite his problems, he managed to get them all in, then cranked up the outboard and away they went.

"It's what the doctor ordered," Janelle said contentedly while laying stomach-down on a huge beach towel, sunning her back. While waiting for a reply, she looked in Tanya's direction to make sure she hadn't strayed too far.

"You can say that again," Phillip agreed lazily while stretched out in a low-slung lounge chair, reading a recent copy of the *Wall Street Journal,* the one he had purchased in George Town several days ago.

"Don't go in too far," Janelle suddenly called out upon seeing Tanya enter the water.

"All right, Mamma," Tanya called back, acknowledging her mother's warning.

"You worry too much about her. She'll be all right. Just let her alone," said Phillip as he dropped his paper to look around, seeing his wife's shapely body in the process.

The sight of her evoked tantalizing thoughts, something he couldn't afford right now; it wasn't the right place or time. So he went back to his dull paper, and before long, pulled it over his face, closed his eyes, and dozed off. It wasn't for long, however, as metallic sounds soon disturbed the silence.

"Clank! Clank, clank, clank!"

Both Janelle and Phillip stirred, Phillip more so than his wife. Slowly he pushed his paper away to see if he could locate the origin of the noise. Another clank followed; it came from Tanya's direction.

"What's that noise?" asked Janelle without moving.

"I don't know," replied Phillip as he rose from his low-slung chair and peered into the distance to see what she was doing.

She was further out in the lagoon now than where she had been earlier. The tide had receded and she had simply followed it. That was okay because it wasn't very deep where she was, but what bothered her father most was the strange object protruding out of the sand that she was striking over and over again. It was silver, reflecting the sun's rays like a polished mirror. Some of the rays glanced off the object and struck Phillip in the eyes, momentarily blinding him.

Curious, he walked toward Tanya while telling Janelle where he was going. "Be right back," he said.

"Okay," she replied groggily without turning around.

Clank! Clank! Clank!

Phillip increased his pace to a fast walk. As he moved in closer to Tanya and the object, panic struck him.

"TANYA! STOP! Don't hit it!" he cried at the top of his lungs, racing toward her like a leopard in pursuit of a fleeing gazelle. He yelled again when he saw her raising her shovel for another try at the object. "TANYA! STOP!"

She heard him this time and looked his way, puzzled by his frantic motions.

In the distance, shaken by the loud yelling, Janelle looked up in time to see her husband making a frantic dash toward their daughter. Once there, he picked her up and carried her to a spot far from where she had been.

Sharks! thought Janelle until she realized Tanya hadn't been in the water, only on the water's edge. *So what's the fuss all about?* To find out, there was only one thing left to do—go see for herself.

"What is going on?" she asked upon reaching them.

"Do you know what your daughter was doing?" asked Phillip, still panting from his long run.

"How do I know? You're the one who went to see," said Janelle.

"Well, she was pounding on a torpedo."

"A torpedo!" cried Janelle. "Where?" She looked around, while grabbling her daughter and holding her tight.

Phillip pointed to the water's edge. "Over there," he said. "It's that silvery object out there, the one that's pointing its head out of the sand like it's part of an overgrown cigar."

"Good Lord!" exclaimed Janelle. "How in the world did it get here. Is it dangerous?" she asked all at once.

"Could be . . . unless it's a dud," he replied.

"What's a torpedo, and a dud, Daddy?" Tanya asked.

Phillip looked down into his daughter's innocent eyes, then offered an explanation. "Honey, a torpedo is something like a bomb that could kill people, and a dud is something that doesn't work anymore," he added, pointing at the object she had been trying to open. "It could be dangerous and kill people, or it could be a dud."

"Which one is it, Daddy?" Tanya asked.

"That's something only the experts can determine," replied her father as he put his hand on her head. "Thank God, you didn't hit it anymore because we could have lost you."

"See why it's important you always let us know where you are and what you're doing," said Janelle as she knelt near her daughter and hugged her.

"You two, stay here," said Phillip. "I need to take a look at that thing."

"Don't go," warned Janelle as she held Tanya's hand.

"Don't worry; I won't get too close. With all that pounding by Tanya, if it hasn't gone off by now, it's not likely to do so now . . . providing I don't move it."

"Just the same, be careful, dear," insisted Janelle. "I'm too young to become a widow."

Phillip smiled, then walked away. He knew a lot about military weapons, but not much about torpedoes, yet enough to know there as a variety of types from the standard torpedo having a nose propeller which activated the device after a certain number of turns to the type that honed in on its quarry by electronic means. This was the first kind. *So, that's what she was after,* Phillip thought upon seeing the bent nose blades. Tanya was trying to knock it free. *Thank God she failed!* He turned and walked back to his family, grateful he still had a daughter.

"Well?" asked Janelle.

"It's a torpedo all right."

"Is it a dud?" asked Tanya.

"Can't tell, honey. We'll have to notify the authorities so they can make that determination."

"We can't stay here with the thing around!"

"We can't leave it either. Someone could get hurt," said Phillip. "It's got to be destroyed. I'll notify Caymanian port authorities by radio to tell them what we've found. I'm certain they'll have an answer, so we had better gather our things and head back to the boat for now."

"Oh, dear! What a way to start a vacation," moaned Janelle as she turned and walked back to the camp with Tanya firmly in hand. Phillip followed close behind.

It took the better part of an hour to raise Caymanian port authorities, with much of the dialogue between Phillip and the radio operator on the other end being garbled by static. Eventually, he reached them, conveying the unwelcome news.

"Roger, it's a torpedo of some sort. Phonetically, T for Tommy, O for Obo, R for Roger, P for Peter, E for Easy, D for Dog, and O for Obo—T-o-r-p-e-d-o, over."

A voice crackled on the other end to confirm what had been said.

"Torpedo. Is that cor. . . rect? Over."

"Roger," Phillip replied, relieved. "Over."

"Are you certain, sir? Over."

"I know a torpedo when I see one, sir. Over," Phillip replied while the radio crackled. He was getting frustrated with all the questions, yet he knew the interrogating officials wanted to be certain he knew what he was talking about before making plans to come out.

Again Phillip described the object.

"Very well, sir, (crackle), we will (crackle) (crackle) shortl. Over."

"Say again, over," Phillip repeated. This time their message broke through the atmospheric disturbance.

"We'll be there as fast as we can, sir. By helicopter most likely. Over."

"Why so long? Over." asked Phillip.

"It take some time to alert the demolition team, since they will have to come from Jamaica. And after that it will take additional time to fly over. Anywhere from (crackle) 4 to 6 hours . . . more or less. Can you remain on the beach until we get there? Over."

225

"Roger, will do. We are self-sufficient. Over and out."

"Roger. Over and out," replied the voice on the other end.

"They seemed skeptical at first," said Janelle.

"Can't blame them. A torpedo isn't something one runs into every day—in these waters especially, though I suspect it'd be more likely to be found here than elsewhere," Phillip replied wearily.

"What makes you say that?" Janelle asked as Tanya listened with typical childish curiosity.

"Because this was a war zone during the Second World War. A lot of ships were sunk in these waters by German submarines, U-boats. Sooo, if I were to venture a guess, I'd say that that thing out there on the beach is a leftover from WWII. The only thing that puzzles me is that it looks new—like it had been put there yesterday unless, though we don't know for certain, it is new and this island has—and is—being used for a military target practice range."

"I doubt that," said Janelle. "If that had been the case, wouldn't the George Town authorities have warned us? I can't imagine anyone sending innocent tourists to a potentially hazardous area."

"I agree," Phillip replied, "but people do make mistakes. In the meantime, however, all we can do from now to the time the experts arrive is wait. After they take over, perhaps we'll have the answer."

Tanya took her father's meaning to heart. Like a spring, she bounded out of the cabin onto the open deck, then back into the dingy. Her parents followed.

As they approached the shore, the sun had already passed overhead. In fact, lunch time had come and gone without anyone noticing. The excitement of finding the torpedo had made everyone forget their gastronomical needs—until they reached shore, that is. Hunger soon dominated the scene when Janelle opened the lunch basket and set the food before them.

They ate until they couldn't eat anymore. Then drowsiness set in, affecting everyone. Four hours wasn't too long to wait, so they all agreed to take a nap under nearby trees. Phillip was the first to doze off. Tanya was next, followed by her mother, who simply could not surrender her "mother hen" role, especially now with so much danger around!

The thub, thub, thub sound made by helicopter blades woke Phillip with a start. It was a welcome sound like those he and his comrades in Vietnam had eagerly welcomed years earlier. For a moment, he thought he was there, but his senses returned and he woke Janelle and Tanya.

"They're here," he said.

They got up, then searched the sky for the approaching craft. Before long, it was hovering near them, whipping stinging grains of sand in their direction. It didn't land right away because its pilot wanted to find a suitable place to set down. Once he found it, he slowly let it down. A number of men exited, one of them in a Royal Navy nniform.

"Mr. Northam?" inquired the officer, upon approaching the family.

"That's me," Phillip answered.

"Leftenant Osgood of the Royal Navy," said the man extending a hand.

"Phillip Northam, sir, and my wife, Janelle, and daughter, Tanya."

"Pleased to meet you, Mrs. Northam . . . and you, too, young lady," the kindly officer replied before getting to the point. "I understand you've had a bit of a problem? Torpedo of sorts?"

"It's over here, sir," Phillip replied as he led the way. Though the tide was rising now, a good portion of the torpedo's nose was still visible above the water.

Janelle and Tanya wanted to follow the inspection party, but the officer in charge wisely and politely insisted they remain behind. So from a safe distance, they watched the men as they worked in and around the gleaming torpedo. The wind carried their voices.

"It's a torpedo, all right," said one. "From the looks of it, I'd say it's a World War II T5—a *Zaunkonig*—the acoustical type used by German U-boats toward the end of the war."

"My thoughts exactly," agreed Leftenant Osgood as he thumbed through a naval manual to make comparisons.

"How do you suppose it got here?" asked another man as he scratched his head, puzzled by its presence.

"Probably fired at a merchant vessel years ago and missed. When it ran out of steam, it ended up here in the cove," another man speculated.

"As good an explanation as any," replied another technician as he surveyed the area.

"U-boats were quite active in these waters at that time," continued the technician as he studied the torpedo. "What I don't understand, however, is how this one was able to remain in perfect condition. It's as if it was manufactured yesterday," he added while rubbing its smooth and shiny surface. "Not a sign of barnacles either."

"That's not so strange," another man interjected. "Probably got buried during a hurricane, where it couldn't be touched by organisms.

Then, when another one came through, like the one that hit this island a few weeka ago, it got uncovered. . . ."

"Sounds plausible," the officer in charge agreed while making adjustments to his camera so he could get good photographs to take back to his superiors. While doing so, he looked around. Evidence of a passing hurricane was everywhere, from splintered palm trees to scattered floatsome which had been washed ashore. But as he was quick to notice too, nature had a way of rejuvenating itself. Sprouts were springing up everywhere, patching up the damage.

"Lucky the blither didn't go off," said another man, making reference to the torpedo again.

"You can say that again, mate," his associate replied.

"Better search the area in case there's more," ordered the officer in charge, "though I doubt it."

Instantly, two of his men stripped to their waists and walked into the deepening water. Fortunately, it was still quite shallow and they could see just about everything within the reef. They found nothing within their search area and returned.

"Not a thing anywhere, sir. Not even a stray doubloon," one of the men reported.

"Very well. Set the charges, and let's head for home. It's getting dark, and we want to be out of here before it gets too dark."

While several technicians strapped explosives to its side, the officer in charge joined the Northams.

"What are they doing?" asked Phillip upon observing a rash of activities around the torpedo.

"We're going to blow it up electronically," said the young officer before advising them they would have to return to their yacht for a while.

"Will the explosion be large?" Janelle asked, concerned for Tanya and everyone else's safety.

"It could very well be, ma'am," the young officer replied, "if the original charge within the torpedo has not been damaged by water or decomposition."

He looked toward the horizon; the sun had already dropped beyond the horizon and darkness was rapidly closing in. His eyes searched the shoreline where his men were completing their assignment. Within a minute, they raced back to the helicopter and boarded.

"Well, it's time for all of us to go," said the leftenant. "I'll detonate the torpedo from the air, and if everything goes as planned—and I believe it will, there will be nothing left of the torpedo. After that, you'll be able to resume your activities. "

Leftenant Osgood saw the Northams safely to their Zodiac, bade them all good-bye—with a sweet parting salute for little Tanya, then hastened back to the waiting helicopter whose pilot was complaining bitterly. His major complaint centered around his fear of flying over water in pitch black nights and recent PIREPS—pilot reports—about a squall line coming their way.

From the air, Leftenant Osgood watched the Northams board their yacht. Once they were safely aboard, he directed the pilot to hover nearby while he activated his detonation device. A red light flashed, showing it was ready for use. He pushed it firmly. Instantly, an explosion rocked the place where the torpedo had been. Shock waves followed which buffeted the helicopter, but not too hard. As for the Northams, they were unaffected because a small island in the middle of the lagoon absorbed the brunt of the blast.

The last thing the Northams saw of the helicopter with the demolition crew was its quick but short flight over the detonation site, where the leftenant conducted a quick survey. Upon seeing debris scattered over the beach, he concluded his mission had been satisfactorily completed and ordered the pilot to fly back to Grand Cayman, but not before making a quick and low circle around the *Lucky Streak* as a gesture of farewell.

"Whew! That was quick," said Phillip and he and his family waved at the helicopter's occupants before they disappeared from sight.

"If this is what digging for treasure is all about," replied Janelle, "I'll take my chances in New York's subways any time."

"Aw, come off it, Janelle," urged Phillip. "Finding the torpedo was coincidence, that's all . . . ."

"That may very well be true, Phillip, but if anymore of those . . . those watchamacallits. . ."

"Torpedoes. . ." Phillip interrupted.

"Well, if any of them show up again, we're going home!"

Phillip laughed. He felt certain Janelle was kidding, but then again he could be mistaken. What mattered most to him was their marriage, and he wanted to preserve it.

"Honey, I can assure you, it was a freak occurrence," he said. "Like the lieutenant said, it was a leftover from World War II."

"But how did it get here?"

"The lieutenant thought it had been fired against Allied shipping during WWII and it missed its mark, ending up on the beach here. And it's been here ever since. . . ."

Janelle accepted his explanation. *After all,* she thought, *Phillip isn't responsible for that monstrous thing being here.* "You win," she said after planting a loving kiss on his lips. "We stay!"

Everyone slept well that night including Tanya, who did a little bit of snoring herself. She was exhausted from all her running around and the late evening meal. Her dreams were as pleasant as everyone's, and somewhat similar.

Tanya saw herself on the beach, filling her pail with sand. Her mother saw the sand in another way; she was lying on it and getting a golden tan. On the other hand, her father saw himself searching the sand with his new metal detector. In his long dream, when the detector's light flashed and its alarm buzzed, he saw himself grabbing Tanya's shovel to dig where the instrument indicated. Regrettably, his physical body did not detect the difference between the dream and reality until pain ran through Phillip's left hand, following a collision with the bulkhead.

"OW! Oh! Shit!" he cried aloud before realizing what had happened. He looked around to determine if he had been heard. Fortunately, he hadn't been so he went back to sleep, only this time, with a bruised and throbbing hand.

Phillip wasn't in the best of moods when it came time to wake up; his hand had swollen during the night. Upon seeing this, Janelle asked why, then got a grumpy explanation.

"Ice cubes is what you need," she insisted as she went to the small gas-operated refrigerator and withdrew a tray.

She put them into an ice bag then over the swollen area. A towel came next, and Phillip fussed. His concern was over being able to use his hand to operate the boat and metal detector, but his fears were soon allayed when the pain started to recede after he swallowed several aspirins.

"See, big boy," Janelle added with a motherly tone, "we all need someone to lean on."

"But it was a terrific dream," Phillip replied, "and I had the treasure in my hand when. . . ."

"Forget it. Enjoy yourself first. Then later if you happen unto something valuable, then chalk it up to Providence."

She was right, of course; there was a thousand to-one chance he might find something valuable, but then again, he did buy an awful lot of equipment which needed to be used.

Breakfast was served this morning with more pleasantry than in the past few weeks. Something had come over Janelle. It wasn't confined to her alone; it had gotten to Phillip, too. The closeness of the two, something they hadn't experienced in years, was beginning to kindle the old spark that drew them together originally.

"I'll operate the Zodiac this morning," said Janelle as she refilled Phillip's empty coffee cup, "if it's all right with you."

"What's gotten over you?"

"You don't know?" she replied before planting a kiss on his lips.

"Tell me."

"It's you! You're becoming like your old self again. More relaxed too—except of course your obsession over finding treasure."

"Well, I'll try to do better from this day forward, I promise."

"We'll see, but I have hopes for your redemption," Janelle interjected with a smile as she poured more orange juice into Tanya's half-empty glass.

"I don't want anymore, Mamma," Tanya protested.

"Hush, dear. You need your vitamin C."

Tanya took it reluctantly. She drank it all at once to get it over with, and as an indication of her defiance.

"Good girl, now run along and get your things," said Janelle, ignoring her antics.

With her mother's permission, Tanya dashed away from the small cabin table and up the stairs leading to the main deck. She was soon ready to go—sand pail, shovel, and all. Her father was close behind.

"Leave the dishes for later," he called back. "I'll help you wash them later."

Janelle scoffed, but hoped he meant what he said. She was willing to give him a chance and raced after him.

As Janelle started the Zodiac's engine, Phillip untied the lines as best as he could. Within minutes, they raced away and were back at the favorite beach, where Phillip carefully unloaded his prized metal detector.

"What about your hand?" inquired Janelle when she noticed the difficulty he was having.

"A little sore, but I'll get along."

"Let it rest for a while; you have all day to search," she suggested.

Phillip considered her words. It was true, there were many hours left, both for work and play, though he doubted treasure hunting was work.

"You're right!" he agreed, carrying his treasured equipment to their camp site, where he deposited them carefully beneath the canopy of the large beach umbrella they had left the previous day.

231

Janelle, carrying her own things, walked with him up to the umbrella, then promptly spread a large beach towel on the surrounding sand. She laid down, stomach up this time.

Tanya, who followed close behind, had her plans, too. "Mamma," Tanya asked, "is it all right if I play on the beach where I played yesterday?"

"I don't know, dear," Janelle replied. "Better ask your father. He should know if it's safe or not."

She turned to her father.

"Daddy—"

"Perfectly safe. Go right ahead, but be careful," he said with his head buried in his metal detector instruction handbook.

"But don't go in the water and stay where I can keep an eye on you," added Janelle as she lay with her eyes shut.

That's all Tanya wanted. In a split second, she was gone, singing and dancing all the way until she came to the spot she wanted and started picking up things.

"Kids! They sure know how to pass the time," Phillip commented loud enough for his wife to hear while watching his daughter happily picking up things he thought to be sea shells.

"One child is enough," said Janelle in response, "unless I decide to retire and you decide to change your way of living."

"You mean that?" Phillip responded, excited over the possibility of having another child, a boy this time.

"I know what I told you in the past, but that could change," hinted Janelle. "After all, times have changed. Over the past few days, I've had a chance to think . . . about my career and our marriage. It's been a compromise at best, with a child to raise as the same time."

"I'm happy to hear you say that," said Phillip. "I have to agree. It was a problem . . . picking up Tanya each day, then returning home to an apartment devoid of a mother."

"I know," Janelle agreed. "When it was my turn, I felt the same emptiness. But now. . . ."

"Things are getting better," Phillip interjected as he reached over from his beach chair and tapped her affectionately.

"Later," she said without looking up.

"Shucks," replied Phillip with a horsey laugh before returning to his instruction booklet.

The Northams could not have asked for a better day. A squall had passed through during the night, which made the anchorage a bit unsteady during the early morning hours, but after its passage, everything returned to normal to bring back bright blue skies, clean and cool fresh air, and a welcome breeze to blow the flies away.

But something else was of interest, too— Little Tanya, her golden hair glistening in the sunlight, singing happily as she danced from tiny object to object, most of which glittered brightly. That tranquil scene lulled her father into a partial slumber, and he wouldn't hear her voice again for another hour or so. . . .

An hour passed without incident, during which time Janelle managed to get baked on one side and had to shift to the other to balance her color. Occasionally she would look Tanya's way to make sure she was all right. After that, she would slap more suntan lotion on the exposed surfaces of her body.

Her husband didn't have that problem. He felt all danger had passed and Tanya didn't need watching. That was true until Tanya came back to show him what she had found. She was within five feet of him when rays of light struck him in the face, causing him to seek its source.

"Tanya, what's that in your pail?" he asked.

"Gold, Daddy," she said quite frankly. "That's what I've been picking up all morning."

Phillip laughed, then said loudly so Janelle could hear. "See, hon, what'd I tell you. Like father like daughter."

"It figures," replied Janelle in a sleepy voice. She was much too content to turn over and look.

To humor Tanya, Phillip motioned for her to come closer so he could examine her treasure. As she did, more bright sparkles of light jumped out at him, attacking his retina. He winced, then took the bucket from her and turned the other way.

A loud gasp escaped his lips. The bucket contained hundreds of pieces of bright yellow metallic fragments which really looked like gold!

Phillip jumped up. "Where did you get these?" he asked excitedly.

"Over there," Tanya said as she pointed to the place where she had been playing.

"OOO-eeeeee," Phillip shouted as he raced to the place Tanya pointed out.

His outburst woke Janelle. "What's the matter with your father?" she asked.

"I don't know, Mummy," Tanya replied quite casually. "All I did was show him my gold."

"Gold?" scoffed her mother, thinking she was being teased. Her thoughts didn't have time to gel when another loud shout followed. In

233

the distance, Phillip was jumping up and down like he had lost his mind or had a sun stroke. On second thought, he hadn't been in the sun like her, so she decided to go look.

"Have you gone mad?" asked Janelle breathlessly after racing to his side.

"Look!" said Phillip as he pointed to thousands of metal fragments which covered the sand on which they stood. "It's gold! And it's everywhere!"

"Are you sure it's not something else? Like pyrite, for instance?" questioned Janelle. She did have to agree with him, however, there was something strange about the sand compared to the previous day, but what was it? *Surely, it can't be gold?* she thought.

"Honey, believe me. I know gold when I see it," insisted Phillip as he palmed a few pieces of the gold-colored metal. One piece in particular caught his attention. It had the letters *RB* stamped in one corner of its smooth surface. The whole thing to Phillip's eyes and mind looked like a chip off of something bigger. What that was he didn't know nor could he venture a reasonable guess. He turned to Janelle.

"Look at this one, honey," he said excitedly. "It's got letters stamped on it."

Janelle and Tanya looked.

"It stands for Red Beard, the pirate," Tanya said unexpectedly. Her wit surprised her parents.

"You mean, Blue Beard, don't you?" her father corrected.

"It's got to stand for something," said Janelle. "Any idea what it could be?"

"At this point I'm not certain," he replied.

"You know, if this is real gold, it had to have come from somewhere—but where?" said Janelle.

"We won't know whether it's real gold or not until we can find someone who knows something about precious metals," said Phillip. "But, as to how it got here, your guess is a good as mine, dear. Like you, all I know is that it wasn't here yesterday."

A thought struck both of them at the same time. "The torpedo!" they shouted together.

"Or something under the torpedo," qualified Phillip, offering an option.

Broad smiles covered their faces when realization of what could have happened struck them. While it didn't answer everything, it did bring them closer to solving the mystery of the torpedo and the metal fragments which covered the sand before them. It didn't explain how the torpedo got there nor why it looked like new when found, but it did provide the Northams with the opportunity to speculate.

A good guess concerned the hurricane which had recently passed through the Caymans, hitting Little Cayman quite badly. It was logical, therefore, to conclude that the torpedo had been unsanded, so to speak, as the storm passed through, and the explosion set by the demolition team unexpectedly uncovered a horde of pirate treasure or the remains of a Spanish galleon that might have washed ashore centuries before.

"Think of it, Janelle!" Phillip said excitedly. "We've struck a bonanza! No more worries over investments—somebody else's especially!"

"If it's really gold—"

"I know it's gold!" interrupted Phillip. "What else could it be?"

Before his wife could answer, Phillip's eyes chased after Tanya who had seen something in the nearby sand and had hastened to get it. She picked it up and ran back to him, asking him to open it.

"What have you got, Honey?" he asked as he took the small battered box from her outstretched hands.

With great care he pried the box open, only to find a box within a box—fully intact. The inner one was miraculously undamaged and more ornate than the one in which it came.

"Good Lord!" said Phillip unbelievingly. "It can't be real?"

"What is it?" asked Janelle as she pressed in closer.

"It's an antique watch of some sort!" Phillip said excitedly.

The watch appeared to be made of solid gold. Encrusted jewels encircled it as did engravings and designs of exquisite workmanship. Phillip pressed a tiny button on its side. Surprisingly, its cover snapped open revealing an ornate inscription, written in French.

"What does it say?" asked Janelle, knowing Phillip studied French in college.

"Just a second," he replied. "I'm not current, but I think I can read it." After a brief pause, he came up with the interpretation. "To my darling Nicholas, Czar of all the Russias, on his 35th birthday. Alexandra."

"Oh, my God!" Janelle responded in shock. "It belonged to the Czar of Russia!"

"How in the world did it get here?" Phillip asked, puzzled by its discovery. Remembering something, he added, "Well, there goes our Spanish galleon theory. We're back to ground zero again."

"I agree," said Janelle, remembering her history, "The czar—this one anyway—came long after the Spanish galleons disappeared from the seas."

"Any other ideas?" asked Phillip.

"Blue Beard," suggested Tanya.

"No, honey," said her father, "but keep trying; you might find it before we do."

Satisfied, Tanya went off again to look for more things.

"It had to come from some place," said Phillip while pondering the watch.

"That leaves only one place —the torpedo," said Janelle. "None of this stuff was here yesterday until they blew it up. So where else could it have come from?"

Before he could answer, Tanya came running back carrying something again.

"Mummy, look at these," she said excitedly. "I know where the tooth fairy keeps all the teeth he takes from little children."

"Teeth?" both parents replied simultaneously. It was a strange thing for her to say, so they decided to look. Janelle looked first and was the first to react.

"Aiieee!"

"For Christ's sake! What's wrong now?" Phillip demanded as he rushed in to see what Tanya had given her that was so frightening.

"Throw them away! Ugh!" Janelle repeated.

"Here! Let me see," said Phillip before realizing he shouldn't have asked.

"Yuk," he said after viewing what appeared to be a handful of gold teeth and an odd assortment of gold coins bearing various mint marks.

"Did pirates have gold teeth?" Janelle asked reluctantly, hoping she was right.

"I don't think so," Phillip answered, seconds before his daughter presented him with another surprise.

"There's a lot more where these came from, Daddy," Tanya said with sweet innocence. "They're everywhere," she added.

"There's something sinister about this," cried Janelle as she pointed to the surrounding sand, glittering brightly. "Something tells me we're walking amongst the dead, and we're stealing from them!"

"Don't get hysterical," cautioned Phillip. "There's a logical explanation for it all."

"Are you trying to say I shouldn't be concerned about our daughter finding hundreds of teeth with gold fillings?"

"I'll admit it's strange, but they're here, and there's nothing else we can do but pick them up."

"Not me!" Janelle protested.

"Well, if we don't, someone else will," replied Phillip in an effort to get her to cooperate.

"Never!" she replied, resisting vigorously.

"That's funny," Phillip countered after recalling something. "If I remember correctly, didn't I hear you say that, if we find gold, it would be providential?"

"I'm sorry I said that!" Janelle admitted as she turned and walked away.

"All right! Go! Leave us! Me and Tanya, we'll pick'em up if you won't, won't we, Tanya?" said Phillip, addressing his puzzled daughter who still thought she had found the tooth fairy's cache.

"No, she won't!" Janelle responded angrily, stopping in her tracks. She stomped back, then grabbed Tanya's hand and dragged her back to the shade of their beach umbrella.

"Women!" Phillip muttered to himself as he walked unhappily to the place where Tanya had found the teeth and coins. "Just because there's a few teeth scattered around the place, irrespective of their value and everything else, they're ready to pass up a fortune! How ridiculous!"

Upon studying the site, Phillip knew he was going to experience difficulty in retrieving the teeth and coins and was grateful he had bought the metal detector. The problem was the incoming waves. Their rushing in and out were burying—and unburying—coins and teeth, making a complicated recovery. In time, if not retrieved quickly, all would sink deeper and no longer be seen.

He picked up several coins and studied their markings. They were minted in many countries and most carried dates back to the late 1700s. He couldn't believe his eyes and wondered what it all meant—the finding of the treasure—and where it all came from? *If it didn't come from some sunken galley,* he thought, *then it could only have come from one other place—the inside of the torpedo! Unless there's some other explanation?*

He didn't dwell on it long because the gleaming sands reminded him of a job which needed to be completed, retrieval of every piece of gold he could find, and the only way to do that was to use his metal detector. With that, he ran back to the place where he had left it, gathered some containers, then returned to the beach. Moments later, his machine was buzzing incessantly.

For a long time, Janelle refused to help, believing she was right that the treasure was tainted, though deep in her heart she hoped Phillip was right about the gold-looking objects possibly coming from a pirate ship. As to the presence of the teeth, that was another story.

Its answer eluded her, causing a gnawing within her that something was wrong.

However, after watching her husband working so hard under the broiling sun, she felt guilty not helping him, so she relented and decided to lend a hand. With Tanya in tow, they returned to the beach and pitched in by filling containers he had brought, most of which were emptied into the bottom of the Zodiac because he didn't have enough containers to hold what he was finding. The remaining they buried until they could return after learning more about what they had found.

"I'm glad you changed your mind," Phillip remarked.

"Well, I had some time to think," said Janelle, referring to the origin of the coins, teeth, and gold watch. "Maybe you're right about taking it before others do. Anyway, I hope you're right."

"It's a chance we've got to take," replied Phillip after stopping to wipe the sweat from his face.

"You are going to inform the authorities, aren't you?"

"Hell no!" came Phillip's quick reply. "We're the ones who found it! Not them! If we tell them anything, the first thing they'll do is to confiscate everything!"

"Didn't they say what we find is ours?" she asked.

"I think we got a qualified guess," replied Phillip. "Until we know otherwise, I want to keep this between us. Like the California gold rush, we want to avoid claim jumpers."

It sounded reasonable to Janelle, so she went back to her work. However, when coming across large pockets of gold-filled teeth, she'd refused to touch them, leaving those for her husband. While performing her tasks, she thought about the previous day's activities, especially about the explosion which followed the detonation of the torpedo. It wasn't as big or as awesome has she had expected. The navy lieutenant had said it would be huge, providing its warhead hadn't been ruined through corrosion or decomposition.

As she walked alongside her husband, helping him carry one of several containers to their rubber boat, a load which he said would be their last, she decided to ask him a bothersome question.

"When are we going back?" she asked.

"Why?"

"Because I don't feel comfortable here anymore," she replied.

"But it's beautiful, peaceful, and isolated . . . like we wanted," countered Phillip.

"Just the same," insisted Janelle, "I think we need to go. Before anything else happens."

"All right, we'll go," Phillip agreed without argument, "providing wind conditions and the weather as a whole are okay. Will tomorrow morning be okay? It's too late now," he added while pointing to the darkening sky.

As a seasoned sailor, too, Janelle knew he was right and conceded to his suggestion. That wasn't so for their daughter.

"I don't want to go," said Tanya after overhearing part of their conversation. "I like it here, and besides, there's lots and lots of things to find."

"Sorry, but we have to go, honey," replied Phillip. "But there are other places just as nice as this—and even better," he said to reassure her.

At first, the Northams thought she was going to cry and have a temper tantrum, but it didn't happen. To their mutual surprise, her whole reason for wanting to stay was her desire to keep some of things she had found.

"So long as they're not gold teeth and the metal pieces," replied her father, "because we don't want anyone to know anything about what we found."

"They're only shells. See!" said Tanya with a big smile on her face. While her parents looked on, she pushed her sand pail into their faces. What she didn't say was that she had hidden something at the bottom.

"Good," said her father after a quick inspection.

By eight the following morning and within two hours of waking and enjoying a wholesome breakfast, the Northams were ready for departure. Their destination: Hog Sty Bay, Grand Cayman Island.

As Phillip winched in the stern anchor, Janelle waited for his signal to winch in the one off the bow. Neither one of them was easy to remove because they had gotten hung up on some coral. After some backward and forward movement of the boat through use of its inboard engine, the anchors finally broke loose, and the yacht moved freely first into crystal light-blue waters, then into dark water, an indication of the growing depth. At the proper time, the sails were raised high into the bright blue sky overhead, where puffs of white clouds floated lazily, and the yacht continued its course for Grand Cayman.

On board the vessel after the basics were done, Phillip took a moment from his chores at the helm to finger the small metal chip he saved—the one with the letters *RB* on it. It had become his lucky piece and he didn't want to part with it, though he knew he would have to show it to someone in George Town to learn more about it and to verify its authenticity. What he didn't know was that on the deck below, Tanya had similar plans for the roundish gold object bearing odd symbols she had found earlier. With great care she wrapped it in a piece of tissue paper, then stuffed it under her mattress for safekeeping.

On deck, her father beamed with delight as he guided the *Lucky Streak*, a most propitious name, out to sea again. His thoughts were on one subject: Gold!

Chapter 20

The Watchmaker

George Town—1990

he *Lucky Streak*, her sails full of the prevailing wind, reached her destination in record time, a fact which surprised even its owners. Before entering Hog Sty harbor, Phillip had lowered the vessel's sails automatically, then started its small diesel engine. He engaged its single propeller after Janelle assured him all sails and lines had been secured. After that, he guided the sleek vessel into the tranquil harbor to its preassigned mooring buoy.

Their return went almost unnoticed. The arrival of a Norwegian luxury liner had upstaged their entry by an hour; it was anchored offshore, busily engaged in ferrying its tourist passengers for a shopping and sightseeing tour in George Town. There anxious vendors and cabbies wasted no time hawking their wares and services.

"It's the same everywhere," Phillip remarked when he noticed the fanfare.

Janelle watched for a while too, but quickly went back to her own

At a watch repair shop in George Town

chores—primping—in anticipation of their own trip to shore. They would go there an hour later, lost in a crowd of excited visitors, some of whom had also arrived by plane.

It took the better part of another hour before Phillip found what he was looking for, a small watch repair shop. It was located across the street from the public park next to the town square. It wasn't a fancy place like many of the nearby shops, but it was centrally located.

After peering through the plate-glass window, Phillip decided they should go in. He could see a man, his back hunched over a desk on the other side of a counter. A tiny bell sounded as the Northams walked in, causing the frail old man to look up.

"Do you repair watches? Antiques?" asked Phillip.

"Yes," answered the old man in a foreign accent. "Most of them, *anyvay*," he added while pushing his spectacle-mounted magnifying glass out of the way to more appropriately address his customer. "Do you have it *mit* you?"

"Here," said Phillip as he reached into a small hand bag Janelle had been caring, to withdraw the watch he had found the day before. It was now carefully packed in a new box.

With great care, Phillip opened the box and gently removed it. He held it before the watchmaker to remove, then watched as the man carefully withdrew it.

"My," the man remarked softly. "It most certainly is old. I haven't seen *von* like *zees* before."

"Really?"

"Oh—yes," the man repeated quickly. "*Zat* is *zo*," he added while continuing to finger the watch before opening it.

"You speak with an accent. Is it German?"

"*Jah,*" the old man answered almost as if he were reluctant to say so.

"Oh, I thought so," replied Phillip, hoping to strike a friendly relationship. The man's failure to say more, however, was inducement enough for him not to press the subject, especially when he spotted a series of numbers tattooed on his forearm.

The old man seemed awfully slow, thought Phillip, as he and Janelle watched his movements. They attributed some of it to his advanced age, the rest of it to the thoroughness with which he examined the watch.

"Have you had *zees* long?" the old man asked as he removed the back cover.

"A little while," replied Phillip.

"*Wunderbar*! Beautiful!" the old man gasped as he studied the complex works. "Such a movement—*wiz* so many jewels."

"It is, isn't it?" agreed Phillip as if he knew beforehand.

"Where did you get *zees*?" the man asked again in a manner designed not to minimize his true interest.

"I found it on the other side of the island while using my metal detector. It was buried in the sand," lied Phillip.

"*Mein Gott!*" exclaimed the man. "On zees island? You are most fortunate because it is very valuable!"

"Like how much?" asked Janelle, now fully alert.

"*Zat* I cannot *zay*," the watchmaker replied, "but I know it is worth much money."

"Will it take long to fix it?" asked Phillip.

"A day at *zee* most," the old man replied as he put his magnifying glass to his face and peered down into the fine works. "A spring has come loose, and with a little cleaning and oil, it will be as *gut* as new."

"Should we leave it?" Phillip asked Janelle.

"I don't know. You think it'll be safe here?"

She looked at the old man, not certain what to do.

"You found it here—on Grand Cayman Island?" the watchmaker addressed Phillip again.

"Just like I said," answered Phillip.

"There have been many valuable things found on this island, but never before anything like this, I can assure you," said the watchmaker. "*Vas* it near?"

A worried look crossed Phillip face, much like the one on Janelle's. He wasn't sure he should answer, but since he had said he found it on the island, wisdom seemed to dictate an answer of some sort.

"Yeh, at Gun Bay," he finally replied, the beginning of a fabricated story he was now bound to follow. "I just thought I'd try my luck with my metal detector, and then I heard this loud buzz. . . ."

"I *vouldn't* tell anyone where," the old man cautioned. "There might be more treasure, and it'd be all yours . . . so long as it's on the land."

The man's reassuring comments prompted the Northams to rethink his offer to repair the watch. After all, he looked like a legitimate businessman, and he most certainly didn't have anything to gain by cheating them.

"How long will it take to get it in good shape again?" asked Phillip.

"If you leave it now, I can have it ready for you by tomorrow afternoon," the old man replied as he snapped the cover shut and handed the watch back to Phillip in case he decided to keep it.

"Shall we?" asked Phillip.

"I don't see any reason not to," Janelle answered while anxiously peering through the shop's plate-glass window to keep a watchful eye on Tanya who had gone across the street to play in the park.

"Okay, she's yours—to fix, that is!" said Phillip as he handed the watch back to the man.

With tortoise-like movements, the old man searched through a pile of papers near him. With some difficulty, he finally found what he was looking for, a small carbon-backed receipt book. In the same way he examined the watch, he filled out the form, adding particulars about the watch. He signed it, then tore the original off the pad and handed it to Phillip.

"For your protection," he said. "Be sure to bring it with you when you return. I wouldn't *vant* someone else to claim it. It's too valuable—physically and historically."

"Oh?" said the Northams almost simultaneously.

"Historically! In what way?" asked Janelle.

"Madame," the gentle old man replied as he peered over his half-moon glasses directly into her eyes. "One needs only to look at the inscription on the inside cover, and to whom it was presented to know it is an antique of immense value. And besides, it is made of solid gold and precious stones."

He didn't say anything after that; he didn't have to. The Northams' thoughts were racing wildly, again causing them to reconsider leaving the watch in a stranger's hand.

"Are you insured?" Phillip ask.

"Yes, sir. Up to a million dollars, U.S.," the old man responded. "But you need have no fear; we have no robberies here. And besides," he added while pointing to a large steel safe near his desk, "I lock up everything in there."

"What the earliest you can fix it?" Phillip asked again.

"Without complications, by two o'clock tomorrow afternoon. That's the best I can do."

Phillip thought for a while while looking at his wife. He whispered something in her ear and she responded with an affirmative nod.

"It's okay with us," Phillip replied. "We've still got a few errands to run anyhow, so we'll see you tomorrow afternoon."

With that, the old man tagged the watch, then set it in his open safe. He returned to shake their hands, a custom quite typical of Europeans.

"Good-bye. *Auf wedersehen*," said Phillip, proud to be able to demonstrate some knowledge of German.

"*Danke*.. Thank you, sir," the old man quickly responded, but without a great deal of enthusiasm when German was used.

Phillip linked the man's reticence to the tattoo on the inside part of his forearm. It was a mark of a barbaric past against his person, and for the sake of decency, Phillip felt it would be better to let the past alone. He walked out with Janelle to the park where Tanya was having a great time with some local children.

It was late morning when Hans Schumacher lifted his weary body from off his bed; he had overslept. With an angry grumble, he dragged himself into the living room and promptly picked up the phone. It was almost nine when he dialed.

"Chief Inspector Gilford, *bitte*—please," the old man said nervously while fingering a set of polaroid pictures he had taken after the Northams left. It was a precaution he always took when anything of value was left in his care, but he hadn't expected to take them home as he did until a question of the watch's origin triggered something in his mind.

After hours of research, Hans Schumacher, a former death camp inmate of Auschwitz, found what he was looking for. It was in a massive dust-covered book entitled *Stolen Nazi Treasures*, a publication compiled by the Allied War Crimes Commission shortly after completion of the Nuremberg trials of Nazi war criminals.

Needless to say, Hans was ecstatic over what he had found, but frightened at the same time. The watch—originally the property of the Soviet government—had been taken to Berlin after the siege of Leningrad, where it was deposited in the Reichbank for safekeeping. It disappeared after that—without a trace.

After thinking about the implication of his discovery for a while, Hans had come to the conclusion the chief needed to be notified. He didn't think the Northams had anything to fear but that they were merely innocent tourists who just happened to find the watch, a watch whose history they knew nothing about, much less its value. Otherwise, why did they dare take it to a watchmaker for repairs?

Calling Chief Inspector Gilford, an old friend, was Han's first thought, though he had considered calling Johann Liebermann, too, a long-time acquaintance who had settled in the Caymans about a year after his own arrival. Johann had been an inmate too, but in a different camp.

"He's not in, Mr. Schumacher," the chief inspector's secretary said sweetly after recognizing the caller.

"Oh, my," the weary man said. "Do you know when he *vill* be in?"

"I'm afraid not, sir," the lady replied. "To my knowledge, he's still sleeping. Was out most of the night . . . investigating a theft at one of the hotels. Shall I have him call you when he gets in?"

"*Jah, Jah,* with all urgency," Hans replied.

"Can anyone else help you?"

"No, thank you," the old man replied somewhat irritably, partly because he was exhausted and hot. The morning sun was bearing down on his poorly ventilated house, and his air conditioner was on the fritz, causing waves of sweat to pour down his forehead and body. He brushed some of it away with an equally sweaty hand. It didn't help much.

"If it's an emergency . . . ."

"No, it—can wait, but not too long. You *vill* tell the inspector it's a matter of utmost importance, *jah?*"

"Of course, Mr. Schumacher," the lady replied. "Where will you be?"

"At my shop—he knows the number."

"Very good, sir," the young lady replied. "I'll see that he gets your message."

With the call out of the way, the watchmaker left for his small shop. A number of customers had come and gone by the time he got there. Of those who remained behind, he saw to their needs immediately. There was a reason for this: He had decided to call his friend, Johann, to seek his advice, too. *After all,* he thought, *Johann's much more knowledgeable about such matters than me. And he'll be able to help me contact the Mossad,* to see if they're interested.*

When he was alone again, the watchmaker picked up his phone and dialed. A gruff voice answered.

"Johann, *meine freund,* it's me—Hans!" Hans said excitedly. "Can you come over . . . *schnell?* I have something to show and tell you. It is most important. More important than anything you can imagine!" He listened to what his friend had to say, expressing disappointment upon learning his friend could not come right then. So they agreed on a time.

After that, he put the phone down, then went over to his safe, where he removed the watch he had repaired the previous evening. He studied it for a while, then put it back in the safe when another customer walked in. After the customer left, his thoughts turned to his friend, the chief inspector. He should be calling momentarily. He looked up at a wall-mounted clock. It was just past noon.

Inspector Gilford rushed into his office at the police station

*Israels counter-intelligence agency

shortly after noon, a diet Coke in one hand and a sandwich in the other. He'd gotten both from vending machines in the hallway outside his office. As he entered, his secretary was quick to draw his attention to pressing business, the note being one of them.

"You need to call Mr. Schumacher."

"Oh?"

"He said it was urgent."

Gilford hurriedly munched the sandwich, then picked up the note. He sat down and studied it while taking occasional sips from the can before deciding to dial. A familiar voice answered.

"Hans, did you call?" asked the chief inspector.

"*Jah,*" replied Hans. "About two hours ago."

"I'm sorry about that, but I didn't get in until now. Suzie left me a note, however, saying it's urgent."

"*Jah,* it's a matter of grave importance, so important I must see you right *avay.*"

Inspector Gilford wavered when he heard that. He was already late for another appointment. "Can we talk about it over the phone, or can it wait?"

"*Nein!*" Schumacher replied instantly. In all the years the inspector had known the old man, he had never known the watchmaker to be so blunt. He was about to comment, but was stopped.

"*Eine moment*—one minute please, Peter," the old man interrupted. "Someone is coming in. I must see who it is before we can talk."

Inspector Gilford pulled his ear away from the phone when the old man unintentionally let his receiver fall heavily on his work bench. A few muffled voices could be heard, enough to tell him it was someone the old man knew. He heard other parts of the conversation after the watchmaker returned to the phone to continue his conversation. This part was clear: "I'm so glad you came. Come, wait, you'll never believe it! I've got the chief inspector on the line. You *vill* hear it all."

"You there, Peter?" the old man asked after retrieving the phone, breathless with excitement.

"I am. What's this all about?" the inspector asked.

"Stolen Nazi treasure! Here in the Caymans! And what's more, I have proof of it in my safe!" he said in an excited and quivering voice. "That's why you must come immediately!"

"Nazi treasure! You can't be serious," replied the chief inspector, doubting the man.

"Oh, but it's true!" the old man replied vigorously. "Come see, and I will prove it!"

A noisy shuffle was heard just then, followed by a loud horrifying cry: "Oh! *Mein Gott*! No! *Vat are you—*"

"Hans! Hans! What's the matter? What's going on?" yelled Gilford. He heard the cry, then a loud thud, and after that, silence, before the phone went dead. He redialed the number, but got a busy signal, then tried the operator, who confirmed there was trouble on the line.

"Suzie! Call my driver," Gilford called out, "and have him meet me at the front entrance. It's an emergency."

While the secretary scrambled to her desk, the chief inspector grabbed his holster and strapped it around his shoulders. As he raced out of the door, he grabbed a light tan jacket which he had hung on a coat rack minutes earlier. He bounded down the stairs of the two-story police station to the front of the building where his driver and police car were waiting.

The vehicle's siren wailed as they raced through the streets to the town square a short distance away. It took longer than expected to reach the shop because of all the tourists. He could have gotten there sooner had he elected to run.

When they got there, a crowd of people was milling around the shop, stretching their necks to see what they could. A lone policeman kept them from going further.

"Damn!" cried the inspector as he waved his driver to double-park so he could exit quickly. Other officers arrived on the scene about the same time. At his direction, they ordered the crowds to disperse. A few obeyed while the more nosey ones watched from behind a hastily erected barrier.

"Which one of you got here first?" Gilford asked several uniformed policemen, the ones who had preceded him.

"I did, sir," answered a tall black Caymanian officer. "Minutes before you arrived."

"How did you find out?"

"I heard a woman scream and ran over."

"And—?"

"She told me that she had just gone into Schumacher's watch repair shop to get a new band when she found him lying in a pool of blood."

"He's dead?" asked Gilford, not wanting to believe his ears.

"I'm afraid so, sir. His skull's crushed!" the officer replied. "When you go in, you'll see exactly what I mean. Nothing's been touched."

Gilford took a quick glance, but another thought struck him.

"That woman witness, where is she now?"

"Over there, sir," the officer pointed. "I told her to wait."

The inspector looked to where he pointed. An anxious middle-aged woman of mixed extraction was looking on.

"Hold her until I can question her. In the meantime, I'll take a look inside."

"Very good, sir. Shall I accompany you?"

"No. Just keep the place clear of busybodies."

He turned and walked in just then, hoping he wouldn't find what he expected. It wasn't likely. On the floor between his work bench and open safe, lay the lifeless form of the old man, lying in a pool of coagulated blood. The inspector could not help but cringe at the sight. Hans' last words and death cry echoed painfully in his ears.

As the chief inspector surveyed the room, mixed feelings flowed through his mind—pity, but also anger and revulsion. The crime seemed senseless. What could have been so important that it justified the taking of a human life? It didn't make sense.

With great care, he stooped down to study the victim. Near the man's head, he found a large metallic statue; its base was covered with blood and strands of hair. *The murder weapon,* he thought. Upon further study, he saw where the blood came from, a huge laceration and depression on the side of the old man's skull, slightly above the right ear. Then again, another thought: *Crushing blow to the head caused by a blunt instrument. That's what the coroner's report will say.* It was almost cynical, but he didn't mean it that way. He was merely remembering how homicide reports treated victims—more like inanimate objects than human beings! Disgusting!

As the inspector's thoughts were gearing up, his driver ran in, interrupting them.

"Anything I can do to help, sir?"

The inspector looked up for a moment before answering.

"Yes, call the coroner—and notify homicide. Tell them to get here quickly . . . while everything is fresh. Might find some prints."

"Yes, sir," the driver replied. He looked for the phone, but found it had been pulled from the wall.

"Did you see this, sir?"

"Yes," replied the inspector. "Whoever did this tore it out, so use the car radio."

As the man raced out, Gilford continued his search. Outside of the dead man, the blood-tainted statue, and the blood-soaked floor near the desk, everything else seemed to be in order. Disorder was the more appropriate term for the old man's housekeeping efforts, but that was normal.

One thing caught his eye just then. The back door some thirty feet away was partially open and a narrow stream of light was filtering through.

"Sergeant, come here," the inspector called to the first officer on the scene. He had entered on the heels of his driver, observing in silence.

"Sir," replied the man as he rushed forward.

"That door back there, did you open it?"

The officer looked before replying. "No, sir. As I said earlier, I arrived only minutes before you. All I got to see was old Schumacher lying here on the floor."

"Well, it's open."

Both men, with the inspector leading, walked cautiously toward the back door with their pistols drawn. They were careful to observe everything, yet disturb nothing. To get to the rear door, they had to squeeze through a long narrow aisle littered with boxes of what looked like ordinary junk. Often they would have to grab hold of shelving as they stumbled over unseen objects. When they reached the back door, they found it slightly ajar and no one around. A lock used to secure it was found hanging on its clasp, indicating someone had unlocked it to get out, or let someone in. What really happened had yet to be determined.

"When the homicide team gets here," ordered the inspector as he and the officer reholstered their weapons, "make sure they dust everything, including the cabinets we just touched. Whoever it was could have left some prints."

"I will, sir," the officer replied.

He didn't have to relay the message. Just as they were returning to the front, members of the homicide team entered. The coroner was with them.

When the police photographer finished taking his shots, it came time for the coroner to examine the body. Besides the skull-crushing wound, it didn't take him long to find the tattoo. He drew the inspector's attention to it.

"I know all about it," Gilford said sadly. "It's exactly what you think it is. Ironic, isn't it? He escaped the death camps only to come here to meet his end."

"Inspector," interrupted an officer. "the director of tourism and members of the council are waiting outside. They want to know if you can spare a moment to talk with them."

"Oh, all right," the inspector fussed as he wiped his hands clean

251

with a handkerchief he always carried in his back pocket. Without saying anything else, he headed for the front door where he was met by the nervous delegation.

"Gentlemen," he said, "you wanted to see me?"

The director of tourism was the first to speak. "Is it true?" he asked with a nervous twitch disturbing the contours of his face.

"Depends upon what you've heard?" Gilford replied.

"That the old man has been murdered?"

"It's true all right. A person, or persons, unknown did him in. And that's all we know at this time."

"Oh, how terrible!" one of the island's councilmen exclaimed, a sentiment quickly voiced by other members of the fold. Something else was on his mind, however. He expressed it plainly, "You know, this could hurt tourism!"

"We've got to squelch this thing right away," said another official, expressing his concerns. "If we don't, our economic base could be seriously affected!"

"What are you going to do about it, Inspector?" asked a member of the Legislative Assembly, worry clearly on his face.

Chief Inspector Gilford knew the man and why he was so concerned. It had to do with next year's elections and how the people would vote if this case wasn't solved to their satisfaction.

"I'm not a Sherlock Holmes," Gilford shot back, almost angrily. "Give me time! I just got here, and the crime is only minutes old!"

"He's right," interrupted the director of tourism after sensing their approach had been premature and lacked sensitivity. He turned back to Gilford after that. "You do understand the problem, don't you? All we're asking is that you keep us abreast of your progress. The crime— if that's what it is—must be put behind us as soon as possible. And, of course, we will need to inform the governor general—as a matter of courtesy, naturally."

"I understand and can appreciate your concern," acknowledged Gilford. "I'll let you know as soon as I can."

"The one thing we don't need, to put it succinctly," admitted the director of tourism, "is bad publicity, so please do keep that in mind. It's bad for business."

"No need to concern yourselves, gentlemen. We're right on top of everything, and we have some clues to go on. We'll need more time to check them out, however."

"Anything you can share with us?" the legislative councilman asked, hoping to pry something loose.

"No, sir, it's much too soon for that. And in fact, some of it is quite bizarre, so it's better we say nothing at this time."

His comments seemed to satisfy them, and they departed. With them out of the way, he walked back to the storefront to give last-minute instructions before interviewing the woman who had discovered the crime. As they spoke, a couple with a child approached the barrier in time to see ambulance personnel loading a sheet-covered body into their vehicle.

While Janelle and Tanya looked on, Phillip asked a nearby spectator, "What's going on?"

"A man died," he replied.

"Heart attack?" ventured Phillip.

"Would have been better for the island had that been the case," another spectator interjected after overhearing the conversation.

"What do you mean?" asked Phillip.

"It's shameful! The poor fellow was murdered!" the well-informed spectator added. "That's what one of the policemen told me."

"You're not talking about the watchmaker, are you?" asked Janelle.

"Yes, ma'am, that's the one," he replied. "I can't believe it. He was liked by everybody."

"Oh, my God!" Janelle cried as she looked in her husband's direction.

Phillip took longer to react; his mind was asking many questions. Besides concern and sorrow for the old man, he was worried about the watch they had left. "Was it robbery?" he asked.

"Not from what I've heard," the spectator replied. "According to the police, nothing seems to have been taken. The cash register hadn't been touched at all. It still had money in it."

"I need to talk to somebody," Phillip told the man. "It's about something we left in his shop yesterday. Can you direct us to someone?"

The man pointed to a middle-aged Caymanian man holding a light tan jacket over one shoulder. He was a handsome figure of a man, noted Janelle, tall, of mixed African-Caucasian descent, about thirty-eight, and he most certainly was in command of the situation, judging by the way others responded to his commands. Phillip tried to cross the barrier.

"I'm sorry, sir," said a most courteous black police officer in impeccable English. "You can't come in just now. This is a restricted area for the time being."

"I don't want to go in," replied Phillip, "but I do need to see that man." He pointed.

"Chief Inspector Gilford?" the officer asked after noting to whom he was pointing.

"Yes, that's him."

"He's busy now," the officer replied. "If it has something to do with the investigation, I could deliver a message to him."

"I don't know about the investigation, but I must talk to him about something else. About something I left there yesterday. It could have been stolen."

The officer thought for a moment, thinking at first he wouldn't bother. His police training intervened. On second thought, he decided the smallest clue might possibly come from an inconsequential source—a tourist!

"I'll see if he'll speak to you," the officer said politely, before walking toward his superior. He waited until the inspector turned to him.

A brief conversation followed with the inspector looking in Northams direction. Phillip motioned he needed to see the man by putting his hand in a prayerful position—clasped—in front of his chest. His request was acknowledged when the inspector motioned him through.

"Thank you for seeing us," Phillip said after introducing himself and his family with a cordial handshake.

At first, the inspector seemed irritated at being bothered. His disposition changed when he observed the man's beautiful blond wife. There was no doubt in his mind she was a beauty beyond anyone he had seen on the island—his wife included. When his eyes fell on the pretty little girl holding her hand, his thoughts returned to normal.

"What can I do for you, Mr. Northam? As you can see, I'm quite busy."

"It's about our watch . . . the one we left yesterday . . . with the watchmaker," Janelle replied first in a sweet voice.

Gilford smiled. He liked her right away. *Oh, heck,* he thought, *what's a few more minutes, even if it does delay the investigation?*

"If you left it with the watchmaker, you're just going to have to wait," he said. "There's nothing we can do until the investigation is over."

"But—" Phillip protested. "If the old man was murdered, as everyone is saying, someone could have stolen it."

The chief inspector smiled. "Not likely, sir. From what we've determined so far, robbery wasn't the motive since nothing seems to be missing. We won't know that for certain, however, until an inventory has been taken."

"God!" Phillip protested. "That could take weeks, and we haven't got that kind of time to play with!"

"That's not true, Phillip," countered Janelle as she tried to hang on to Tanya's hand. Tanya had spied some of her friends from the previous day and was anxious to join them. "Not now, Tanya!" Janelle scolded. "We've got other things to do."

"Well, several weeks anyway," Phillip conceded, somewhat embarrassed at having been contradicted.

Sensing a need to pacify the tourists before him, Gilford decided to accommodate the Northams, Phillip especially. He pulled out a pad and pen. "If you'll be so kind as to give me full particulars, I'll have my men make a special search."

"Oh—you're so kind," Janelle cooed. It was an offer equally appreciated by Phillip, who wasted no time giving his boat's name, berth number, and a better-than-average description of the watch they had left.

"Sounds like a valuable antique to me," Gilford said, not knowing he was hitting at a truth the Northams were hoping to conceal.

"Yes. It had been willed to me by Aunt Martha. That's why it's so important. An heirloom, you understand," Phillip lied without a trace of deceit. Though shocked by his outright lie, Janelle managed to hold her tongue. She didn't know why, but she knew she was going to find out!

"Well, we'll do everything in our power to find it for you. Do you have a receipt?"

Phillip reached into his back pocket and withdrew his wallet. After a brief search, he withdrew the receipt the watchmaker had given him and handed it to the man.

"Here," said the inspector after scribbling something on a sheet he tore from his pad.

"What this?" asked Phillip.

"A receipt."

"Oh!" replied Phillip, now fully relieved.

"Call me in a day or so," the inspector added as he handed Phillip one of his cards. "By then, we should have located it."

With that he offered his hand, first to Phillip, then to his wife, and last of all, to their young daughter. "Pretty girl. Wish she were mine," he said before turning to walk back into the shop to confer with his associates.

"Such manners," teased Janelle, drawing her husband's ire.

"Don't rub it in," argued Phillip. "Let's see if he's as good as he looks."

They walked back to the barricade, crossed over the banner lowered by the police officer, then went on their way, hoping to shop as they had planned.

"He'll find it, I'll bet," Janelle said, hoping to get in the last word. Phillip's reaction was simple. "We'll see!" he said.

"And oh, by the way," said Janelle, recalling something. "Why did you mislead to him?"

"Do you want everybody to know where the watch came from?" whispered Phillip. "For the moment, it's none of their business."

"I hope you know what you're doing," challenged Janelle without saying more. Wares in store windows distracted her, but only for a moment; she couldn't shake what had just happened.

Phillip became quiet, too. Hand in hand with Tanya dancing along the way, they walked back to the bay with the intention of remaining on board their yacht for the balance of the day. The idea was good, but it didn't last long. Phillip had a better idea.

"Let's go to the other side . . . to get away from it all," he said after a long silence.

Janelle's face lit up, as did Tanya's. It was a good idea. Their gait picked up, and soon they were on the boat heading for Gun Bay!

Chapter 21

Scotland Yard

Gun Bay—A Week Later

ear an isolated beach halfway around the east end of the island, ship skeletons—rusting hulks of what had once been ocean-going vessels—dotted reefs which not only surrounded them, but refused to let them go, much like a protective parent intent on discouraging unacceptable suitors.

In a sense, that was the way it was for the Northams as they tried to enter the narrow but treacherous opening through the east end channel off the beach. From Hog Sty Bay, the trip to the opening took them the better part of an hour because shoals and other obstacles posed a number of frightening difficulties.

The *Lucky Streak*, with her keel fully withdrawn to permit a safe transit and powered by the diesel auxiliary instead of sails, didn't come through unscathed because the vessel's depth gauge was giving inaccurate readings. As a consequence, a number of large gouges were left in its fiberglass hull.

She got through finally, but not without injury to her owners pride also! While searching for a safe haven, they sulked over the damage, Phillip more than Janelle. He had only come to build an alibi not to harm his new pride and joy.

Janelle had argued against building an alibi for as long as she could, using the premise that the "building of one falsehood upon another could only lead to disaster," but her words found no acceptance in Phillip's ears. He was adamant about carrying out what he considered to be a minor—and not harmful—subterfuge so as quickly as he could, he put his plan into action, starting with the moment they laid their things beneath a row of coconut palms lining the beach they had selected.

It started with the metal detector, followed by the digging of numerous holes in the sand, then scuba and snorkel diving in the deeper part of the channel, which gave passersby—tourists and locals alike—the impression that someone was intent on finding treasure, artifacts, or both! Naturally, that's what Phillip wanted—a front of credibility, so when a district police officer stopped by one day on a friendly visit, that's the impression he got. He went away chuckling to himself, thinking he had seen it all.

The facade had side benefits for others. On the second day, while Phillip was out in the bay diving, Janelle and Tanya decided to do a little exploring on their own. Using Phillip's metal detector, they scoured the sand, striking pay dirt—so to speak—when it gave off high-pitched squeals. They squealed, too, over having found something. While it wasn't gold or anything of value, but just finding something made them feel good. Success inspired them to continue. An old axe, minus its handle, some modern-day coins, bottle caps, earrings, plus a ring of questionable worth were among the items recovered.

For a while, Tanya participated in the searches but later decided to collect shells from among submerged rocks in the shallow sections of the secluded bay. Seashells fascinated her inquiring mind; she could spend hours doing nothing else. Later, she was to learn the hard way that the animal within each shell needed to be removed, or they would leave a horrible stench after they died. The odor was so bad, that for hours after removal of the shells from her bunk, no one could enter the cabin until it had been properly ventilated. That's when Tanya decided to collect only dry, empty shells like the ones lying all over the beach.

As the days passed, Phillip decided he would turn a facade into something worthwhile. Every other day for almost a week, he alternated between using his scuba gear and snorkel. With the scuba gear, he would search the bottom for signs of metal, just in case something was there. With his snorkel and fins, he would free-dive to harpoon fish or catch lobsters with a gloved hand. His catches were all large and plentiful. What he didn't like were the eels; they would pop out of their holes unexpectedly. Caught off-guard, he would shoot to the surface, though he knew never to do such a thing, from a deep dive especially.

Janelle worried when he was out diving alone because there was no way for her to help him if he got into trouble, but he insisted he knew what he was doing and dived anyway. It was that way everyday, and today was no different except she was getting upset because it was noontime and he promised he would return in time to eat lunch.

As she always did, Janelle ran to the water's edge to see if she could see him and get his attention. Fortunately, he had just emerged from a dive and was climbing into the Zodiac. She waved frantically while trying to call over the noise of the surface, but to no avail. Phillip had his back to her and was busy tuning his portable radio to the local station. A familiar piece was just finishing when the announcer broke in.

"We interrupt this program to bring you this special announcement: The murder of well-known watchmaker Hans Schumacher, who came to our lovely island some forty years ago, has police baffled. This, according to Chief Inspector Peter Gilford of the George Town Criminal Investigation Division. In an exclusive and candid interview this morning, he said the police have ruled out robbery since nothing seems to be missing other than an old watch of questionable value which had been left by a tourist for repairs.

"According to the inspector, the watch, in and of itself, may or may not have any connection to the case, but they are looking into the matter just in case there is some remote possibility. When asked about possible clues or leads, the inspector indicated they had a few, but declined to say what specifically. He did say, however, that officials at Scotland Yard had been contacted for assistance.

"When queried as to what—if anything—would be his next step and what—if anything— could we, the general public, do to help solve this terrible crime, the inspector had this to say: 'Our first step is to find the motive. Rarely, if ever, is a crime committed without one. Once that's been determined, our job becomes easier though it may take a considerable amount of time and effort to put the pieces together, but we will persist until we've apprehended the person— or persons—responsible for this senseless crime. As to your second question, concerning citizen participation, I would answer in this way: A criminal is not always the sole source of information. Often times, innocent people inadvertently gain access to information. It is to these people, then, that I direct my message. Specifically, if there is anyone listening in today who fits this description, I urge them to call my office immediately and ask for me. All contacts will be kept strictly confidential.'

"Well, folks," said the announcer, "you heard the inspector, so if this fits any of you, here is your chance to do something good. Remember, everything will be handled with the strictest of confidentiality." He concluded his message by saying, "We now return to our regularly scheduled program."

"That's got to be mine!" Phillip exclaimed as he snapped off the radio. "Of questionable value, hummph! That's not what the old man indicated! Wait till I get hold of that inspector. I'll tell him a thing or two," he muttered before having second thoughts. "On the other hand, it'd blow my cover, and I can't do that! Not now anyway."

In his excitement, he stood up and nearly toppled out of the Zodiac; its pliable rubber bottom wasn't built for that. He knew better, but other things had suddenly clouded his mind, in particular, Janelle's warning which he chose to ignore because he felt he had the answer to her misgiving about how to handle the watch problem.

He looked to shore then, knowing he needed to tell her the news. That's when he spotted her, waving frantically, not because of the special news report, but because of lunch. Fear gripped him. As a marital pact, a treat, he had promised her faithfully, as long as he was around, the family would eat together for the sake of unity and peace. After all, she was the one who always prepared the meals, and if there was anything she hated, it was a hot meal turning into a cold one for the lack of someone to eat what she had labored so hard to prepare. But now the treaty had been violated!

He waved back, acknowledging he had seen her, then quickly started the Zodiac's outboard before raising its anchor. As he motored toward shore, his mind also searched for answers to the watch dilemma. *What do I do next?* he asked himself. *If I approach the inspector and tell him I hadn't told him all there was to know, what excuse could I use for telling him such a deceitful tale?* Phillip knew then that he shouldn't have changed his story from the one he had given the watchmaker earlier, even though it was not correct either. But having regret over something that old was too late. *On the other hand,* he thought, *maybe it's not my watch. In that case, I could be worrying about nothing! And for all I know, it could be someone else's watch! But then again . . . ?*

The more he tried to figure things out, the more confused he became. That's when his eyes shifted to the shore and he became conscious of the gnawing feeling in his stomach. It growled unbelievably like his wife as he jumped from the boat to the shore and to her side. Like an old trooper, he took his well-deserved lumps and apologized, swearing to be more attentive in the future. Then he quickly informed Janelle about the special news bulletin.

"So? What do we do now?" she asked as they walked to the picnic table, where lunch was ready. Tanya was already there, munching away.

"Call the inspector I guess . . . in case the missing watch turns out to be ours," he replied.

"Anything else?" she pressed.

"Like what?"

"Telling the whole truth and nothing but the truth," she said, making it quite clear by her inference he should avoid more plots.

"To some degree, but—" he added, reluctantly. "I have no choice but to stick with the story I told him earlier about inheriting it from my widowed aunt, but I won't tell where it really came from. He doesn't have to know that."

"I won't go with you unless you agree to tell the inspector the truth," replied Janelle.

"You think I'm crazy?" Phillip answered.

"It'll only come back to haunt you if you don't!" Janelle insisted.

"That's not the way I see it!" Phillip countered. "What's ours is ours! And you know perfectly well we don't have to tell anybody anything."

"I don't know anything about that," replied Janelle, finally giving in, "so don't blame me when all your best laid plans fall apart."

A victorious smile crossed Phillip's face. He felt certain he was right in protecting their secret. *After all, it was for their own good,* he thought.

Minutes later, after considering their options, they were back on the *Lucky Streak.* After hoisting her anchors while engaging her inboard engine to propel her slowly through the difficult channel and back into the open sea, where sails were again unfurled, they set her course for George Town.

Soon, the vessel with the Zodiac trailing behind it were nothing more than specks on the horizon. If everything went well and the winds were with them, the Northams would arrive in Hog Sty Bay in an hour and a half. Irrespective of weather, Phillip was bound and determined to reach his destination as planned even if he had to fire up the diesel to get there. If that failed, he felt determined enough to get out and kick.

Hog Sty Bay, George Town

He was lucky! George Town came into view as expected. By ship-to-shore, radio contact was made with port authorities, who cleared them directly to their mooring buoy. An hour or so later, the Zodiac raced to shore, carrying Phillip and his family and a number of suitcases. Once there he wasted no time getting to a pay phone where he promptly deposited some coins, then dialed the Holiday Inn reservation desk. Only one other call would have to be after that, and that was to the police station.

While waiting for his call to go through, Phillip noticed Crazy Joe sitting on a bench at the end of the dock, sipping a bottle of beer. His disarming, toothy-white, "Welcome back" grin covered his face. Phillip was glad to see him.

"Get a taxi, Joe," he called over, just as a woman's voice answered his call. In a flash, Crazy Joe was gone, allowing Phillip to make his reservations. When that was over, he dialed his second number.

"Criminal Investigation Division," a woman answered. She put him on hold after he announced he had to speak to Chief Inspector Gilford and that the subject matter was quite urgent.

"Chief Inspector Gilford," came a prompt reply on the other end.

"Inspector Gilford, this is Phillip Northam. I hope you remember me, sir?"

"Oh, yes," the inspector replied. "I'm so glad you called, Mr. Northam, because we've been trying to find you for days. Even tried our port authorities, but they said you had gone sailing around the islands somewhere and you were out of range of their radio."

"Sorry if we've caused you any inconvenience, Inspector," replied Phillip, "but we wanted to do some treasure hunting, and that's what we did. We just got back."

"No harm done," replied the inspector, continuing. "By chance have you been listening to Radio Cayman—to the news?"

"About your investigation—and the missing watch?" questioned Phillip.

"That's the one," replied the inspector, pleased that he had.

"Have you found our watch?" asked Phillip cautiously.

"Not quite, but that's what I wanted to talk to you about," replied the inspector. "While we haven't found it physically, so to speak, we

262

have found something else. It's a series of polaroid photographs of a watch resembling the one listed on the receipt you left with me last week. We'll need you to confirm whether they are one and the same. Can you come by?"

"Photos? We didn't take any photos!" said Phillip.

"They were taken by the watchmaker," the inspector corrected. "It was something he always did when anything of value was entrusted to his care. I know this because he was a friend of mine and he once told me about his procedure."

"Oh! I see," Phillip replied.

"Well? Can you come over?" the inspector asked.

Phillip's heart jumped. He was worried now. Not because the inspector considered him a suspect, but because he feared the consequences of the lie he had built. Once again his wife's words rang prophetically. "Women's intuition," he said aloud, forgetting himself.

"What did you say?" asked the inspector, overhearing his comment.

"Oh! Nothing," Phillip replied quickly. "I was just thinking aloud. But now, as to your question. Yes, we will be able to come by, but not today because we're moving into the Holiday Inn just now to get away from the boat for a while. We expect to remain a week at least."

"When can you come?" asked the inspector.

"Would it be all right if we stopped by in the morning?"

"Fine with me, providing it's not too early," replied the inspector. "For me the best time would be around 9 a.m. after I've gotten routine things out of the way."

"Nine it is," Phillip replied happily. He needed more time to perfect his next story.

"And, oh, by the way," interjected the inspector before cutting off, "thank you for calling."

"You're entirely welcome, sir," said Phillip as he returned the phone to its hook with a feeling of uneasiness. It was much like what Janelle had been feeling, and he didn't like it because it raised questions. For example: Was the watch which had been stolen really theirs? If it was, why in the world would anyone want to kill for it?

"Taxi ready, boss!" cried Crazy Joe from the dock's edge while motioning to the upper street where his taxi driver associate was anxiously waiting.

The Northams raced over, then vanished in the milieu of taxis, all busily going in different directions. The motel was located along

Seven Mile Beach not too far away and they were anxious to get a good night's rest.

Holiday Inn, Seven Mile Beach—Next Day

Janelle was apprehensive even though she had slept comfortably. Breakfast in bed added to her comfort, but it didn't quell her mounting fears over the upcoming visit to the police station, in particular, those caused by her husband's bulldog insistence to tell an untruth.

It wasn't that Phillip was greedy or that their family was in need. To the contrary, they were well-off, comparatively speaking. Both worked and had accumulated a nice nest egg over the years, so it wasn't that. The cause, as she saw it, centered around personal loans made to friends, relatives, and some associates, most of whom defaulted, leaving him to bear the losses. With that went old friendships and relationships, and those losses left their marks. Yet, despite it all, Phillip was generous to a fault. He continued to tithe and contribute to his favorite charities and other worthwhile activities.

The watch was discussed heatedly, and at length, in Tanya's presence. It couldn't be helped, so when she attempted to get involved by supporting her mother's position, she was bluntly told by her father to stay out of it. She almost cried then, but stifled it. Stubborn like her father, she felt she had something to say, and she tried again.

"But you always told me to tell the truth, Daddy! No matter how much it hurts," she argued.

Her father gave her a hard look, making her wish her hotel-sponsored baby sitter would whisk her away; she was due momentarily. Upon realizing how harsh he had been, Phillip knelt next to her to make amends.

"Honey, please forgive me, but there's something about this you just don't understand. It . . . it's something that requires careful handling, and it's so important that no one must know where we got it until it's time to do so. Trust me, that's all I ask. If you don't, we could lose everything—like that neat little package you stuffed under your mattress."

"Daddy! You didn't!" Tanya shouted.

"No, I didn't," he confessed with a laugh. "But you see what I mean, don't you? I didn't tell anybody about what you have, so why should it be any different for me?"

"You didn't open it, did you?" insisted Tanya before answering his question.

"You can be sure of that, honey," he replied. "Why should I? It's yours—not mine! Besides, I would never open it without your permission."

"Okay then," Tanya said with a happy smile on her face, accepting what he said. That didn't apply to her mother, however, who still felt uneasy about the whole thing. Before Janelle could say anything, a knock sounded on the door, followed by a women's voice.

"Sitter!"

"Run along, dear, and remember to behave," said Janelle as she hurriedly ran a hair brush through her daughter's golden hair. "There! Now, give Mamma a kiss before you go."

Tanya quickly complied, then ran over to her father and gave him one, too.

"Remember now," cautioned her father before he let her go, "you're not to mention a word to anyone."

"On my honor as a Campfire Girl," Tanya replied soberly seconds before leaving with her sitter, a sweet-faced black lady, who took her by the hand and led her down the long hallway, filling it with happy chatter as she went.

Police Station—George Town

The island rent-a-car people were prompt. Within minutes, the Northams were speeding on the left side of the road, heading for the police station. Along the way, Phillip kept thinking, *Think left, drive left*, so he wouldn't swing into the right-hand lane in which he was accustomed to driving.

The drive to the station, which wasn't long, took them from their hotel on Seven Mile Beach to the town square, then left and right a few times, and they were there. Inside on the second floor, a talkative but courteous secretary directed them into the inspector's office, where introductions were made.

After shaking their hands, Inspector Gilford motioned for them to take seats opposite his desk. For the first time since they met, the Northams noticed he spoke with impeccable English, shaming them somewhat.

"Concerning your watch, Mr. and Mrs. Northam," the inspector said right off, "we've done what you've asked. And what we've uncovered so far isn't exactly what we expected. In fact," he said while eyeing the couple, "it's most confusing and we're not certain which way to go at this point."

"What do you mean?" asked Phillip as he turned quickly to analyze his wife's reaction.

"Your watch—if it is your watch—" the man said pointedly, "seems to carry some form of liability."

A twinge of nervousness swept the Northams, making them feel they were suspected of some major crime, but that wasn't the case.

"I—we don't understand," Janelle interjected while exhibiting a quiver in her voice as she spoke. It was detected by the inspector, but he said nothing. For the moment, its meaning seemed to hold no priority.

"Was it our watch?" Phillip countered.

"That's what you must tell me," the inspector replied. "Search as we did, we couldn't find it though we did find the receipt book showing you had left it with him."

"And—?" asked Phillip before being cut off.

"So when we couldn't find it, we decided to conduct a search of the victim's home. And that's when we found these."

As the couple looked on, the inspector placed a series of polaroid photographs on the desktop near them. He watched for their reaction.

"That's it!" Phillip replied excitedly.

Janelle looked, too, bouncing back with the same discovery. "So where is it?" she asked, a question echoed by her husband.

"That's what we don't know," the inspector said, adding, "and that's what bothers us. There's something peculiar about the whole thing, and we're desperate to learn what it is."

Janelle looked at her husband just then, as a worried look crossed her face. Upon seeing it, Phillip shrugged his shoulders in bewilderment, adding to her discomfort.

"Could it have something to do with its value Or origin for example? And someone stole it?" Janelle asked all at once. She was hedging she knew, hoping against hope not to give their secret away. After all, she had promised Phillip she would hold her tongue.

"Was it worth much?" the inspector asked. "I'm not an expert on watches—antiques especially."

"We're not sure," Phillip answered. "It's never been appraised before, but the watchmaker—Mr. . . . what's-his-name—"

"Schumacher," the inspector offered.

"Oh, yes, Mr. Schumacher," Phillip continued. "He said it was quite valuable. Exactly how valuable we don't know because he said he was going to look it up . . . in some old books of his."

"I see," the inspector replied before continuing. He leaned back in his comfortable leather chair and thought for a while before speaking again. "Care for a Coke—or something?" he asked.

"No, thanks," said Phillip, forgetting he was only speaking for himself.

"Well, I would like one. A diet drink if you've got it," said Janelle.

The inspector motioned for his secretary to answer the intercom.

"Yes, she answered.

"Suzie, get us a couple of diet sodas. One for me and one Mrs. Northam here," the inspector directed over the intercom.

"With or without cream?" she snapped irritably, not expecting an answer.

"She got a problem?" asked Phillip upon hearing her response.

"Mad at her boyfriend again, I presume," the inspector replied. "She'll get over it; she always does. Anyway," he continued, "while we're waiting for her to come back, why don't you tell me what you know about the watch?"

The look on the couple's faces didn't escape his notice this time. There was something strange about the way they reacted to what seemed to be an ordinary, straight-forward question. He decided to try something.

"It is your watch, isn't it?"

"Oh, yes," Phillip responded nervously before adding, "My aunt left it to me as part of her estate."

When Janelle frowned, the inspector felt he had touched upon something, but wasn't able to decipher its meaning, so he pressed on, taking the answer at face value for the moment.

"But why did you bring it here to a remote corner of the world? Certainly not to get it repaired?"

"It was operating until the other day," Phillip lied, getting himself deeper and deeper.

At that moment, as the inspector searched him with his piercing greenish-brown eyes, he began to squirm. His chair was no longer comfortable.

"For God's sake, Phillip! Tell him!" Janelle exclaimed unexpectedly, breaking her promise. "If you don't, I will!"

Inspector Gilford was caught by surprise. *What are they concealing?* he thought to himself while waiting for what might come next.

"Oh, all right!" Phillip replied angrily as if caught with his hand in a cookie jar.

"Is there something I should know?" asked the inspector, baiting the hook.

"In a way, yes," admitted Phillip, "but we only did it to protect ourselves, that's all."

"In what way and protection from what?" asked the inspector, more confused than ever.

"The truth of the matter is that we found it—the watch," Phillip admitted as a tinge of crimson traveled across his handsome but proud face, "and we thought if we told anyone, it could be taken away even though we found it buried beneath the sand."

"You found it? Where?" the inspector asked as he pushed forward in his chair, his interest clearly peaked.

"On the beach—at Gun Bay," Phillip lied through his red face, again throwing Janelle off guard. This time though, she didn't contradict him. Though she didn't approve, she decided to go along with his charade awhile longer, most of all to keep from embarrassing him any further.

"Is that right, Mrs. Northam?" the inspector asked, now turning to her as if Phillip had lost his credibility.

"It's Janelle," she corrected to make things more personal and friendlier.

"All right . . . Janelle," the inspector agreed with a gentle smile while waiting for her to answer his question. "Is that true?"

"Yes," Janelle replied. "It's as he said."

"Why didn't you tell me this in the first place? We could have saved a lot of time," said the inspector.

"It's like I said," replied Phillip. "We thought some unscrupulous official might lay claim to it, and we'd be minus a valuable watch."

"I understand," said the inspector, "but we don't work that way here, though we do have certain laws governing removal of such items."

Janelle looked at her husband, but wisely chose not to rub salt into his embarrassed wounds.

"If what you're saying is true," continued the inspector, "we've got a long way to go if we expect to solve this case."

"I—we don't understand," replied Phillip, speaking for Janelle as well.

"Just this," added the inspector. "There now seems to be a definite link between your missing watch and the murder of Mr. Schumacher. And whoever stole it is the murderer."

"It's not possible!" exclaimed Janelle. "No one outside of ourselves—and the watchmaker—ever saw it before, so how could anyone have known?"

"I disagree, Mrs. Northam—Janelle," replied the inspector politely. "In view of what I have just learned concerning its origin, plus some other facts which I'm not at liberty to reveal at this time, I would say there is more than a remote possibility the two are connected."

"Why shouldn't we know what you know?" asked Phillip. "After all, it is our watch."

"For the time being, the less said the better," replied the inspector. "As you know, this is a small island, and secrets—no matter how small or inconsequential—travel quickly." He motioned to them to turn around and look through the large plate-glass window separating his private office from the working staff outside. It was full of people, all milling around and getting in each other's way.

"So?" said Phillip.

"Everybody's related to somebody, and no one—unless it's quite serious—wants to see a family member go to jail."

"Then you do have crimes? Lke robberies?" asked Phillip.

"Of course," the inspector answered with a laugh. "What gave you the idea we're any different from elsewhere?"

"One of your former residents, but it doesn't matter any longer because he's dead," said Phillip, referring to the watchmaker.

When the inspector didn't pickup on his statement, Janelle had one of her own. "What do you want us to do?" she asked.

"A good question," Gilford replied as he pushed back into his chair. First of all, I need to know everything you can tell me about the watch."

"There isn't more to tell," replied Phillip, again avoiding details about their Little Cayman experience, which infuriated Janelle.

"Phillip!" she exclaimed, hoping he would reveal the truth.

"Oh, yes, there was something else," he said as Janelle and the inspector looked on expectantly. "I found this, too," he added as he tossed a small gold-colored metal fragment on the inspector's desk.

"What is it?" asked the inspector as he reached for the tiny object to look it over.

Janelle cringed again when thoughts of Shakespeare's immortal words ran through her drama-oriented mind, *Oh, what tangled webs we weave, when first we practice to deceive.*

"I don't know, but I think it's pirate gold. There's a lot of it around here, so we've been told," replied Phillip.

"At one time, perhaps," replied the inspector as he examined the fragment more closely, "but not as plentiful as before. The tourists and locals have found most of it."

As the Northams looked on, he reached into a desk drawer and withdrew a magnifying glass, then carefully studied the fragment.

"Mmmmm, what do we have here?" he said after a thorough examination. "There are some letters on it . . . *R* and *B*."

"We saw the same thing," interjected Janelle.

"Any idea what it stands for?" asked Phillip.

"No, but I know some people who might," the inspector replied. "A minter's mark probably. May I keep it for a while?"

"I—" Phillip hesitated.

"Of course, you can, Inspector!" Janelle broke in. "If it'll help solve the case, why not?"

"Tell you what," said the inspector as he looked at his watch. It was almost noon. "Let me take you to lunch. I'll treat."

"Splendid!" Janelle replied quickly. Phillip had no choice in the matter, she had made up his mind.

"Good, then we'll continue our talk during lunch," the inspector added. "There's got to be an explanation to all of this."

"What about those clues you spoke about?" said Phillip as the inspector politely directed him out of his office, then down the flight of stairs.

"A few," the inspector conceded, "but as I said before, it's better nothing be said until each lead can be checked. Don't you agree?"

"Of course," replied Phillip and Janelle together. They went outside to a beat up rusting hulk of a car in a nearby parking lot.

"Mine," the chief inspector said. "Can't afford another just yet," he smiled. "With the salt air, a new one would only corrode anyway. But it gets me from here to there," he joked.

There was nothing pretentious about the man. By his demeanor alone, the Northams could see that, in addition to being well-educated, he was every bit a gentleman. This made him all the more acceptable to the Northams, and they felt comfortable in his company.

With a trail of black smoke blowing out of the car's leaky exhaust system, the trio raced off.

"How about lunch at Gun Bay?" the inspector asked as they dodged around corners. The silence which followed took a long time to undo, but it had its effect. "I'm only kidding," he admitted moments later, just before the car turned into a highway they knew; it led to the waterfront.

Within minutes, they were seated behind a large plate-glass window in a delightful upstairs dining room which provided an unrestricted view of Hog Sty Bay and harbor. In the water nearby, a number of tourists undergoing scuba diving instructions could be seen going in and out of a flat-bottomed boat.

"Now, let's go over your story again," the inspector said, addressing the Northams. He hoped to learn more, like small details they might have overlooked. As a detective, it was a natural thing for him to do. Doubting truth until proven otherwise was part of his basic training. Like a hunting dog, he doubted almost instinctively.

Once again, Phillip repeated his version of the truth, minus major details, which he didn't think the inspector needed to know.

The inspector accepted what he said, but reserved the right—in his mind—to accept or reject what he had been told. They parted after that with both parties agreeing to keep in touch.

Inspector Gilford's Office—Next Day

The following morning, there was only one thing on Chief Inspector Gilford's mind. When he dashed in and shut the door to his office, everyone knew something was up. Within minutes, instructions to his secretary to call a colleague in London followed.

His activity this morning was the result of a lot of thinking. Now the only way for him to prove his theories was through contact with a former mentor—now a colleague—at a world-renowned institution of Her Majesty' government—Scotland Yard.

Years earlier, at the expense and with the blessing of the council, Gilford had been sent to England to attend an advanced course in criminology. It was a program specially designed for police officials belonging to the British Commonwealth system. For the Grand Cayman Island Council, it was a deal. Cutting down crime through expert police work meant job security and a healthier economy for a lot of people. It benefited Gilford, too. He was promised an increase in and a promotion if he passed. He passed, got the promotion, but the pay did not materialize. Anyway, he didn't care, he had a job.

"I have the Earl of Olive on the line—I mean, Sir Oliver," Gilford's secretary joked as she notified him his call had gone through.

"Funny, funny," he said while theorizing correctly, "I see you've made up with your boy friend again."

"Last night," she said dreamily. "And—"

"Not now, Suzie, I've got too many important things on my mind. Put the gentleman through, and for God's sake, be sure no one is listening in. Know what I mean?"

"Are you implying—?"

"I am," the inspector replied bluntly, infuriating the woman. She clicked her telephone off with a heavy thumb. When the light went out, Gilford began.

"I say, Oliver, are you there, ole boy?" The inspector asked

271

eagerly, anxious to hear his friend's voice. He loved the British accent and tried to use it wherever possible, especially when talking to Englishmen.

"Jolly well, ole chap," came a friendly reply. "And you, ole fellow, have things been going well with you?"

"Couldn't be better, but I've got more important things on my mind right now. It's about the fax I sent you last week . . . the one containing copies of polaroid snaps. Have you learned anything?"

"Indeed I have, old boy. And I must say, they were most interesting, to say the least."

"In what way?" asked Gilford. Small talk was okay, but now he was in a hurry to have an opinion and his friend's usual modus operandi was just the opposite of his.

"You've really hit upon a big one this time. Never dreamed we'd find one of the pieces out your way."

"Don't keep me biting my nails, Oliver. What in the hell are you babbling about?'

"Well, quite simply, it's stolen merchandise all right. Been gone a long time."

"You don't say?"

"I do indeed."

"Dammit! Oliver, get on with it! I haven't got all day. These calls are expensive, you know, and the council audits every one I make."

"Cheap bastards, I'd say," his colleague replied quite humorously before continuing. "Don't they know investigative work is time- and money-consuming?"

"They do, but they insist on balancing the budget," Gilford replied. "But you still haven't answered my question. Are you going to tell me what you learned or not?"

"For the moment, I can't, old chap. The subject is too sensitive to discuss over the phone."

"You must be joking? Or are you?"

"To the contrary. In fact, I'm deadly serious. But I can tell you this much, Interpol has been contacted."

"Interpol!" Gilford whistled. "It's that important, huh?"

"And more," his colleague continued with great calm. "Surely you must have suspected something when you sent us your fax, or didn't you?"

"Yes. Yes, of course," Gilford pretended. True, he had some suspicions, but they seemed so unreal at the time, though he couldn't overlook anything, and that's why he contacted the Yard.

"And—?"

"Well," Gilford admitted, "it was only a guess at first, but then yesterday, the pieces really began to fall together after I interviewed an American couple who claimed they found it at a local beach. It happens all the time, but never like this."

"Are they suspects?"

"At this point, no, but something's missing. I haven't been able to figure it out as yet, but anyway—to get on back to the story—my big break came through yesterday evening after another search of the victim's home."

"Tell me what you can without compromising our call," his friend advised.

"It's quite simple really, but I'm disgusted I hadn't stumbled across it the first time."

"What?"

"The book! It was there all the time, lying cover-side down on the floor next to the table where I found the snaps. Can you imagine that? Clumsy of me."

"What kind of book?" his colleague asked with an urgency in his voice.

"The key to it all," said Gilford, "A book about loot stolen by the Nazis, most of which has never been located. It was produced by the U. N. War Crimes Commission over forty years ago. . . ."

"Go on," his friend urged.

"Well, when I opened it, then flipped through the pages, I ran across a series of underscored paragraphs. There were photos, too. When I compared what the old man had marked to the snaps, I knew I had found the motive, not all of it perhaps, but good enough for the moment. So the snaps you have match what I found in the book—unless there are others?"

"You have stumbled across something all right," his friend agreed. "It coincides with a finding of our own, but I'm not at liberty to speak about it this time."

"Oh? Why not?" Gilford asked.

"Because we're planning a visit to your island within the next few days. Would have told you sooner, but I only got the word this morning."

"What's going on? I'm in the dark."

"'Trust me, friend," the Englishman replied. "I can't tell you anything more at the moment, but you'll get a complete briefing upon our arrival. Our itinerary will be faxed to you with instructions it is for your eyes only. You'll see to it, won't you, ole boy?"

"Of course," replied Gilford, "but this sure comes as a surprise.

Anything else?"

"Yes. One other thing. "

"Go on."

"Would you mind making reservations for a party of ten?"

"Ten! Whose coming?" Gilford asked, shocked by the number.

Oliver laughed, then gave the answer. "Let's just say they're a party of tourists. Okay? And by the way, whatever you do, please say nothing to anyone about our conversation. There's a lot more to this case than you realize, believe me."

"You have my word on it," agreed Gilford. "Nothing will be done until you get here except other efforts to find more clues."

"Super," his colleague replied. "We'll see you in a few days, then. Will that be convenient?"

"No problem at all. I'll confirm your reservations as soon as I get your itinerary."

At a moment when the conversation was to end, another surprise came from the lips of Gilford's colleague, once again causing the inspector to realize how complicated the case was becoming. "Oh, by the way, ole chap, don't be surprised if a deluge of unexpected foreign visitors should suddenly appear on your shores."

"What do you mean?"

Sir Oliver laughed. "You'll find out soon enough, ole boy, so don't lose any sleep over it. Tah, tah for now."

"To you, too," Gilford replied as he put the receiver back on its cradle. He pondered the last statement, not certain what it meant. *Oh, well,* he thought, *what's another surprise?*

The bespectacled and balding, middle-aged man placed his call through the Cayman international operator, using a credit card sponsored by an organization in Mexico. Of course, the operator didn't know this as she dialed the number he had requested. The phone on the other end rang with a quick burst.

"*Hola. La Institucion de las Mayas.*"

"*El Senor Martinez, por favor.*"

"Who may I say is calling?" the answering party asked in Spanish.

"Just tell him it's Senor Rodriguez, who wants to discuss *El Projecto 1945* with him."

There was a silence on the other end. "Has there been a breakthrough?" the party on the other end asked in an excited voice.

"*Jahwohl*! There's no mistake about it, and I wouldn't be calling about it if it wasn't so," replied the caller.

"*Un momento, por favor,*" replied the man. "I'll get the chief right away. I know he will want to speak to you," said the party in Mexico as he set the phone down and raced away. Unfortunately, in his haste to notify his chief, the phone fell to the floor, hurting the caller's ears.

After that, a cacophony of sounds followed, some of them resembling the scuffling feet of running men. A voice came back on—a different and much older sounding one.

"Rodriguez—in the Caymans?"

"*Jah.*"

"Any chance you're mistaken?"

"I've got the proof in my pocket, but it took some doing to get it."

"What do you mean?"

"Can't tell you now, but it was found by an expendable . . . if you get the gist of what I'm saying."

"I do. How soon can you get here?"

"Tomorrow if I can get a flight to Jamaica with a transfer to Mexico City."

"Good. Call when you're on the final leg, and we'll send a plane to meet you at the general aviation terminal."

"I won't be able to bring the proof with me, though."

"Why not?" demanded the man on the opposite end.

"Let's just say it's inadvisable, but I will take some photos which you can develop when I get there. Is that all right?"

"Well, we've waited all this time; a day or two more can't hurt anything so long as you're right. So make your plans to get here as quickly as possible. I can hardly wait. *Adios* for now, Kamerad."

"And to you, *mein* . . ." The caller stopped there, cursing himself for nearly uttering something which was restricted. There was an uneasy pause on the other end, but when the name failed to come out, the tension was relieved. "Till tomorrow. *Adios.*"

George Town Police Station—Four Days Later

The fax machine buzzed, prompting Suzie to run over to it. Inspector Gilford had warned her to be on the lookout for a very important message and to let him know when it came in.

The phone light was on, indicating the recipient should pick up the phone first.

"Grand Cayman Criminal Investigation Division," answered Suzie.

"This is Sir Oliver, chief, Security Division 3, Scotland Yard," replied the party on the other end. "If you will be so kind, please put Chief Inspector Gilford on the line. He's expecting my call."

"Yes, sir! Immediately," replied Suzie, who dashed into her boss's office to tell him about the call. This time she didn't dare ask what was going on because she had been warned by him days earlier about putting her nose where it didn't belong and about the penalty for eavesdropping—termination!

It didn't take Inspector Gilford more than three seconds to reach the fax machine, where he promptly picked up the phone.

"Gilford here," he said, anxiously while looking around to make sure no one was listening in.

"That you, ole boy?" asked a familiar voice.

"Yes. What's up, Oliver?"

"You'll hear and know in a moment, old chap, but I urge you to handle everything with extreme caution," his friend said with an ominous tone. He offered an apology at the same time. "I'm sorry I can't say more at this time. Security you know, and damned high at that!"

"Is it that important?"

"Indeed it is, ole chap. And by the way, before I transmit my message over your fax, please make certain no one is near you. We don't want anyone to see what we're sending. Beyond that, I can't say more. In the meantime, keep well, and we'll be seeing you soon, ole chap. Ready for the message?"

"Let her roll," said the inspector as he put his phone back on the fax machine and pressed the receive button. At the same time, he looked around the room to make certain no one was in seeing distance. Except for Suzie who was still in his office, the room was empty. The others were on their fifteen-minute coffee break.

The machine buzzed again, showing a "fax connecting" message in its tiny window. Seconds later, it spewed two continuous pages from its guts. Gilford removed them quickly, then raced back to his office, dismissing Suzie in the process.

"It's all yours," he said as he passed her, referring to her work space and fax machine.

The contents of the message caused Gilford to whistle in disbelief. What had started out as a simple homicide case had suddenly become internationally important. Why, he still didn't know, but from the looks of the impressive guest list, something big was brewing. What surprised him the most was the composition of guests. In addition to security agents representing the U.S.A., Great Britain, Germany, and Israel, a number of others were coming from the now defunct countries of East Germany, the Soviet Union, and former eastern block nations. The fax ended with warning, "Caution! Imperative customs be advised personnel named herein—including those without diplomatic passports—be permitted unhindered entry. Baggage checks prohibited! Foreign office approval granted. Make all necessary arrangements. Arrival time and dates will vary for different members, as provided herein."

"What in the hell is going on?" Gilford asked himself aloud as he reread the message. What he was being requested to do was unprecedented in Caymanian history. He was willing to do it, however, since he trusted his friend explicitly and he knew Sir Oliver would never have made such a request without being absolutely certain that what he was doing was justified. So all he could do from now to then was to make sure the instructions were carried out as delineated.

His intercom buzzed just then.

"Anything I can do for you, sir?" Suzie asked politely.

"Yes. Just keep your mouth shut about the call I just received."

The intercom went dead, bringing a satisfied smile to Gilford's face. He looked up through the front office pane at his secretary. She was pouting and furiously pounding her typewriter to get rid of her anger.

Gilford smiled, then tucked the fax in his pocket and walked out of his office to make the arrangements Sir Oliver asked for. *Boy*, he thought to himself as he passed his gloomy secretary, *perestroika has sure come a long way. I wonder what we all have in common.*

Inspector Gilford meeting "Mort" at the airport

Chapter 22

Protocol

ay I have your attention please?" said a sweet voice over the airport's public address system. "Cayman Air Lines, flight 330 from Miami now arriving. Passengers expecting to board for the return flight are reminded to have their visa cards, passports, and customs declaration slips ready."

"On time for once," Gilford said to his assistant, Charles Ebanks, as they waited in the customs office overlooking the open bays where the disembarking passengers would pass. In his hand, he held a number of photographs, all sent by special courier from London.

"Who's coming on this one?" asked Gilford's assistant, who was patiently waiting at his side.

"Israeli agents—incognito... like the others," replied Gilford as he watched a string of new arrivals enter the customs section where they got into different lines, those for residents and those for visitors.

As they filed through, customs agents were quick to identify the three passengers Inspector Gilford and Ebanks had been waiting for.

Just as quickly, they led them passed the customs checkpoint to the customs office where they were promptly greeted.

"Mr. Joachim, I'm Chief Inspector Gilford, and this is my assistant, Charles Ebanks," said Gilford with an extended hand. He had recognized the man from a photo he had been supplied.

"It's Mort," the short, stubby, balding man replied as he grabbed the extended hand. Then he moments introduced the two young men who had accompanied him. "These are my trusted associates, Eric and Yitzak," he added. "No need for last names," he said, "since you won't be seeing much of them. They've got a lot of things to do from now until whenever it is we leave."

Gilford and his assistant shook hands with the men. He noted how young and physically trim they were, but their purpose for being here escaped him. He had never been told.

"If you don't mind, gentlemen," Mort interrupted quite quickly, "they need to retrieve our baggage as soon as possible. It's important we lose nothing."

"Of course, I understand," said Gilford before directing their attention to his assistant. "Mr. Ebanks will help you. Just follow him."

As the two men went out, Gilford watched curiously. They were friendly enough, but terribly job-oriented. Even before airport personnel could offload the baggage car, both men raced up to it and removed a series of heavy, well-sealed cartons. What they contained Gilford did not know nor did he ask since he had been told to allow them through without question.

Moments later, the two young men and their escort, Charles Ebanks, left the building and boarded the unmarked vehicles. They sped away after that, leaving their much older boss, a man about sixty—more or less, talking with the inspector.

"What about the others? Have any of them arrived?" asked Mort after they were out of sight.

"Two groups so far—Germans and Russians," Gilford replied correctly.

"To make amends, I guess. . . ," said Mort, speaking softly as if to himself.

"Who?" asked Gilford, overhearing his comment.

"The Germans, of course," he replied.

"I don't understand."

"Slip of the tongue—an old habit," he apologized. "I can't get used to the idea they've changed—the Germans—though I have my reservations."

"I still don't follow," said Gilford, not certain he understood the man.

"Sorry. I was referring to old days, Nazi days, and some painful memories which are hard to shake," explained Mort. "But, who knows, they might be of some help to us. Anyway, we'll see in due time. After all, we can't hold all Germans responsible for the sins of their fathers, now can we?"

"I agree," replied Gilford, understanding better.

He directed Mort, who was now sweating profusely from being too heavily dressed, to follow him to a junker of a car in a parking lot located next to the busy terminal. As he opened the door, Mort wondered if he could push his flabby frame into the compact car. It was a tight squeeze, to say the least, but somehow he managed to get in, heading for town.

Police Headquarters—Same Day

At the station, Gilford hurried the man upstairs without bothering to introduce him to his nosy civil service secretary. With the door closed, he offered Mort a seat opposite his own, then got down to business.

"You have weapons, I presume?" asked Gilford, mindful of his duties when dealing with visiting law enforcement officers or other special guests.

"Of course," Mort eagerly replied, "but don't ask me to turn it in because I can't do that."

"I won't," Gilford replied, "but we do have laws requiring the registry of all firearms. May I see what you have?"

Mort reached into his bulky coat pocket and pulled out the bulge that had given it away. It was a Belgian-made pistol, minus its clip, which Mort said he kept separate during air travel.

"Nice," Gilford said as he looked it over. While Mort looked on, he pulled out a note pad and wrote down its serial number and description before handing the weapon back to him. "No offense intended, but I'll have to have a list—with serial numbers—of the ones your associates have with them."

"Of course, and none taken," Mort replied as he stuffed his weapon into his tight-fitting coat. "I'll bring them with me tomorrow."

"Good, and while you're here," said Gilford, "I need to advise you of something."

"Like what?" asked Mort, quite casually.

281

"That your weapons—outside of life-threatening situations—are not to be exhibited, drawn, or used while you are operating in the Cayman Islands," said Gilford with a serious look on his face. His eyes met Mort's, registering his feeling.

A smile crossed Mort's face. "You can be certain of that, Inspector," Mort replied, matching the stare.

"Good," said Gilford, relieved it had gone so well. He articulated a though, "What I can't understand is why you even brought them . . . your weapons?"

"Didn't Scotland Yard tell you?" asked Mort, perturbed by the question, which in his mind should have been answered earlier by others.

"All I know is that you—and your associates—have been sent here to assist us and that you're a Nazi hunter instead of a Mossad agent as we'd been led to believe earlier. Is that correct?"

"As far as representing Israel is concerned, let's just call it a 'reciprocal' arrangement between my government and Her Majesty's government," Mort replied tactfully, avoiding everything else. His answer confused the inspector.

"Reciprocal? In what way?" asked Gilford.

"Mind if I smoke?" Mort asked as he pulled out a long Havana and sniffed it as one would sniff a rose.

"No, not at all," Gilford replied. He didn't smoke himself but tolerated those who did.

"Now, as to your question," Mort said as he sucked in and emitted small puffs of smoke from his mouth while holding a lighted match beneath the cigar's tip. "You may not understand this, but it's a long and complicated story, one that goes back many years—to the fall of Hitler's Germany and his Third Reich."

"You must be joking," Gilford said with a disbelieving smile.

"I don't blame you for responding as you have," replied the fat small man, "but believe me, it's quite true."

"Are you trying to tell me that this murder—on our little island—has something to do with a war that took place over forty years ago?"

"Incredible as it may seem, it's true nevertheless," Mort replied without blinking an eye even when puffy black smoke obscured them momentarily. He leaned back in his chair, uttering words of pleasure. "Ah, there's nothing better than a good Havana to relax one's thoughts like my Yiddish papa used to say."

Gilford wanted to laugh, but he couldn't. The subject matter seemed way out, yet the man before him came with the blessing of the Israeli and British governments, so he had to be credible. He thought on while the contented man took long drags on his long expensive cigar, taking his time to spring other pertinent questions.

"Is that why we're having this strange gathering of international security representatives? Not to mention the CIA and God knows who else?" Gilford asked.

"A common interest, regrettably," Mort admitted, leaving Gilford to ponder his meaning.

"Is the missing watch responsible for all of this?"

"That, my dear friend," replied Mort with great vigor, "is what we want to know and what we've come to find out."

Mort looked around the room for a second to see if anyone was listening in. He noticed Suzie outside, but she was bent over her typewriter punching away, leaving him to say safely what was on his mind.

"As you will find out tomorrow, my friend, when we get together with all the others—though I don't really care to—there is much more to the murder than a missing watch. In fact, all evidence seems to point to something much bigger and we're not certain where it will all end."

"Is that why you're involved and why you're here?" asked Gilford, getting more personal.

"Partially, but more so to match pieces we've been collecting for over four decades with those of the others."

"Four decades! That's a long time," replied Gilford, confused once again.

"But a short time in the history of man," Mort qualified philosophically as he took another deep drag on his cigar before blowing small rings of smoke into the air. "In time, we'll find what we're looking for."

"And where do you think it'll lead?"

"For the moment, we don't know, Inspector," Mort replied honestly, "but we do have some thoughts on the subject, the latter of which I dare not mention at this time."

"Secrets!" complained Gilford mildly.

"Yes," agreed Mort while adding cautiously, "it's because we want to be absolutely certain our information is correct before we draw conclusions. Beyond that, I can say no more."

Gilford accepted the answer. He had been advised earlier by his English colleague that he'd be told what he needed to know upon his arrival. That's when an alarm sounded in his mind. He had forgotten Sir Oliver, whose plane was due in shortly. In a panic, he looked at his watch.

"Good God!" he cried out while grabbing his coat off the coat rack near the door through which he was trying to depart.

"Something wrong?" asked Mort.

"I've got another plane to meet, and it's due in right now," he explained.

"What about our meeting?" asked Mort, getting up.

"It will have to wait until tomorrow after we meet with the other delegations."

"That's fine with me," agreed Mort. "I've got enough to do anyway. So if you'd be kind enough to have someone take me to our apartment, I won't burden you any longer."

"I'll have my secretary take you," replied Gilford, "but I must warn you, don't say anything in her presence you wouldn't want repeated. She blabs too much."

"Like my second wife," replied Mort humorously, "before I divorced her. Been single ever since." He didn't elaborate.

The two men shook hands and walked out of the office together, where Gilford introduced Mort to Suzie. At the same time, he instructed her where to take him.

"The Royal Palm Arms would have been much better," said Suzie, incurring her boss's wrath.

"Suzie!" he bellowed before making hasty departure.

"Me and my bloody mouth. When am I ever going to learn?" said Suzie as she picked up the phone and called for transportation.

Mort smiled upon hearing her remarks but said nothing. Fatigue had set in and he needed some rest before the following day's meeting. *It should prove interesting,* he thought.

Owen Roberts Airport Terminal

Inspector Gilford got to the terminal by breaking speed limits, something he rarely did. His watch revealed he was late, but he should have known and remembered that Caymanian Airlines didn't always leave or arrive on time. He cursed after running into the terminal only to find the plane was overdue and wouldn't be in for another half hour. So he waited in the air-conditioned terminal and went over the dossiers which had been sent to him about his incoming visitors so he would know how to deal with them upon arrival.

Igor Michailovich Pederosky, a mature man with a thick crop of graying hair, of average height and weight, was leader of the Russian Republic delegation. To those who worked with him, he was known as a man given to detail, so when first approached about the project he was now on, he looked at it with mixed feelings. Nothing like it had ever happened before!

The request sent to his office in Moscow had cleared through the highest echelons in his government, a surprise itself. Even more intriguing was the fact it originated in both Germanys—East and West—before they were reunited. As such, the whole thing was startling, to say the least, just as much as Gorbachev's political reforms—*glasnost* and *perestroika*—when first introduced, had startled the free world. Eventually, of course, it led to dissolution of the once all-powerful Soviet Union and its Warsaw Pact allies. That was in the background now, and Pederosky had been selected to head this group.

When it came to sleuthing, Igor, a man in his late fifties, had a lot of experience. Often he was called upon to solve difficult cases, most of them dealing with Nazi war crime activities, so when the East— now merged with the West German—government agreed to ask the new leadership of the KGB for assistance in finding Nazi-era documents, President Yeltsin—like Gorbachev before him—agreed.

Specifically, American, British, German, and Israeli governments wanted the Russians to search their archives for Nazi shipping records previously stored at Peenemuende, Hitler's infamous rocket development factory on the Baltic. They had fallen into Soviet hands at the end of the war, and almost everything within—personnel, records, supplies, and research materials—had been shipped to the Soviet Union to help develop its own rocket capability.

This coordinated international front was something new for Igor and his comrades, all of whom had previously been trained to betray nothing, but listen much. From such experiences, they carried some predetermined attitudes which were not easy to keep in check. Now, however, he, like the East Germans had to reverse their thinking. Their work was difficult, but they managed even though they had to resort to hand-sorting as opposed to what the West Germans had done through use of highly sophisticated mainframe computers and software technology. For the latter, fify years of Nazi-era records which had been entered into computer banks over the years could be screened for just about anything.

Fortunately for Igor, part one of the original request for assistance could be met without too much difficulty. All confiscated Peenemünde records where kept in one place—at the record center headquarters for rocket development on the outskirts of Moscow. When it came to the second request, the identification of a gold watch purported to have belonged to Czar Nicholas, his—and the KGB's— attention was significantly increased especially when reference was made to the Allied War Crimes compendium on stolen treasures. The KGB knew all about that book and about treasures secreted out of Nazi Germany before and after her defeat, most of which had never been found.

Then came a break! An unexplained shipment of unidentified cartons from Peenemünde in early 1945—weeks before Hitler's suicide—to a port in Kiel, Germany, was uncovered among a mass of documents long stored in military archives. Of equal importance, though no one quite knew why, was the discovery of a list of missing concentration camp inmates who had been sent to Peenemünde about the same time, but had never been found. What did it mean? Was there any connection between the crates and the missing prisoners? Were rockets involved, though it didn't seem so, since no rocket launching facilities existed in the Kiel area? Again, what was the significance? And why had the questions been posed? Igor did not know, nor did his comrades, but they were eager to find out, and the seeds sown by *glasnost* seemed the best way to learn.

Helmut Grundig, the Bonn representative, and Franz Joseph Koehler, his East German counterpart, a former member of that country and its secret service—*STASI,* shared a room in the far end of the townhouse complex which housed other members of the European delegation. They hadn't met the others yet, much less knew what they looked like, but all had come armed with information.

Helmut had been the instigator behind the West German push. He was happy Interpol wasted no time contacting his office when they discovered a link between the watch and previous Nazi activities, but that's all they had! It was up to Helmut to find the rest. He did it by putting his computer operators, some of the best in Germany, to the test. Their work brought surprises they hadn't expected, and it was all because of his highly sophisticated software programs which took years of trial and error to perfect. With uncanny speed, they were able to correlate unrelated facts involving time and space differentials which would have defied recognition of key data by those using hand processing methods.

Like the Russians, in their discovery of unexplained shipping cartons, the Germans were now anxious to see if the cartons related to missing treasures taken from the Soviet motherland. The united Germans, who were now cooperating to help overcome a forty-five-year-old stigma which plagued their respective consciences, had run across something which had no explanation until recently.

As the computers scanned hundreds of thousands of stored Nazi data, investigating teams from both countries began to notice the appearance of certain letters and numbers—*U4R*. It was unimportant at first until more references began to surface and in many places—commissary records, to name one.

Then as the weeks passed, pieces to a much larger puzzle began to fall in place after the Germans—with help from the Russians—uncovered similar references. Again, the meaning escaped everyone though nearly all felt a connection between the *U4R* symbol—a code perhaps—and the watch. A few laughed, saying it was ridiculous to draw such a conclusion. After all, the watch was found on a beach thousands of miles away in a remote place of the world!

"So what?" Helmut had argued at the time when someone joked they were chasing ghosts of long-dead Nazis. "If this case has anything to do with that cursed generation—alive or dead—then we must at all cost eradicate its memory. Otherwise, we Germans will never regain our honor or our rightful place among the nations of the world."

His message struck home and his staff dug in more until they ran across a name which was little known to them: General Ernst Wilhelm von Kleitenberg, a relatively young and obscure man who rose quickly to the top to head a special *Aktion* division within Hitler's SS guard.

The man disappeared weeks before the fall of Berlin, taking with him trusted members of his elite unit and a number of young volunteers. Where they went no one knew, but it had been presumed they were numbered among the unidentified casualties defending Berlin though no one ever proved it.

The last piece of information to fall into place came from naval archives, those dealing with emergency around-the-clock overhaul of several unidentified U-boats at the Luebeck repair yards weeks before Germany capitulated and of the boat's last-known departure port as recorded by witnesses—Kiel. By itself, this information would have meant nothing, but what drew attention to it was the lack of U-boat identifying information, a most unusual oversight—or was it? It was strange indeed because the Nazis were known to be sticklers when it came to record-keeping—witness their detailed records on concentration camp inmates whom they sent to the ovens.

A follow-up was made with naval office personnel. This brought some initial disappointment when it was found all U-boats had been accounted for at war's end even those that surrendered to foreign nations. So what did it mean? Again the team went to work, more zealously this time. Where did von Kleitenberg go? And his men? Were they killed as presumed? What about the watch? Was it just a coincidence it was found in the Cayman Islands? And was it the same watch Alexandra had given Czar Nicholas?

All these questions plagued the teams, many of whom were schooled in brainstorming techniques. It paid off finally, but many questions were left unresolved because they didn't seem to fit the pattern though intuition kept telling many that a connection—no matter how remote—existed!

The payoff came when an another message was passed from Scotland Yard to Interpol in Paris, then to German authorities. It seemed inconsequential at first until fax copies arrived showing a gold fragment bearing the letters *RB*. Helmut exploded with excitement when he first saw it. He didn't have to be told what it was; he knew! The team went back to work, culminating finally in an agreement they needed to go to the scene of the crime.

Hitler's Reichbank, its gold, and other reserves were high in the thoughts of everyone though there still wasn't enough information to show any connection between all they had found so far.

What they did know, however, was both historical and factual: that a jewel-encrusted gold watch which once belonged to the czar of Russia and reportedly was stolen from the Reichbank had been found again on a remote Caribbean island before being stolen again. At the same time, adding to the mystery, a fragment of a Reichbank minted gold bar was also found. Also significant and mind-teasing was the fact that the original losses coincided with last-minute activities of loyal Nazi followers in Berlin at the time the Reichbank's treasury was removed! Beyond these facts, which were self-explanatory, no room for philosophical thought was needed.

In a spirit of cooperation, the Russians were told what had been found, causing them to respond in kind—to a point. What they didn't tell the Germans added another dimension to the story: A former Peenemünde scientist who had been captured and encouraged to help the Soviets in their rocket-building industry recalled a highly unusual activity which followed the sudden arrival of elite SS troops. When interrogated further, the aging German recalled an entire building set aside for some kind of "top secret" metallurgical work. What it was he never knew because he wasn't one of those selected. Like the workers who later hauled out a series of elongated cartons, he recalled they simply disappeared. Killed in the war was his thought though he could not confirm it from actual knowledge.

Again, the Russians were puzzled yet happy about another break in the search. What it meant they didn't know. And the only way they could learn more was to share what they knew with the others.

Helmut and his colleagues were grateful for everything they could get or learn. What he, his associates, and the Russians didn't know—though they asked about it, too—was whether anything unusual or different had been stored in those cartons. No one could give them an answer, so all they could do was speculate.

"A new type rocket or torpedo perhaps," suggested one of his associates, little realizing how close he had come to the answer, "but it came too late in the war to help them."

"Maybe," agreed another, "but that doesn't explain the missing unidentified U-boats and their whereabouts."

"Or no connection at all! Coincidence?" interjected Helmut. "We can overspeculate," he cautioned, "but then again we can't overlook anything. We're on to something I know, but it 's eluding us."

"Treasure anyway," replied an assistant. "Small as it is," he said, referring to the gold fragment. "It's a link to the past, and without doubt, was minted by the Reichbank."

"*Jah,*" another member replied, "but then again, it could be just that—a fragment. With all the bombing that took place, someone could have picked it up and used it as a lucky piece, then lost it while on vacation."

"Two things at once? Not likely," scoffed Helmut. "And let's not forget the murder, and the last statement made by the dead man . . . about stolen Nazi treasure. That's too much of a coincidence for me."

His analysis struck home, making it clear a meeting between interested parties was necessary if the truth was to be weeded out. And, by luck, if his thoughts were correct, the solution could not but help the German Federal Republic's image; it had been tarnished far too long in his estimation by its predecessor and had to be changed

At the Airport—Same Day

Inspector Gilford went through the same routine he followed earlier by waiting in the customs office, the one overlooking the processing area. Within minutes, he and his long-time friend, Sir Oliver, were reunited. They shook hands first, then embraced each other warmly before turning to other matters.

Of importance was Sir Oliver's luggage. He was careful to insist that no one open any of them. When his bag was safely back in his possession, Gilford led him to the parking lot outside where they were to wait for other members of his team. Like a blow torch, the offensive heat caused them to perspire instantly, but it didn't keep them from talking about old times since they hadn't seen each other for years. In time, however, the subject was bound to switch to the purpose of everyone's being on Grand Cayman Island.

"Have they arrived?" Oliver finally asked, referring to the other guests.

"Safe and secure," replied Gilford confidently. "And what a day it's been. I don't speak Russian or German, but thank God, they speak English."

Oliver laughed. "We're on to something, ole chap, and it's important we not botch anything, especially during critical times like this . . . internationally speaking, of course."

"I don't follow," said Gilford.

"You know—the world situation and all—following the demise of the Soviet Union and her satellites. With each going its own way and the emergence of factions, one can never tell what they might do. It could pose a problem for us if one emerging country or the other decides they're now anti-West instead of pro. Should that happen," he said in a near whisper, "then our efforts to solve this case will be dreadfully compromised."

"I see—"

Before Gilford could complete his statement, their conversation was interrupted by the arrival of Inspector Ebanks and other British team members. As before, Ebanks had helped the arriving team pass through Customs.

Sir Oliver introduced them to Gilford, then turned their future over to him.

"Everything is in readiness, and there's a nice comfortable place waiting for you," he said. "So if you would be so kind as to follow my assistant to the waiting vehicles, he will see to your needs."

With that, everyone except Sir Oliver turned and walked away. As they were driven away, Sir Oliver articulated his thoughts.

"I still can't get over it," he said thoughtfully. "All this started through the reporting of a missing watch."

"A murder, actually," Gilford corrected.

"Oh, yes," Sir Oliver agreed, "though one could argue which one came first, like the chicken or the egg."

Gilford smiled; the man was correct.

"We'll know better by tomorrow after we compare notes, that is, if the Russians haven't forgotten their old ways, that of listening one hell of a lot while saying little or nothing in return," replied Sir Oliver with a serious look on his face.

"Let's hope they've changed," agreed Gilford while thinking

about other matters. "I'll be damn glad when this mess is over because my council is driving me nuts. A day never passes before one or the other rings me up for the latest developments in the case."

"You don't tell them anything confidential, do you?" asked Sir Oliver as he picked up his bag and briefcase and followed his friend to his trusty rusting car. Sight of Gilford's junker of a car made him wince, but he said nothing. He had seen worse—at the battle of El Alemain in North Afric, where thousands of burned-out tanks and armored vehicles lay in ruins over a sand furnace desert.

"No, of course not!" Gilford replied quickly. "I just tell them to hang on, that we're still following leads which look promising. That's all!"

"Excellent," replied Sir Oliver as they drove off, heading out of town instead of to it. Gilford told him why. They were to meet the others for a get-together party at a secluded spot on the other side of the island.

"Is there anything you can tell me before tomorrow's meeting?" asked Gilford as they drove.

"Like what?" asked Sir Oliver. There were a number of things he could have told the man, but he felt it better the question be more specific.

"Like why in the hell representatives from NATO and former Warsaw Pact nations have suddenly converged on our peaceful little island?" replied Gilford.

Oliver looked at the man next to him before answering. Gilford hadn't changed. He was the kind of person who wanted to get to the bottom of things as soon as possible and waiting wasn't his way of doing things.

"They're on a vacation or haven't you heard, ole chap?" replied Sir Oliver, teasing him a bit.

"Now come off that," responded Gilford, detecting the humor. "Whose leg do you think you're pulling? I know better than that!"

"You're quite right, of course, Peter. The truth of the matter is this, subject of course to your keeping your word not to divulge anything I tell you until told otherwise. . . ."

"You have it!" Gilford replied quickly before his colleague had finished talking.

"Good. Then here it is," said Sir Oliver. "It concerns the murder victim, whom we believe knew he had discovered a piece of missing treasure which in reality was part of a much larger cache, one secretly removed from Nazi Germany before it crumbled."

"That doesn't explain how the watch got here," challenged

Gilford.

"Quite so," the man responded. "That's the part we haven't figured out yet though we have some plausible theories, some a bit absurd perhaps, but with a little more research and time on our part, we should be able to confirm or reject them."

"Well, I hope it's soon," replied Gilford. "Like I said before, I don't know how much longer I can keep you and your delegation's presence a secret."

"Patience, ole chap. It'll all bear out. Mind if I smoke?" he said as he placed a large-bowled pipe with a curved stem in his mouth where it partially covered one of his most prominent features, a deep-set dimple in his chin.

"No, go ahead. I don't smoke myself, but many of my friends do, and I'll probably die before they do—of cancer, a consequence of breathing in all their exhaled gunk," he said wryly.

"Touche, ole fellow," Sir Oliver replied, undisturbed by his concerns. "Tried to kick the habit a number of times, you know, but never could muster the will power to fight temptation. Oh well, what's a little vice anyway? After all, I don't go chasing females like some of my friends. Besides, my wife wouldn't like it, so I squander my time in my work and a pleasant pipe."

"To each his own," Gilford replied before continuing his query. "Anything else on the case?"

"Nothing—other than the fact we're looking into some U-boat activities which took place in and around the Caymans during and after the war."

"You must be kidding!" Gilford said with an incredulous look.

"I never joke about such matters," came a quick and serious response. "It's all part of our game plan—to overlook nothing no matter how insignificant or remote. Remember?"

"Sorry," Gilford replied after being reminded of his training in the yard. "You're right, of course."

"Didn't mean to be hard on you, old boy, but—ridiculous as it sounds—preliminary studies indicate possible Nazi criminal activity in this region—even now, perhaps, and the reason for your recent homicide. Anyway, we're checking it out with others."

"Unbelievable! Others?" Gilford said and asked all at once. "What others?" he pressed, thinking it his duty to persist.

"Former British, Canadian, and German officers and seamen who were stationed in the immediate area during the last days of the war," came the answer.

"You don't say," Gilford replied, shocked by what he was

learning.

"Quite so. In fact, we've reason to believe the British admiralty's previous beliefs that all German U-boats had been accounted for at the end of the war was a gross misstatement of fact."

"Meaning?" pressed Gilford.

"No one in the admiralty considered the 'X factor,'" replied Sir Oliver, deliberately delaying the answer Gilford was seeking.

"I'm stumped," Gilford admitted. "What's the 'X factor'?"

"Simply this, ole boy. It's our belief that the gold fragment and the watch were all part of a treasure carried by escaping U-boats. And somehow if our theory is correct, they ended up here on your island a long, long time ago. . . . "

"That's heavy stuff!" groaned Gilford. "It's like a fairy tale. You think it's buried here? On this island?"

"There's a flaw in the theory, however, much like a hole in a bucket allowing its contents to leak out," Sir Oliver added.

"Like what?" asked Gilford, hoping the flaw wasn't serious.

"The existence of German U-boats in this area, following the end of World War II. Our admiralty says all U-boats have been accounted for to their best belief and knowledge. And that's where the rub comes in," said Sir Oliver before stopping to relight his pipe.

"If what the American tourist told you about where they found the watch is accurate," continued Sir Oliver as he sucked on his pipe before blowing sweet-smelling smoke into the air over their heads, "then we must conclude the admiralty was mistaken."

Gilford didn't know what to say next. The story seemed too incredible, unbelievable, like a chapter out of a fiction novel, matching in some ways Robert Louis Stevenson's *Treasure Island.*

"What's the matter?" asked Sir Oliver after noticing his colleague's expression.

"It's almost too much to comprehend," Gilford replied, referring to the U-boat theory. "As to the Northams, the folks who found the watch," he added, "all I can tell you is what they told me."

"Who? The tourist finders?"

"Yes," replied Gilford. "They said they found it at Gun Bay, a secluded beach not too far from here. We can't go there right now, but we can run out there later if you like."

"Okay by me," replied Sir Oliver, "but I would like to look it over."

"Historically," added Gilford, "Gun Bay was frequented by pirates because it offered a safe haven for their many exploits and a good anchorage, too."

Gilford made a left turn at a crossroad, stopping all conversation for a moment.

"How interesting," replied Sir Oliver. "And that's where the Americans found the gold fragment, you say?"

"That's what they told me," replied Gilford, "though I'm beginning to have doubts."

"You've got to give them the benefit of the doubt," said Sir Oliver. "After all, they could be telling the truth unless they have something to hide. However, if pirates used the place at one time, then it's conceivable modern, Twentieth Century ones—like escaping Nazis, for instance—might have done the same thing."

"We could still turn back," offered Gilford, his imagination now fired up.

"Later," replied Sir Oliver as he mulled over the question. "We've got more important things to do for the moment."

"On second thought," Gilford said suddenly, "there's a drawback to Gun Bay."

"Explain yourself," said Sir Oliver.

"It's too obvious. If the treasure and whatever else accompanied it were buried there long ago, it'd probably have been found by now by anyone on a treasure quest."

"That does pose a problem, doesn't it?" Sir Oliver replied.

"Given present circumstances, yes," Gilford answered. His thoughts were now on the Northams and what they had told him. *Could they have been lying?*

Silence swept through the car, allowing both men's thoughts and eyes to wander—Gilford's to the setting sun, which caused him to speed up before the legions of mosquitoes descended upon their meeting place, and Sir Oliver's upon the joy of being far removed from his stuffy office and pressures of the day.

At a crossroads where a sign was marked with the highway number A4, Gilford made a left turn. Further on, he made another turn in the direction of an arrow pointing toward Rum Point, their final destination.

They arrived five minutes late at a nice residential home set beneath and between a host of ironwood and coconut trees. Other members of the team were already there, eating a feast set before them in an adjoining pavilion. It was fully screened to ward off thousands of mosquitoes which were swarming everywhere.

What followed after that was inconsequential since everyone suffered from jet lag and mosquito bites. Gilford said his peace, bid them good night, then returned to his home, equally exhausted. What he had learned, however, did not allow him much sleep that night, a fact attested to by his wife the next morning while he was eating breakfast.

"What's this about a treasure?" she asked innocently and totally unprepared for what was to come next.

Her husband choked on a piece of bacon then yelled, "Good God, Emily, where did you hear that?"

"From you! You talked in your sleep last night. Why? Is something wrong?"

"Promise me, dear," he begged, "you won't say a thing to anyone about what you heard. Okay?"

"What's this all about, Peter?" she demanded, upset over his response.

"I can't tell you. Not yet anyway," came his reply. "It's a matter of grave importance. That's all I can say."

He gave her a quick hug and a warm kiss, then flew out of the side door leading to the carport. Moments later, his clunker smoked away.

Emily stood watching. Though confused, she had consented to his request.

Police Headquarters—Same Day

In his car, Gilford was more worried than ever before. If word got out about what he and the others were doing, Grand Cayman would be swamped with tourists, many of whom would be undesirables. *Of course,* he thought, *when it comes to tourists, the council would love that, but, oh, what havoc it would bring.*

The station loomed into sight just then, causing him to reject everything that would turn Grand Cayman into a pit of holes. He had had enough of that especially those inconsiderate metal detector tourists who thought nothing about going into someone's yard to dig.

"Go easy," a councilman urged, following one such arrest. "Just give them a warning ticket, then a free meal at the Grand Old House— at the council's expense. We can't afford to antagonize our meal tickets."

He walked into his office grumpier than usual, only to be confronted by Suzie.

"You've got some calls sir. One is from the Northams and the others from Sir Oliver and Mr. Mordeciah."

"It's one of those days," he complained as he pushed past her and plopped wearily into his comfortable leather chair. He sifted through the messages then dialed the most important caller first. The phone rang, and a familiar voice answered.

"Oliver, are you ready?"

Chapter 23

The Summit

A Private Residence—George Town

here are your assistants?" asked Inspector Gilford as he greeted the bulky Israeli representative on the driveway outside a large white residence not far from the townhouse complex the man had occupied the night before.

"They've got their assignments," replied Mort, "but I brought what you requested." He handed Gilford a piece of paper with a series of numbers on it.

"You can't be serious?" questioned Gilford as he pushed his hat back on his forehead. "They're—"

"It's what you wanted, isn't it?"

"Yes, but I didn't think they had an arsenal with them."

"Can't ever tell what we'll run into," Mort said slyly without so much as a flinch.

"But these are Uzi's—submachine guns!" Gilford protested. "Not ordinary pistols or revolvers, as I expected."

"A gun is a gun even if it's automatic," Mort replied.

A gentle breeze rolled through just then, bringing with it the sweet fragrance of tropical flowers. It helped ease the tension in Gilford, most of which was caused by last-minute changes in location after earlier arrangements fell apart. While looking around and thinking about an appropriate response to Mort's statement, he was distracted by the mimosas. They were everywhere, bright pink and in full bloom like the abundance of royal poinciana's scattered throughout the manicured estate. Other plants and flowers were in bloom too, including hibiscus of many varieties. He turned back to Mort, clearly showing his frustration.

"Anything else I need to know about?" Inspector Gilford finally asked.

"Like what?" said Mort, asking rather than giving information.

"Like the bulky stuff your men were anxious to protect when they got off the plane?"

"Oh," said Mort, a sly smile again crossing his face. "You're very observant, I see, but if you remember, those items were exempt from search and registry—all except for small arms carried on one's person, that is."

"Did the others do the same thing?" asked Gilford.

"I don't know. You'll need to ask them," replied Mort, suspecting they did.

"I have! Like you, most of them came with diplomatic passports and sealed valises."

"Sorry, but that's the way it is," replied Mort nonchalantly. "Wouldn't have it any other way. Security, you know."

"Oh, very well," Gilford replied, giving up. "Let's go in. It's getting hot out here. And . . . besides, you're late. The others arrived some time ago."

"Do they know I'm here?"

"Not yet, but they'll know soon enough."

As they walked onto the green-painted veranda, Mort looked around. A number of plain-clothes men were posted around the building making odd attempts at being inconspicuous. A gardener with shiny black shoes seemed out of place, causing Mort to inquire, "One of yours?" he asked.

"Unfortunately," Gilford replied, a bit chagrined. They walked through the double doors of the yellow-trimmed house, then down a large carpeted hallway to another set of double doors halfway down. There they took a right, straight into a huge palor full of dense smoke and people speaking in subdued voices. Again, Gilford cringed. He didn't like smoke of any kind but had to endure it nevertheless.

The talking stopped when Gilford and the stocky man entered. Mort had arrived with a half-burnt cigar stuck between the fingers of one hand, reminding everyone who saw him of someone quite famous though now long-gone, Winston Churchill.

"Gentlemen," Gilford interrupted. "May I introduce Mr. Mordeciah Joachim, an independent representative for the Israeli government?"

Upon hearing the word "Israeli," the Germans stiffened uneasily but showed remarkable restraint as they politely walked up to introduce themselves.

As for the Russians, no one within their group moved until their leader, Igor Pederosky, gave a friendly *"Da,"* signaling his approval to greet the new arrival.

"Glad you could come, ole fellow," Sir Oliver said as he walked up. "We understand you've been involved in many cases like this."

"Depends upon what you mean," Mordeciah replied.

"You know, Nazi hunting and all that. . . ." He stopped, suddenly conscious he had said something at the wrong time and place. He turned to face the Germans, who appeared slightly embarrassed. "Sorry about that," he apologized. "No offense intended, of course."

"Not at all, Sir Oliver. We're quite used to it," Helmut answered quite diplomatically in behalf of his associates, too. "It's the unfortunate part of our life, but we've learned to live with it. Like everyone here, we despise anything having to do with the Nazi era."

"Good show," Sir Oliver replied before being reminded by Gilford it was time to start.

As he moved away, the CIA representative, Joseph Rosenkranz came up and shook Mordeciah's hand with great vigor. "I've heard a lot about you . . . . "

"It's Mort for short," Mordeciah replied as they exchanged greetings.

"Mort, you've quite a reputation . . . like Simon Wiesenthal. I sure hope we'll be able to work together," Rosenkrantz said in hopes of developing a relationship in which they had a common base—their Jewishness.

"Not likely," said Mort, totally indifferent. "We can't afford foul-ups."

As the startled agent tried to regain his composure, a distinct English voice swept through the room, bringing a hush with it.

"Gentlemen, if you'll please take your seats at the table next to those windows over there," said Sir Oliver, "the sooner we'll be able to get on with things."

At the end of the room, near a long row of louvered windows—

all open to allow a cool breeze to flow through—was a large rectangular table, 4 feet across by 20 feet long. To nourish the guests, fresh fruits and refreshments had been set upon it along with seating arrangement cards for each country and person represented, Mort's assistants included.

"Sorry," he apologized when queried about their absence, "they've more important things to do at the moment. Besides, they've nothing to contribute . . . not yet anyway."

Sir Oliver accepted his word and motioned for everyone to be seated. A mixture of sounds followed: snapping briefcases and valises, rustling of papers, and the scraping of wooden legs against the parquet floor. Silence came next as Sir Oliver, a dignified white-haired man from Great Britain, took his place at the head of the table. Behind him and to his side were a projection screen and blackboard, both ready for use.

Like everyone before him, he snapped open his large briefcase and quickly withdrew a pile of documents, all of which he promptly circulated. He waited patiently until everyone had received his copy.

"Gentlemen," he began slowly to allow everyone—the interpreter included—time to get used to his linguistic pace, "if you'll note, at the top of each document there is a security classification. It's marked in large red letters. Documents having the words "Top Secret" written upon them must be treated with the utmost of care. Should their contents be leaked we might as well go home because our mission here will have been compromised. Do I make myself clear?"

He looked around the room to see if everyone understood. When they said they did, whether by word or sign, he started his portion of the program with a brief history of the case to date, backed by a montage of films from different sources, "to offer continuity of subject matter." That was the way Sir Oliver explained it before he ordered his assistants into action.

"Mr. Jones, if you would please," Sir Oliver said to a man stationed behind a large projector at the other end of the table. To another, he gave the task of pulling down the blinds and turning off the lights.

A muffled silence followed when a long beam was projected onto the screen. Before long, everyone heard a scratching sound track playing *Deutschland Uber Alles*. It introduced the title: *A Legacy in Terror and Deception*. Scenes from a 1939 Berlin military parade came next, revealing thousands of jack-booted soldiers goose-stepping to the delirious cheers of banner-waving masses. On a large balcony along the route and high overhead stood Adolph Hitler and his entourage, smiling and waving to an admiring people they would eventually bring to ruin.

"Please note this man, the one directly behind Hitler and slightly to the right," said Sir Oliver as he drew the audience's attention to a figure on the screen through use of a long pointer. He ordered the projectionist to rewind, then freeze the frame. "If you don't know who he is, I'll tell you. It's Martin Bormann, one of Hitler's closest confidants. Note the tall, handsome, blond man too. That's OberFührer SS Hermann Fegelein. Both men deserve your serious attention."

"Bormann I know, but who's the general? I've never heard of him before," said a voice from the back of the dark smoky room, momentarily interrupting the speaker.

"His name is Fegelein, originally an insignificant horse trainer and part-time jockey with little or no formal education who just happened to meet the right people at the right time. On such persona was a certain Christian Weber, a grotesque hulk of a man who was one of Hitler's early supporters. Weber introduced Fegelein to higher-ups like Himmler, and away he went. Within a matter of years, because of his impressive riding skills, he was promoted to brigadier general, OberFührer SS, and made inspector over all calvary units. In 1943, he was sent to the Russian front, was wounded, then sent back to Germany for rehabilitation. Upon recovery, through some sort of manipulation, he managed to get an appointment as Himmler's SS liaison officer to Hitler himself. Pretty good for an uneducated country bumpkin, wouldn't you say?"

"Why is he important to us?" someone asked.

"Because he's one of the men, along with Martin Bormann, who vanished right after Hitler committed suicide."

"That name is familiar, " a member of the German delegation said aloud. "Isn't he the one who married Eva Braun's sister, Gretl?"

"You're quite right, my dear fellow," replied Sir Oliver. "It was a marriage of convenience requested by Hitler upon learning Gretl was pregnant. Whether by him or someone else no one really knows since she had a reputation for being quite a socialite. In any event, as far as Fegelein is concerned, he was supposed to have been executed."

"I remember reading about him!" replied Gilford. "He was shot for desertion after being caught wearing civilian clothes and carrying a lot of foreign currency."

"Not to mention, in the company of his mistress, too . . . a Hungarian baroness. Or was she British?" added Sir Oliver thoughtfully. "No matter because his court martial and execution, if such a thing ever took place, remains unproven. In fact, to go one step further, we have no proof of his demise before a firing squad outside of the Führerbunker either by way of witnesses and the like or skeletal remains. The same applies to Martin Bormann."

"I'm afraid you're mistaken, Sir Oliver," said Frederick Rosenkrantz, the U.S. CIA representative to the meeting. "Bormann's bones—along with those of another Nazi—were unearthed in Berlin several years ago if I'm not mistaken."

"Hah! A smoke screen," roared Mort as he blew a defiant ring of smoke into the air near the agent's face. "Don't you believe that garbage!"

"I beg your pardon!" the CIA agent responded in shock.

"No offense taken," replied Mort, giving way to the speaker.

"I share your opinion, Mr. Mordeciah," Sir Oliver quickly interjected. "While it's true a number of forensic experts have examined skeletal remains purporting to be those of Bormann and a doctor, we—my staff and I—are of the opinion they're mistaken."

"Are you saying they're not dead?" asked Igor Pederosky, the Russian leader.

"That's precisely the point I'm trying to make," answered Sir Oliver. "We have reason to believe that the two men just mentioned might still be alive and living under assumed names."

"Is there any evidence to support your theories?" asked Gilford.

"About General Fedelein, yes. But that can only be done through review of our remaining films, if that is all right with the members present?" replied Sir Oliver.

"All right with me. I've got nothing but time on my hands," said Mort.

"How about the rest of you?" asked Sir Oliver.

Da's and *jah's* followed, along with *Yes's* and *Oui's*, clearly showing everyone was in agreement.

"All right, Harry, roll her forward to the frames we picked out. A bit more. Yes, yes—that's it," said Sir Oliver before addressing the audience. To them, he said, "If you will look closely, you will get a better glimpse of Fegelein in this frame."

Sir Oliver used his pointer again to single out one of many Nazi officials in general's uniforms. When all eyes were upon the man, he added, "Please take note of his features. You'll need to remember them when it comes time to examine a number of photographs which recently fell into our hands."

The scenes changed often after that to Hitler's rocket testing facilities on the Baltic, Peenemünde, then on to Dieppe, France, where V1 "pulse jet" buzz bomb launch sites had been constructed to bombard London. Later, the film showed a massive network of underground tunnels dug deep into the heart of the Harz Mountains of southern Germany near a sleepy, picturesque village called Nordhausen. There, with the help of slave labor, the Nazis had constructed a sophisticated factory for building V1 flying bombs. Dr. Werner von Braun and hundreds of his assistants had been sent there to continue Hitler's rocket development program after things got too hot for them in Peenemünde. They were to leave again when the Allies began closing in.

As the projector whirred, more scenes followed, capturing everyone's attention except Mort's. With the curtains drawn and the room stifling hot, he had fallen asleep. Disturbing snores gave him away. He apologized, "Sorry, it's the heat—and jet lag."

More scenes flashed across the screen, showing shipbuilding, repair, and harbor facilities in Hamburg, Kiel, and other locations. Next came views of bomb-proof U-boat pens throughout France and Germany and a final view of Hitler's infamous Reichbank before and after its destruction by Allied bombers.

Though the program was longer than expected, no one seemed to mind. It's contents were not only informative, but intriguing, tiring no one. Their response and attentiveness pleased Sir Oliver because he and his staff, in cooperation with members of Britain's Secret Service, MI-5, had spent a great deal of time developing the program.

The final presentation combined Allied and captured German films, many showing hidden caches of Nazi loot, like the millions of dollars of gold bullion hidden by the Nazis in various salt mines throughout western Germany. Where much of it came from was shown, too: concentration camps. Therein, carnage was everywhere as was an abundance of loot SS troops had been unable to cart away before deserting the camps. Examples included barrels of unprocessed gold teeth; personal belongings such as wedding rings, broaches, and jewelry of all sorts and sizes; negotiable instruments; and a variety of precious art treasures much like those found in Hermann Goering's palatial homes and rail cars of his personal train following Germany's collapse. A lot of sad faces could be seen in the room as the films ground on, those of the German representatives in particular. Often, while hoping others wouldn't notice, they'd look the other way to wipe an occasional tear.

When Sir Oliver and his group had finished their presentation, the Russians began theirs. Like the British before them, they too had materials to present from slides to films and records. They had more of the latter, and surprisingly, willingly shared what they had with

303

everyone.

"All because of *glasnost*," Igor added at one point before going on. "What puzzles us the most, however, is the continuous appearance—and reappearance—of something we can't identify, the letters *U-4R*. They show up everywhere even where we least expect them."

"*Jah*. It was the same for us," Helmut Grundig interjected excitedly. "Our computers found them, too! At first, we didn't pay any attention to them. It was so subtle . . . almost unnoticed until. . . ."

"Go on," urged Sir Oliver, anxious to hear more.

"Until we found this," Helmut added. As everyone watched, he removed something from his valise and held it up for everyone to see. It looked like an old manuscript cover. Though badly faded, everyone could see what appeared to be a large silver-embossed eagle, the symbol of Hitler's Third Reich. Right below it, again in faded letters though quite large, was a title: *PROJEK U4R*.

"What is its significance?" asked Sir Oliver.

"We can only speculate," said Helmut, "but we feel certain it contained something important, for the Führer's eyes only. A secret plan perhaps. . . . "

"How did you get it?" asked Sir Oliver.

"It was found by one of our researchers when he was given the task of screening some old SS printing records which had been turned over to us after our country became a member of NATO. And regrettably, like many other important and unidentified records, it's been gathering dust in one of our warehouses all this time."

"Outside its ornate cover, there's little here to indicate it has any connection to what we're talking about," continued Sir Oliver.

"On the surface, yes, but the date, if you will notice, which is also embossed at the bottom, leads us to think it was part of a secret package delivered to Hitler—for his signature, perhaps—just before Bormann, Fegelein, and other high-ranking Nazi officers disappeared from the Führerbunker."

"That's still speculative," replied Igor, head of the Russian delegation.

"Yes. We know," agreed Helmut, "but far too much care was put into its creation, which makes it suspect. And then there are those mysterious letters, *U4R*, which kept showing up in our computer readouts, to which we can now add an antonym, the German word *PROJEKT*, or "PROJECT" to those of you who understand English. All together it gives us something called Project U4R!"

"That is most interesting and revealing, and I agree with your hypothesis, Herr Grundig," interjected Sir Oliver. "Here, take a look at these," he added as he reached into his briefcase to withdraw a number of worn documents. All eyes followed his movements.

"What is it?" asked Igor Pederosky as he and other members of the group reached for copies which Sir Oliver was circulating.

"It's an old inventory of the contents of an SS vault in the Reichbank just before it went out of business."

"What's the "X" mark for?" asked Gilford as he slithered over to the German delegate, the only one who could read it.

"*Mein Gott!*" exclaimed Helmut while noting the date of the withdrawal. "It's a description of a gold watch like the one reported missing!"

"Precisely," commented Sir Oliver. "Just like the one reported stolen here in Grand Cayman."

"And . . . and the date," Helmut stumbled. "It coincides with the cover. By a day anyway. . . ."

Sir Oliver smiled, then reached into his back pocket and withdrew a small leather pouch, the one in which he kept his special blend of tobacco. He refilled his pipe just then and relit it, blowing out sweet-smelling smoke in the process.

It smelled so good, Gilford didn't complain even when the smoke blew his way. Perhaps it was because he was intent on learning more about the inventory list and its full meaning to the case. Whatever the reason, he pressed on.

"Let me get this straight," he asked Sir Oliver. "Are you trying to tell me the watch listed here in the inventory is the same as the one which was left at the watchmaker's?"

"What else?" replied Sir Oliver. "They're identical, and we know for certain only one was ever made. And because of these records, it's obvious the bloody watch was once part of the Reichbank treasury before the greedy SS made a hasty withdrawal."

"Incredible!" replied one of the delegates in the room, an expression shared by others.

"If that's true, how did it get here?" Gilford demanded.

"Gentlemen," interrupted Sir Oliver loudly. "There's still more, and you're missing it!"

Everyone looked his way, unclear as to his meaning.

"Look at the bottom of the each list," he urged, "at the recipient's name and signature."

Again eyes turned to the document. This time Helmut spoke out. "It's signed by an OberFührer Ernst von Kleitenberg, whoever that is . . . ."

"Never heard of him," interjected Mort with sudden interest.

"Neither had we, at first," replied one of Sir Oliver's assistants. "Which is what makes it so interesting."

"You have an explanation?" asked agent Rosenkrantz.

"Possibly, but that will have to wait for later since we've much more to cover," replied Sir Oliver.

"I see a connection!" exclaimed Igor excitedly, his eyes full of fire. "It's the Peenemünde records!"

"And the U-boats! The ones without identification numbers!" interjected Helmut Grundig suddenly. "Don't you see? They're intertwined! Is that how you say it?"

His thoughts trailing far behind, the former East German, Wolfgang Koehler, asked a question which embarrassed his counterparts. "Did they put the treasure in the rockets then fire them out to sea where they could be recovered by U-boats?"

"*Nein,* that wouldn't have worked. The VIs and 2s were too imprecise for such work. Besides, it would have been too risky and the treasure could have been lost for all time," explained Grundig to his less-technically sophisticated associate.

"But they could have worked things out," Koehler argued before being cut off.

"*Mein herre,* gentlemen," Mort interrupted after tiring of their conversation. "The whole damned thing is quite simple really, but you've got to pay attention to the signs."

"What signs?" asked Gilford, a question shared by others.

"U-boats without identification—and a general no one ever heard of!" replied Mort with a boldness which drew respect. "Think of it! As meticulous as the bastards were, the Nazis, that is, when it came to record keeping, it's inconceivable they would omit something as important as an identification number. It's totally out of character, unless it was intentional. Make sense?"

"In a way, yes, but how do you explain it . . . the U-boats and a general few if any ever heard of?" asked agent Rosenkrantz.

"Salvaged vessels. What else? No doubt secretly recovered from the bottom of the sea so no one would find out. It's been done before," Mort replied.

"And the general?" Gilford asked.

"Could be the one we referred to earlier," said Sir Oliver with his crisp British accent. "You know . . . Fegelein . . . the general supposedly shot for desertion? At this point, it's all theory, however, but in time it may all pan out, like missing pieces to a jigsaw puzzle."

A hush fell over almost everyone except those in the group who needed to study the documents more closely. After that, they joined the others in silence, too, but it was not for long. Mort broke the silence.

"Let's go over this Peenemünde thing," said Mort. "Perhaps our Russian friends here can fill us in on a few details since it was they who occupied the place and had a few years to study what they found."

"*Da.* That is true," admitted Igor. "I agree with the German and English delegations, that here does seem to be a connection. To what extent, I am not clear since we have conflicting information."

"Like what?" asked Sir Oliver.

Igor pulled out a folder just then and flipped through its pages. "I have here a sworn statement," he said, "from a former Peenemünde scientist, a German who was captured at the end of the war and taken to the Soviet Union for questioning."

"He's still there no doubt," said agent Rosenkrantz, jokingly.

Before the Russian leader's interpreter could translate his off-color remark for those of his group who did not speak English, Igor gave a surprisingly good answer, embarrassing the CIA agent and challenging him at the same time.

"Yes, and he's now enjoying a very good pension, courtesy of the Soviet, the Russian peoples. But since you mentioned our prisoners, what about your own? Take Dr. von Braun and his former assistants for example. Didn't they get good-paying jobs and pensions?"

"Touche!" replied Rosenkrantz before being interrupted by Sir Oliver who felt it expedient to act as a moderator.

"Gentlemen," he said, appealing to their sense of reason, "may I remind you we have no need for rivalry? What must take precedence above everything is a spirit of international cooperation."

"My apologies," said agent Rosenkrantz with a sheepish grin as he faced the Russian. "I'm sorry."

"Accepted, and you have mine, too," said Igor.

"Shall we continue, Igor," asked Sir Oliver, "with your report on Peenemünde?"

"Ah, yes," Igor replied, picking up where he left off. "About six months or so before the war ended, the witness I mentioned claimed a detachment of SS troops arrived at their camp in early February 1944 and immediately went to work establishing a highly sophisticated metallurgical research department. It was so secret that even Dr. von Braun and his staff, had they not been transferred to Nordhausen in southern Germany, would not have been allowed access to it."

"Strange, yet not so strange," said Sir Oliver, "when it comes to an understanding of how the Nazi mind worked—around secret projects especially. But do go on, ole boy," he urged after interrupting.

"Thank you," said Igor, agreeing with the Englishman on both accounts. "We do not doubt the Nazis were working on a secret weapon, but we still do not have a clue as to what it was or might have been. What we do know, however, is that a series of unmarked boxes—the size and shape of rockets or torpedoes—were taken out of the facility at Peenemünde and shipped by rail to Kiel. The SS razed the factory after that, leaving nothing to indicate what they were doing."

"Rockets perhaps, but not torpedos. Peenemuende was a rocket test site," said Grundig after weighing the information.

Sensing they had hit upon something, Sir Oliver cut him off, then turned to the Russian. "When did those crates go out?" he asked.

"One or two days before Hitler died," he replied. "And, oh, yes, there's something else I almost forgot," added Igor. "Of all the people known to work in that facility, and that includes the scientists, technicians, and slave laborers, no trace of them has ever been found."

"God!" exclaimed Gilford. "All this is like something out of a James Bond movie."

Sir Oliver smiled, then turned back to Igor who was trying to figure out who James Bond was. His interpreter didn't know either until Mordeciah whispered in his ear in Russian.

"Anything else?" asked Sir Oliver.

Before Igor could respond, two smoke rings raced across the table, giving everyone the distinct impression Mort wanted to say something.

"Typical! Do the dirty work, then bump them off. As for the cartons . . . torpedoes probably, in which to store the treasure and anything else of importance to them."

"Like what?" inquired Gilford.

"Ah, that is the question as put so aptly by Shakespeare," responded Mort, happy to answer. "Why go through all that crap at Peenemünde when they could have easily gutted a regular torpedo? They had plenty of them stockpiled, so it had to be something else and the facility on the Baltic was the vehicle for carrying it out."

"Your point is well taken," agreed Sir Oliver. "Weight might also have been a deciding factor, too, don't you think?"

"Perhaps," agreed Mort, "but even that seems trifling as reasons go. The Nazis never did anything in a small way; it was always big— remember? So from what I can determine, there's more to those mysterious cartons than we know. I'd bet a box of my best Havanas on it."

"To carry bullion is my guess," Igor interjected. "We have the missing watch and the gold fragment to support such a theory," he added before directing a side remark to Mort.

"By the way, Mr. Mordeciah, I don't agree with your assessment of post-Castro cigars. A friend sent me several boxes not too long ago, and they were quite good, believe me. Here, have one," he said as he pulled a long, brown, twisted piece of hemp from his coat pocket and handed to him. He smiled while doing so, leaving Mort to appreciate his sense of humor.

"What about the murder?" interrupted Gilford, "and the arrest and apprehension of a person—or persons—who committed the crime? While everything seems to point in one direction, I must admit it's hard for me to believe all this stuff about Nazi thugs transporting their loot to this island over forty years ago!"

"Don't let it bother you, sonny. I've run across stranger things than this before," Mort replied in a very casual manner. "It's Nazis all right, and they're here! Can smell them, like that butcher Adolph Eichmann and Klaus Barbie, until we sniffed them out." He inhaled through his nostrils, making the German delegation squirm uneasily.

To avoid a confrontation which seemed imminent, Gilford saved the day. "If you're right, what's next?"

"Check the watchmaker's friends for someone he was close to," replied Mort while offering a precaution. "Without revealing what's been going on, of course."

"I want this case solved—not jeopardized!" replied Gilford, adding, "It's still going to be tough because Hans had a lot of friends— me included."

"All right, make yourself a suspect," Mort joked before continuing in a more serious vain. "A man like Schumacher must have had a confident. A foreigner perhaps . . .like himself."

"There are a few," agreed Gilford after thinking it over.

"And you might consider someone who emigrated here after the war," suggested Sir Oliver. "With an island as small as yours, it shouldn't take long."

"True," agreed Gilford. "We've got to start somewhere and our home ground is as good a place as any, providing the murderer has left."

"Glad you think so," said Mort before giving way to Sir Oliver again.

"Peter," said Sir Oliver in a questioning voice, "that young couple you told me about, the ones who found the watch and fragment. Why don't you contact them again?"

"I'm not so certain that'd do any good," came his reply.

"Why not? Surely, if made aware of the gravity of the matter, it would seem they'd agree to cooperate."

"The wife, perhaps," replied Gilford, "but as to the husband, it's ify. He's been very cautious—too cautious, in fact—like he's hiding something. Can't put my finger on it yet unless . . . unless he's found more than what he's admitted to date."

"That's a curious thing to say," remarked Mort. "Any reason for that?"

"A good one. He's lied once already, right after the murder. Said the watch had been willed to him by a loving aunt, only to change his story later when his wife contradicted him. Now he's claiming it was found at Gun Bay some miles away from here . . . along the east side."

"Is that unusual, given all the treasure that's been found throughout the islands?" asked Sir Oliver.

"For Gun Bay, yes, like I said yesterday. It's been picked clean. Gone over and over again by hundreds of locals and tourists, which makes the likelihood of him finding something of value out there—in a raked-over beach—as remote as finding the bones of a prehistoric dinosaur."

"Oh! I see," replied Sir Oliver. "Now I understand why you've been reticent from the start to accept their story. Any ideas?"

Gilford thought for a while before answering. "Yes. The weak link is his wife. If she could be approached without him being present, she might be persuaded to tell the truth. I know she's fed up with the whole mess by the way she reacts, but he's the boss."

"Then try him again," pressed Sir Oliver. "If he sticks to his old story, single her out."

"Or the little girl. . . ." Gilford replied, having a suddenly thought.

"Who?" asked Mort.

"Tanya—their eight-year-old daughter, a cute blond thing with sky-blue eyes. She's been with them all along. Must've seen or learned something."

Gilford's mind raced. He was happy with himself though he could have kicked himself for not thinking of the child earlier. Kids weren't good at keeping secrets, especially those involving adult games of deception. Case in point: his own children. He learned the hard way one day after one of his daughters revealed details of a case she had overheard him discussing. It taught him a lesson: Say nothing in front of children!

"A good idea," said Gilford after thinking about Mort's suggestion. "I'll try the father first, then the mother. If that doesn't work, I'll take on the child . . . with help from one of my children perhaps, if you know what I mean." He winked in Mort's way.

Mort blew a large smoke ring above the table this time, showing his approval, though one didn't always know what he was thinking. Like the Soviets, he listened a lot and spoke very little.

"Gentlemen," announced Sir Oliver after looking at his watch. "It's getting quite late, and I believe we've covered enough for today, so if you have no objection, may I suggest we adjourn until day after tomorrow, which should be sufficient time to allow you to contact your governments to advise what we have accomplished to date. And, hopefully, enough time to receive information from them that might have been uncovered during your absence."

"Here, here," replied a happy British subject.

"Fine by us," agreed Rosenkrantz, representing the CIA. "What we've learned so far is invaluable and a couple more days to sort things out would help. Besides I'm on per diem."

"For us, too," replied the interpreter for the Soviet delegation for his superior, "but I'm sure our reimbursement expenses aren't so liberal as yours."

"And for us," answered Helmut Grundig for his group, anxious to avoid international rivalry.

"Very well then," said Sir Oliver, overlooking the sly remarks as he searched the room for those having other thoughts. "Since there are no objections, we stand adjourned." He turned to Gilford, "Think you can arrange things?"

"No problem. The owner's in Miami for a week. We can have the place until then."

Chairs scraped the floor noisily again, and briefcases snapped loudly as the Russian and other delegations eagerly gathered handouts to carry back with them. It had been a fruitful day for everyone, and they were satisfied with the day's program.

The delegations were divided into small groups to minimize drawing attention to their departure. While leaving the patrolled grounds, several members were overheard asking the guard at the gate for directions to Seven Mile Beach; they wanted to bask in the sun on its white sand beaches, then swim in its crystal-clear waters. Others had different plans. They were the ones—as noted by Mort and Gilford earlier—who wasted no time marking their Grand Cayman Island highway maps after learning of the spot where the gold fragment and watch had allegedly been found.

Gilford couldn't help thinking about them as they drove away. At a crossroads a quarter of a mile down the road, he could see them turning to the left instead of the right, confirming his suspicions.

Fools! he thought to himself while shaking his head in disappointment. *What do you think you'll find?*

He didn't have long to think about them before his attention was drawn to the street beyond the gate. Unlike the British who knew the proper side to drive on, one of the delegations had taken the wrong side, nearly causing a head-on collision. Seconds later, loud cursing and the screech of angry tires reached his ears.

You need to think left and drive left, sonny, he thought to himself as he walked to his clunker car parked near the entrance and got in. By then, his old thoughts were impervious to everything and everyone except a new one: *Well, Mr. Northam, let's see what you've got to say this time.*

The man parked in the shade down the street hadn't drawn any attention because he seemed harmless. Besides, his car was too far away to cause concern. Yet had anyone investigated, they might have learned otherwise.

Just before Gilford's car chugged by, trailing a thick cloud of black smoke, he had carefully repacked a set of earphones to his highly sophisticated eavesdropping machine. Earlier, its parabolic microphone had been aimed at the curtained windows outside the private residence, recording what it could. When the last guard drove off, leaving the way clear for him to leave without danger, the nervous man made a sharp U-turn and drove away. Minutes later, he reached his destination—a set of public phones.

"Operator, a credit card call to Ciudad del Carmen, Mexico. Person-to-person, to Señor Martinez, please."

After hearing the number, the operator dialed, putting his call through in record time.

"Who's calling?" asked a gruff voice on the other end, first in Spanish, then in English.

"Señor Rodriguez in the Cayman Islands," replied the anxious caller through the operator.

"I'm sorry, operator, but Señor Martinez is not here."

"Not there! Where is he?" the caller panicked. Before the operator could stop the conversation, the party in Mexico gave the answer.

"He's taking a cruise in the Caribbean, if you know what I mean," the party on the other end replied quickly.

"But—"

"Don't worry. Plans have been made, and his associate, Señor Ramos, will be arriving in George Town tomorrow morning aboard Air Jamaica flight 247."

"Sir, sir . . . ," said the operator in a futile attempt to stop the unexpected conversation.

"Oh! Thank God!" said the caller. "I was worried . . . because important things have been happening."

"Tell Mr. Ramos when he gets there," the man on the other end replied, a moment before the frustrated operator cut in.

"Sir, if you wish to continue this conversation, I must make a charge. Do you wish to speak to your party in Mexico?"

"No, thank you, operator," the caller replied. "It's no longer necessary." He put the receiver on the hook just then as did the party in Mexico.

The clicks angered the operator, causing her to violate company policy. She yelled loudly, "Cheap skates!"

John Hankins

Chapter 24

New Dimensions

Owen Roberts Airport—George Town

he short and stocky old man with the Mexican passport didn't appear Spanish or Mexican, but that didn't bother customs agents because Anglo-looking people from Mexico were quite common. In fact, many were descendants of Castillian Spaniards who originally settled the country while others came from France, Germany, and other European countries.

He passed through customs without difficulty, bringing a feeling of relief. Johann Liebermann, whose real name was Johann Steinmueller, waited for him outside the Customs clearing point. Johann had seen him a week ago and was shocked to learn his once-vigorous chief was now using a cane. That really wasn't so unusual' since many years had passed since they had seen each other. And besides, he too had lost some of his own hair.

Liebermann couldn't complain, however. After his initial training as a *Hitler Jugen* volunteer, he had accompanied his chief and other high-ranking Nazi official's, like Martin Bormann, aboard

315

U-4R2 after the fall of the Third Reich. His payment for Cayman Island services had been more than adequate even though his duties required frequent travel throughout the Caribbean, much of it in search of the missing U-boat, *U-4R1*. Now, however, after years of frustration, the break they had been waiting for had finally come. What was fascinating about it all was that it came through a most unlikely source—a Jewish watchmaker!

In some ways, Johann was sorry he had to kill the man because he had come to know and like him. It was part of his job to infiltrate the local scene and become one of its respected citizens. Making friends with a supposed fellow inmate was part of it, a role which came easily because he had assumed someone else's identity. Though he didn't have a Jewish name, he had passed himself off as a persecuted *Mischling** and tried to act the part by appearing introverted and unwilling to speak about the atrocities he supposedly endured in a concentration camp. Naturally, his deceit was readily accepted by the old watchmaker for he too, didn't like to be reminded of his miserable past.

In recalling the killing of the watchmaker, Johann, a man now in his sixties, was reminded of something drummed into his head by his socio-political science instructor at the Institute of the Mayas in Mexico years earlier. As a bright-eyed student leader of the schools newly formed SS Warrior brigade, he was eager to learn everything. Killing others was one of them.

"It's the nature of war," his instructor bellowed, "and duty comes first, taking precedence over everything, friendships too . . . which is only a transient thing anyway."

The message was vivid as though given yesterday, making him feel better. He turned to greet the new arrival, the man who had been his mentor, Sturmbannführer Reiter—now a general.

"Any trouble, Mr. Ramos?" Liebermann asked, knowing full well he couldn't address him any other way.

"Nothing except the usual customs check in Mexico City. A little *moneda* here and there sped things up, however," replied the man as they hurriedly exchanged amenities.

"Any baggage?" asked Liebermann.

"My briefcase, the clothes on my back, and a carry-on bag," his chief replied as he motioned for a porter to set it beside him.

Lieberman tipped the man, then said, "Traveling light?"

"The rest of my bags will arrive shortly. By sea, if you get my meaning."

"Ah, yes," smiled Lieberman, showing he understood. He added,

316

"I'm glad you're here. A lot of things are going on. . . ."

"Must be important," Reiter replied as Liebermann, after picking up his superior's carry-on bag, led him outdoors to a bright red convertible—a Porsche—in a nearby parking lot. After helping him get in on the left side, he ran to the other door and got in.

"British influence, I see," said Reiter with contempt.

"We will need to act quickly," said Liebermann the second he got behind the wheel, leaving his boss somewhat confused.

"Why the urgency?" asked Reiter who hadn't been fully briefed about the previous day's eavesdropping.

"Because we're facing a Normandy all over and the Allies have landed again!"

"Be specific, Kamerad! Remember, I don't know all you know," complained Reiter.

So Liebermann told him about the secret meeting at a private residence. He learned about it by chance, after taking a table in a Hog Sty Bay waterfront restaurant, right next to an anxious young man who was upset because his date was late and he had to get back to work. As it turned out, he knew the young woman. She worked at the police station and gave as an excuse for her tardiness, the arrival of an important message from Scotland Yard, for the eyes of her boss only Chief Inspector Gilford. The answer satisfied the young man, but left Liebermann with a lot to worry about, so he stalked the inspector for several weeks until mixed groups of Europeans and Americans began arriving.

"And that's why I'm concerned," said Liebermann. "The place has been invaded by foreign dignitaries and agents belonging to the CIA, KGB, Interpol, SDD, *STASI*, Scotland Yard, and God knows who else!"

Reiter was incredulous. "I . . . I can't believe it," he replied. "Why didn't you tell me . . . before I got here?"

"I tried to, but you were already gone, sir," replied Liebermann. "But don't worry. From what I've learned, they haven't found anything yet, not even my identity or location of the treasure."

"You sound mighty sure of yourself," said Reiter. "How can you be so certain?"

"Because I know, though it doesn't mean they won't find out in time."

"What about the site? Do you know where it is?"

"Not exactly—" replied Liebermann.

"That's not a good answer," replied Reiter.

"For us it's good," Liebermann argued, "because we know more

317

than the authorities at this point. Oh, yes, they know the names of the people who found the watch and fragment, but so far they haven't learned where it really came from."

He pulled out a pack of cigarettes, and offered one to his chief.

"Nein, danke," said Reiter with a shake of his head. "I gave it up years ago. Bad for your health, you know? As for young people these days, in spite of cancer warnings, they continue to follow the tide which is the strongest. A pity," he said almost nostalgically.

Liebermann didn't seem bothered by his remark. He took one for himself and lit it before starting the car and driving off. They semicircled around the airport, then raced off toward George Town.

"Why do you suppose the couple haven't told the authorities everything?" asked Reiter as they raced through the maze of small streets.

"One of two possibilities," answered Liebermann. "For one, because they might want to keep everything, and secondly, maybe that's all they found."

"Good God! I hope not!" Reiter exclaimed. "We've wasted too much time and money already!"

"Frankly, I think they've got it," Liebermann replied. "If you find one piece, it's only logical to conclude the other parts are nearby too, don't you agree?"

"Yes, I do," agreed Reiter, "but like you said earlier, we can't afford to wait. If what remains of the U-4R1's cargo is here, then we've got to get to it before the others."

The Porsche roared up to a stop sign near the tourist-crowded seawall on the bay, and there Liebermann made a quick right turn. Two miles down the road, along Seven Mile Beach, Reiter spoke out.

"I know this place," he said, pointing to the beach on their left side. "Studied it for days, so I'd know how to get around. Can't be too careful, you know."

"Very wise," Liebermann said as he made another right-hand turn into a peaceful residential subdivision. He swung left into a circular driveway leading to a modest cottage. "My place," he said. "We'll stop here for a while."

They got out and walked into a spacious air-conditioned home. The cool interior brought a sigh of relief from Reiter as he limped toward a large sofa and plopped down. Liebermann left him for a minute and returned with two bottles of beer.

"Steinlager," he said as he handed a frosty bottle to his boss who was resting his head on a large pillow. Lieberman settled into his favorite platform rocker next to his boss.

Reiter pushed forward and patted one of Steinmueller's knees. "You know, Liebermann . . . ah . . . Steinmueller, you were one of my best students and I'm proud of you for your diligence."

Before Steinmueller could reply, a twinge of pain shot across Reiter's face, causing him to cry out.

"Are you all right?" asked Steinmueller with a worried look on his face. He hoped the man wasn't having a heart attack. If he did, he was in deep trouble and would have to hide the body.

"It's a pinched nerve. At least that's what Doktor Heim tells me. But I'm used to it," he continued while seeking the correct position to alleviate the pain.

"Goodness! Is he still around?"

"Getting older and a little forgetful, but otherwise all right," replied Reiter. "Now, as to what we had been talking about. . . ."

"Oh, yes," continued Steinmueller after being assured everything was all right. "About the delegation which just arrived. From what I've learned they've decided to reinterrogate the man who found the watch in hopes he'll change his story. If he doesn't, they'll try his wife, then their daughter."

"Daughter!" Reiter exclaimed as if struck by a bolt of electricity. He pushed forward even further, ignoring the pain which racked his joints.

"Yes. The chief inspector is of the opinion she knows as much as they but has been told to say nothing."

A sinister smile crossed Reiter's face. "How clever," he said as he sat back to think a bit. Steinmueller watched him, his own thoughts swirling.

"Where are they staying? The American family?" Reiter finally asked.

"Nearby—at the Holiday Inn."

"Good, then that's where we'll start. The girl is the weakest link in the whole chain, irrespective of what the authorities think," Reiter said. "Is there anything else about which we need to concern ourselves?"

"Yes, my future here."

"Why? Is it in jeopardy?"

"Not now, but it soon will be because the police have been encouraged to contact the watchmaker's friends, close ones especially. Since I'm known to be one of them, I know they will be calling soon."

"You don't expect trouble, do you?"

"Only if they make a computer check of immigration records, like they did when discovering *PROJEKT U4R."*

"Hmmm, I see what you mean," replied Reiter, showing concern. "Yes, that could be serious, but totally unimportant if we get to the site before they do. After that, we'll all be gone. In the meantime, however—as you said—we must act quickly."

"Two weeks is about all we can hope for," replied Steinmueller as he looked around the home he would be leaving.

"What's their name . . . the family you spoke about?"

"Northam," replied Steinmueller.

"Are you sure they're still at the hotel?"

"Yes. No problem there. Beside, they can't leave until the police finish their investigation."

"That's even better," Reiter replied cheerfully, causing Steinmueller to wonder what was going through his conniving mind. He knew it was conniving because he had once overheard General von Kleitenberg talking about it.

"My friend," he said at long last, "we have work to do but not before we have dinner. After that, a nice warm shower and then we talk."

"My place is yours, sir."

Holiday Inn—Seven Mile Beach

It was 8:45 in the evening when the phone in the Northam's hotel room rang. The entire family was watching TV at the time.

"Yes?" answered Phillip while reluctantly lowering the TV's volume with his hand-held paddle. Tanya let out a disapproving moan.

"Mr. Northam, this is Chief Inspector Gilford. I'm sorry to bother you at this late hour, but something important has come up and I wonder if we could get together."

"What's it about, Inspector?"

"I'm sorry, but it's something we shouldn't discuss over the phone," the inspector replied.

"It's not about the watch and case again, is it?"

"Partially," admitted Gilford, "but there's much more, really."

"Look, Inspector," argued Phillip, "I—we've told you all we know."

As they spoke, Janelle listened with anxiety. Tanya, on the other hand, was fiddling with the TV's push buttons, hoping to raise the volume a little.

"That may be so, sir," Gilford countered respectfully, "but there's still a number of questions which we must review and we feel certain you and your wife might be able to help."

Phillip froze. More than anything else, he didn't want his wife interviewed; she might have another pang of conscience and spill everything. As for himself, he knew he was being misunderstood. It wasn't that he was greedy. To the contrary, he was only being cautious about his find. Unfortunately, his delay in cooperating with the police was becoming complicated, something he regretted. Even Janelle misunderstood his intentions, though he knew his best interest was hers.

"Is it that important?" he asked in a final effort to keep from going.

"I wouldn't ask you if it weren't," came the inspector's quick response.

"Oh, very well. When do you want us?"

"In the morning, around nine? Like I've indicated before, I usually think better after I've had my cup of coffee."

"Hold on," said Phillip as he cupped his hand over the mouthpiece to address his wife. "They want us down at the police station around nine tomorrow morning. Can we make it?"

"Why?" Janelle asked nervously.

"Something important, that's all I know," replied Phillip. Janelle thought before answering.

"Yes," she said finally. "Tanya's baby sitter will be here by eight, and . . . if we have breakfast by seven, it should work out all right."

"Inspector," said Phillip back into the mouthpiece, "it's okay. We'll be down after the baby sitter picks up Tanya. She gets here at eight."

"Super! I appreciate that," replied Gilford. "Till tomorrow then, and please do enjoy the rest of your evening."

"You, too," replied Phillip as he put his receiver down carefully, thinking all the while.

"I hope they haven't found out," Janelle said, interrupting his thoughts.

"I don't think so," replied Phillip. A thought rolled through his mind just then. He stepped over to Tanya and knelt beside her.

"Tanya," he said softly.

"Yes, Daddy?"

"Remember what we spoke about a few days ago after we found all that yellow stuff on the beach on the other island?"

"The ones made by the bomb?" she asked innocently.

"Well—yes," he replied, stunned by the truth. He took another tact.

"You still want me to keep it a secret?" Tanya asked.

"Yes, I do, honey. Because it's more important than you know."

"But that's lying, Daddy," Tanya argued, almost hurt by having to remind her father.

"In a way it is, dear, but there's a reason for it, and you've just got to trust me until I tell you it's okay."

"Why, Daddy?"

"It's just that we don't want anyone to know anything about it just yet because a man's already been killed because of it."

Tanya knew about the murder but only what her parents wanted to her know. Now, for the first time, she was learning more. Fear crept over her tiny angelic face, showing her father she understood his warning.

"Will they catch him? The man who did it?"

"In time they will, but in the meantime, honey, just promise me and your mother you won't say anything to anyone. Will you do that?" her father asked sweetly.

"If you say so, Daddy," came her gentle reply.

"Good! Then that's that," said Phillip as he stood up and walked back to his chair, plopped in, then pushed a button on his TV remote control paddle.

A war movie was on, *The Dirty Dozen.* As the volume went up, the protagonist and antagonist—American soldiers against the Nazis —were mowing each other down in a hail of gunfire. Phillip cheered at one scene, the pushing of a German armored car over the wall of a bridge.

"Don't you ever tire of war movies?" asked Janelle irritably. "They're so depressing."

"It's a good movie . . . quite realistic, but not as bad as Nam.... "

Phillip's last words evoked a painful memory. To little Tanya's dismay, he pushed the paddle's "off" button, then walked out onto the balcony where he did nothing more than look out over the moonlit sea. A whitish streak in the distance caught his eye. He couldn't make it out. *A fishing boat,* he thought, before taking a seat where he sat silently.

"He needs time to himself," Janelle explained to Tanya. "It's Vietnam. He hasn't quite gotten over it."

At her mother's urging, Tanya stopped complaining and went to bed as directed. She was too exhausted to have seen the entire picture anyway.

Holiday Inn—Next Day

"That's them!" Steinmueller said. "The ones getting in the yellow Honda rent-a-car."

"You certain?"

"No mistake. And that's their little girl, the one with the Caymanian baby sitter.

"She looks like pure Aryan stock," replied Reiter as he studied the golden-blond child being led away by a black lady.

"I thought the same thing," replied Steinmueller.

"A pity," replied Reiter. "If they cooperate, there'll be no reason for her not enjoying a long life." He smiled when he said that, then turned his attention to the taxi in which her family was departing. "Know where they're going?"

"Wait here," said Steinmueller before walking toward a bellhop he recognized. They exchanged a few words and he came back shortly.

"They're on the way to the police station," Steinmueller reported anxiously.

"All the more reason for us to get moving," Reiter said with an urgency in his voice. "The authorities are moving in obviously and we need to get the information they're after before they do!"

"I agree," Reiter replied as he kept one eye on the baby sitter who was escorting the child toward the sandy beach behind the hotel.

"We'll wait until she heads for the bathroom for a soda machine by herself," Steinmueller suggested, "before we make our move."

"Is everyone ready?" asked Reiter as he looked around to a salt-corroded van parked nearby. Several men could be seen inside. He smiled.

"Yes, ready and waiting," Steinmueller replied. "Thank God they got here when they did. Otherwise. . . ."

"Never otherwise," corrected Reiter. "Always on time. That's our motto!"

Steinmueller smiled, agreeing in principle though he knew that even members of the SS made mistakes.

The men in the van were getting edgy as time passed. They had been told each minute counted and that the abduction had to be performed without witnesses or sound. There was no second chance.

Steinmueller and Reiter, in the meantime, had taken seats under a beach umbrella near the pool, sipping soft drinks. As the minutes passed, their concerns increased. The child seemed to have no

323

inclination to relieve herself, yet there was nothing for them to do but wait.

At long last, what Reiter and Steinmueller had hoped for came, moments after the pretty blond child approached the baby sitter with a request to go to the bathroom. She drew a nod and a few precautionary words from the lady, then raced off, leaving the sitter resting comfortably beneath a large beach umbrella.

Right then, Reiter passed a signal to the three men who were waiting near the women's bathroom. One of them stopped the little girl and asked her a question. When he appeared not to understand her directions, he asked her to guide him, a scene which didn't seem out of the ordinary. Together they walked around a corner, followed by a second man. A third had to intercept a tourist who was about to follow in their path.

As the third party engaged the tourist, the remaining two men quickly subdued and gagged the child, then bundled her up in a carpet and quickly carried her to a beat-up van not far away. Reiter and Steinmueller were in the van by then with Steinmueller behind the wheel. Within minutes, they passed through George Town, heading in an easterly direction. The child's muffled whimpering was overshadowed by the van's noisy muffler.

"Once she's aboard, we can breathe easier," boasted Reiter as they drove down a highway past a small town, "and they can search all they want, but they'll never find her."

Steinmueller was all smiles, too, though somewhat ill at ease. There were things yet to be done, some of which depended on luck and timing.

"I only wish it were evening, though," he complained. "I'd feel better then. After she's off the island."

"So would I," agreed Reiter, "but that's the chance we've got to take." He looked at his watch. "How much longer?"

"Ten minutes at the most, then another five to the shack."

"Get a move on then," urged Reiter.

"I can't," cautioned Steinmueller. "It's important to stay within the speed limits or risk being stopped by the police. We can't afford that, can we?"

Reiter agreed, though reluctantly, as his eyes studied every segment of the road ahead. Fortunately, police cars were absent, allowing them to reach their destination safely. Upon arrival at the small beachfront house, he—along with the others—hastily removed the frightened child from the back of the van and carried her into the main room. Once inside, they removed her blindfold, then her gag.

"I want my daddy," Tanya cried hysterically. Reiter moved to her side in hopes of calming her. With one fast movement, he struck her flat across the face and demanded she stop crying. When she didn't, he slapped her harder. The blow nearly toppled her and the chair in which she was sitting. A soft whimper followed, pleasing Reiter.

"See?" he said, directing his words to those around him, Steinmueller in particular. He had moved away to a spot near a large open window. On the reef beyond, a graveyard of abandoned ships caught his eyes. He looked at his watch, causing Reiter to do the same thing.

"Something wrong?" queried Reiter when he noticed the strained look on Steinmueller's face.

"We're running out of time. I need to cover our trail and get back to town . . . to make that call."

"You'd better go then," Reiter agreed while motioning for him to go.

Both men looked around the room just then, in the direction of the child. She had been securely bound and qa vwubf guarded by the other men.

"Our pawn," Reiter snickered.

Satisfied everything was in good order, Steinmueller raced out and got behind the wheel of the van. When the highway was clear, he drove out of the clump of bushes and turned right, heading toward the north end of the island. Five minutes later, he pulled into another clump of bushes and abandoned the van but not before wiping it clean of prints. After that, he took a brief hike down the road to another clump of trees and drove off to George Town in the vehicle hidden there.

Chapter 25

Kidnapped!

George Town Police Headquarters

hief Inspector Gilford glared at the couple before him, but more specifically and intently at the man before him. "Mr. Northam, I don't know how to tell you this except to tell you straight," said Inspector Gilford as he sat on the edge of his desk looking down upon the tense man and wife seated before him.

"I don't know what you mean," Phillip replied as his wife looked on nervously.

"It's that story you told us about finding the watch and gold fragment out at Gun Bay. It isn't standing up."

"Are you calling me a liar?" Phillip protested.

"It's not my intention to do so, sir, but we know every inch of Gun Bay and nothing of value has been found there for over fifty years, which makes us suspicious about your claim."

"Well, I can't help that," Phillip protested. "Maybe they weren't looking in the right place."

"Perhaps," agreed the inspector, "but we think otherwise. In fact, we have reason to believe you are holding something back though you're fully protected, that is, unless the find is part of stolen loot."

"Loot!" the Northams exclaimed together after a startled glance in each other's direction. They pushed nervously back into their chairs, trembling slightly.

"What do you mean by that, Inspector?" Janelle asked reticently.

"Just a guess," replied Gilford, pretending he hadn't noticed their earlier response. *They know something*, he thought. *Otherwise, why are they squirming?*

"Inspector," said Phillip after regaining his composure, "I thought you said everything we found is ours."

"It is, so long as the recovery fulfills certain local laws . . . like not being stolen property, or something like that, or fitting within the description of being permissible salvage in Caymanian waters," replied Gilford before realizing he had given part of the truth away even though it applied to crimes committed some forty years earlier.

"Does a murder disqualify us, providing everything else is kosher?" asked Phillip.

A wave of exhilaration swept through Gilford. Phillip appeared ready to change his story. Before he could gain the momentum, however, the intercom on his desk buzzed. With fire in his eyes, he peered hotly through his plate-glass window in the direction of his secretary. She, in turn, seemed equally exasperated at having found it necessary to disturb him. Despite her fears, however, she persisted in motioning to him to take the call.

Gilford walked around the desk and pushed a button while the Northams watched dejectedly.

"All right, Suzie. It'd better be important," he said brusquely.

"It is, Chief. It's an emergency call for the Northams. The hotel is on line one. Can they take it?"

Gilford motioned to the Northams. "An emergency call from the hotel."

"Tanya!" exclaimed Janelle before knowing for certain. She flew out of her chair and grabbed the phone from the inspector before her husband could get there.

"Yes?"

"It's me, ma'am, Esther, the babysitter," said a nervous voice on the other end.

"Is something wrong?" asked Janelle anxiously, suspecting the worse.

"Tanya's missing. She left me to go to the bathroom and never returned."

"She couldn't have gone far," replied Janelle in an effort to remain calm. While waiting for an answer, she quickly told her husband and the inspector what she had been told. So they could all hear, Gilford pressed a key which opened the circuit.

"Have you checked our room?" asked Janelle.

"Yes, ma'am. Right after I checked the ladies room on the ground floor, but she wasn't there either," the sitter replied. "I don't know what to do. I've looked everywhere."

"She may have just gone for a walk," Inspector Gilford interjected, hoping to calm the situation.

"I don't think so," said the sitter. "I told her not to go anywhere without telling me first."

"Esther," asked Phillip from where he was standing, "how long has she been gone?"

"No more than a half hour," came the reply.

"Well, she couldn't have gone far," said Phillip. "Where are you now?"

"At the front desk," replied Esther.

"Wait there. We''ll be right there," said Phillip.

"She couldn't have gone far," said Inspector Gilford who managed to grasp what was going on. "She ever do anything like this before?"

"No, never!" replied Janelle. "She's been warned never to wander off. We live in New York City, you know, and she knows better."

"Well, what are we waiting for?" asked Phillip as he grabbed his wife's hand to lead her outside. He apologized to the inspector for leaving so abruptly. The inspector offered assistance, but they politely refused.

"Well, allright," replied Gilford, "but if you need me, you know how to reach me."

"Thank you," the Northams replied before running out.

Gilford watched them leave. He felt confident the child was safe but was perplexed at having lost time in his investigation. He knew for certain he was on the verge of learning the truth about the missing watch and the murder, but now everything was on hold again, all because of a babysitter failing to perform her duties properly.

After the couple had been gone a few minutes, he walked over to his window and peered downward into the parking lot. The Northams had just entered their small island rental car and were preparing to drive off.

"Did I do the right thing, Chief?" asked Suzie nervously from behind while he was still looking down.

Gilford turned. "For once, yes," he sighed.

"Something cold to drink?" she asked.

"Why not? My day's ruined anyway."

At the Holiday Inn Lobby

"Esther, have you found her?" asked Janelle as she ran past the chief bellhop to the worried baby sitter.

"No, ma'am," Esther replied. "We've looked everywhere, but there's still no sign of her."

"We'd better call the police—the inspector," Phillip urged, seconds before one of the clerks behind the desk sent a bellhop to tell him there was a phone call for him at the guest phone in the lobby opposite the restaurant.

"They say who it is?" he asked.

"Only that it's a man and he says it's urgent," replied the bellhop.

Phillip looked at his wife. "It could be about Tanya," he said before running off.

"Wait for me," Janelle insisted before directing Esther to keep watch just in case Tanya showed up.

"Hello. Phillip Northam here."

"The father of Tanya Northam?" asked a muffled voice on the other end. It was distinctly foreign.

"Yes, speaking. Who is this?" asked Phillip somewhat suspiciously.

"A messenger of good news," the other party replied almost cheerfully before turning the conversation around. "You do value your daughter's life, Mr. Northam, don't you?"

"Of course I do! And who is this anyway? Is this some kind of joke?" demanded Phillip all at once.

"It's no joke, I can assure you," replied the voice on the other end.

"Then what is it you want?" Phillip demanded.

"Just this," the muffled voice replied. "We have your daughter. She is alive and well. And if you love her as you say you do, then you will do exactly as I say."

"What! Who are you? And what have you done with our daughter?" insisted Phillip.

"It doesn't matter who I am," the man replied. "What matters is your response to our demands. Do you understand?"

With Janelle trying to hear what was being said, it took everything Phillip had to remain calm so he could comprehend the gravity of the man's words.

"What's going on?" she said loudly, demanding a reply. Her raised voice drew the attention of others, causing Phillip to squeeze her upper arm after the caller said gruffly, "If that's your wife, tell her to keep quiet or suffer the consequences of your daughter's death."

Nothing could be plainer to Phillip. Instantly he brought her close and whispered in her ear to remain quiet. It was imperative and he would explain.

"All right. I'm listening," said Phillip. "What do you want? Money?"

The man laughed, angering Phillip. "Much more," the man said, "but you will learn about that shortly. In the meantime, I want you and your wife to return to your room and wait for my return call."

"Why not now?" demanded Phillip.

"It's too risky," the man replied. "Just do as I say and all will be well for you and your daughter. I will call you back in fifteen minutes, no sooner nor *spater* . . . later," the man corrected, leaving a curious thought in Phillip's mind concerning the use of the German word *spater* for its English counterpart *later*. It was definitely German. "And, above all," the caller added, "do not under any circumstances attempt to contact the police. Do I make myself clear?"

"Yes . . . of course," Phillip replied weakly while clenching his wife's arm to keep her from overreacting to what was happening. A second later, he returned the phone to its cradle, giving Janelle the license to besiege him with questions.

"Not now," he replied firmly as he directed her to the elevators near the restroom where their daughter had last been seen. "I'll tell you when we get back to our room."

"Not until I know what's going on!" she shouted angrily while trying to resist being dragged to the elevator. Their struggle drew attention, embarrassing Phillip, so he whispered in her ear, hoping the worst would not occur.

A loud screech, then: "Tanya's been kidnapped! Oh, my God!"

Before she could let out another scream, Phillip clamped a heavy hand over her mouth, almost suffocating her. She became limp and nearly fainted. With help from Phillip, she was half carried to a secluded spot around the corner where he tried to reason with her.

"For God's sake, Janelle, don't bug out on me! Not at a time like this," he begged. "Get yourself together, please. Tanya will be all right so long as we keep our wits about us and do as they say."

"They? Who?" asked Janelle.

"I don't know. All I know is that it was a man with a foreign accent who said he'd call us back in fifteen minutes at our room." Time suddenly became important. Phillip glanced at his watch. "Oh, God, ten minutes left," he said as he directed Janelle back to the elevators. She went readily this time.

"My baby," Janelle sobbed. "Why?"

"I don't know and he didn't say," answered Phillip. "But it doesn't seem to have anything to do with money . . . so he said."

When assured Janelle had regained her composure, they entered a crowded elevator and pressed the button for the top floor. They got off minutes later and reentered their room to await the promised call.

Waiting fifteen minutes was like fifteen hours and the Northams felt every long minute. While waiting, they discussed everything they knew, or thought they knew, about the probable cause.

"To kidnap a child on an island this small is ludicrous," reasoned Phillip. "There's no place for them to go! Or is there?"

"Could it have something to do with all the stuff we found and the watchmaker's death?" asked Janelle.

"Your guess is as good as mine," said Phillip. "It doesn't seem likely. Besides, how could anyone know? To my knowledge, we're the only ones who . . ."

"Maybe," interrupted Janelle, "but somehow I think there's a connection."

"Ridiculous! If that were true, they'd have to know who we are first."

"Who says they don't? After all, we did leave our names with the watchmaker."

A silence fell over them just then; the subject was too much for them to comprehend in so short a time, and besides, everything that passed through their minds and lips during those tense minutes—something they both knew—was speculation at best, so they waited for the call which was to come at any moment.

The phone rang.

Phillip grasped the receiver and pressed it to his ear. "This is Phillip Northam."

"Have you spoken to anyone since I called you last?" asked the caller.

"You think I'm crazy?" Phillip answered hotly upon recognizing the voice.

"Good, then listen carefully because I'm not going to repeat anything. And above all, keep your mouth shut, or your daughter will never be seen again, *verstehen sie?* Understand?" the man quickly corrected, once more confusing Phillip. A slip of the tongue or

332

deliberate? No time to speculate. An answer was required. "Explicitly," came Phillip's reply. What he was to do came next. The conversation was over in three minutes.

Phillip looked at Janelle, then told her what had transpired. Both were now deeply distressed. Separately they wanted to go to the police, but the caller had warned against that by saying their every movement would not go undetected, causing them to reconsider any improper response. Uppermost in their minds was Tanya's safety. Options were discussed. They decided on one.

"Is there any other choice?" asked Phillip.

"None," came Janelle's reply.

Phillip looked at his watch. It was near noontime and the inspector would no doubt want to know the outcome of the sitter's call. He picked up the phone.

"What are you doing?" Janelle asked when she heard her husband ask for Inspector Gilford "You're not going to tell—"

"Of course not," Phillip said, cutting her off. "He's got to be told something, and I'm going to give him what he needs."

"Like what?" questioned Janelle.

"That she's all right. Just wandered off. So keep cool while I get him off our backs."

Janelle went into the other room as he dialed, not certain she could keep from crying. The inspector's voice resounded over the phone.

"Hello, Inspector Gilford? This is Phillip Northam. I thought I'd call to bring you up to date."

"She's back safely then?" said the inspector.

"Oh, yes. Just wandered off. Had to confine her to her room for the day for not listening to her baby sitter."

The inspector seemed satisfied with the answer from what Janelle could tell, allowing her to get hold of herself. What came next, however, bothered her.

"No, sorry, but we can't make it today," said Phillip, responding to the inspector's request they come back in. When asked why, Phillip concocted another lie. "It's just that we're still upset over what happened a while ago. Tomorrow perhaps. Okay?"

"Mr. Northam," the chief inspector said over the phone after sensing an unexplainable delay, "need I remind you we still have a police matter before us and that I do have the authority to send people to the hotel to bring you in?"

"I know, Inspector, and believe me we do wish to cooperate, but we just need a day of rest. Surely, that can't be too much to ask? And besides, we have a few family matters to settle. Rather delicate, if you know what I mean. After that, we're all yours. Will that be all right?" The use of the word "family" caused the inspector to change his mind. One more day didn't really matter, but no longer. After all, others were waiting for developments in the case and progress could be made only if the Northams really had a story that could be changed.

"Oh, very well, one more day," replied Gilford. "I have a family, too, and know private matters need special attention."

Phillip could hardly contain his joy. His play on words had struck out, giving him and Janelle time to decide what their next move would be. It was noontime now, and in six more hours, they would go to an out-of-the-way public phone and wait for the kidnappers to tell them what to do next.

Townhouse—Israeli Delegates

Yitzak Goldstein, a tall, dark-haired young Israeli who had just turned twenty-two, was the first to tell Mort what he had observed earlier.

"Before I could get to my own car," he said breathlessly, "the van was gone. Along with it went the child, still dressed in a yellow bathing suit."

"Damn!" cursed Mort.

"I'm sorry," apologized Yitzak while his associate, Eric Hoffmeir, listened in dismay.

"It's not your fault," said Mort. "After all, how could you have known they would pull something so daring. Anyway, it's good you didn't follow them. Without backup, they could have killed you and the child."

"Did you see the men who grabbed her . . . what they looked like?" asked Eric.

"Young and blond, that's all I could see. They were gone before I knew what they were up to."

"What about the driver and his passenger?" asked Mort.

"The older one walked with a cane, and the other drove. I saw them from a distance only . . . seconds after the two young men tossed the carpet containing the girl into their van."

"Audacious!" remarked Mordeciah. "To think anyone would do anything like that in front of everyone!"

"They were clever and careful, though," said Eric, "like they had been planning the abduction for years."

"Not if they're experts—trained to carry out such tasks," commented Mort as he rubbed his round face before putting his unlit cigar in his mouth to think about what he had been told. "I wonder what they're up to?" he said loudly.

"Who knows?" replied Eric as he thought about the Northams and their immediate isolation after receiving a call in the hotel lobby. "Haven't heard a peep out of the Northams since that call."

"They went immediately back to their room, you say?" asked Mort with more fire in his eyes than in his cigar.

"The last time I saw them anyway."

"That means they're expecting something or someone," Mort theorized. "A phone call perhaps . . . telling them what to do or where to go."

"Makes sense," replied Eric. "After all, whoever is behind it all can't risk detection. The island's too small."

"That's what makes this case more interesting," added Mort. "If you were they, where would you hide a little girl especially if the police were alerted?"

His associates thought for a while before answering. When the answer came, their thoughts were identical. "Not on the island!" they said simultaneously.

"Precisely!" replied Mort jubilantly, thinking aloud. "There were two submarines which left Kiel, right? And just suppose that only one of them got through safely. What then?"

"After all these years?" Eric responded.

"Why not? If old sailing ships are still sailing the seven seas today, why not a U-boat?" Mort replied with musical zeal.

"Incredible!" one of the other men replied, too speechless to say more.

"My friends," Mort said softly as he drew them close to him, "if what I think is true—and there's every reason to believe it is—we must act quickly or lose what we've come after. And I don't want to wait another forty years."

As heads nodded, he directed his assistants to take places around a large circular table in their condominium where they were to study a large map of Grand Cayman Island. They parted company after that, each to new duty assignments. His last words of caution that night stuck in their minds, "Wait until the fish comes for the bait, then pull it in after it's been gaffed."

Holiday Inn—Early Evening

It was almost 6:00 p.m. when Mort knocked on the door to the Northams' suite. Solomon, the agent who had relieved Yitzak earlier,

335

had told him they were still in, though he suspected they were about to leave. When asked why, he said they had called the front desk to hold a taxi for them. The fact they had a rented car made the request suspicious.

"Who is it?" came a man's voice on the other side of the door.

"A friend, Mr. Northam," replied Mort.

"Do I know you?" asked Phillip.

"Not directly," replied Mort, leaving room for thought on the part of the Northams.

sensing what they were thinking. "For the time being, it's better they don't know though I am working with them on a cooperative basis . . . with 95 percent my way."

Janelle and Phillip relaxed for a moment, but only for a moment. A glance at their watches, which Mort caught, told him he had come at the right time.

"You going to meet their contact?" he asked. He surmised correctly when their faces dropped.

"I—we can't tell you that!" said Phillip.

"Folks, let this old boy from the Bronx tell you something before you leave," said Mort, throwing them off guard. "Never trust a Nazi."

"Nazi!" both replied.

"Who's talking about Nazis?" demanded Phillip, incredulous at the thought.

"I am," Mort replied bluntly. "If you don't know by now who you're dealing with, then it's time you learned."

Janelle was the first to look at her watch. "But we've only got twenty-five minutes left before we're to make the first contact!" Like her husband, the subject of Nazi involvement in their problems went over her head. Besides, it seemed too far-fetched!

"Good, because I need much less than that," said Mort as he pushed his heavy frame into the room and motioned for the two to sit down. The explanation was brief and simple, bewildering both of them. In turn, and now more cooperative, they agreed to tell him what little they knew and whatever else they would find out after making their initial contact except for details about what they had found on Little Cayman.

"Then it's settled," said Mort after looking at his watch to determine the remaining time. "You can get there in less than five minutes, with five to spare."

"You won't tell the police, will you?" asked Janelle for reassurance.

"Madam, do I look like a blabbermouth?" replied Mort with a

humorous smile. "I might be heavy-set, but I'm not a tale carrier," he added, bringing hope to her fearful heart.

As they left the room, leaving him to trail behind as he had agreed, he left them with one thought, "Don't worry because my assistants are nearby. And for goodness sake, don't strain my Jewish heart by trying to figure out who my agents are. You could be mistaken."

As the taxi sped away, Eric watched their departure. Mort joined him seconds later and told him to follow and to do nothing unless attacked.

"Where are you going?" asked Eric before leaving.

"In there," Mort replied, pointing to a disco, "to get a good stiff drink while waiting for your report." The young man threw him a finger, then ran off.

"Kids!" complained Mort. "No respect for their elders." Disco music caught his ears and away he went. Before long, several unaccompanied ladies who had just arrived for a weekend took a seat next to him. One took a fancy to the friendly overstuffed fellow with dancing eyes.

"May I have this dance?" she asked.

"With pleasure, madame," replied Mort.

The Taxi—Five Miles Away

The cab taking the Northams to the public telephone booth was a familiar one. It was chauffeured by Crazy Joe's business partner and friend. He hadn't taken them around since they rented a car and was surprised when he picked them up in answer to a call from the hotel.

"How have you folks been?" he asked innocently.

"Just fine," Phillip replied for the two of them.

"Strange things going on in the islands, you know?"

"Like what?" asked Phillip to pacify the man's enormous curiosity, a fact of which they were fully aware from previous trips.

"The murder of old man Schumacher . . . and the devil fish that nearly killed my partner, Crazy Joe, many years ago."

"Where's he now—Crazy Joe?" asked Phillip as Janelle listened in. Actually her mind was on other things, but she pretended to listen for the sake of courtesy.

"He went out to the other side to see his friend, Scavenger Jones, the fella who said he just saw it."

"Is the story true? That is, about him almost being eaten by some sea creature?"

"Yeah, mon. That's what he say, and I believe him. He's a pretty smart guy, my partner, though he drinks too much."

The taxi took a quick left, then sped on to the location given earlier by the Northams.

"Why you stop here?" asked the man curiously.

"To make a phone call," answered Phillip as the taxi came to a stop near a small store.

The taxi driver was bewildered. "Hey, sir, if you wanted to make a call, you could have made one from the hotel."

Phillip was upset by the man's inquisitiveness and showed it. "Just remembered something, that's all," he answered.

The driver wasn't so sure because Janelle raced after him. During their short ride, not a word about making a phone call had escaped their lips. Strange! Nevertheless, he waited patiently as they waited near the phone. That's what bothered him the most, their waiting. They were supposed to be making a phone call, not waiting for one.

At exactly 7:00 p.m., just as they had been told, the pay phone rang. Instantly—while the driver watched with curiosity—Phillip jerked the receiver off its cradle. Janelle pressed in closer, her head near the receiver pressed to her husband's ear.

"Northam here," said Phillip.

"Anyone around?" asked the familiar voice.

"Just the taxi driver, and he's out of listening distance."

"Good."

"Good nothing," Phillip said sharply. "Why have you taken our child?"

"Because you have knowledge as to the whereabouts of something which belongs to us."

"What knowledge, and who is 'us'?" demanded Phillip.

"It doesn't matter who we are, but what it is we need from you," the man replied gruffly.

"What could we possibly have that would be of any value to you?" Phillip asked, playing dumb. Mort had instructed him wisely and had informed him of some things concerning Nazi involvement although very little. He had planned it that way.

"You're a fool, Mr. Northam," the man chided. "Apparently you've forgotten the watchmaker and what happened to him."

"You mean—?"

"Of course! He was stupid and deserved to be silenced. And the same thing will happen to your daughter if you don't cooperate."

"What do you want?" Phillip demanded. He raised his voice momentarily, then dropped it when he noticed the driver looking their

338

way.

"We want to know where you found the watch and gold fragment."

"Oh, so that's it!" responded Phillip. He turned to his wife to answer a whispered question. "They want to know where we found the watch and fragment." Like his wife, he was shocked to learn the man knew about the fragment, too. How, he could only guess, and Inspector Gilford's secretary, Suzie, was his prime suspect.

"Are you there, Mr. Northam?" the man asked when a brief silence followed.

"Yes, yes. I'm—we're here," Phillip said nervously.

"Well?" demanded the man, waiting for an answer.

"What about our daughter, Tanya?"

The man chuckled. "We're not unreasonable people. After we've gotten what we want from you, you can have her back in the same condition we found her."

"That's not good enough," argued Phillip, feeling certain now he couldn't trust the man. After all, they had—if it was true—killed the watchmaker. Mort's warning was still in his mind: *You can't trust Nazis.*

"If I tell you where we found it, you might not keep your word," argued Phillip.

"True," the man replied, "but we're prepared to make a deal, one that would satisfy both parties."

"Like what?" Phillip demanded.

"First of all," the man replied, "we can't just take your word without knowing whether the materials we are looking for are there."

"And?" pressed Phillip as Janelle pushed in closer. She wanted to say something, but Phillip cautioned her to remain calm and silent.

"Secondly," the man added, "we've got to have someone with us, just in case."

"Not Tanya!" Phillip cried, upsetting Janelle who heard part of the conversation."

"What choice do we have?" asked the man.

"But they weren't—" Phillip caught himself in time to avoid saying the items had been found on another island. A slip like that could have been disastrous, and more than anything he couldn't reveal the truth—not now anyway.

"Is there a problem, Mr. Northam?" the man asked coolly, totally unnerving Phillip.

"Yes," he replied quite frankly. "I don't trust you."

"That's your problem, isn't it?" the man countered just as a thought struck Phillip.

"Hang on a minute, okay? I've got to talk this thing over with my wife. She's standing next to me."

"Take your time," replied the man, making it clear he didn't want them to play tricks.

Phillip cupped the mouthpiece, then turned to Janelle. "They won't let her go unless we tell them where we found the stuff."

"Do it!" she urged, forgetting Mort's warning.

"I'm not so sure," replied Phillip. "This guy—and God knows who else—killed the watchmaker. You hard him say so, didn't you? What makes you think they won't do the same thing to Tanya after they've gotten what they want? After all, she could identify all of them."

"Oh, dear God!" Janelle whimpered. "What do we do?"

"Whatever we do, it can't be under their terms," replied Phillip. "You heard what Mort said. They can't be trusted!"

"He should know, I guess. . . ," Janelle agreed.

"Let me think," Phillip said before asking the man for more time. A minute later, he had a thought. He uncupped the mouthpiece. "You still there?"

"Of course," the man said confidently. "Have you made up your mind?"

"Yes. My wife and I have talked it over and agree that you—and whoever else is working with you—can't be trusted." The man on the other end was startled and had to search for an adequate reply.

"Oh, come now, Mr. Northam," he finally countered. "We're honorable people."

"Not if you're Nazis!" Phillip shot back spontaneously, something he didn't expect to do. A long silence fell before the man spoke.

"Who told you that?" he demanded. By his strained response, Phillip knew Mort had correctly identified the culprits, so he promptly played his ace-high hand. "That's our secret, and it'll remain that way until we work out arrangements for our daughter's safe return."

"Impossible!" the man bellowed unexpectedly, experiencing a dilemma he hadn't anticipated.

"See what I mean," said Phillip vehemently. "You can't be trusted."

A silence followed before the man spoke again, making the Northams fearful. "All right, I concede you have a point. What do you have in mind?"

"An exchange. My daughter for me!"

"You can't!" cried Janelle when she heard his offer before he cupped the phone to keep the man on the other end from thinking they had nothing with which to bargain.

Phillip cupped the phone again and whispered to his wife to keep her from worrying too much. "I'm stalling for time. There's nothing else I can do for the moment. If I don't give them what they want, they'll kill her."

"Then do what you must," urged Janelle, "until we can confer with Mr. Joachim. He said he'd help."

"Mr. Northam!" the man on the other end said loudly. "Are you there?"

"Have you considered my offer?" asked Phillip as if he were the one in charge.

"Yes, but I'll have to talk to my chief first," replied the man, giving Phillip more to think about. "On second thought," the man added with an irritating and deceitful chuckle, thinking he had struck upon a valid answer, "perhaps we don't need you at all. Your daughter must know as much as you?"

"That's what you think, buster!" Phillip shot back instantly, a ploy designed to confuse the man. "What she knows isn't enough to fill a jigger of whiskey."

Phillip's sudden bravado and unexpected challenge threw the caller off-guard again. A temporary state of speechlessness followed, which allowed Phillip time to say something else.

"Don't think you've got all the cards stacked on your side because we have a few, too."

"Such as?" the man finally asked.

"One phone call to the police, and everything would be lost."

"For your daughter, too," countered the man, equal to the challenge.

"True," agreed Phillip, "but you'd be out of whatever it is you want so desperately and I'm not so sure that would fit your plans."

"Can you afford the loss of your daughter?" the man challenged again.

"No more than you over whatever it is that you're after. Can you afford the loss?" countered Phillip in a bold display of courage quickly conceived to portray a semblance of strength on his side.

The bluff worked!

"What do you mean?" asked the bewildered man.

"Without me, you've got nothing," Phillip replied boldly, knowing he had gotten the man's attention.

What he had done was worth the risk. After all, his daughter's life was at stake, and if he didn't handle the matter correctly, she might never return. So far, from what he could determine, her kidnappers had goofed, and badly at that. While Tanya might be able to tell them something about the treasure, they could never be certain she was directing them to the right island in sufficient time to allow them to proceed with their work before being detected, that is, unless a quicker and better way could be found.

"One word from me to the police and it's all over," Phillip reiterated, knowing he didn't really mean it, but he had to explore the other side's weakness.

"You wouldn't—?" replied the man, clearly disturbed.

"I will if we can't come to terms," replied Phillip with a vocal and inner strength which surprised even him. "As I said before, I don't trust you, no matter what you say."

A silence followed. A standoff had been reached. Neither side could afford their losses, making it obvious to the contenders that negotiations were in order.

"I'll speak to the chief," the man answered after a long pause. Uncertainty was in his voice.

"When?" asked Phillip without pressing too hard.

"Tomorrow sometime," the man replied. "He's unavailable for the moment. I'll call you at the hotel tomorrow evening around six p.m." "What will I tell the police if someone tells them our daughter is still missing?"

"That's your problem," the man replied, giving the impression he was back on top again. "Tell them anything. You seem to be good at deceit."

"Tomorrow evening but no later," replied Phillip, ignoring the man's dig. "There's only so much a person can do when others know something about a matter."

"Sounds reasonable," the man agreed. "Till tomorrow, Mr. Northam. And, oh, please remember this: Your daughter's security is only as good as your ability to keep what you know about us a secret. And that goes to whoever it is that told you about us. Do I make myself clear?"

"Don't try to frighten me, you lousy bastard!" Phillip cursed. "I know what to do! You do what you've got to do, and I'll uphold my end of the bargain."

"*Gutten tag,*" replied the man in German, a split second before his end of the phone clicked.

Phillip returned the receiver to its cradle and looked at Janelle. She was visibly shaken and depressed. "We've given them something to think about. It's our only hope for the moment."

"But you'd be in danger, too!"

"Maybe, and maybe not," Phillip replied as he nudged her back toward the waiting taxi. "Let's see what Mordeciah has to say."

The taxi drove off with them again back to the hotel. The couple's strange behavior puzzled the driver, making him determined to tell Crazy Joe about it. Outside of what he observed, there really wasn't much else he could say, but it would be good conversation anyway.

Eric was on hand the minute the Northams arrived, but by split seconds only. He had followed them on a motorbike to a spot near the booth, then back again when nothing challenging happened. When they stepped out of the taxi, he—a total stranger—had walked up to them and promptly informed them where to find Mr. Joachim. Before they could ask questions, he was gone again.

In the smoke-filled disco, Mort was showing wear and tear. To his disma, before the Northams barged in, he had found the lady with whom he had been dancing intent on making him her third husband.

"Sorry, sweet lady, but I'm afraid I wouldn't be good for you. You see, only recently have I learned that I have been afflicted by an incurable disease—AIDS."

"Oh! How awful!" exclaimed his companion before she staggered back to the table she had left earlier, the one from which her envious friends watched as she applied her charms. Their eyes all turned in Mort's direction when she related how close she had come to disaster.

"Wouldn't you know?" remarked one of the ladies as he passed by quickly. "And he was so cute."

As Mort passed by with the Northams, they wondered if the people with him knew of his terminal affliction.

"Where to?" asked Phillip.

"Your room, where it's safer," Mort replied as he wiped his forehead with his handkerchief. "You know," he added when they were back in the hotel lobby, "I've faced a lot of things in my life, but I've never received a proposal of marriage in a disco before."

His remarks escaped the Northams. They too had a lot of things on their minds, most of all, the need for a plan of action. Mort—they felt—could provide it.

"A good counterbalance," said Mort after listening to what the Northams had to say. "Hit them where it hurts the most."

"I learned a few things in Vietnam," replied Phillip. "Most of all, not to panic in the face of the enemy or underestimate their cunning either."

"Good advice. Kill a few in the process?" asked Mort, referring to Phillip's Vietnam experiences and also to understand the man better. After all, from what he could see, they would be working together for a while.

"More than I care to admit," Phillip replied soberly. He went silent after that.

"War is never pleasant," admitted Mort, sensing some of Phillip's emotional conflicts, "but oft times we have no choice except to fight back. Israel's a good example. . . ."

"True, but for the moment I—we're concerned about Tanya," said Phillip, changing the subject.

"In my opinion, she's safe for the moment," Mort replied confidently. "And from what you've told me, they've been dealt a blow they hadn't expected though they're not likely to change their recovery plans whatever they are. Also, they now know it's you they really need. And that's good; it gives us more time to plan."

"If he were to go," said Janelle fearfully, "how can we be certain they won't go back on their word and hurt my husband after they've gotten what they want?"

"You can't," Mort replied bluntly. "That's the risk he has to take if they decide to accept his offer."

"I don't like it—it scares me," Janelle responded.

"You have a better idea?" asked Mort as he reached out gently and touched her hand in a demonstration of understanding and compassion.

"She hasn't any, and neither do I," Phillip interjected, speaking for both of them. "Anyway, there's really nothing we can do until we hear from them."

"To a degree, yes," responded Mort, "but there are options, and as I've said before, I didn't come empty-handed. Even as we speak, my assistants are already at work trying to locate their base of operations."

"Like the guy downstairs?" asked Phillip, referring to Mort's assistant, Eric.

"He's one of several," acknowledged Mort without saying more.

"Got to hand it to you," Phillip said. "I'd have known it if he hadn't come up when he did."

"Don't get overconfident," warned Mort. "On cases like this—Nazi hunting—one never knows what he'll run into. The opposition is usually well prepared and armed."

"What do you want us to do?" asked Phillip, seconded by his wife.

"Beat them at their own game," replied Mort while taking a drag from his cigar without asking permission. As smoke gathered in a swirly mass over his head, his thoughts raced through the labyrinths of his mind. For a long while, neither Janelle or Phillip moved for fear of disturbing his thoughts. In time, however, a break came.

"When did he say he'd call?" Mort asked unexpectedly, referring to the kidnapper's spokesman.

"Tomorrow evening . . . around 6."

"Good. If they'll do what I think they'll do, we'll have sufficient time to counter whatever it is they're planning."

"And if you—we fail?" Janelle questioned nervously.

"I see you're not an optimist," said Mort as he looked into her worried eyes. "Mamma," he said affectionately as he hugged her, "it's important we maintain a positive approach. We don't have a choice. No matter what we do, someone or something is at risk. Make no mistake about it. This includes me and my men as well. There are no guarantees, remember that."

"I . . . I'm sorry," Janelle replied, "for being so thoughtless and selfish. You're right, of course."

He released his grip and gently stroked her cheek, making her feel better. "Don't worry, dear. We'll get Tanya back safely, provided everyone maintains a cool head and properly carries out his specific roles."

Mort walked toward the door just then, preparing to leave. Before doing so, he reached into his pocket and pulled out a small notepad. He scribbled a number on one sheet, tore it out, and handed it to Phillip.

"Call me at this number when you hear from them again. It's possible they might try to contact you sooner, though I don't think so. They're methodical and cautious."

He shook Phillip's hand warmly, then kissed the back of Janelle's hand in typical European fashion before leaving the room with a final good night.

"*Shalom.*"

John Hankins

Chapter 26

Cayman Sunset

East End—Four Days Later

ven though he had been caught red-handed by harbor authorities trying to sell a boatload of goods taken from the hold of a wrecked ship, Gun Bay locals didn't consider Scavenger Jones a thief.

Gun Bay at the east end of Grand Cayman Island had, for as long as local inhabitants could remember, been a coral reef graveyard and final resting place for sea-going vessels from pirate ships to modern-day steamships. Historically, vessels met their demise as a consequence of unexpected storms, errors in navigation, a combination of these or other factors, or by calculated intent—losses often referred to by the police as "suspicious." Whatever the case, in the past anyway, such mishaps often proved a boon to the local economy despite the legitimacy of the shipwreck. Investigations by the police were of no concern to the local inhabitants.

Procedures for the handling of ships gone aground were simple. If notice of a shipwreck reached port authorities in time, they were the first to investigate. The owners or their agents along with insurance adjustors and salvage crews generally came next, most hoping to minimize their losses through the successful refloating of the distressed vessel. Almost without exception, the converse became the case in that the ravenous reef upon which the unlucky vessel had come to a rest usually responded like a protective mother refusing access to her newborn child. After that, a predictable course of events followed: salvage by the rightful owners, oftentimes with the unwanted assistance of local residents who had developed an uncanny ability to strip a stricken vessel during the middle of the night. All along, nature helped, too. Eventually each vessel would turn into rusting hulks and erode away until nothing was left but the skeletal remains of its keel. In time, the keel too, would disappear, allowing the reef to wait for another morsel to devour.

Scavenger Jones, a short, friendly, wiry black man, barely five feet tall and weighing not more than a hundred pounds, was one of the self-made salvors. The police had given him the name following his first shipboard misadventure. Jones preferred being called a "salvage specialist" because it sounded better, but it wasn't to be—despite vehement objections.

Jones's career started somewhat haphazardly, months after he had been jailed for drunkenness, in the big town, George Town. In view of his repeated offenses, the judge banished him from the city for two months in hopes he would stay sober and never come back. While waiting for his sentence to expire, Jones took up residence on a beach at Gun Bay, using a makeshift lean-to for his temporary quarters. It was sufficient for his needs, except for money; that was always in short supply. Thus, to remedy the situation, he decided to go into business for himself. The hulks which occupied his seaward view every waking day whetted his appetite for exploration. Unfortunately, the very day he attempted to develop a new occupation was the same day the harbor patrol decided to check out the wrecks.

"I was only looking," he told the arresting officer.

"A likely story," countered the man as he carted him off to the jail after finding Jones's boat loaded to the gunwales with merchandise taken from the new wreck. What was disturbing to port authorities was the fact it hadn't been surveyed yet either by its owners or insurance adjustors, thereby making his initial offense all the more repugnant.

"Two months in jail," ordered the judge as he pounded his desk with his gavel after hearing Jones's "not guilty" plea. Within minutes, Jones was whisked away to beginning serving his sentence.

Confinement didn't curb his pilfering appetite, however. In time, he was back to his old habit and haunts. He was safe from arrest so long as he practiced his new profession in a reasonable manner, that is, not to take items which were readily traceable. Unfortunately, that type was far more plentiful and valuable than the other, so he had to consider alternatives. That's when an old drinking buddy, a well known character around George Town, came to mind—Crazy Joe! Together they concocted an ingenious plan. On items which could be easily traced, Scavenger Jones would bury them on nearby beaches, then advise his friend where they could be found.

Not-so-Crazy Joe would then offer his nominal guide services to unsuspecting and gullible tourists, who always ended up at the pre-selected site. Then, while his charges swam and picnicked, he'd go treasure hunting with his cheap metal detector, and *voila!*—a treasure—all fully witnessed! Consequently he and his partner made a lot of money to the chagrin of local police. Though the latter suspected something was amiss, they couldn't prove it. Discoveries in the sight of credible witnesses were the best defense the partners could want. After all, what sane politician would dare allow the police to challenge the integrity and veracity of money-spending tourists who just happened to be present?

After a while, the pickings got leaner, partly because harbor authorities had posted "danger" signs on most of the wrecks (they were beginning to fall apart) and partly because newer satellite navigational and radar aides were being used by shipmasters to help them steer clear of the reefs.

Those restrictions bothered Scavenger Jones, but despite the warning, when desperate for cash, he'd go back out to the wrecks. That's what he was doing four days after the first meeting between police authorities investigating the watchmaker's murder case and the visiting foreign dignitaries.

On that day, in the late afternoon and at high tide, Scavenger Jones had gone out in a outboard-powered fiberglass runabout to search an old wreck. Weeks earlier, he had boarded the vessel but had to abort his salvaging activities when port authorities made a surprise visit. He got off quickly and pushed out to sea a bit where he promptly dropped a series of fishing lines. When the authorities came alongside and interrogated him, he told them he had been fishing all afternoon. They didn't believe him because he didn't have any fish in the bins nor any fish bait with which to catch any, but they couldn't do anything because they could not prove he had broken any laws!

This time out, he expected things to be different. Before leaving for the abandoned vessel, he had called Crazy Joe in George Town to learn if port authorities were planning a visit. They weren't. A half hour later, his white, blue, and green-striped boat, painted that way to make it less visible, was tied alongside the seaward side of the stranded ship.

Like a monkey, Jones scaled its tall steel plates through use of grappling hooks and knotted lines, then went about his business of selecting choice items. Removing bulkhead-mounted objects like clocks, barometers, and water coolers then lowering them over the side took much longer than he had expected. In fact, by the time he finished, the sun had set and the moon was rising in a partially overcast sky, making view of the shoreline difficult. This worried him because patrol cars were known to cruise the nearby shore, so he decided to make a quick check. With a pair of high-powered, night-viewing binoculars, he raced to the other side to study the shoreline. To his shock, he saw a car, its headlights blinking on and off as if signaling someone, but who?

His question was partially answered when he heard a strange muffled hub-dub-dub sound. "No!" he said fearfully to himself as he crouched and ran to another position near the aft foc'sle to see what it was. "It can't be the port authorities. Joe said they weren't coming!"

As he searched the silk-screen moonlit sea with binoculars pressed hard to his eyes, his mouth dropped. About 200 hundreds yards away in the deep part beyond the reef, the waters began to part and burble. Seconds later, a massive black object, its upper section coming out first, burst out of the sea in an ostentatious display of foamy, white fury. While this nearly caused the little man to jump out of his twine-tied trousers, what came next was even more frightening. Emblazoned in white on the vessel's superstructure—as if able to see through its eyeless sockets—was an enormous, gruesome-looking skull with crossbones. It frightened the little man so much he had trouble thinking coherently. It took the better part of five minutes for him to recover, and many things went on during that time.

Despite his fear, Jones saw it all through his binoculars; he didn't have a choice. Before his startled eyes, a swarm of black-clad figures emerged from the vessel's crimson-lighted fore, aft, and conning tower hatches like angry bees protecting their hive. Then like ants, they scurried obediently across its decks to their preassigned posts, some to deck guns and others to storage places beneath deck plates where they removed and inflated a small rubber boat of the Zodiac type while still others manned lookout stations next to their white-capped captain who was busy triggering his hand-held signal light. Without doubt, every movement was well orchestrated as if those involved had rehearsed the scene over and over again.

"A submarine!" Scavenger Jones finally exclaimed through chattering teeth after regaining some composure. He muttered to himself, "What the hell's going on?"

What happened next might have been the answer he sought, but given his understanding of the matter, there was no way for him to comprehend anything. After the crew had inflated the rubber boat, they launched it. A lone seaman jumped in, started its outboard motor, then maneuvered it through the turbulent surf toward a small shore-based signal light.

Again Jones slipped quietly back to his previous position on the shore side of the vessel, where he refocused. More than ever before, he appreciated having the binoculars even though he had wrongfully appropriated them from another wreck some years earlier; their owner's name was still engraved on their side. Anyway, and to his surprise, he could see a number of men waiting on the shore. They were struggling with something, a small bag or something. Whatever it was he couldn't tell. As he continued to watch, the boat pulled in. At that point, several men ran up and got in, carrying their package with them. Soon they were on their way back to the sub. As for those who remained behind, they stayed a little longer before returning to their car and driving off, leaving Jones again to speculate what it all meant.

It didn't take long for the boat to pass near the wreck. As it headed toward the stern, Scavenger Jones ran back to his safe lookout spot near the aft foc'sle in hopes of getting a better view. Without light from the screened moon, he wouldn't have seen anything, the bright yellow dress especially.

"I must be seeing things," he said while questioning his eyesight. It had never failed him before. He looked again, this time believing what he saw. "It's a little girl, all right, but what's she doing out here . . . with all those men?"

A cry pierced the night air just then, clearly that of a young child. A harsher one followed, "Shut up!" At least that's what Jones thought he heard though he couldn't be certain since the noisy outboard motor and pounding surface distorted everything. He questioned his ears this time, for a moment only, until a bustle of activity swept across the sub's deck. This time, crew members were performing their duties in reverse. When everything was secured, they slipped back into the vessel's belly; their captain followed minutes later, pulling the hatch cover shut as he descended. With the closure went the ominous beams of crimson light which earlier had illuminated everyone passing in and out of it's many hatches.

Within minutes, the U-boat's diesel engines pulsated louder and it began to move forward. It dived after that, but not before the surrounding sea churned frothy-white, indicating valves had been opened to let air escape through the top of its ballast tanks on the one hand while letting water enter from the bottom on the other.

Soon everything but its snorkel, a tall mast-like object with an odd-shaped dome on its top, was all that was left to see. As it sliced through the water, breathing heavily and expelling gases from its exhaust system like a dying man in respiratory distress, a phosphorescent wake marked its path. It reminded Scavenger Jones of something he had often seen: the temporary footprints of a man pressed into a smooth, white sand beach moments before an incoming wave washed them away. That was enough to trigger his anxious thoughts. Softly he said to himself as he turned and ran, "I'm getting out of here. This place ain't safe no more!"

He had to make a safety check of the shore side first to be certain it was safe to leave. After that, he went back to the other side and quickly lowered himself into his loot-loaded boat. What he had taken meant nothing to him now. Eagerly he committed to the deep everything he had taken. Uppermost in his mind was his strong desire to survive, to return safely to his tiny lean-to not far away.

As he raced for shore, he couldn't help pondering recent events, the condition of his nerves included. To calm them, he took a big swig from a flask he had hidden beneath the transom.

"What am I going to tell the police?" he muttered to himself while imbibing. "If I tell them where I've been, they're sure to arrest me. And Crazy Joe, what am I going to tell him? He's going to get angry with me for tossing the stuff over the side! Oh, me, what a day!"

He didn't lack thoughts. As the next one surfaced, he said loudly, "Lord, could that be the sea monster my pal Joe has been babbling about all these years? The one he said he'd kill if he ever saw it again? Anyway, it sure matches his description."

There was only one thing—or two—left for him to do for the rest of the evening. With childhood catechism lessons in mind, he put the flask down then quickly grasped the large crucifix which hung around his neck and prayed. Just as quickly, he released it and reached for the half-empty flask near his side and pushed it to his awaiting lips. Morning was still many hours away he knew, and there were many things he had to think, pray, and drink about before dawn.

Chapter 27

The Plot Thickens

A residence—Seven Mile Beach

t's too dangerous, and he's smarter than I thought," said Reiter after being informed by Steinmueller of the Northams position. "Regardless, we must accept his offer before the others can get organized. Otherwise we will have wasted all these years in search of something we cannot have."

"That would be disastrous," agreed Steinmueller, acknowledging the problem. "But what I don't understand is how they knew about us? Do you think it has something to do with the group which just arrived?"

"It's obvious," replied Reiter. "They're being coached by someone. Perhaps by someone in the group which arrived yesterday."

"Like who—?"

"Israeli agents."

Steinmueller gasped. "Nazi headhunters! Here?"

"Why not? Anything is possible these days, and I haven't forgotten, nor should you, that it was an Israeli group who tracked down Eichmann—poor soul—before giving him the *coup de grace*. And if that's the case, then that's all the more reason for us expediting our efforts before the those on the other side can act."

"Surely, you don't think the Israelis have arrived, do you?" asked Steinmueller, hoping he could be wrong.

"Don't be naive," responded Reiter. "We're still at war, and the enemy is all around us, ready to devour us if they can." His thoughts wandered for a moment before he added, "If there's anything I learned from the Führer and General von Kleitenberg, it's this: Never take your enemy for granted."

"So what do we do now in view of the potential danger facing us?" asked Steinmueller.

"Exactly what I said before. We'll take the American up on his offer and make the exchange."

"Suppose it's a trap?"

"Perhaps, but not likely. But to be perfectly secure, it will be us—not them—who will establish the time, place, and conditions."

"And if they don't agree?"

"It will be all over for the girl."

Northams' Hotel Suite—Next Evening

RING!

"That must be them," Phillip said anxiously as he lifted the phone off its cradle. "Phillip Northam, here."

"Mr. Northam," a familiar voice said. "After some deliberation, we accept your offer."

"When and where?" asked Phillip while motioning to his wife to remain calm.

"I cannot tell you that over the phone for obvious reasons," replied the man. "You know, too many ears, and besides, we feel the same way about you as you feel about us—distrust."

"Get one thing straight, buster. My daughter's safety is more important to me and my wife than your opinion of us, so let's get on with it. What do you have in mind?"

"Don't get excited, Mr. Northam. After all, much is involved and we do not want the authorities involve—if you get my point?"

"Go on," urged Phillip.

"Tomorrow, at noon precisely, you are to go to the main lobby of the hotel and wait there for someone to contact you."

"Who?"

"You don't need to know that," said the man. "The rest will be made clear after you receive our message."

"Anything else?"

"Yes. Under no circumstances are you or your wife to divulge the nature and content of the message to anyone. If you do, our arrangement will be over and your daughter will suffer the consequences of your decision. Is that understood?"

"Yes, but we might be late," replied Phillip after being reminded by Janelle they had an appointment with the chief inspector the same morning. He explained their predicament to the man.

There was a silence on the other end as the caller considered the problem. After a while, he offered an alternative. "All right, let's make it 3 p.m. at the latest, but no longer. And," he warned vehemently, "if you reveal what has happened to your daughter, she's dead!"

"You bastard!" cursed Phillip, clearly upset by the threat. "We're not stupid enough to do a thing like that, so lay off the threats!"

"We're not taking any chances, that's all," replied the man. "We know you're receiving advice from someone, and we don't want any interference from them, whoever they are."

"What makes you think that?" asked Phillip, suspecting his earlier slip of tongue had given part of Mort's involvement away.

"Come now, Mr. Northam. How else would you have known who we were?"

"A guess," said Phillip, thinking quickly, determined to keep Mort's involvement secret.

"Hah, you expect me to believe that?"

"Think what you like," replied Phillip, "but that's the way it is and there's no one helping us."

"Have it your way," warned the man, "but remember what I said. No one is to know anything about this. All we want is what we came for. After that, you can have your daughter back."

"How long before we get together?"

"At the earliest, tomorrow evening, if everything goes as planned. Do we have your agreement to abide by our rules?"

"Agreed," said Phillip, while adding a warning of his own. "Remember, Kamerad, I hold high cards in this stake too. I'm willing to give up what I found and know, but it's contingent on my daughter returning safely. And don't you forget that."

"Your point is made," replied the man. "Until tomorrow then. *Auf wiedersehen*." He terminated the call, leaving Phillip and Janelle to ponder their future actions. Their first thought was to call Mort.

"Stay there," he said to the Northams. "I'll be there in ten minutes. We'll talk then."

Police Headquarters—The Next Morning

"How is your daughter?" asked Suzie before hurrying the Northams into her boss's office.

"Just fine," replied Janelle, showing a coolness toward the young woman. Phillip had warned her about saying anything critical in her presence because he feared she was the source of a leak involving the gold fragment.

"Why didn't you bring her with you?" asked Suzie, trying to bridge the gap which hadn't been there previously.

"Because she's being punished for disobedience, and we've confined her to her room for the rest of the day."

"kids," said Suzie, understandingly. "They're all alike, and you've got to watch them every minute."

"Tell us about it," agreed Phillip in an effort to take the pressure off his wife, who found it difficult to play out her role as she followed the woman into the inspector's office and took a seat opposite him.

"Coffee?" he asked after getting up to greet them.

"No, thanks. Have had my quota for the day," replied Phillip.

"And you, Mrs. Northam?"

"Nothing, thank you," replied Janelle, struggling to keep her composure, a fact which did not escape the inspector's eyes.

"Something wrong?" he asked.

"Why? Do I show it?" she replied, feeling she had given her concerns away and now had to act more convincingly about everything being in order.

"A bit. Your daughter all right?"

"Why . . . why, of course," Janelle stammered while struggling to find a way out of her dilemma.

Phillip came to her rescue. "She had a hard time sleeping last night. Tanya's disappearance and misbehavior had a lot to do with it. She'll feel better once she get's some rest."

"Your daughter," pressed the inspector. "She's all right, isn't she?"

"Of course," replied Janelle, much more believably this time. "But she did give us a scare."

"Being a father myself, I can understand," said the inspector. He fiddled through some papers on his desk, and took his time before readdressing them. His delay tactics, or whatever it was he was employing, made the Northams uncomfortable. It was exactly what he wanted, since he was determined to learn the truth about the watch and where it came from. It's was passed time he knew.

"I'd like to begin where we left off yesterday if you don't mind," he began, moments before recounting Phillip's modified version about how and where he really found the watch.

"It's true," replied Phillip, reaffirming his previously stated position. "We found it at Gun Bay along with the fragment, and there's nothing else to say."

"All well and good, Mr. Northam," countered Inspector Gilford, "but like I said yesterday, before being interrupted by your unfortunate family problem, it doesn't hold water."

"How can you say that?" asked Phillip, pretending to be offended.

"I've lived here all my life, Mr. Northam, and I know this island from one end to the other. And . . . if there is any spot that's been worked over and over again by local and visiting treasure hunters, Gun Bay is it!"

"Well, you're mistaken!" replied Phillip hotly. Sweat ran down his once-calm face, not from the heat but from nervous tension. "It could have been overlooked, you know."

"That's possible, of course," admitted the inspector, "but not likely."

"What else can I tell you?" replied Phillip in a most convincing manner, causing the inspector to stop his inquiry momentarily. What Gilford did not know was that Phillip had no other choice than to continue with a deceit he wanted to abandon.

"You agree with all this?" asked the inspector, hoping to coerce Janelle into contradicting her husband.

"Yes, of course," she replied. "Phillip is the one who found it, and I was there when it happened."

"At Gun Bay?" he asked again, determined to break her composure, but she wouldn't budge.

"Well, then, if that's all you have to say, there's only one thing left to do."

"Do?" inquired Phillip.

"We'll need written statements from the two of you—for the sake of record, of course—as to how you came to find the watch along with its description, so that in the future—should it be found again—it can be returned to you as its rightful owner." It was a lie, of course, since he already knew to whom it belonged, but he couldn't tell them that for fear of revealing what was really going on.

"Now?"

"Yes. Why? Is there a problem?" asked Gilford.

"No. It's just that we have another appointment, but it's not until mid-afternoon."

"It shouldn't take more than a half hour at best," replied the inspector. "Depending upon how much detail you give, of course. After that, you're free to go." He motioned for his secretary to come in.

"Suzie, find a spot in one of our offices where the Northams can complete separate statements about their recent experience, will you?"

The Northams breathed more easily then. As they stood up to walk out, the inspector extended a hand. "Sorry to have detained you," he said, "but I had no other choice but to do my duty as I saw it."

"No apologies necessary," said Phillip as he grasped the other man's hand in farewell. A thought struck him then; he whispered it into the chief inspector's ear. "By the way, Inspector, you were right."

"About what?" Gilford replied softly.

"About Suzie. She does talks too much."

An astonished look crossed Gilford's face, leaving him confused even though he agreed with the man who was just walking out with his wife. *Why in the world did he say that?* he asked himself.

The Hotel Lobby—3 P.M.

The Northams had finished earlier than they expected and had time to kill after leaving their signed statements with Suzie. To review their strategy before heading back to the hotel, they decided to have lunch at a newly built waterfront Burger King. Once fully reinforced, they got in their island rent-a-car and headed back to the hotel lobby where they waited as told.

"Hey, mister," asked a little Caymanian boy who walked straight up to them. "Is your name Northam?"

"Yes," replied Phillip.

"Good, then this is for you," the youngster said, handing Phillip an envelope with his name printed on it.

"Where did you get this?" he asked, delaying the youngster who was eager to leave.

"A man gave it to me," the boy replied as he looked outside the lobby as if trying to find someone. "He was right there ... but he's gone now."

Phillip looked in the direction the boy pointed, but saw no one except taxi drivers and hotel personnel.

"What did he look like?" pressed Phillip, hoping for some means of identification.

"Like you," said the boy. "A little shorter, but about your size."

"Anything else?"

"No, sir," the boy replied. "But he gave me a dollar for bringing the letter to you. I've got to go now."

"Thanks for your help," said Phillip as he motioned to the boy he could go after convincing himself he could learn nothing else.

"Open it," said Janelle anxiously.

"In our room," cautioned Phillip, leading her by the arm to a nearby elevator.

The message was typed and was clear as to how, why, and where the Northams were to go to begin negotiations with Tanya's kidnappers. What surprised them most of all was the statement they would be meeting one of the kidnappers—in person—at the Tropical Gardens restaurant, a short distance away.

Why in person, they pondered, *since the contact risked being permanently identified and captured.* Whatever the reason, they had to accept the fact that such factors had to have been considered by the kidnappers too, otherwise they wouldn't been so bold.

How the Northams would respond now depended upon how Mort would respond. They called him again. And again he said: "I'll be there in ten minutes. Wait for me."

That was all they could do anyway.

George Town—Same Day

Scavenger Jones was beside himself. All day he had been searching for his friend Crazy Joe but to no avail. As a last resort, only because he had forgotten about him, he approached Joe's business partner, the taxi driver.

"Haven't seen him for days," said the man. "Probably on one of his binges and passed out, and God only knows where. Why? Is he in trouble with the law again?"

"No, but I've got important news for him, but he's nowhere to be found."

"If I see him, I'll tell him you're looking for him. Any message?"

"Yeh. Tell him I know where to find his devil fish."

"It's for real?" the taxi driver asked, admitting he heard a rumor earlier in the day, but really didn't believe it. He didn't believe it even now, for that matter.

"Well, it's true," replied Jones, upset over the man's questioning. "And I saw it with my own eyes, but I don't want to tell anyone else, not even the police, until I've had a chance to talk to Joe. And then— mind you—everybody will look up to Joe with respect."

"That'll be the day," the driver scoffed though privately he hoped it could be true since his partner had long been ridiculed by many of the more astute of the island's inhabitants. To prove Crazy Joe had been right all along would be a boon to those who had befriended him for so long.

"You will tell him, won't you?" pressed Jones.

"If I see him," agreed the driver. "And where will you be in the meantime?"

"At my shack at Gun Bay," came the reply. Jones ran off, looking every which way in hopes of seeing his friend, who could be mingling among the crowds in search of new clients. He left the taxi driver where he found him, parked along the waterfront waiting for potential fares.

Tropical Gardens Restaurant—That Evening

Janelle felt awkward all dressed up compared to what she had been wearing previously, but the message insisted she wear something red and yellow to help the agent who was to meet them recognize the couple. Her husband, likewise, had to wear something white with a red tie to match instead of the typical casual wear seen everywhere. As recommended, they sought a secluded spot for a party of three in the restaurant, where some semblance of privacy could be enjoyed.

Every face and body which popped in raised their expectations until they gave up trying to guess who it was they were to meet.

"I don't like his colors," complained Janelle while waiting, referring to the colorful dress the note suggested she wear; she liked more subtle colors.

"Not bad from my point of view," remarked her husband as he surveyed his newly purchased outfit. "It's the tie I don't like."

"I thought red was your favorite color?" said Janelle.

"Yeh, but not as a tie," mussed Phillip as he looked around the room again, hoping for a sign.

A tall young man with crewcut hair, blond as blond could be, walked in just then and spoke to the receptionist. She turned him over to a waitress who took him to a vacant spot in the crowded room.

When that happened, Phillip looked away, thinking, *So much for that man.* He went back to door-watching again, growing more impatient with each passing moment. To pass the time, he and Janelle ordered drinks, a mai tai for her and a bourbon and seven for him.

Minutes after the cocktail waitress delivered their drinks, to their surprise, the young man who had entered earlier approached their table.

"Mr. and Mrs. Northam?" he asked politely and quite softly.

"Yes," answered Phillip while his wife looked on.

"I believe we have an engagement," the man replied.

In Phillip and Janelle's eyes, he couldn't have been more than twenty years old, too innocent-looking for works of intrigue and deception, but he had to be the man they were waiting for. *How clever,* thought Phillip as he eyed the young man before him.

"May I sit?" he asked after failing to receive a reply from the Northams.

"You can't be—," said Phillip before being cut off.

"I'm afraid so, sir," the man answered politely.

"But you're so young."

"And idealistic too," replied the young man, making it clear he was without question the one they were waiting for. "Shall we get down to business?"

Before he could say anything else, a short, heavy-set, balding waiter, rather slovenly in appearance, walked to the table, disrupting further talk.

"Your order, please," he said.

"Please. The treat is on me," the young man said in flawless English.

It took a lot of strength on the part of the Northams to maintain a serious face while at the same time not laughing at the fat waiter—or what appeared to be one—as he fumbled with the menu.

It bothered Mort to perform such a menial task. He hadn't waited on tables since college days and had vowed he'd never do it again, but here he was, scribbling everything down before running off to get the order filled.

The young man was irritated by his clumsiness, and even more so when the waiter spilled a glass of water on his neatly pressed suit.

"*Dumkoph!*" yelled the young man before correcting himself. "Don't you know how to pour water!"

"I am sorry, sir," said Mort as he grabbed a towel and started dabbing the man's suit while at the same time attaching a small listening device with an adhesive band attached to it to the underside of the table nearest the man.

"Get us another waiter," the irritated man demanded, completely dissatisfied with the service he was receiving.

"As you wish, sir," replied Mort. It didn't matter to him at this point who served them. He left then to send a real waiter to take his place.

The new waiter arrived fifteen minutes later with a steaming platter of mixed seafood, the majority of which went uneaten by the Northams. Their concern was for Tanya, and they were anxious to hear what the man had to say, but he was playing his part as he had been ordered to do—by acting quite ordinarily. In fact, he seemed to be enjoying the food quite well as if he hadn't eaten such excellent food for sometime.

"Can we discuss terms now?" asked Phillip.

"We need to know *something*," urged his wife.

The man took one big swallow from his wine glass, wiped his mouth, then glanced around the crowded room quickly before answering them. Had he looked a little further to his left, he might have abandoned the meeting then and there. Mort, as great a planner as he was, hadn't anticipated a visit to the restaurant by members of the delegation.

"What are you doing in that outfit?" one of them asked, ready to say more.

Like a greased ball-bearing, he whisked them out of the room to another section, where he had to confide he was involved in some undercover work. Naturally, they wanted to know more, so he told them only as much as he needed to, but that only helped to stimulate their curiosity and they refused to leave. They promised not to disrupt his investigation while jokingly adding, "Providing you continue as our waiter." To the suggestion, Mort's answer was concise: "Go to hell!"

When they insisted he bring them up to date at the next day's meeting, he had to agree since they were entitled, by reason of their position, to be informed. To what degree was a matter of opinion. He had his own ideas beyond those he represented.

Back in the Northam's corner of the room, while the young man engorged himself, Phillip decided to push the question, "Can the exchange be done this evening?"

"Yes. Within the hour if you listen to my instructions and do not deviate from anything I tell you."

The Northams felt somewhat better, but apprehension was still with them. Phillip's future was questionable though there was a good chance, as they had decided earlier, the kidnappers would not harm him. All they wanted from him was information as to where he found the watch and the gold fragment, so they said. That part puzzled the Northams since logic said the other side should have known where to find it. They dropped the subject for want of an answer.

"What do we have to do?" asked Janelle as she squeezed her husband's hand for reassurance.

"Do you have a car?" asked the man.

"Yes. It's parked outside," replied Phillip.

"Good, then that will make it easier for all of us." He pulled out a map and stretched it out before them, then looked at his watch. "In twenty minutes, I will leave you to join my friends. Ten minutes after that it will be your turn to leave." He pointed to the marked map before them. "You will go along the routes shown, from here at Seven Mile Beach to here," he added. The stopping point was a spot on the opposite side of town.

Phillip said he knew the spot and could find it even in the dark since he had passed that way before. It was at the juncture of two major roads, both leading to the east side where Gun Bay was located.

"Make sure you are not followed because we will have people watching you, just to see that we aren't betrayed. And when you get to the spot we have marked, remain there until you see another car pull up a hundred meters or so away. You will know it is the right people when you see them blink their headlights off and on three times. Is that understood?"

"Perfectly," said Phillip. "Then what?"

"You will walk halfway and stop. After that, your daughter will be brought halfway on the other side of the street, where she will be released to join her mother."

"How do I know you won't keep the two of us? Or double-cross us in anyway?"

"Your wife will still be some distance away, and if anything goes wrong, she can always race away," said the man. "But that won't be necessary because we know how much this means to you and how much our part means to us, so it's an even trade."

It made sense and Phillip, after talking it over with Janelle, agreed they had little or no choice but to go along.

"Is it acceptable?" the young man asked, now looking at his watch more frequently and with some anxiety.

His concerns hit the Northams too. A plan had been made with Mort, and they were obligated to carry it out.

"It's time to go," the youthful man said as he rose out of his chair and dropped two one-hundred-dollar bills on the table. "This should more than cover the sumptuous meal and the delightful company," he said as he walked way.

The Northams didn't move for a good ten minutes, fearing they were being watched though they didn't know if it was true or just a ruse to throw them off. The fact was that they were, but not by the ones they expected.

On the other side of the room, many eyes—some German, others American, and still others Russian—followed their every move from behind menus or cocktail glasses. Mort had told them just enough to keep them busy while he puttered away on a motorbike far too small for his frame.

It was something he had to do since he knew approximately what route the Northams were to follow. While they were talking, Eric had taped the conversation between the Northams and the young Nazi. He didn't need the map because Phillip had been sufficiently briefed to verbalize what he was being shown or told, making it easy for Mort —and anyone else listening in—to know where to go, thanks to the listening device which functioned marvelously.

When their ten-minute wait was up, the Northams got up and left, leaving delegation members to ponder their movements. Regrettably, some of them were more curious than they should have been and decided to follow, complicating Mort's investigation. In desperation, Eric called the police station anonymously, advising them that a hold up was in progress at the restaurant and men brandishing weapons were holding customers at bay.

Within minutes, a band of patrol cars and policemen erected roadblocks on either side of the restaurant, blocking traffic. Bullhorns announced their arrival which petrified everyone inside the restaurant, until the level-headed proprietor managed to convince the police the whole thing was a mistake. Thwarted in their attempt to leave, some of the curious delegation members were left with no choice except to visit the bar. A few of the more adventurous ones, however, refused to quit and went out after a cold trail.

While the Northams were taking a circuitous car ride through the streets of George Town to throw off would-be followers before heading for their final destination, Mort was puttering his way past the police station to the hospital road, not too far behind the Northams' vehicle. Being on a motorbike in the dark night made him quite inconspicuous despite his large size.

While motoring past police headquarters, he thought he recognized the inspector, racing to a waiting car. It passed him, going in the direction from which he came, its siren wailing and lights flashing. A smile crossed his face. *One less person to worry about*, he thought as he twisted the throttle to make his tiny bike go faster, but it had a governor, specifically installed to keep tourists from racing on Grand Cayman Island's narrow, pot-holed streets.

After passing the hospital, the red taillights of the Northams' car brightened. It had made a quick stop at an intersection, then proceeded slowly from that point on, after making a left turn. Its occupants were obviously looking for something. Mort followed close behind, only this time with his lights off to avoid detection. It was a difficult thing to do on such a dark night, but an occasional street light gave some illumination.

Minutes later, the Northams' vehicle came to a stop near another intersection, the main highway leading to the east end of the island. At that point, the Northams got out and stood alongside their car. Upon seeing this, Mort moved in cautiously, using clumps of trees to hide his approach. Within minutes, another car, one that came from the east end, parked on the embankment a hundred yards away. Its driver blinked its headlight three times. In turn, Phillip Northam reached into his car and did the same thing. The driver of the other car signaled again, this time with one blink. Phillip blinked his twice, and the activity for the evening began.

Phillip kissed his wife before walking forward. From the opposite direction, a man holding the hand of a little girl walked toward him on the opposite side of the road. Behind the man and girl were several other men, who trailed behind the two, but kept a reasonable distance away. Then, at a point halfway between the two vehicles, Phillip and the man with the girl stopped, making Mort, who was watching it all from a safe distance, breathe more easily.

A voice rang out just then. It was Phillip's.

"Let her go to her mother."

True to their word—which surprised him—the man holding Tanya's hand released it and directed her to go directly to her mother.

Tanya obeyed and went screeching to her mother, who stayed a safe distance away, just in case the men on the opposite side decided to change their minds. They didn't and Phillip, after turning to make sure, walked toward them. Instantly, he was whisked away, leaving Janelle to fret over his safety.

"Don't hurt him," shouted Janelle to the departing vehicle as it made a sharp 180-degree turn and raced into the night.

At that point, Mort made his appearance. "Janelle! It's me—Mort. Don't give way to panic, honey. Everything will be all right. . . ."

"Who started all this?" demanded Inspector Gilford as he queried some of the Tropical Gardens employees.

"I don't know," most of them answered until he came to their employer, who ventured a guess.

"It could have been that fat man who passed himself off as a waiter as a joke on some of his friends," he said.

"What fat man?"

"Never saw him before, but he gave me a hundred dollars to let him do it. It was perfectly harmless. All he did was to spill some water on one of our customers. No harm done."

"Can you describe him?" asked Gilford.

"Short, fat, balding, a big paunch, and likes cigars. And talked like he was from New York."

A bell clanged loudly in Gilford's head. The description was too familiar. "Mordeciah!" he said loudly, sensing he was right.

"Who?" asked the bewildered proprietor.

"Inspector!" called a voice from the bar, interrupting the interrogation.

Gilford looked around. Nestled in a corner were several members of the delegation, all looking glum. He walked over. Rosenkrantz was the man who got his attention.

"Surprised to see you here," said Gilford, refusing a drink handed him by one of the Russians. "On duty. It's against regulations."

"You missed all the fun," said Rosenkrantz. "The Israeli guy, Mordeciah, just left. On the heels of the American couple you've been dealing with . . . a beautiful blond and a tall, dark man about my height."

"Damn!" cursed Gilford. "What in the hell is he up to?"

"I don't know, but he was sure in a hurry," replied Rosenkrantz.

"Know where they went?" asked Gilford while trying to ignore a side attraction, a member of the Russian delegation doing a high flying dance on the dance floor to the delight of the patrons who had never seen a real Cossack dance before.

"All I know," replied Rosenkrantz, "is that we caught him posing as a waiter and he told us not to interfere because he was engaged in some undercover work. And that's about it."

"Anyone else with them?" pressed Gilford like a true detective seeking out clues.

"Oh, yes," answered Rosenkrantz. "There was some good-looking young fellow with the couple. Clean cut, crew-cut, well- dressed, and nice in appearance ,but he left ten or fifteen minutes before Mort and the couple. Why?"

"Can't say for certain," replied Gilford, "but it appears Mort is working independent of any of us and that's not good."

"Anything we can do to help?" asked Igor, who had listened much but spoke little during the exchange, a pattern which everyone now recognized.

Gilford thought for a while. "Did you all see the man and woman clearly so you can recognize them if you saw them again?"

"I—we think so," answered Igor for everyone. "The woman was beautiful. A man would have to be out of his mind to forget such a person."

"Well," said Gilford, "since you are about the only ones who know what they look like, I'm going to ask for your assistance in finding them if they haven't gone back to their hotel, that is. In the meantime, wait here while I make a call."

"Strange man, this Mordeciah," said Igor, remembering with a smile how ridiculous he looked in his waiter garb. "You think he's on the trail of Nazis?" he asked, not knowing how close he had come.

"I wish I knew," replied the CIA agent, "but it was quite clear he didn't want us around."

"He's is known for such things," the Interpol representative, a Frenchman, suddenly interjected. "Rumor has it he was involved in the apprehension of Klaus Barbie, a Nazi who ordered the executions of many of my countrymen during the last world war."

Gilford came back just then. "They're not there!"

"Which means?" asked the CIA agent.

"He's hot onto something, and we're being left in the dark. And I don't like it!" said Gilford. He addressed the members of the delegation just then, "You fellows still ready to help?"

"That's what we're here for," said Sir Oliver, who just arrived on the scene from an extended tour of the john. Beer just didn't agree with him and he had tried to empty himself before returning.

"Goodness," said Gilford, shocked at seeing his old mentor in an inebriated state. "I didn't know you were here."

"Well, I only came for the ride, but I'm afraid, old chap, I've overdone it, don't you think?"

"Yes, and that's why you're not coming," Gilford said authoritatively.

"As you say, ole boy," replied Sir Oliver as he pushed his way to the nearest chair.

Gilford motioned to one of his officers to join him. "Take him to his apartment at the Charleston Arms. Room 312. You can get a key

John Hankins

at the desk."

Sir Oliver sang happily as the officer and his companion helped him to their patrol car.

"Hasn't had a good time in ages, I'll bet," said Gilford as he watched the patrol car drive away before turning to the remaining members of the delegation. "Wait here. I'll have several patrol cars pick you up to drive you around the city and island. If you spot any of the people you've described to me tonight, tell my officers and they will radio me. I'll take over after that."

His words were interrupted by an announcement over the public address system. "Call for Inspector Gilford at the front desk."

"Who in the hell wants me now?" asked Gilford, exasperated by the interruption. He had more things to do than answer phone calls. He excused himself, then raced to the desk so he could get it over as quickly as possible.

"Inspector Gilford, here?"

"This is Scavenger Jones, Inspector," said a nervous and weak voice over the phone. "Remember me?" he asked.

"You're not in trouble again, are you?" asked Gilford irritably before he knew what the man had on his mind.

"No, but I've got something important to tell you, Chief, before he gets himself killed."

"Before who gets himself killed? You haven't been drinking again, have you?"

"A little, but I ain't drunk, Chief—"

"Inspector," corrected Gilford.

"It's my friend Crazy Joe. You know, the one who's always getting locked up for trying to kill the devil fish that he says chewed him up."

"Look, Jones," Gilford replied. "I've got more things on my mind than chasing the figment of someone's imagination."

"But it's true, Inspector," insisted Jones. "I've seen it myself and they was taking a little girl out to it. And Crazy Joe, after I told him about what I saw the other day, he went crazy and wouldn't call you like I told him to. So I called you instead to keep him from getting himself killed."

"Girl? What girl?" asked Gilford, his thoughts now running wildly.

"The one in with yellow hair and a matching bathing suit, the one the men took out in the rubber boat before it dived. She was cryin' all the time."

My God! thought Gilford, suddenly remembering something. *If*

368

*he's talking about who I think he is, the Northams have lied to me
about their daughter being found and Mordeciah and his men knew
it all about the time!*

"Jones! Now listen to me," demanded Gilford. "I want you to tell
me exactly where this all happened and anything else you can
remember."

Gilford listened, rarely missing a word. When Jones finished, the
inspector gasped. The case he had been working on was unfolding
before his very eyes, and he didn't know a thing about it until now
through the eyes and words of a well-known thief.

"Forget it! More important things have surfaced," said Gilford
upon return to the waiting delegation. When asked why, all he could
say was, "Something more important has come up, demanding my
immediate attention."

He was gone after that, but not before stopping at his office to
acquire an assortment of handguns and automatic weapons, plus a
number of police officers to assist him. When they were gathered, he
advised them what to look for but could promise nothing beyond that
since too much time had lapsed since the meeting between the
Northams and the mysterious young man.

On the Road Again—Bodden Town

While Gilford was instructing his men, Mort was following the
vehicle which had driven off with Phillip. He would lose them often,
then try to catch up, but the distance between him and them began to
increase until he lost them altogether.

In one instant, while driving through the illuminated streets of
Bodden Town, a small community halfway between George Town
and Gun Bay, he was almost run over by a noisy, battered old pickup
which seemed held together by bailing wire. Its lights were out of
alignment, allowing the driver to see to the right only or upward
toward the sky.

Mort caught a glimpse of the man behind the wheel. From that
split-second look, he thought he recognized the man. On a lunch break
in George Town several days earlier, one of his assistants had pointed
him out, saying that was "a man with a most interesting history." Like
everyone who heard the story, Mort listened but attached no significance to the man until now. What passed through his mind during the
next few minutes joined past events to the present, making it imperative he reach his next destination as quickly as possible. From the look

on the pickup driver's face, as briefly as Mort saw it, he felt certain he needed to get to the other men before the driver did. Unfortunately, that wasn't possible since his motorbike couldn't go faster than 30 miles per hour while the pickup could go beyond 50.

Mort's heart sank when he finally caught up with the vehicles he had been following. They were parked alongside Gun Bay Beach, lights on and engines still running. As to their former occupants, they were nowhere in sight, so he ran down to the beach, searching for signs of them.

Footprints were everywhere, going from the abandoned vehicles to the side of a series of skid marks, the kind made by the dragging of a rubber boat. At the water's edge, both types disappeared.

Mort swore, disappointed he had missed his quarry. As he did, another sound, one coming from a behind a clump of trees and bushes, caught his ear. With his weapon drawn, he ran in its direction in time to see a man whom he guessed to be the driver of the pickup, guiding his boat through the surf toward something in the sea beyond.

Mort tried to get the man's attention, but the pounding surf drowned his words, leaving him nothing else to do but watch the departing boat. To his surprise, it was following in the wake of a large black object, one that was slowly sinking into the sea. The more it sank, the more Mort thought he heard loud muffler-like sounds coming from the monster.

"Submarine!" Mort exclaimed. "So that's how they did it!" he said to himself while racing back to his bike to return to town. He changed his mind after seeing the abandoned vehicles. He took the closest one and drove off, just in time, too.

Heading in his direction, their sirens blowing and red and green lights flashing, were a number of police cars. As they passed, Mort noticed the man in the lead car—Inspector Gilford. He winced. He should have included the man in his plans, but time had prevented that. At least, that's the excuse he gave himself.

At this point, there was nothing else for him to do but to get back to town as quickly as possible to assemble his men for a quick and dangerous flight. Again, he hoped he could beat his opponents to Little Cayman, where they were bound to go. Of that he was certain since the Northams told him that was where they had found the watch and gold fragments, plus much, much more. . . .

Chapter 28

A Desperate Chase

Beyond the Reef

efore heading out to sea, the first thing Crazy Joe did was to check the outboard motor's fuel tank to see if it—and all the other gas containers on board—had been topped by his pal Jones like he had insisted upon time and time again.

Running out of fuel on some of their more interesting ventures was something they had learned to avoid quite early in their midnight appropriation careers after nearly being caught stripping several beached vessels.

To his delight, Scavenger Jones had not done as he had in the past, used the gas money on booze. This time everything was in order. Every container, including the outboard's main tank, was full, leaving Crazy Jones to do but one thing: concentrate on his pursuit of the fleeing U-boat, the one he had for years upon years thought was a real live monster though after many years he was beginning to have his doubts.

"I'm going to get ya, you lousy bastard," he cried with vengeful

371

enthusiasm as he directed his boat through rough waves near the reef he had just passed through. Not far ahead of him was the black monster he hated. It had submerged to periscope and snorkel depth, leaving a frothy white trail in its wake.

While Crazy Jones did not know where the sea monster was going, an inner sense told him it was heading for Little Cayman, site of a forty-year-old tragedy. The thought pricked his heart to the point of bursting. This time, the monster would pay for its fateful intrusion into his once-peaceful life. If he failed, life would not be worth living, and he would willingly throw his body into the sea rather than suffer emotionally as he had most of his life.

His tiny boat was a modified Boston whaler which had been purchased by Crazy Joe from its original owner after it suffered a major mishap on the other side of the island. Now as it broke through the high waves outside the east end of the reef, which tended to impede his progress, very little if anything could be done by the wiry man to shield himself from the stinging salt spray which peppered his body like tiny steel pellets.

His resolve was the single most important factor which kept him going. He persisted when others would have given up, but then no one besides himself, so he told himself often, had reason enough to do what he was driven to do.

Within an hour after departure, using the head of the snorkel as his guiding point, he began to worry because the U-boat wasn't heading in the direction he expected. Why, he didn't quite know, but he was determined to follow it as long as he could because there was a mystery surrounding it which needed answers, in particular, answers to the story told to him by Scavenger Jones whom he chanced to meet days after recovering from another binge. It was about a young girl who had been taken aboard against her will.

Sput-t-t-ter, sput-t-t-ter.

His outboard died as he was closing in on the snorkel which was only yards away from his grasp! He only wanted to attach a line to it until to save fuel and see exactly what it was going to do. But before that could happen, tragedies of tragedies! Dead in the water! He wanted to cry—to bellow like a madman bent on destruction, but there wasn't time. A cool head and reason needed to prevail. All was not yet lost. "Find the cause, stupid," he said to himself. "Check the tank first." Knowing how careless Scavenger Jones was with gas drums, water could have gotten in the fuel.

"Tools! Tools!" he cried out. "I hope he had sense to leave them alone!" In desperation, he tossed things here and there, using his flashlight to help him see. "Thank God!" he cried again, breathing more normally now after finding what he needed. "I've got to check the line now . . . and drain the bastard. If there's water, I'll kill the bum," he said, referring to his pal while selecting the proper wrench to unfasten one of the lines. He looked out in the distance, his heart pounding hard. The snorkel was now heading in another direction and was slowly disappearing from sight. In minutes, it was gone except for a light white trail which almost pointed to Little Cayman. Again he cried out, but this time with glee.

"Oh, ho, you big, black bastard. Now I know where you're really going. I'll get you yet. Just you wait!"

The fuel line came loose, and just as he suspected, there was water in the outboard's tank, enough to fill a tiny drinking cup he had brought along. He cursed, but continued draining until the water, which was heavier than gasoline, was no more. Then, to be certain the plugs were not fouled, he unscrewed each one and flushed their cylinders with fresh gasoline before trying to crank them again.

"Start, Angeline!" he cried, using the name he had given his faithful engine, before pressing the starter button. Black smoke, a cough, and a sputter immediately followed by a magnificent purr brought tears to the little man's eyes. He kissed the top of the motor, the put engaged the props again, and sped off in the direction of Little Cayman. He knew the way by heart, irrespective of the time of day or night.

As he traveled over the surface and was buffeted by the rough seas, numerous thoughts ran through his mind. Most of them centered on revenge, but others were on the more current situation: getting to Little Cayman before the U-boat even though the belligerent sea seemed to want to challenge him every nautical mile.

George Town—Grand Cayman Island

While Eric was banging at the door of the man who owned the best dive shop in town, telling him he would make it worth his while to open up his place and that his needs constituted an emergency, his partner, Yitzak, a funny name for an Irish-American Jew now from Israel, was out looking for a large pickup to carry the equipment the Israeli team had brought with them and whatever else they needed from the dive shop.

When the happy man received the generous payment, Eric received the keys to the dive shop and away they went, first to the private aviation part of the airport where they were given the name of a competent helicopter tourist pilot, whom they contacted immediately by phone. In the process, they found he was the only charter helicopter pilot on the island and didn't like flying at night. To counter his objections they offered him a bonus, but he refused by countering with an outrageous quote which he felt would discourage them. Not to be outdone, they accepted, leaving him with no choice except to meet them at the airport.

"Wait for us at your chopper," said Mort. "We'll be along shortly. Have to get our night camera equipment," he lied, just to keep the man from knowing where they were really going. Had Mort told him, he would have no doubt gotten a rejection because Little Cayman was too far, so he kept mum until it was time to spring his surprise.

Five minutes later, they were on their way to the dive shop, where they quickly loaded two wind surfboards, diving masks with snorkels, shark knives, and a number of other essential items.

Every time the proprietor asked a question, hoping to know what they were up to, he always got the same answer. "It's a secret. You'll probably read about it in the morning papers." Little did he—and they for that matter—realize how prophetic those words were.

They left after that, leaving the proprietor counting his money, and still confused over their frantic efforts to get to the airport. That much he knew, but the reason why eluded him.

"You the fella that called?" asked the pilot looking cautiously over the men who had just raced onto the tarmac.

"Yes. You the pilot?" asked Mort, the first to reply.

The pilot looked at the equipment and supplies in the back of the pickup and shook his head. "I hope you're not thinking of taking all that stuff?" he asked.

"Why not?" asked Mort.

"Too much. And besides we'd be overloaded," replied the man. "You'll have to leave some of it behind. The wind surfs especially." A thought struck him then. "Hey! Wait a minute. You're not planning to take those wind surfboards, too, are you?"

"We are," replied Mort.

"We can't do that," said the pilot before remembering something. "Hey, didn't you say you just wanted to take pictures."

"True," replied Mort, "but I'm afraid we've had a little change in plans since we last spoke."

"Not in my bird," replied the pilot. "Find someone else who's crazy enough to carry them."

"Why? Is it because you think you might have weight and balances and other aerodynamically unsound flight characteristics?" asked Mort, surprising the man with his aeronautical knowledge.

"Well, yes," replied the pilot, surprised Mort could speak his language.

"Forget it then," said Mort, "because I know your ship is large enough to handle everything we have, including the windsurfing boards, so long as they are properly lashed to your skids."

"You might know a lot about flying, mister," argued the pilot, "but the answer is still 'No!' I own this plane, not you!"

"In that case," said Mort without batting an eyelid, "I think I have something to change your mind."

Before the pilot knew what was happening, Mort pressed the cold barrel of his automatic against the man's forehead.

"On second thought," the pilot said, acquiescing, "your point is well taken."

Mort smiled. "I knew we would come to terms."

Within minutes, everything was loaded, including the windsurfing boards. In the latter case, the pilot personally got involved to make certain nothing would interfere with his craft's ability to maneuver. He started the helicopter's engines, turned on its radios, then went through his call-up routine.

"I'll need to tell the tower where we're going," said the pilot. "It's routine."

"It's Little Cayman," replied Mort with the straightest face the man had ever seen.

"Thank God," the pilot replied in relief. "For a minute I thought it was Cuba for certain. Or a big drug deal or something, but not Little Cayman! Why in the world would anyone want to go there? At this time of night especially?"

"You'll learn soon enough," said Mort as he nudged the man to prepare for flight.

"Cayman Tower, Tango Two Whiskey, filing flight plan to Little Cayman. Estimated flight enroute forty-five minutes, barring headwinds. Souls onboard four, including pilot. Over."

"Tango Two Whiskey cleared for take-off. Barometric pressure 30.03, winds 45 at 8 knots, visibility indefinite."

"Roger Cayman Tower. See you guys later . . . I hope."

The tower operator laughed, thinking the man whom he knew quite well was joking.

375

"All right, Pat. Have your fun. See you later."

"A slip," the pilot apologized to Mort after being reminded by the barrel against his temple as to who was really in charge.

"I can accept a mistake one time, but beyond that, nothing," Mort advised the man through his in-flight intercom. "Now get on with your business," he said as he withdrew the weapon to allow the man to get on the proper radial out of the Owen Roberts Airport to Little Cayman.

As the man fiddled with the frequencies, the familiar automated dot and dash pattern identifying the local VOR—direction signal transmitting station—filled the cabin. After that, following a few turns of a dial, the needle in the navigation radio window centered, showing it was on a course leading directly from the airport VOR to Little Cayman.

"Satisfied?" asked the pilot, knowing Mort understood every move he had made.

Mort smiled. "You're doing better."

Into the night the helicopter flew, fighting headwinds most of the way, until Mort suggested a different altitude where they would be less forceful. Within minutes, the speed increased and the distance to Little Cayman decreased.

Later, as the helicopter drew in closer, the pilot tuned his ADF, automatic direction finder, and followed the needle directly to the radio beacon located next to a small grass strip at the southern part of the island. A few lights in the distance could be seen, but outside of that, everything like the dark midnight sky was pitch-black.

Mort wouldn't let the man touch down. Instead, he directed his attention to a small reef-surrounded lagoon in the center of which was a small island. While enroute, using the pilot's maps of the area, he had made quick calculations as to how much time it would take the U-boat to reach the island as opposed to the time it would take to reach the same place by helicopter. To his great pleasure, they had time to spare, and he directed the pilot to set his bird down on the lagoon's beach.

"I don't know what you guys are up to," said the pilot carefully, "but you must be nuts for coming out here and commandeering a helicopter to do it! Because there's no place to go. Unless . . . that is, you're going to meet someone out here. . . ."

"Shut up and get us down," said Mort as he coached the man to find a decent landing spot.

Within minutes after turning his landing lights on, the pilot found such a spot and with great precision put the plane down safely. It was unloaded quickly with the pilot pitching in feverishly. By now, however, he no longer feared his captors. They seemed not to be the criminal type, so he pressed his luck further.

"This some kind of secret operation?" he asked, guessing correctly, though he didn't know it.

Mort let down his guard down and apologized but not before pulling out his credentials, which showed he and his assistants were representatives of the Israeli government as well as guest of the Crown.

"Whew!" the man gasped. A larger gasp followed when Mort filled his pockets with bands of hundred dollar bills to make him forget his anguish and promised he could check with the authorities when he returned to Grand Cayman to verify the truthfulness of his statements. Chief Inspector Gilford's name was used frequently, though often out of context. With so many important names and titles being tossed at him, the pilot could not help but be impressed and readily agreed to help in any way possible.

While the pilot and Mort discussed possible courses of action, Eric and Yitzak searched for places where they could safely hide their equipment until ready for use. The best spot for them since they worked in pairs was behind clumps of banyan trees which lined the perimeter near what appeared to be an uninhabited beach. They told Mort about their plans.

"Oh, but there are people," interrupted the pilot who overheard their conversation. "Some of them live not too far from here."

"That's all we need!" said Mort in near panic. "Tell me about them," he directed, "so we can decide on a logical plan of approach."

The helicopter lifted off minutes later, heading for the airstrip, where it sat down again. The pilot's instructions were clear: Run as quickly as you can up the dirt road leading to a small tourist cabin located not too far from the airstrip and warn everyone you can find about the need to stay out of sight until the danger had passed. Mort refused to say what that was, but he assured the pilot he would know everything he needed to know by morning, provided everything went as planned. On the other hand, if things went sour, Mort instructed him to get in radio contact with Grand Cayman authorities and tell them what he knew.

"All right, Eric, Yitzak, you know what to do. Get your equipment ready and wait for my signal."

The two young men ran off, leaving him in the darkness to wait patiently for a U-boat to rise out of the sea.

On Board *U-4R2*

Phillip's captors didn't seem to care whether he saw everything they were doing or not, nor what it was they had whisked him away in, causing him reservations about his future. In his mind, what he was seeing and experiencing was a lot more than a hostage should have been seeing, especially someone who was supposed to be released later. His uneasiness started with his first glimpse of the submarine after the men who escorted him, rather roughly at first, removed the blindfold and handcuffs they had placed on him right after their Zodiac touched the hull of the huge, freshly painted U-boat.

At that point, they nudged him to climb the Jacob's ladder, then shuffled him quickly to a hatch on the forward end of the boat. He got a quick glimpse of the bridge and a number of men who were watching intently as he came aboard before being told in broken English to descend. Men with pistols drawn were waiting for him below decks. They promptly pushed him forward; past a pantry, small dining area, and wardrooms, and finally into what appeared to be the main operating section of the boat.

Many eyes glared at him as he was pushed forward near what he recognized as being the housing for the U-boat's periscope. A man was waiting there for him. He was an old, thin, tall, prominent-looking man, whose once handsome face had been marred by a number of small scars. As for his other features which Phillip confined to memory, his hair was yellowish-white and thinning rapidly, but still quite prominent for an old man. Of interest was his uniform. It was coal black with silver-thread embroidered embellishments on his collar and sleeves. They all made him stand out from the rest of the men in the room—officers and enlisted men. The latter wore neat uniforms too, but not quite as ornate. Common to everyone, Phillip noticed their armbands—a black swastika on a circular blood-red background.

Nazis, thought Phillip, *just like Mort said!*

"Welcome to our humble abode aboard *U-4R2*, Mr. Northam," said the tall, old man. "I am General Ernst von Kleitenberg, head of this noble expedition."

"What's so noble about it?" asked Phillip as he looked around the immaculately clean control room and into what seemed to be an endless composition of youthful faces who looked at him as if he were an animal in a cage. There were a few exceptions, some older officers, but not many.

The general laughed. "You Americans, always joking," he said.

378

"I like Americans really. They've been very resourceful throughout their history, very much like my own people, and our dear Führer of course before his superb work was brought to an unfortunate and regrettable end. But what he did is not forgotten, and we are his successors."

"Well, what does that have to do with me?" demanded Phillip.

Again the man laughed. "More than you can ever imagine, Herr Northam. Phillip, isn't it?"

"Yes, but—?"

"Don't concern yourself with trivialities," interrupted the general as he motioned to a man with a white cap standing beside him. "Kapitän, you may get underway. Take her down to snorkel level," he said.

As Phillip watched, the captain, a young man in his thirties, issued orders to other men who issued more orders to even younger men, causing to them to secure hatches, open and close valves, turn wheels, and trip electrical circuits while monitoring a series of intricate dials. The control room became a beehive of activity. When the air sounds dissipated, valves were again turned and the U-boat began to tilt, nose down, gradually dropping into the depths of the sea. At that point, the room was filled with the sound of pounding diesel engines and the sucking sounds made by its snorkel as it inhaled fresh air and exhaled exhaust gases.

"Come with me, Mr. Northam," said von Kleitenberg above the noise as he motioned for the newcomer to follow him into another compartment to a space which doubled as the officers' mess. Several officers and a man in civilian clothes were already there as were a number of armed guards. The general motioned for Phillip to take a seat, which he did.

"Well, let's get down to business," said the general as he pushed his thin body into a position opposite Phillip. "If I understand right, you are the key to something we lost many years ago."

"It's more like forty-four years plus, isn't it?" replied Phillip.

"I see you have discernment," replied the general with a smile on his face. "That's something I like in a man—boldness. Too bad you're not on our side because I could use a man with such qualities."

"Let's not waste words, general. Tell me what you want and let's proceed from that point," said Phillip.

"Ah—another fine attribute," said the general, undisturbed by his arrogance. "You're right. Time is a commodity of immense value, " added the general who was quite astute at handling hotheads. "Before I do that, Mr. Northam, let me remind you of the necessity to uphold your portion of this agreement as we did when we let your daughter go."

"You want to know where I found the watch—"

"And the gold fragment," added the general. "Where you found one, you also found the other."

"If you hid them, why do you need me? You could have gotten them yourself."

"I wish that were so," replied the general, his grey-blue eyes piercing Phillip's brown ones, "but unfortunately, fate intervened during those crucial days and we were forced to jettison our cargo on an island somewhere in this general area in the middle of the night with no reference points to follow. That was over forty years ago and we've been searching ever since. Until you came along, that is."

"I found it within hours," remarked Phillip with a smile on his face, "and I wasn't even looking for it!"

"Fate again," replied the general with a sly smile. "So now if you would be so kind, Mr. Northam, my staff and I would appreciate knowing where you found our property."

"What assurance do I have you will not eliminate me if I tell you?" asked Phillip.

"Come now, Mr. Northam," von Kleitenberg said as he looked in the direction of his guards, a serious smile on his face, "we're honorable people. After we reclaim what is rightfully ours, you are free to go."

"That's no assurance," answered Phillip.

"I agree, but what else can I tell you other than to say your release will in no way be of any consequence to us, so why should we commit a totally irresponsible and an immoral act?"

The general's argument was persuasive, but Phillip doubted his sincerity. He thought to himself, *I still don't trust the bastard—or his goons—but I'll play along and be on the alert for an opportunity to escape. After all, where we're going, I know the place better than they.*

"Well, what do you say?" asked the general, showing a great deal of patience.

"You've got a deal," replied Phillip.

"So where on Grand Cayman Island did you find our property?" asked the general.

"Who said it was on Grand Cayman?" asked Phillip with a chuckle.

"Why? You mean it wasn't on Grand Cayman?"

"Heck, no," came Phillip's reply. "It was found on Little Cayman sixty miles or so from here."

"You certain of that?" asked the general, shocked by the revelation.

"Look, General—or whatever you are, you and your gang have put me and my family into a lot of turmoil over these last few days not to mention what the Grand Cayman police did to us before that, so why should I lie to you? After all, you have the advantage. Either I'm lying, or I'm not!"

"You're quite right," admitted the general. "It's just that everything happened on your island and we had little or no information to rely on until your discovery."

"Yeh, but Grand Cayman doesn't resemble Little Cayman in anyway or size other than being a long, flat island."

"True, but we didn't know that then because it was too dark when we fired our torpedoes. . . ."

"You mean there were more than one?" asked Phillip. "All loaded with stuff. . . ?"

Phillip's statement excited the general. It was the most positive thing he could say.

"No one could have told you that, Mr. Northam, unless he had first-hand knowledge, and I believe you."

At that moment, he motioned for the captain to come foreword. "Good news, Kapitän. Bring your maps of the area so we can determine how to make the recovery.

"Aye, Herr General," replied the man. He returned moments later carrying a large nautical map showing details of the Cayman Islands, then spread them before his superior.

"It's all yours," said von Kleitenberg as he pushed the maps in Phillip's direction. Other members of the general's staff moved in to get a better view.

Phillip felt nervous, but did as asked. After a quick review, he pointed a lone finger to a reef-surrounded lagoon on Little Cayman, within which was a small island.

"We anchored off the reefs here, then took our Zodiac—rubber boat—past this tiny island and to the beach which is here. And about here," he added while pointing, "is where my daughter found your damn torpedo."

"So near yet so far," sighed the general as he shook his head in disbelief. "It was near us all the time, and we didn't know it!"

"I'm sorry we did," said Phillip glumly.

"Oh, come now, Mr. Northam, don't be so negative. You had the easy part. It was I who had the worst experience. How would you like to have been dragged down toward the bottom of the sea, torn and

381

bleeding from various wounds caused by a British destroyer, and upon escape from the sinking U-boat, being confronted by man-eating sharks who were already feeding on the flesh of your dead comrades?"

"I wouldn't have liked it," answered Phillip, "any more than you would have liked being in Vietnam fighting a war you couldn't win because of politics."

Von Kleitenberg said nothing for a while. Phillip had taken some of the wind out of his sails, but he respected the man because it was obvious he had a military background steeped in combat.

"So . . . you were in Vietnam? Were you there very long?"

"Long enough," said Phillip, stopping there.

Von Kleitenberg stopped his questioning just then to readdress his captain. "What's our present course?"

"Circular, and around the island as you directed earlier, Herr General. That is, until you instruct me otherwise. . . ."

"Good, then alter your course immediately for Little Cayman. We need to get to this cove as quickly as possible."

"Aye, Herr General, immediately," replied the captain. He gave the general a quick salute, then hastened back to the control room where he issued a series of orders over the sub's public address system.

"He's quite good," von Kleitenberg said proudly, hoping to impress Phillip.

"I've seen better flunkies," replied Phillip.

"Flunkies?" asked the general, showing a weakness in his vocabulary. An aide stooped and whispered in his ear, eliciting an angry blush which the general quickly suppressed. In the general's mind, honey was preferable to vinegar unless all reasonable steps failed. Of course, it could have been easy for him to have had the crap beaten out of Phillip to get what he wanted, but he—like many before him—had learned long ago that coercion didn't always work, especially around strong-headed people. The man before him, a combat veteran, was such a person. And besides, if he had given in to his basic impulse to pulverize the man, such an act would have been in violation of a major principle expounded in one of his book chapters, "The Art of Persuasion: Diplomacy versus Force."

Everyone's thoughts were interrupted by commands sweeping through the boat's public address system. "Hard aport, left full rudder! Maintain depth, watch your depth gauges. That's it! Bring her around quickly to a heading of . . . ."

Again more sounds, all deafening, which bothered Phillip's shell-shocked ears. He plugged them with his fingers for a moment, then released them when the pressure in the boat abated after a slight down-dipping closed off the air intake to the snorkel. It was scary at first for everyone, but the chief engineer was quick to avert a compounding problem.

"How did you come to be a general in charge of a submarine?" asked Phillip after things quieted down. "It's a strange combination if you ask me."

The general smiled through his scarred face, then answered, surprising Phillip.

"Mr. Warrior," he replied after remembering something he had said years earlier before he and his new cadre departed from Kiel, "it's a story of the century, one unparalleled in the annals of modern warfare. Would you like to know more?"

"Well, if I'm to be subjected to more of this, then I might as well know why my life has been so adversely affected."

"You have a point," agreed the general. "I guess there would be no harm now in acquainting you with a little of our past."

From this unexpected beginning, von Kleitenberg began relating the history of PROJEKT U4R and its purpose. While the staff gathered nearby quivered at the thought he was giving information away which could be detrimental to their future, he ignored their motions to desist. What they didn't know was that the general was testing Phillip Northam's reaction to his grandiose plan for a Fourth Reich, variously known by many people throughout the world as "The New World Order" or the neo-Nazi movement. "The fomer should not be confused with a contemporary movement having a similar title," explained the General.

"But how can you tell the difference?" asked Phillip.

"Hah. That's the good part. Both bring light and hope to the world—at least for those who want something better, no matter how diluted or deluded their beliefs. Thus everything good that happens strengthens us."

"False light," you mean," responded Phillip quickly, almost as if he had been given the tongue of a prophet. "As a shade of darkness, false light can never replace true light, which deceives no one."

His words left the general momentarily speechless, but when he answered, it was with a firmness grounded in his beliefs. "Oh, but you're quite wrong, my impetuous friend. National Socialism is the light—the beacon of understanding through which social justice and equality can be established throughout the world and through which one's genetic heritage can be protected!"

Oh, oh, thought Phillip. *It seems to me I've heard this line before.*

Caution, boy, caution! Don't get caught in his fanaticism and idealism!

"Get my point, Mr. Northam?" asked the general hoping for a positive response to bolster his ego in the front of others.

Phillip played along, but chose a different path. "You could be right, general, but you're way over my head. I'm not a philosopher like you, I'm afraid. It's beyond me."

"It doesn't matter," replied the general. "You and others like you will be the ultimate beneficiary as long as you keep your blood pure. You don't have Jewish blood in you, do you?"

"Two-thirds Scotch-Irish, with a tinge of French" said Phillip. "The French part comes from my mother's side, a Louisianan cajun who went north after the Civil War."

"Enough Teuton in you to pass," said the general. "Your Scot-Irish ancestors are descendants from the Celts—Germans, you know?"

"So I've heard," replied Phillip, showing little or no interest.

The general turned to his captain again as he entered the officers' mess, a very narrow and crowded cubby hole in the forward section of the submarine.

"In view of our change in course, we estimate another hour or so at this depth. We're running into a contrary current which is slowing us down."

"Can we go lower?"

"It might be the same thing down there, and we would lose more time than it would be worth since we'd have to lower the snorkel first. Do you want us to try?"

The general thought for a moment. "No. Keep your course, but add speed if you can."

"We're tops now, sir," replied the man. "Remember, the snorkel can only withstand a certain amount of pressure before it gives away. And we wouldn't want that to happen as it did to you. . . ."

"Don't remind me," said von Kleitenberg with a noticeable quiver in his voice. "That's an experience I wouldn't wish upon anyone."

That was a part of the story the general hadn't related before, giving Phillip more insight as to the vulnerability of the boat he was traveling in even though it had been modernized to a great degree. Whether he could use the information or not he didn't know, but he stored what he learned for future reference. His ears where continually open, hoping for more tidbits which could possibly help him should he need it.

"You have a large complement," said Phillip, referring to the many men he saw moving in and out of the passageway which was part of the section he was in.

"A few, including the men who recently joined you, the ones responsible for locating our lost property and for your daughter's abduction," replied von Kleitenberg.

"They're here?" snapped Phillip as he looked up into the faces of the men near him as if he would know who they were.

The general smiled as if playing games with him. "Of course. You didn't think we would leave them behind, did you?"

Phillip didn't answer, his mind was on the abductors. "Who—where are they?" he demanded.

"Obersturmführer Reiter, step forward," said the general as he motioned to a short, balding, and slightly obese man standing near the hatchway to come closer. "Otto is the architect of your daughter's abduction and my faithful assistant for many years. In fact, he's one of the founding fathers of our new order. Third in line to me." Von Kleitenberg didn't say who was second.

Phillip wasn't impressed by the man's appearance; he was stocky, aging—almost as old as the general—and didn't appear too bright though he had all the appearance of a fat-headed, obedient slob.

"What about the other man, the one who killed the poor watch-maker?" asked Phillip.

"Meet Herr Johann Steinmueller," said the general as he motioned for another man—a slim, balding man who had been standing in the background saying nothing—to come forward. Obediently, the man pushed forward to a spot opposite Phillip.

"Herr Steinmueller here," continued the general, "is an agent of ours who has been a resident of the Cayman Islands for over forty years, representing our interest under an assumed name. He is the one, I'm proud to say, who found our missing watch."

"A murderer would be more descriptive, wouldn't you say?" replied Phillip caustically as he tried to get up to punch the man. Several guards intervened and pushed him back down.

"Let's not be too harsh on the man," said von Kleitenberg in a condescending manner. "After all, Mr. Steinmueller is a soldier and was only doing his duty as he saw it. Surely, you can understand that?"

"Call it duty if you want, but in my book it's called murder," replied Phillip as he looked into Steinmueller's eyes, throwing optical daggers of hate which the man could not help but feel.

In his own defense, Steinmueller started to respond, but the general waived him off. "You must forgive the man, Steinmueller. After all he does not have your orientation or zeal."

Steinmueller stepped back, and disappeared into the control room from whence he had come, where he could vent his anger. While he was going, a petty officer raced past him, carrying a message.

"Excuse me, Herr General," the man said, interrupting the conversation. "The first officer manning the periscope says there's a small boat following in our wake."

"Small boat?" repeated the general before giving the matter more thought. "It could be a fisherman who spotted our snorkel and decided to investigate," the general said aloud. "How many occupants?"

"Just one man, sir. That's all he could see," reported the petty officer.

"It might be coincidental, but we can't take chances," said the general, addressing the U-boat's captain. "Let's go down," he said, "and be sure to drop the snorkel. I don't want to hit another fisherman like the one we hit forty some years ago . . . ."

What the general said was in German. Though Phillip understood part of what the man said, he didn't get it all because of the engine noises, but he had heard enough to know that there was a connection between Crazy Joe, the man he had doubted earlier, and the general who commanded the U-boat. How it all came together he didn't quite know, but felt he would learn shortly.

Again orders followed, and down, down went the U-boat, leaving no trace for anyone on the surface to follow.

George Town—Police Headquarters

"Gentlemen, we have a problem." That's the way Inspector Gilford addressed what remained of the foreign delegation who had gathered in the police conference room after his mad dash to Gun Bay.

The whole matter turned out to be a fiasco when he got there. All he could find, outside of footprints in the sand, were a number of abandoned vehicles. The motorbike which Mort had used was found, too, though Gilford did not know that at the time of its discovery.

In an attempt to get to the bottom of what was going on, Gilford had radioed headquarters demanding an all-out search be made of the island for Mordeciah and his associates and the unidentified young man who sat at the Northams' table before they disappeared. Included in that request was an order to find Scavenger Jones and bring him immediately to headquarters.

Scavenger Jones was waiting for Gilford when he arrived and promptly clarified what he had seen yessterday, apologizing all the while for not telling anyone except Crazy Joe until now, because he was too scared to tell anyone else. Then, when Crazy Joe told him to tell no one, he did as he was told, figuring the man knew what he was doing. And even if he didn't, he still deserved the first chance to "kill the bastard fish," as Crazy Joe stated so emphatically.

"That's obstructing justice!" Gilford shouted angrily. "I should throw you in jail." The tiny man trembled all over, saying he was just doing what he thought was right.

"Even so, it was wrong!" said Gilford as he poked a long finger in the man's face. "So where is he now?" he demanded, referring to Crazy Joe.

"I . . . I don't know," came the weak reply.

"Damn! Just when we're beginning to get our act together, everything blows apart," groaned Gilford as he paced his office. He glanced out of his office window from time to time as if trying to see the men he was looking for.

A short time later, a commotion in the hallway outside his office captured his attention. A robust black sergeant popped in just then to make an announcement. "They're here, Chief, a little under the weather perhaps, but they're here . . . in the conference room as you asked."

"Good, I'll be right there," came his reply before turning to Scavenger Jones. "Stay here and don't go anywhere," he said. "Got it?"

"Yes, sir, Chief. I won't go nowhere until you say so."

The Conference Room—Police Headquarters

"Why have you sent for us, Peter?" asked Sir Oliver, showing he was still quite capable of conducting business despite the few drinks he had consumed.

"You have found something, yes?" asked Igor on the part of his delegation.

"Where in the hell is our Israeli sleuth?" asked CIA agent Rosenkrantz after noticing his absence.

"Gentlemen, gentlemen, one at a time," interrupted Gilford abruptly. "You'll know what I know in a minute, and it's not much."

"Well?" another voice, that of the Interpol representative, called out in a thick French accent. "We're anxious to hear what you've found. The last time we saw you, you were out chasing Mordeciah and that American couple while we had to stay behind. I don't think that's ethical nor professionally correct."

"That may be so," replied Gilford, answering the last person, "but I simply had no choice. I was about to put some pieces together when the false alarm came in about a robbery in progress. Had that not happened, it's possible much of what we've experienced tonight could have been averted and the parties involved apprehended before they left the island."

"Left? How?" asked a number of excited voices.

"I hate to admit this, gentlemen, but it seems they left by boat."

"A submarine, most likely," Sir Oliver interrupted. "Why not? It all makes sense now."

"I—we don't follow," said Gilford, backed by others.

"Well, don't you see?" he said. "This case has tentacles reaching into the past . . . when certain U-boats, identities unknown, left German waters at the end of WW II carrying large sums of money and other assets like jewelry, objects of arts, or negotiable currencies and God knows whatever else! And to make it even more interesting, no one has seen them since!"

Heads stopped bobbing right then as the brains within them began sifting through the information they already had while merging it with what they had just received. A sign of recognition fell on almost everyone's face.

"It's too incredible!" exclaimed the CIA agent before being cut off by his German colleagues.

"Not at all," Helmut said. "The pieces are really falling together, especially when one considers the flurry of activity—and the mystery surrounding it—which took place only days before Hitler's Reich fell."

"World War II U-boats—here?" asked another to be certain he was hearing correctly.

"If not U-boats, perhaps a submarine from some other source outside of Germany."

"Not likely in view of something else which just came to mind. I had forgotten about it until now, though I did mention it to you earlier . . . if you will recall," said Sir Oliver, attracting everyone's attention.

"Like what?" asked Gilford.

"An interview my staff and I conducted after locating the original commander of a British destroyer, the HMS *Winston*, I believe, which sunk a German U-boat in this general area over forty years ago."

Gilford wanted to smile, but there was something in his former mentor's voice which gave the impression he was quite serious. The others listening felt the same way.

"The destroyer was commanded by a Canadian captain serving in the Royal Navy and operating out of Jamaica. Its last wartime job was to track down a maverick U-boat—possibly one of two, so I remember him saying, which had been suspected of having sunk a Brazilian freighter a day earlier. And, think of this, the sinking took place some two months, more or less, after the war."

"I've heard of things like that happening, but do you think this one is connected to our case?" asked agent Rosenkrantz.

"The more I think of it, the more I'm convinced it is," replied Sir Oliver while lighting his pipe again. Everyone waited tensely as he lit it. "I say this because there are too many coincidences to ignore, in particular, what happened to the other submarine, assuming there was one, since we already know that emergency repair work done near the end of the war at Luebeck was done on two U-boats, both having no recorded identification and both of which simply disappeared. That leads to only one conclusion, does it not?"

"In a way, yes," agreed Gilford. "What's the link?"

"A cook," said Sir Oliver before taking a deep draw on his pipe, then exhaling its sweet-smelling fragrance.

"A cook?" a number of startled voices responded.

"Yes, indeed. A cook—or one who had identity papers purporting he was one and the same—after he was rescued by the men on the destroyer that sunk his U-boat off these shores. In fact, he was the only survivor outside of a little boy who was found adrift in what remained of a small fishing boat."

"If the sub went down in the Cayman trench, which it probably did," said Gilford, unintentionally avoiding discussion of the boy since it didn't seem relevant, "he's lucky to be alive because it's over 5 miles deep."

"And now, as I think of it," added Sir Oliver after being interrupted, "and I'm taking all of this from memory, of course, since we didn't think to record what the captain said—which I now regret—his description of the cook fits someone we've already spoken about— General von Kleitenberg, though I could be mistaken. But why not, since he, like so many other former Nazi leaders, disappeared about the same time and their last steps can be traced to the Kiel area."

"Kind of far-fetched, I'd say," replied agent Rosenkrantz, bypassing discussion of the general. "That was a long time ago. If the cook had been captured, his true identity would have been discovered in due time, if that were the case."

"You're right . . . had that been the case," replied Sir Oliver.

"What do you mean?" asked Gilford, seconded by Igor.

"Simply this. When the cook was first taken aboard the destroyer, he was found to be critically injured. To save his life, the ship's doctor, a psychiatrist-turned-surgeon, was forced to perform an emergency procedure. Later however, complications from an infection set in so the destroyer was diverted to the U.S. Navy base at Guantanamo Bay, Cuba, where he was taken off and entrusted to the care of doctors at the navy hospital. After that, because he required more intensive care, he was airlifted to a navy hospital in Maryland—Bethesda, I believe—where he was to undergo further treatment. Upon recovery, interrogation was to take place, but he escaped before that could happen. To date, no one knows if he was really who he claimed to be or someone else. All trace of him has vanished and no one knows where he went."

"These things only happen in movies," said Gilford, bewildered by the complexity, yet still not certain the illusive cook had anything to do with the subject they were on, nor that he was the missing SS general.

Sir Oliver knew what he was thinking and added several other provocative thoughts, "How else do you think the watch and fragment got here?"

"I don't know," admitted Gilford.

"By U-boat, of course," said Helmut, convinced Sir Oliver was on the right track. "It fits, the timing and all. . . ."

"Up to this time," asked Sir Oliver, pressing Gilford to search his mind, "have there been any other incidents around this island—marine types, for example?"

"None that I know of," came his response. "We try to keep things quiet around here, even if we do have some incidents," he added. "It's bad for tourism, not to mention our world-known off-shore banking. A hint of scandal could do us in since we have no manufacturing or other capabilities."

"I understand," said Sir Oliver, nodding his head.

"I could ask our president, Boris Yeltsin," interrupted Igor Pederosky eagerly, "to send a submarine, the hunter type, to look around the island. I'm sure there's one or two nearby. . . ."

"That wouldn't be wise," interjected Rosenkrantz quickly. "We don't need more incidents, and besides, we have a few of our own in the area."

"I was only trying to help," countered Igor, showing he was sincere, "just in case we have a boat or two still left in Cuba. But your point is well taken, so I withdraw my offer. We are still friends, yes?"

All faces turned to see Rosenkrantz's reaction. He was quick to nod his head while giving a not too enthusiastic reply, "Yes, of course."

"What about unexplained incidents?" Sir Oliver asked again, hoping to jog Gilford's mind.

Gilford's thoughts dug deep, showing that through his wrinkled forehead. *Who in the world—on this island—would know such matters outside of the police? On the other hand, the police aren't always informed about what goes on in other departments. Especially on marine problems.*

"Oh, my God! Why didn't I think of them before?" said Gilford loudly. "On marine problems, contact the Port Authority!"

As everyone in the room watched, Gilford turned quickly and asked the sergeant near him to call the man in charge. "Get me Ralph Wrongtree," he said, drawing an unexpected fit of laughter from several people in the room in the meantime.

"I hope we're not barking up the wrong tree," joked agent Rosenkrantz upon hearing the name. His words meant nothing at first to the Russians, French, or Germans until someone in their group explained. After that, they all laughed.

"He can't help it, but that's his Christian name," explained Gilford, anxious to put a damper on the levity since what he was doing was quite important to them. "Hold it down," he urged. "It's quite late and I'm sure he's not going to be to anxious to talk to me."

He called for a coffee break just then to allow everyone a moment of rest until contact had been made with the Port Authority head. The call came in moments later.

"He's hot as hot can be," warned the sergeant as he directed the inspector to the blinking phone near him, "but I explained it was an emergency and he's quieted down a bit."

"Thanks," said Gilford as he motioned for everyone in the room to keep quiet.

"Sam?" asked Gilford.

"It better be good," said the sleepy and grumpy man on the other line who was barely able to speak coherently.

"It is, and I need to know if—within the last month or so, for examples—you have had any unusual situations occur around the island, in particular, anything that would have been ill-advised to notify the public about."

"Why do you ask?" said the sleepy man.

"I can't tell you that. Not now anyway," replied Gilford.

"So why should I tell you our secrets if you don't tell me yours?" argued the other man.

"Come off it, Sam! I promise you, I'll tell you later, but right now it would be inappropriate, though I can tell you this much—it's of international importance. Okay?"

"Well, all right. What do you want to know?"

"What I asked earlier. Has your agency experienced anything out of the ordinary . . . over the last month or so?"

"Nothing except a few disabled fishing and sports craft drifting out to sea. Otherwise everything's been quiet on this island."

Gilford's hopes plummeted. "You sure?" he asked until a thought struck him. It was worth a try, so he pressed forward. "How about on the other islands like the Brac or . . . ."

"Now that you mention it," replied the man, recalling something too, "but no, that couldn't be what you're looking for. . . ."

"What? You've thought of something?"

"Yeh, but it wasn't much, and we took care of it weeks ago and no one was the wiser right after we received the radio message from Little Cayman."

"Come on, out with it! What may not be important to you might be quite important to us."

"Us?" inquired the man.

"Yes, but I can't tell you anymore than that. Like I said before, it's hush-hush for the moment."

"It was a little brush with a WWII torpedo, which a couple of tourists found several weeks ago."

"Torpedo!" exclaimed Gilford, now drawing equal excitement from those gathered near him.

"Why? Is that important?" asked the man, getting interested himself.

"Depends," said Gilford in an attempt to minimize his interest. "Tell me about it, so we can make a determination."

"Well, there wasn't much to it actually. We had a demolition team fly in from Jamaica and sent them by helicopter to help destroy the thing just in case it was armed and still dangerous."

"And?"

"That's all, really. The Royal Navy lieutenant who headed the team said it was an old WWII German torpedo which probably beached itself after missing its target though he did say, as I recall, that he had never seen one quite like it before. Said it look like new, like it had just been uncrated."

"What happened to it?" asked Gilford, becoming more interested by the second.

"The lieutenant said his team wrapped it with plastic explosives and blew it to kingdom come. They left after that, but not before reassuring the young American couple and their little daughter who found it that they were perfectly safe. It was considerate of the lieutenant, doing that. After all, as you know, we've got to protect our tourist trade."

Gilford jumped out of his chair and looked at everyone as he shouted into the phone. "Young couple? With a little daughter? Was the girl about eight years old and blond as blond can be?"

"I don't know," replied the man. "I never saw them. You'd have to ask the lieutenant, but he's long gone."

"Anything else?" asked Gilford while trying to control his excitement.

"No. The matter is dead as far as I'm concerned," replied the man, yawning.

"Thanks, Sam, you've been a great help. Go back to bed and say nothing to anyone, okay?" He put the phone down after that and turned to face everyone, excitement bristling in his face. "Eureka!"

"What is it?" asked Sir Oliver, knowing full well he had stumbled onto something.

"I was right! They misled me—dammit!"

"Who?"

"The Northams—the American couple. But why I don't know. They found the watch on Little Cayman, not this island, and it came from the insides of a German torpedo."

"Hold on! What's this about a torpedo?" a member of the group asked.

"I haven't got time to explain right now," replied Gilford, "but this much I know. It's all coming together . . . the murder, the watch, and all." He turned to his sergeant, saying, "Let's go!"

"Hey! What about us, and where are you going?" asked Sir Oliver as he watched Gilford remove his pistol from its holster to see if it was fully loaded and if he had sufficient shells for reloads.

"To the airport to catch a helicopter ride," he called back while racing down the hallway opposite the conference room, heading for his patrol car in the street below. Those he left behind ran for the door to watch him leave, disappointed he wouldn't let them follow.

"He's going to the other island," replied Sir Oliver, slightly taken aback too, but he understood. Too many cooks could spoil the soup, especially if the peas in the pot had difficulty communicating.

John Hankins

Owen Roberts Airport—General Aviation

"They're all down for repair except for the one that left about an hour and a half ago," said the security guard.

"Damn the luck! At this time of night?" Gilford said, suddenly realizing it was strange that a helicopter should be flying around at night. Yet he remembered that while returning to George Town after returning empty-handed from Gun Bay, he did see a chopper flying overhead, its strobe lights blinking brightly. *That's strange,* he thought. *I thought Pat didn't like to fly at night, especially over water.*

"Who was flying?" he asked.

"Pat Michaels," replied the guard.

"But he doesn't like to fly at night," said Gilford.

"That's what I thought, but he did anyway. Saw him leave with three men and a pile of stuff."

"Can you describe them?"

"Not too well," replied the man, "because they were down at the other end of the hanger where I don't usually go. But I did see one of them up close as they passed by in their pickup truck. He was pretty chunky."

"And the others?" pressed Gilford, thinking he knew who they were.

"Tall, young, and thin, that's all I can say."

"Mordeciah and his associates!" exclaimed Gilford. "Damn their hide! Now what do I do?"

"You might check with the tower," suggested the man who knew nothing at all about the inspector's concerns. "You can call it from here if you like."

It was a good idea, and Gilford wasted no time making the call. "Tower, this is Chief Inspector Gilford on a very serious matter."

"What can I do for you, Inspector?"

"I'm looking for Pat Michaels. Have you any idea where he is at this time?"

"No problem. He just filed a VFR flight plan for Little Cayman and is on his way. Had a total of four souls on board. Anything else?"

"No, but thanks for your help," said Gilford, putting down the phone dejectedly.

His thoughts twirled desperately like the air speed indicator next to the building weathervane. He had to do something, so he thought, but what? It was late and even the airlines were closed not to mention the little interisland feeder plane service which made daily flights to the outer islands.

Maybe I can get the interisland boys to fly me over, he thought, until another thought, one far more realistic, countered the first. *No, they won't do it because it's too risky. All they've got out there is an unlighted grass strip, and no one in his right mind would risk a landing under such conditions. So, that's that! Until early morning anyway!*

John Hankins

Chapter 29

A Night to Forget

Reefs off South Hole—Little Cayman

ithin an hour after they had parted company, Eric and Yitzak took positions at the farthest part of the reef, where they could kept out of sight. Their only link with Mordeciah was through a portable radio, which they agreed to use sparingly.

"Something's coming," said Mort as he looked beyond the reef. Coming out of the water, reflecting moonbeams now breaking in what had been a cloudy sky, was a huge, black object—a submarine—which churned the waters through which it was emerging into a frothy, white foam, much like the kind one would see on a freshly poured mug of beer. And out of its sides through its many ports came a similar flow, which contributed to its awesome sight.

"Don't do anything until I tell you," ordered Mort, "until I'm certain what they're going to do. There are things we don't know about. Over."

"Understood," said Yitzak. "Over."

"Standby until further notice," replied Mort, ending his transmission.

As Mort watched through his night-vision glasses, the vessel surfaced and pulled in as close to the reef as it could. At the same time, dozens of armed men emerged from its fore, aft, and bridge hatch, where they quickly dispersed. Some ran to the vessel's deck guns while others ran fore and aft to help with the anchorage. Still others helped remove inflatable rubber rafts and outboard motors from their storage spaces before lowering them into the sea, where the boats were quickly manned.

Crackle!

"Y to M?"

"Go ahead."

"They've got an awful lot of stuff . . . men. Maybe too much for us. Over. Hang on, okay? Emergency transmission only," said Mort, now truly worried over the size of the group. From what he could see, there were fifty men or more, and one hell of a lot of gear among which, as near as he could determine, were a number of underwater metal detectors.

He ducked when a bright searchlight struck his position. It swung away toward his associates, then continued until those doing the search felt the area was secure and began lighting up the exterior of the boat while using the searchlights to light the path for the rubber boats to follow.

"They came prepared," Mort said to himself, surprised by their thoroughness.

Moments later, after finding a breech—a low spot in the reef—the sub passed through, slowly at first to avoid getting snagged, then with greater speed shortly thereafter. They passed Owen's Island, a tiny dot in the center of the lagoon, then headed for a sandy beach not far from Mort's position in a clump of mosquito-infested mangroves. He cursed silently as the insects sampled his blood without mercy, but fortunately he had remembered to bring mosquito repellant and wasted no time dousing himself.

"*ACHTUNG!*" a voice called out, barking orders to the men who had just disembarked.

"History repeating itself," Mort muttered to himself. "Germans!" His thoughts went elsewhere when the beach was suddenly inundated with bright lights, all powered by portable generators. Again he was fortunate, almost all were pointed toward the shoreline, where gentle waves moved in and out, making it easy for anyone to wade in.

Under a hastily erected lamp, under which a portable table had been erected, he could see several men going over what looked like a map. One of them pointed, and he focused on his face to get a better look.

"Good God!" he gasped. "It's him! It's him—Phillip! Ohhh, I should be so lucky." His thoughts shifted gears, *But how am I going to get him away from them?*

While considering alternatives, he looked beyond the reef again. On the sub's bridge, several men were intently watching the working parties on the beach as they scoured the nearby sands and the scuba divers as they swam—and sometimes walked—through the shallow water of the lagoon with their underwater flashlights and metal detectors. One of them was its captain, Mort correctly guessed, because he wore a white cap. As to the others, he could not say because they were too far away, though one man seemed to dominate because every time he said something or motioned in any direction, the others jumped.

I wonder who he is? thought Mort before his thoughts were interrupted.

"I found one!" cried one of the scuba divers as he burst to the surface. A rash of activity followed as men with special gear hastened to the spot and started winching a long, shiny object in to the shore.

"M to Z, over."

"Z here, over."

"I believe they've found what they're looking for, so hang on. Don't get impatient. Out."

Again, Mort studied the beach, looking for a chance to wrest Phillip clear of what he knew could be a quick, bloody, and decisive encounter. And the odds, as he knew, were more for the other side than for his.

The hours dragged for Mort, but not for the men working on the beach, moving torpedo after torpedo in specially made inflatable carriers back to the submarine, where they were winched and slipped through hatchways in the sub's midst.

Mort felt helpless, much like Phillip was feeling as he watched his captors recover one torpedo after another. Unlike Phillip, however, Mort and his men came armed with resources—explosives, for example, and a number of Uzis to add sting to whatever they would attempt. Before he could do anything, though, timing had to be considered, so he waited for another thirty minutes before an unexpected break came which caught him by surprise.

"Ich das neutronen kanon gefunden. It's still intact and clearly marked."

"Are you sure?" called an officer who raced into the water—uniform and all—to a lone diver who was excitedly pointing to the water beneath him.

"*Jah*. There is no mistake about its markings," the happy diver replied.

A rash of signaling followed with men being ordered to drop everything they were doing and come over quickly to help retrieve the torpedo.

"A neutron cannon!" exclaimed Mort to himself, showing deep concern and distress.

His eyes fell on Phillip a hundred yards away and the lone guard standing next to him who was now distracted. The officers who had been with him earlier had left him under guard to go and join the others. *My only chance!* thought Mort. *They're too preoccupied to notice my presence. I wonder. . ."*

"M to Z, over."

"Go ahead, this is Z, over."

"We've got problems—serious ones, which changes everything. You've got to go in now and take them out. Over."

"We're outnumbered, over," responded Yitzak in a quivering voice.

"I know, but it can't be helped, believe me. They've got a neutron nuclear cannon of some sort out there, and you know what that means. I didn't know they had it until now. Over."

A silence, then, "I understand. We'll do our best. Over."

"Good luck. Over," Mort responded with emotion in his voice.

It was a sad moment for Mort. His enthusiasm over beating the odds had been greatly reduced, and he knew—though not for certain—only one or none of his party would return. Of course, a surprise attack could possibly succeed, but with so many men in arms against them, their chances were slim at best. His eyes turned to the reef opposite the position his assistants had taken.

Though they were difficult to see at first, his night-vision glasses finally caught sight of them, two figures on sail surfs hastily sprayed black (sails and all) moving rapidly out to sea. After reaching their turning point, they came back again, pushed by the wind toward the U-boat's blind side—the open sea which was unguarded. For a while, Mort lost sight of them until one of the two came alongside the vessel's stern and leaped off, carrying satchel charges with him. His partner arrived seconds later, carrying the same thing, but his target was the bow.

For a brief moment, their presence went undetected until a bumping sound alerted a lookout. To his shock, an armed man dressed in an all-black, neoprene wetsuit which was hard to see was scaling the sub's hull. He sounded a warning and attempted to stop the man but was gunned down before he could fire his own weapon. A series of shots followed after that, lighting up the sky in and around the U-boat like the Fourth of July. It caused quite a commotion on the shore, where officers and ratings (enlisted men) alike stopped what they were doing to respond to the unexpected attack.

Some of the shots came from the bridge where one officer in particular—General von Kleitenberg—took advantage of his elevated position above the intruder to fire his P-38 pistol, the chrome-plated one he always wore, at the man who had dared violate his boat's sanctity. An exchange of shots took place and the intruder went down, but not before felling a number of crewmen who attempted to shoot him.

As for the intruder's companion on the aft section, the last thing Mort saw of him, whoever he was, was when he dropped into the aft hatch, firing as he went. A silence soon followed, causing Mort to fear the worst. He bit his lip to keep from crying because he loved those boys. They had been his prize students, and he had taught them all they knew, and now they were gone!

A horn blared just then, causing everyone on the beach to assemble and to await further instructions, most of which were being relayed by hand-held walkie-talkies. That's when Mort saw his chance to help Phillip.

While his guard's attention was on the beach, where most of the sub's crew had gathered, Mort was racing over the sand in his direction. He was approximately five feet behind the unsuspecting guard when a sailor on the beach happened to look their way in time to see Mort. He yelled a warning, but it came too late.

The guard turned, and Mort fired, dropping the man. "Here, take this," cried Mort as he handed Phillip his pistol. "Hope you know how to use it."

"MORT! How did you—?"

"I'll tell you later," huffed Mort. "Follow me to the mangroves. It's our best bet."

As they raced for shelter, a hail of bullets cut through the air, spewing sand where they had been. With Phillip at his side, Mort fired back, causing those on the beach to duck for cover. Working against Germans were the glaring lights which they had erected earlier to help them in the recovery. It was difficult to see anything behind the lights, so they tried shooting the lights out only to find themselves bathed in darkness.

After a few minutes of confusion, order was restored and the men were ordered to find Phillip and anyone else who might be with him. The U-boat's searchlight was directed toward the shore to help those on the beach find those responsible for the ambush. Unfortunately, it proved to be a double-edged sword, one that tended to reveal their movements rather than those of their opponents.

A volley of bullets followed, downing most of the searching men, until they were called away by von Kleitenberg, who immediately ordered his gun crews to fire their 88mm and twin 20mm cannons at their illusive targets. The mangroves came alive with shells bursting everywhere, but the expected results did not occur; the American and Mossad agent had evaded disaster at every turn by wisely ducking in and out of the many trees. At the same time, they always fired back to confuse the enemy as to their location. In the process, a number of the more daring of the other side swallowed more sand. Phillip claimed at least five, while Mort thought he had gotten that many himself, but they didn't argue about it.

A horn blared minutes later, bringing an end to the firing. Phillip and Mort waited for a moment before sneaking a look. What they saw surprised them. The work crews were racing back to their rubber boats, leaving almost everything they had brought with them,except the torpedoes, scattered over the beach.

"I think they're leaving," said Phillip.

To Phillip's shock, Mort responded like a madman. "NO! They can't do that," he cried. "We've got to stop them!"

"With what?" asked Phillip, just before Mort abandoned their shelter and ran toward the beach, firing his weapon wildly.

"Mort! Get back here," cried Phillip. When he didn't respond, Phillip raced after him.

Mort was still firing when he got there, but most of the inflatables, including the U-boat itself, were too far away.

"Why all the heroics?" asked Phillip as he grabbed his shoulder to shake some sense back into him. "Are you crazy? Can't you see they're too far out? And besides, they can blast us out of the water with their deck guns any time they want."

"You don't understand," said Mort in a distressed voice as he looked out to the sea where activities on the U-boat were being heightened. "They've got to be stopped!" He almost cried when he said that, puzzling Phillip.

"Why?" asked Phillip, demanding an answer.

"Because they've retrieved a neutron weapon of some sort. I heard them talking about it. Didn't you?"

"Oh! So that's what it was," replied Phillip, suddenly aware of something he hadn't understood earlier. He too had heard the cry from the diver, but distance and the noise around him had kept him from learning what had been said.

For a few seconds, Mort remained silent; his eyes and ears were on the departing U-boat. A few men were still on her decks, dismantling the fore and aft hoist which had been erected on its fore and aft deck to help onload the recovered torpedoes. As for the rubber boats, they had abandoned them to the sea, where they drifted with the prevailing current.

"Well? " asked Phillip after a brief pause. "What do we do now?"

"I don't know," said Mort with a heavy heart. It bled for his two assistants. *They weren't supposed to die! They were too young!* he thought before another thought swept the first away because of its priority.

It was about the helicopter pilot he had sent away to advise the island's inhabitants to stay away and of the helicopter itself. *It could be used to get help.* On second thought, even if the pilot was able to get airborne, it would still take a lot of time to get the bird cranked up and ready for flight. By that time the U-boat with all its recovered assets, nuclear cannon, and whatever else it included would be long gone. And to where nobody knew. . . .

As he and Phillip worked their way back to solid ground, they stepped over the lifeless bodies of dead Nazis, all of whom had been abandoned by their comrades. The sight of them enraged Mort, causing him to turn around and fire a volley at the U-boat.

"A good try, but they're out of range," said Phillip with a comforting hand on the man's shoulder. "And by the way," he added, "I owe you and your friends a debt of gratitude."

Phillip was about to add something when another sound caught his ear. Mort heard it, too, and turned around.

In the distance, a small vessel, barely visible were it not for the bright moonlight shining off its shiny hull, was on a collision course with the submarine.

On Board *U-4R2*

Last-minute details were being followed by the first officer whose job it was to check for debris before the vessel could make its final dive. Under orders of expediency from von Kleitenberg, which he claimed were in the best interest of the party, the man pushed the bodies of those who had fallen into the sea. While doing so, a loud crash and scraping noise coming from the bow caught his attention.

To determine the cause, he climbed back to the bridge and illuminated the area with the hull-mounted searchlight in time to see the remains of a small boat passing on either side of the U-boat. No one seemed to be in it, making him think it had been torn from its moorings somewhere and had drifted out to sea, where it crossed the U-boat's path.

Satisfied everything was in order, the man turned the searchlight off, secured a number of other items, then walked briskly to the bridge hatch and yelled to the captain below that everything was in order. What he didn't know was that a tiny man had crept up behind him after scaling the side of the moving vessel. With one swift blow to the head, using the back of his heavy harpoon as a club, the tiny man sent the first officer crashing to the deck, unconscious.

After hours of fighting turbulent seas and contrary winds, Crazy Joe had reached Little Cayman though a little later than he had expected. Bouts with contaminated fuel were equally responsible for his failure to reach the island before the U-boat. Upon arrival, he took a course for South Hole Sound, his grandfather's favorite fishing spot, and the site of a tragedy he could never shake, where much to his surprise, his boat crossed the bow of the departing submarine.

As the remaining half of his boat scrapped its barnacled hull, Crazy Joe barely had time to save his own life, much less retrieve the only weapon he had brought with him, his harpoon. A lucky break came his way when he grasped a safety rail on its afterdeck and pulled himself upward until safely aboard. He proceeded forward and upward after that, careful to avoid the man who was pushing bodies over the side, until he could strike. When the officer fell to the deck, one of his arms fell through the hatchway, causing someone below to call out.

"*Vas ist los?*"

Fearing failure, Crazy Joe decided to see what was below him before deciding to act. As he looked down, first through one hatch, then through another below it, a man—a short, stocky, balding one—was looking up at him. Seconds later, the man reached for his holstered pistol and withdrew it, but before he could shoot, Crazy Joe let his harpoon fly. It traveled downward, through both hatches, before passing through the startled man to the steel deck beneath his feet. Upon contact, an electrical circuit was completed which detonated the harpoon's shaft-mounted explosive charge. A deafening explosion followed.

Barrrooooooom!

Within a minute, Phillip and Mort, who had been trying to see what was happening aboard the U-boat, were knocked to the ground by a series of larger explosions, the last of which blew the boat into many pieces.

"Wha—what happened?" groaned Phillip as he lifted his bruised body from off the sand and dusted the sand off.

"It could only have been Crazy Joe," said Mort. "The last time I saw him, he was chasing after the sub. And from the looks of it, he got what he came after. Thank God!"

Their eyes turned back to the sea to the place where they had last seen the U-boat. It was no more as if it had never existed.

In Memorium
of
Joseph V. Bowman
"Crazy Joe"
The only man to sink
a German U-Boat with
a harpoon. And he got
the "Big One" before it
got him.

Monument to Crazy Joe

Chapter 30

A Fitting End?

George Town—A Day Later

T hey would have killed me had it not been for the timely intervention of Mr. Joachim here and his brave assistants who came to my rescue," said Phillip to a question put to him by members of the press. Most had arrived, compliments of Cayman Airways, on the first morning flight.

After that, Mort was interviewed, but declined saying much because—as he told the press—he was still grieving over the loss of his two friends and assistants.

Not to be denied a story, an aggressive journalist persisted with a question which stunned everyone. "Mr. Joachim, is it true the Nazis were really after a nuclear device of some sort rather than the treasure per se?"

"Who told you that?" barked Mort.

"We have our sources," replied the man as he searched Mort's face for betrayal of his thoughts.

"I'm not aware of any bomb," Mort lied as his eyes, like those of

407

the inspector and Phillip, fell on a secretary who felt her presence in the conference room was not appreciated at the moment.

Still not satisfied, the reporter pressed on. "What about Martin Bormann, Doctor Mengele, and other Nazi war criminals who were supposed to be connected with this plot?"

"At this juncture the only names we know of are those of General von Kleitenberg, Obersturmführer Otto Reiter, and the spy who had been planted here after WWII—a certain Mr. Johann Liebermann."

"He was an investment banker with offshore interests, wasn't he?" interrupted the reporter.

"Yes. It was a cover having two functions. The first being offshore banking responsibilities using stolen assets, and the second, the continuing search for *U-4R1*, which—as you now know—was sunk in these waters over forty years ago while carrying treasure and high-ranking officials of the defunct Nazi Reich to a destination still unknown to us."

"An ambitious project, wouldn't you say?" asked another reporter.

"Conceived by a diabolical genius—General Ernst von Kleitenberg," replied Mort, "but like all schemers, he finally got what he deserved . . . at the hands of Crazy Joe, whom he had injured years earlier . . . from what we have been able to piece together."

"Concerning the U-boat and the men who went down with her, have you any idea where they came from?"

"Again, we can only guess. We know the U-boat's origin, but nothing else. As for the men, that's another question. Only time will answer that."

When Mort refused to say more, members of the press decided to interview the representatives of the European delegation about their contribution to solving the murder and the discovery—even though little if anything had been recovered—of the Reichbank's missing treasury.

In the forefront was Igor Pederosky, who found the notoriety quite exciting. He had never been in the limelight before and enjoyed telling the press of the role he and his associates played in going through old KGB and other files which helped identify specific links in the case. One thing, however, which surprised everyone—including his foreign colleagues—was a statement he made concerning notifying his president of the need for a sub-hunter submarine to help locate the U-boat. When asked if it had been sent, he could only say, "It's on its way, but hasn't arrived."

Not to be outmaneuvered, agent Rosenkrantz of the CIA quickly admitted he had done the same thing, and because events had unfolded quicker than anticipated, he too had no idea where the U.S. sub-hunting sub was located, but a reply was expected momentarily.

The Germans on the other hand gave a sober reply, and by the time the press had analyzed their contribution, it was quite clear to everyone it had been very significant, surpassing in many instances that of Scotland Yard, which had seen the connection between the murder of the Jewish watchmaker and the watch belonging to the czar.

Last on the list was Inspector Gilford, the originator of the investigation. Everyone seemed to ignore him, including the members of the Executive Council who painted a glowing picture about their support of police efforts. Included in their list was a supplemental budget to insure investigative work was not impeded. "After all," one member stated emphatically, "our primary concern is the personal well-being of all those who visit our island!"

Naturally, the last statement added vineger to Inspector Gilford's wounds since he remembered having to justify every call he made outside the island, most of which did not sit too well with certain members of the council.

When it came to a repeat discussion on the subject of the treasure which went down with the *U-4R2*, which everyone now knew about, a number of faces lost their glow—Phillip's more than anyone else's.

"How do you feel about that?" asked a reporter, sensing he was troubled about the loss of so many lives, not to mention having to surrender his share of what he found to local authorities.

"Terrible, in one way," replied Phillip, "but happy in another,, because both were ill gotten to start with and no one but their rightful owners should have them. Regrettably, most of them—to my knowledge— are dead, victims of an inhumane regime which no longer exists."

"Are you sure about that?" asked another journalist, posing an unexpected question.

That's when Mort broke in. "Gentlemen, let me tell you something. These guys—the Nazis—came from somewhere, and there were lots of them. Doesn't that tell you something?" He left them with that thought before excusing himself from the joint interview, saying he had to catch a plane and that this part of the unpleasant case was over.

He kissed Janelle's hand, then lifted tiny Tanya and rubbed her face gently with his unshaved one. She giggled delightfully, making her parents happy and grateful he had come into their lives.

Phillip came next, and while the press took pictures, the two men embraced, saying little or nothing to each other. Their eyes said it all; both had experienced pain again, and words other than "good-bye" and "take good care of yourself" served no useful purpose.

A joint picture of all the participants followed right after Chief Inspector Gilford received a plaque for meritorious service and notification he had been given a long-overdue promotion and raise. He thanked everyone, then went back to his office, driving his smokey car.

Absent from the ceremonies was a man well known to the community, but his picture was there, however bad it was since it was a mug shot taken from police records. Crazy Joe was a hero now instead of the despised town drunk everyone used to talk about. In fact, the tales he used to bother everyone with about a giant "devil fish" were now the talk of the town, and someone even suggested building a monument to commemorate a tale which turned out to be true.

Again cameras flashed, and copies of his likeness, minus the jail identification number, were faxed to newspapers and television stations around the world, heralding Crazy Joe as a hero equal to, if not paralleling, Rudyard Kipling's famous Indian waterboy, Gunga Din.

Later in the evening, long after the reporters had gone, a banquet was held for the visiting dignitaries and the Northams at the expense of the Caymanian Council with a request to stay another week. Unfortunately, most of the guests had to decline since they needed to return to their respective countries. The Northams had planned to leave but decided to stay after being told there would be a monument dedicated to Crazy Joe's memory and that their presence would be appreciated by his many friends.

Coincidently, though no one mentioned it, his monument was to be erected in the same park where weeks earlier, another one, George Town's monument to Shipwrecked Sailors had unceremoniously been blown off its pedestal by a bomb he had made.

The Atlantic—Days Later

Though the Northams missed the Caymans, its people, and the beautiful beaches, they were glad to be on their way home, where they felt certain they could get some rest, and perhaps, even be safer.

Both Phillip and Janelle, after talking things over for a week, realized they had never lost the love they had for each other but had only shelved it to pursue their individual careers. Regrettably, they had allowed dust to cover its sparkle—with dust being the equivalent of too much work and too little play—when far less was required of them by their employers. Naturally, as they both realized, unless they agreed to a reasonable approach, any discord between them would eventually hurt Tanya, a creation by mutual consent.

That very thought brought them together and they agreed to be more mindful of each other's needs or hurts—including Tanya's—in order to develop a more wholesome life for all of them.

It was with these facts in mind, a day later while the *Lucky Streak* was sailing in deep waters in the Gulf of Mexico between the northwest coast of Cuba and the southern part of the United States, that Phillip decided to do something he never thought he would do.

The whole family was in the cockpit at the time looking out over the beautiful sea, where seagulls made diving runs for morsels thrown into the air by Tanya and where porpoises challenged the hull to a race it could not win.

"Janelle," whispered Phillip while nibbling affectionately at her left earlobe.

"Stop it," she squealed, enjoying it though she pretended not to. "What?"

"I've got a confession to make."

"About what?" she asked dreamily, not really paying attention.

"About not fully living up to a promise I made to you . . . back in George Town. I'm sorry about it, and it will never happen again."

"Oh?" She replied in a most casual manner.

"You know the gold fragments we found?"

Janelle turned and looked into his eyes. "You're not thinking about the gold again, are you?"

"Not about what we've returned, but about the ones I didn't give up," he replied softly.

"Oh, Phillip, you didn't!"

"I'm afraid I did," he admitted while bending forward to reach under a nearby transom where he removed a small cloth bag. He opened it in front of her. "I didn't think anyone would really mind."

Needless to say, Janelle was disturbed, but not without understanding. Phillip had paid a price for finding the treasure, but so had they all.

The look in her face was all Phillip needed. At that moment, he stood up, lifted the bag over his head, then threw it as far as he could.

Janelle got up and embraced him affectionately. "I love you. That was such a noble and honest thing to do, and I know how hard it was to do it."

Phillip wasn't so certain it was the right thing to do, but he felt a great deal better even though what he thrown away represented a lot of money—not as much as he earned in a year, but quite a substantial sum when considering the price of gold and precious stones on the world's market.

One thing he didn't tell his wife because he didn't think it important was the palming of a single fragment he had managed to hide before tossing the sack into the sea. He wanted it as a souvenir, but even that was to become a nemesis to him when he made the mistake of peeking at it while looking over his wife's shoulder.

"What's that, Daddy?" asked Tanya, who walked up just then. She had noticed its glint.

Startled, Phillip could do nothing but admit the truth. "Oh—ah, it's a piece of gold bullion, dear."

Upon hearing that, his wife released her loving hold and turned to see what they were talking about.

Embarrassed, Phillip turned to face her while showing the small fragment. "It fell out of the bag, and I was about to throw it away," he said.

Janelle withheld her anger because he could be telling the truth. *After all,* she thought, *the bag did have a lot of holes in it.*

"Are you going to keep it, Daddy?" asked Tanya.

"I'm afraid not, honey. It's going over the side like the bag I just threw away. It's a promise to your mother."

"Why?" asked Tanya with child-like innocence again.

"Because it was stolen from people who died a long time ago and it's wrong to keep it."

While his wife and daughter looked on, he tossed the small fragment into the sea, then turned back to his family, saying, "There, it's done, once and for all!"

A worried look crossed Tanya's face just then, puzzling her parents. "Something wrong?" they asked simultaneously.

Instead of answering, Tanya raced away. While her parents watched, she raced down the stairs to their cabin and disappeared, returning minutes later.

"Here, Daddy," she said while holding up a wad of tissue paper in his face.

"What's this?" he asked, knowing he had seen it before, but still didn't know what it contained.

"You'll see," she replied with an intent look on her face.

While her mother looked on, Phillip unwrapped the ball.

"For crying out loud! It's a doubloon!"

Phillip turned and knelt alongside his daughter. "Honey, where'd you get it?"

"At the same place you got yours," came Tanya's reply.

"Where we found the torpedo?"

"Yes, Daddy," answered Tanya, puzzled by his interest. "Aren't you going to throw it away?"

"Not yet, dear," he said before turning to his wife. "Janelle, do you know what this means?"

"Partially," she replied.

"It's a piece of eight, a gold coin dating back to the days of Spanish treasure galleons—like the kind found by Mel Fisher, Burt Webber, and other famous treasure hunters off the coast of Florida and the Caribbean!"

"So?" she asked disheartened, feeling certain he was getting the malady again.

"Think of it! A treasure-ladened Spanish galleon wallowing off the reef of Little Cayman or pirates who buried their treasure there, never realizing people like us would come along some day and find what they buried!"

"Phi-l-lip!" cried Janelle, upset over what she was hearing. Her rising protest stopped when a sudden rising and falling of the sea on both sides of their yacht caused it to roll from side to side. Moments later, the sea on both sides burst open like a boiling pot and out of it rose two nuclear submarines, larger than anything either one of them had ever seen. One was American, and the other Russian.

"Oh, my God!" exclaimed Janelle, an exclamation shared by her husband. "Who are they?"

"I'll bet they're the ones the CIA agent and the former KGB man were talking about," speculated Phillip after a brief moment of silence.

"If that's so, what're they doing here?" asked Janelle, overwhelmed by their domineering presence. Tanya, on the other hand, was delighted by the spectacle.

"They're huge, Mamma," she squealed fearlessly.

The Northams didn't have to wait long for the answer. Within minutes after their surfacing, heads appeared on both bridges, looking their way.

"Ahoy!" said the first, speaking through an electronic megaphone. "USS *Scorpion. S*orry we missed you in the Caymans. Good luck."

On the opposite side of the *Lucky Streak* came another voice, causing the Northams to look in that direction.

"Greetings from the people of Russia, and our sincerest congratu-

413

lations. Our apologies for missing you, too. Good-bye," called the captain from the other vessel.

Another voice joined his; it came from the mouth of a man who, even from a distance, looked like someone they knew. It was Igor Pederosky and near him were some of his associates, all waving and smiling. "Have a good trip, my friends," yelled Igor. "We are getting a free ride home. Good-bye."

Shaken by their sudden appearance and disappearance, Phillip—like his wife and daughter—stared at their vanishing wake before looking at the coin which had been the subject of controversy minutes earlier. To end it all, he made a hasty decision.

"Oh, hell," he said loudly. "It was fun while it lasted." Then before anyone could say anything, he tossed the shiny gold disc into the sea, where it quickly disappeared.

"You sure?" asked Janelle, suspecting his innermost thoughts.

"As sure as anything," he replied not too convincingly as he picked up Tanya and put an arm around his wife. He brought the two close to him and kissed them one at a time.

"I love you, Daddy."

"Me, too," said her mother.

"Time to go home, eh what?" said Phillip, mimicking an Englishman he had met days earlier.

"Oh, Phillip. . . ."

Cayman Gold

JOHN HANKINS

- If you have enjoyed this book, how about sending a copy to a friend or two?
- Look forward to other books by John Hankins, like Martha's Will, Bouquet Island, and The Spector, all of which will be published shortly.
- If you enjoy poetry, be on the lookout for John's captivating Maid of the Stones and More Poems, plus other poems representing a variety in style and themes.
- You can learn more about the above by going to our Internet Home Page listed below.